RIVER UNDER THE ROAD

SCOTT SPENCER

An Imprint of HarperCollins *Publishers*

HarperCollins books may be purchased for educational, business, or sales promotional use. For information, please email the Special Markets Department at SPsales@harpercollins.com.

FIRST EDITION

Designed by Michelle Crowe
Textures by YamabikaY/ Shutterstock, Inc.

Library of Congress Cataloging-in-Publication Data has been applied for.

ISBN 978-0-06-266005-3

17 18 19 20 21 LSC 10 9 8 7 6 5 4 3 2 1

To Peter Hutton (1943–2016)

Rama, your shadow still falls across the table

Fellow citizens, we cannot escape history. . . .
—ABRAHAM LINCOLN

I found a river under the road.
—ANA EGGE

RIVER UNDER
THE ROAD

Chapter 1

The Farewell Brunch

SUNDAY, AUGUST 29, 1976

You're Invited!
Come for a real New York Brunch at our house and say
Adios Au Revoir Arrivederci Sayonara
to our son—
and to Hell with RSVP.
Just Be There.

THADDEUS SUSPECTED HIS PARENTS WERE DISAPPOINTED he wasn't going further with his education, but he was wrong. Sam and Libby never for a moment thought Thaddeus was going to get a graduate degree, though law school would not have been out of the question. But the life of a scholar? Professor Kaufman? It was not how they saw him. He was charming, he loved fun, pleasure, jokes; he was not the boy of their dreams. In truth, love him as they did, had he not been flesh of their flesh, he was not someone with whom they would ordinarily have been close. Not to mention his mushy liberal politics, his unscientific, unsocialist belief that out of the goodness of their hearts people might share and share alike, live and let live. He was a moderate. A prospector forever on the lookout for common ground. Weeks ago, during the bicentennial patriotic orgy, people his age were insisting that America acknowledge its deficiencies—stop the war, end poverty, own up to epic political corruption—while Thaddeus and his girlfriend spent most of the day in bed, rising only to try their hands at baking a red white and blue layer cake that succeeded solely in bespattering the immaculate Kaufman kitchen.

"Here's what I believe," he had the nerve to tell them, when he had overheard them debating various theories of history. Maybe he was drunk, or high—they suspected he indulged in his generation's rather contemptible distractions. He was draped over the brown sofa. His girlfriend had slipped past them, down the main hallway and into his bedroom. "The whole purpose of history or progress or whatever we want to call it is to create conditions in which people can love each other, and enjoy life. Pleasure is the most we can ever hope for. It's what makes us human. And love, too. Love is the ultimate pleasure. It's the milk and honey of the emotions!"

"Oh please," Libby had said. "Milk and honey my foot. You sound like an idiot."

"It's what I believe," he said, with a lazy grin that struck Libby as distinctly postcoital.

Maybe he was a bit of a fool. They worried over that possibility. As a child there were nights when he literally danced before them, his little feet scraping at the floor, his arms making blurry circles before him. His model was Sammy Davis Jr. Their model might have been any president carved in stone. Sammy Plays Mount Rushmore! They would sit on the sofa, letting him sing and dance, their shoulders back, their chins held high, like Resistance fighters about to be executed. They always clapped too soon, before the finale, which would find him on one knee, his arms outspread. And the jokes! Where did he find them? Did he make them up? Shaggy dogs, guys walking into bars, the talking baby. When he was eleven, Libby found a book hidden under his mattress—*The Toastmaster's Guide to Laffs*—and, her heart racing, her mouth a rictus of revulsion, she carried it to the trash can and disposed of it as if it were the vilest sort of pornography.

And now New York, thus the good-bye brunch they were getting ready to host, in their long, dark apartment, with its preponderance of hallways, its heavy furniture, sagging bookshelves, and murky purple-and-blue Persian carpets.

In a few days, Thaddeus would be gone and they would be alone together. It was not a prospect they dreaded. They would be returned to their original state, living one-on-one, just the two of them. They imagined noontime lovemaking, a luxurious privacy, never ever to be interrupted. Sam talked about learning French. Libby planned to buy a piano.

Not that he would be unmissed. He was their son! And he was good at the shop, a pleasant-looking kid, nice build, square shoulders, black hair, blue eyes, an open face. He had a ruddy, Russian look to him, according to Sam; to Libby he looked like the suitor in a silent movie. But he liked the customers and the customers manifestly enjoyed his genuine friendliness, his interest in them, his warmth, his desire to make them laugh. He remembered so many of their names, a feat that was amazing and a little weird, like double-jointedness. He gazed admiringly at the books the customers chose before bagging them. He flirted with the loveless. He joshed with the infirm. He listened with what seemed like rapt attention to the garrulous. He made calls to other shops if someone couldn't find what they needed at Four Freedoms. He made room on the obligatory bulletin board for the flyers and index cards that people wanted to post, announcing upcoming madrigal concerts or dining room sets for sale. He played with their dogs, slipped pennies or nickels to their children. "That boy of yours could charm the birds out of the trees," a professor said to Libby one day in late July. By then she had heard so much commentary about her son's gregarious, people-pleasing, hail-fellow-well-met personality that her own basically contentious nature sprang to the fore and while she was writing up his sales receipt—Carl Sandburg's two-volume biography of Lincoln—she somehow added an extra dollar to the total.

"I like my birds *in* the trees," she replied, handing him his change.

IN COLLEGE, IT HAD STRUCK Thaddeus as odd and sort of tacky how many people leading comfortable, privileged lives went after their parents with hammer and tongs, swapping late-night stories of idiocy and abuse, portraying the people who gave them life as tax cheats, hypocrites, dumbbells, racists, penny-pinchers, sloppy kissers, warmongers, anal-retentives, or emotional zeros who thought only weaklings cried (his own parents). Maybe his friends had a right to their bellyaching, but that sort of score-settling was not his way, and besides, what would be the absolute worst thing he could say? That Sam and Libby Kaufman made him sad? That there was a stultifying aura of self-denial in their household? That they steadfastly refused to laugh at his jokes? Not his riddles or knock-knock jokes, nor his Jerry Lewis imitations, not even his Lenny Bruce riffs, which he performed for them verbatim until he finally knew better. So his parents were a bit of a *drag*, yet he simply did not have the heart to criticize them. Especially since he knew their lives had been damaged, horribly damaged, perhaps ruined. He could feel what they felt, he could all but *see* the hole that had been bored into the center of their world. Misfortune had slapped the smiles off their faces, shortened their tempers, and fostered in them a resentment of everyday life that was as hard as granite, yet weightless and unacknowledged.

They had a baby and the baby died. A fairy tale composed in the foulest pit of hell: the baby died and they lived unhappily ever after. That's why picnics were a pain in the ass, that's why fashion was for suckers, that's why dancing was for fools, and comedy was for idiots.

Life was endured, like a spanking or a blood test.

It had taken Thaddeus six years to finish college. Actually six and a half—he graduated after summer school and received his diploma in the mail, then stayed in Ann Arbor and worked in a record store and on a novel. He took records home from work and taught himself to appreciate genres that were new to him—opera, bluegrass. More to enjoy! Writing was a kind of torment, but he reassured himself that one day it would bring him pleasure. It would not necessarily make him rich, but there were other rewards—pride, praise. An amazing woman who might think he was a genius.

His return to Chicago was really a first stop—his destination was New York. But first he had to save some money. He moved back home to work at his parents' bookshop, and did not kid himself into believing they were thrilled to have him in their apartment. They were hospitable in a "from each according to their ability, to each according to their needs" kind of way. Sam and Libby Kaufman *did* in fact love Thaddeus to the best of their ability, and as to their needs—well, identifying their needs was a bit trickier. They needed him to be pleasant and courteous and clean and it was the least he could do. They needed him to never mention his sister. And they needed him not to make too many emotional demands on them. From time to time, he wished they would love him a bit more, but their hearts were not whole, so how could he expect them to love him wholeheartedly?

The baby. There was no getting away from the baby. Hannah died when she was five months old, swiftly, horribly. Sam and Libby didn't believe in God, but they had believed in nature, in its logic, its evolutionary journey toward perfection. But this? This was the worst of nature, the very worst. Mother Nature was a filthy beast. Their child. Their baby. Her little body overwhelmed by pneumonia—how not to imagine the bacteria raging through the fourteen pounds of her like an invading army, burning everything in its path? What was the purpose of pneumonia, anyhow? What earthly good did it do? And if it served no purpose and did no good—why did it exist? They were rational people, not scientists but scientific. They accepted disease and death, and they saw the benefits of mortality. It was how the world progressed. Our bodies, like the bodies of monkeys and snails and everything else that lived and died, were the fuel that ran the great engines of evolution. But a baby?

His parents were versed in history, classical music, radical politics. Perhaps if Leon Trotsky had written a pamphlet about infant care they would have known more about that particular field of study, but he hadn't and they didn't. Though Hannah was their *second* child, they didn't know very much about infants and their delicacy—their firstborn had been sturdy and easygoing, he slept through the night, ate happily, never was sick. They didn't realize how lucky they were, and how untested. By the time they realized that Hannah was in the clutches of an infection that she was powerless to fight, and they had stopped trying to bring her fever down with lukewarm baths, stopped chewing up baby aspirins and drooling them down her little throat, and stopped waiting for the pediatrician to return their increasingly distraught phone calls, when they finally had to admit that there was nothing more they could do but take her to nearby University of Chicago Hospitals, leaving their son asleep in his bed, it was already too late. By then Hannah's temperature was nearly 106 degrees. Perhaps out of pity, Dr. Shuster told them that even if they had gotten her to the hospital sooner she would most likely not have survived.

When they returned many hours later, empty and hollow, they found Thaddeus on the sofa with a spoon and a jar of peanut butter, wearing underpants and socks, chortling at some unspeakable drivel on the TV set. He loved peanut butter and it was a treat to have unsupervised access to the TV. Over the years, there was some disagreement as to what Thaddeus was watching when they returned. Sam's version had Thaddeus watching an old *Tom and Jerry* cartoon, shockingly racist, with an ignorant depiction of the cleaning woman in Tom's house shrieking at the sight of Jerry, her polka-dotted bloomers exposed and a pair of dice and a straight razor falling out of her apron. As Libby had it, the boy was watching either a rerun of *Leave It to Beaver*, or *Make Room for Daddy*, or some other nauseating idealization of family life—she couldn't tell the difference between any of those shows. But they both remembered he was there nearly naked and completely content with a tablespoon and a jar of Ann Page, a fat little Buddha with a beatific smile. They might have embraced him; he was all that stood between them and the abyss. But they couldn't, they didn't. *He looked so happy.* Madness to think so, and completely unfair, but neither stricken parent could escape the feeling that there was something wrong with a boy who could be feeding his face and laughing at the idiot box while his sister died.

Of course they never said as much, not to each other, and certainly not to him. Some things don't have to be said.

THE FAREWELL BRUNCH WAS CONVENED at the end of August, on one of those scorching late-summer days in Chicago when the sun felt as if it were trying to force itself into the apartment, a burglar made of flame. An old air conditioner croaked and rumbled in one of the Kaufmans' windows. The curtains were tied in a loose knot chilled and resting atop the Amana like a chignon, allowing the refrigerated air to enter the room, if only it would. The people in attendance were basically Libby and Sam's friends, with whom they had shared their socialist past and with whom they now shared a sense of proud internal exile. To Thaddeus, they were honorary aunts and uncles.

Not everyone who had been invited was in attendance. Sam and Libby had had the idea that the occasion of their son's going-away party might also be an occasion on which old wounds might be healed, or at least soothed. They had hoped to see their old comrade Doris Washington, but she had married a dentist who, while not Nation of Islam himself, took care of Elijah Muhammad, and now Doris was basically Black Nationalist and had cut herself off from the Kaufmans, and, they assumed, her other Caucasian friends. Also absent were Sy and Linda Cohen, who had begun their rightward drift during the Vietnam War and were now great friends of Charles Percy. The Kaufmans considered Senator Percy a country-club jerk, but the Cohens seemed eager to ingratiate themselves with their new Republican pals, and it seemed to have paid off for them—they were planning a move to D.C., where their long-standing anti-Stalinism would presumably be put to good use in one of the new think tanks. An invitation had been sent to Mario Esposito, who'd once had the nerve to fight for leftist principles in the Teamsters Union, but who now heard voices and lived with his daughter, and apparently never left her little town house in Jeffrey Manor. Pierpont Davis, Lucy Medoff, Bob and Kathy Brown, James Komatsu and his unacknowledged lover Allen Watanabe, Cal Harrington, and a half dozen others with whom Sam and Libby had shared so many meals, so many picket lines, so many late nights redolent of Chesterfields and mimeo ink, and who had either drifted away, driven by the steady wind of political defeat, or had stormed away, propelled by irreconcilable differences of theory and practice. Vietnam, Black Power, the rise of Women's Lib, the nightmare of the Cultural Revolution, the outrageous behavior of the new student rebels with their drugs and sexual obsessions, all of these things not only ended socialism as the Kaufmans understood it, but drained the vitality from their social life as well. And as the hour of the good-bye brunch approached and·it was clear to them that Thaddeus's moving to New York was not going to be the momentous occasion that would bring the old bunch back together again, Libby and Sam carried chairs away from the dining table and then pulled the table open and removed not one but two of the leaves.

Nevertheless. Here were the Mendelsohns, both leaning forward on their canes like old, smiling vaudevillians waiting for applause. Margie Mendelsohn, who always sang "We're Here Because We're Here" when she entered your house, had translated *Being and Nothingness* into Yiddish, and Herman, who, though somewhat serious about his Judaism, played organ at the Rockefeller Chapel. Here was Len Wasserman, recently forced out of his position in the economics department at the University of Chicago and now writing a book about Keynes, with his white crew cut and aviator glasses, ferociously fit like Jack LaLanne. Mrs. Thomas was there, their formerly Negro and now Afro-American housekeeper, whose first name might have been Margaret, though none of the Kaufmans had ever used it, considering it condescending to call her anything but Mrs. Thomas. They liked to think of her as a kind of family member, though now that she was here on a Sunday it did occur to Sam that Mrs. Thomas might rather not have been invited to the farewell brunch. She was in her fifties and was there with Mr. Thomas, who worked in an underground parking garage in the Loop, and whose face was speckled, losing its pigment to vitiligo. And here was Stanley Davidson, freelance book reviewer and free-spending customer at Four Freedoms. Rounding out the party were the Gomezes, a relatively young Mexican couple dressed for a dance recital scheduled for later in the day, she in a festive skirt with a multitude of brightly colored hems, he in trousers whose legs were three times broader than his own, both in shiny shoes with Cuban heels.

And then there was Grace Cornell, the twenty-one-year-old girl from the neighborhood who Sam and Libby thought of as Thaddeus's Summer Girl. Because he always had *someone.* He was always in love, or so it seemed to them. The Summer Girl was by all indications friendless. Always a bad sign, in Libby's view. She lived a few blocks away, which was the only logical explanation the elder Kaufmans had for her place in their son's life. As they saw her, Grace was neither beautiful, nor in possession of any special personal qualities. She was not witty or quick, and her politics, if they existed at all, were at best those of the six o'clock news. Nevertheless, Thaddeus had formed a smoochy alliance with her. He gave her piggyback rides around the apartment, scrambled eggs and fried bacon for her, and would not allow her to wash a dish or scrub a pan. He tried to amuse her with funny walks, crazy faces, and barnyard noises, and when she deigned to laugh his face reddened with happiness. He was her tummler, for crying out loud.

And on the subject of crying out loud? Sam and Libby sometimes could hear their son and Summer Girl thumping away. They found the noise intrusive, actually *loathsome*, but they chose to say nothing about it. They could only wait it out, ride summer's slow slide into autumn and peace. Matters concerning sex were difficult for Sam and Libby to discuss, as were all of the other bodily functions, and their reaction to this neighborhood girl bunking in with their boy night after night, using the apartment's one bath, scurrying around in a towel and flip-flops, shaving her legs, applying her mascara, joining them for breakfast, coming home in the early evening with little goodies like soaps and fancy jams pilfered from the hotel where she worked, their reaction to her basically becoming a member of their household was to say nothing. It was a situation with an expiration date; if there was one thing that could be depended upon, it was time passing. They registered their annoyance and embarrassment via long pauses, and the occasional pointed question. Some of these pointed questions were directed at Thaddeus, such as, *How is it you never seem to have money and we've been paying you at the bookshop all summer?* ("Because you put the *mum* in minimum wage, Mum.") But mainly the questions were directed at Grace, and the queries ranged from curiosity about her mother, whom they had yet to meet, her brother, whom they sensed was involved in illegal activity, and her education. She had tried to pass herself off as a student at the Art Institute, which was not exactly the London School of Economics, or the University of Chicago, or even the University of Michigan, but it was, as art schools went, a good one. However, upon further questioning it was revealed that Grace was taking only one summer evening class at the Art Institute. And the kicker was this—the girl had not even graduated from high school.

It was all quite obvious—though more to Libby than to Sam: the girl was a climber, and though the Kaufmans were merely middle class (or maybe a sniff or two higher), to scrappy, skinny Grace Cornell, Thaddeus was a catch. Sometimes she spoke like a girl from Eau Claire, Wisconsin, which was what she *was*, whose *g*'s were lucky to make their way to the end of a gerund, and sometimes she tried to sound like that skin-and-bones actress from *Breakfast at Tiffany's.*

"Grace," Libby called from the kitchen, as she and Mrs. Thomas prepared to bring out the food for the farewell brunch, "I hope you come and visit us at the store from time to time after Thaddeus leaves. Just because he's off in New York is no reason for you to be a stranger."

"Thank you, Libby," Grace said in a quiet voice, as if she did not care if she was heard or not.

"In case you're wondering what kind of Jews we are, here's your answer," Sam said to Grace, with a voilà wave toward the platter of bagels and lox Libby was placing before them. He was dressed for the heat in loose-fitting slacks and a sheer guayabera shirt through which his shaggy chest could not be ignored. He was a large, shambling man, with a high forehead and sleep-deprived eyes. He shaved daily, sometimes twice a day, and never failed to miss a spot.

The bagels, big, bloated Chicago bagels, were ready to eat, schmeared, loxed, onioned, tomatoed, and cut into quarters—no muss no fuss. The guests received them eagerly and with pleasure, except for Mr. Thomas, who frowned at his bagel and pulled it apart to inspect what was inside.

Grace's hand hovered over the platter, deciding which one to choose, and Thaddeus looked on with keen interest. She always tried to choose the best one; she was never on automatic pilot. Libby kept her eyes on Thaddeus while Grace deliberated. *See what you've gotten yourself into?*

"We're bagels-and-lox Jews," Sam said to Grace. He felt sorry for her. Awkward, pretentious little shiksa. Sweet, though. "Here, we're Jews of the belly and the book—but not the Bible, not the Torah, or any nonsense. Real books make real Jews, that's what I say."

"The old Sam Kaufman would have had something to say about that," chided Margie Mendelsohn. "Who used to wear the little beard like Trotsky himself."

Trotskyism ended with Hannah, and by the time of the Chicago riots at the Democratic National Convention in '68, Sam and Libby were no longer calling themselves socialists. They didn't even want to call themselves Democrats anymore—the Dems had seemed weak-kneed and complicit, aiming their outrage at the city's mayor and its police force, who admittedly were ham-handed in the face of student revolt, but the idiot liberals were doing what idiot liberals did best, namely wringing their hands and getting it all wrong. In the case of the so-called hippies and yippies, the liberals failed utterly to realize this new crop of so-called leftists were basically barbarians. Stalinoid, narcissistic, violent, and entitled, antagonistic toward Israel, and actually rooting for a Red takeover of Southeast Asia. Back in the old days, Sam and Libby used to say humanity's choice was socialism or barbarism. Well, socialism was a dead letter but barbarism was alive and kicking.

"So tell me, Grace," said Herman Mendelsohn, who seemed to know a little bit about nearly everything, "are you related to the Cornell after which one of our great Chicago streets is named? That of course would be Ezra Cornell, of Cornell University fame. And who also founded Western Union."

"I've never received a telegram," Thaddeus interjected. He had just noticed Hannah, slipping out of the room, holding a bagel in one ghostly hand, a paper napkin in the other, on her way to wherever it was. He closed his eyes, waited a moment, cleared his throat to make damn sure his voice would be cheerful. "It would be amazing, like being in a Fred Astaire movie or something."

"I don't know very much about my ancestors and all," Grace said. "My brother's going to get some expert to do a family tree for us."

Mrs. Thomas rose to bring pitchers of orange juice and tomato juice from the kitchen, but Libby insisted she sit and enjoy herself. Libby returned just in time to hear the words *family tree.*

"Those family trees," Libby pronounced. She was dressed festively, in turquoise stretch pants and earrings befitting a Mayan god. "All these people who think they're special because some great-great-second cousin came over on the *Mayflower.* Who cares? The Jewish people have been making history for five thousand years, writing law and making breakthroughs in science and industry and music and literature, and I'm supposed to *plotz* over some idiot who takes a boat ride three hundred years ago?"

"I always say, I'm not a Jew, I'm a human being," said Stanley Davidson.

"But you're not even Jewish, Stanley," said Sam.

"I mean if I were," Stanley said.

Sam adopted a more brunchlike tone. "So, how was Montreal?" To the Thomases he said: "He was up in Canada."

Davidson had been there for the Summer Games. In his youth he had hoped to go to the Olympics as a member of the fencing team, but he hadn't made the cut. He'd gotten close, however, and his friends deferred to him about all things athletic, including baseball and chess.

"It was an eye-opener," Davidson said. "I hate to tell you, but the Soviets were very impressive. I'm sorry, but that's just how it was."

"We can live with it, Stan," Sam said.

"I lost count, they medaled so many times. The women fencers, gold gold gold. I never saw anything like it. I don't know what they're feeding those gals. . . ."

Libby had to interrupt. "A steady diet of Stalinist lies, I'd say."

Grace was staring at her plate. As many times as Thaddeus had explained to her that his parents used to be followers of Leon Trotsky and in fact were *anti*-Communist, it still unnerved Grace to hear their guests go on about how wonderful the Russians were. Maybe, she thought, maybe they were all spies and Thaddeus was just too naive and cheerful to catch on?

"You're going to get the real bagels and lox once you get to New York," Margie Mendelsohn said to Thaddeus. She was a fleshy, forgiving woman. Thaddeus had always felt a special bond with Margie. He remembered telling a joke when he was ten or eleven years old to a roomful of his parents' friends and her being the only one to respond, how her great soaring laugh rose like the clarinet in a Dixieland band while all the other musicians sat still with their horns in their laps, scowling at their shoes.

"And where will you be staying?" Herman Mendelsohn asked. "Right in the city?"

"College friend," Thaddeus said. "He's got a place in Greenwich Village." He reached under the table and took Grace's hand, squeezed it reassuringly. "There's a million jobs in New York, and good ones. My friend Kip just got a job as a stockbroker and he majored in comparative lit. He can't even do simple math. I'll get a job and after a couple of paychecks get my own place. I'm thinking editor in chief at Random House."

"Funny, funny," Libby said. "You can always become a comedy writer." She was back from the kitchen again, circling the table with the coffeepot. It was an old tin percolator that looked as if it had been stolen from the set of a cowboy movie. The Kaufmans had been burning coffee in it for at least twenty years. They were not poor. Their shop afforded them a decent living, yet their apartment had a bare and sullen quality to it. It wasn't a form of Early Minimalism— they just didn't believe in squandering money on nonessentials. Why would you piss away your money on butter if you could have margarine for a third of the price? Shampoo? Shampoo was for suckers who didn't realize it was just soap in liquid form. What kind of halfwit would pay extra for Levi's when the store brand at Wieboldt's was just as blue, kept you just as warm, and was probably made in the same factory? This disdain for life's little niceties was a daily, practical application of their otherwise dormant Marxism.

"And what about you, darling?" Margie asked Grace. "Will you be continuing with your studies?"

"I'm not *rilly* sure, quite yet," Grace said. She moved her wedge of bagel and lox around her plate as if guiding a planchette around a Ouija board.

Thaddeus pressed his knee against hers. *I'm right here,* his leg said to hers.

"Is David Sheffield teaching human anatomy over there?" Herman asked. "Such a bright man. And a gifted teacher."

"I'm not *rilly* sure," Grace said.

"That would be a great job," Thaddeus said, his voice booming. "Teaching anatomy. It's not like you'd ever have to revise your syllabus!"

Grace smiled gratefully. It was what he lived for.

"She can't be expected to know the entire staff, Herman," Libby said. "You're mainly a summer student there, isn't that right, dear?" And then, to quickly cover the pettiness of her remark, Libby added, "Have you seen her work yet? It's absolutely breathtaking. You'd think they were photographs—eggs and artichokes and what have you. All done with a pencil. Out of this world. So tell us. When did you start this? Is it a hobby, or is this something you'd like to pursue?"

"Oh pursue, definitely pursue," said Grace. "I've been doing it my whole life. I'm self-taught, I guess. But I do my art every day. Even if I'm sick or having my period or anything."

Libby's eyes widened at the mention of Grace's menstruation.

"Well, you're such a lovely girl," said Libby, the irony in her voice like a concealed weapon. "And pretty girls have so many options."

But Grace was not going to back down. "*Art* is my option," she said. "I'm not in the least bit pretty. I'm a visual person and I see myself clearly. I wasn't cute as a little girl and I'm not pretty now."

"You shouldn't say things like that," Sam pleaded.

"But I don't mind it. It's just a fact. You live in the body you're born with. Anyhow . . ." She glanced at Thaddeus. He was looking at her with considerable amazement, as if the option of not doing everything imaginable to please Libby and Sam was being demonstrated for the first time. "I would love to be an artist," Grace said. "I'll just keep at it and maybe someone will discover me. That would be my dream."

"Dreams are beautiful," Libby said. "I wish we could all live in dreams."

It was suddenly so quiet that when Grace put her coffee cup back down onto the saucer it clanked loudly.

Some of his friends talked about how it felt to be trapped at the parental table, and how mothers and fathers ran guilt trips if the visits were too short. Thaddeus was grateful he didn't have *that* to contend with. He had told his parents that Grace was due at work at 1 P.M. and they were going to have to leave the good-bye brunch no later than noon. Grace worked in the Palmer House, the very hotel in which reporters and Democratic bigwigs watched from the windows in '68 while the police gassed and clubbed the demonstrators on the other side of Michigan Avenue.

AT NOON, THADDEUS AND GRACE stood on the corner of Kimbark and Fifty-Fifth Street, hands linked. Not very far away was Stagg Field, where Enrico Fermi and his coworkers built America's first atomic bomb in the squash court beneath the stadium. Thaddeus always wondered if radiation was running beneath the sidewalk, zizzing through the cement, entering his body through the soles of his feet.

"Was that awful?" Thaddeus asked.

"It was fine. I liked the part when you walked around the table and shook everybody's hand. It was so formal."

"I play by the rules."

"Whose rules?"

"My parents. My poor parents."

"Poor? With that big apartment and air conditioning and a maid?"

"I didn't mean poor in that way. Anyhow, they sell used books. They don't have much."

"They have a maid. She comes every Wednesday at nine and leaves at two."

"Anyhow, we don't call it a maid. Housekeeper."

"Whatever. She's still mopping the floors and cleaning the bathroom. It's kind of funny, them being such Communists and everything."

"They're not Communists. They never were."

"Well, it's still funny. And she never said a word and neither did her husband. I bet they would rather have been spending Sunday with their own people."

Thaddeus wondered if there might be a bit of racism in that phrase: *their own people.* "They're part of our family," he said.

Grace laughed, but let it go at that.

They walked east to catch the number 5 bus downtown. A professorial-looking couple was walking toward them, the man balding, the sunlight throbbing in his little round eyeglasses, the woman with a straw bag and the look of an aging folk singer. They pushed a stroller with their shirtless two-year-old in it, and nodded and smiled as they passed.

"Do you know them?" Grace asked.

"Maybe they come to the store. I don't know."

"People like you, though. I see that. It must feel strange."

"It's fine. Why shouldn't they?"

"People don't like me. I don't rub people the right way."

"You do me," Thaddeus said, wagging his brows Groucho style.

"Strangers then. When people get to know me, it's better."

"That kid liked you. He was looking right at you and smiling."

"What kid?"

"Sitting in his stroller like a little king."

"I didn't notice. Kids are not my thing. It's hard enough for a woman to be an artist."

They were just then passing the building where Grace lived. Thaddeus had yet to see the inside of her apartment. It had seemed awkward and strange before, her refusal to allow him into the rooms she shared with her mother, but he no longer questioned it. He had even stopped imagining what it might be like in there—though he was sure the place was dark, untidy, sad. It had once been the janitor's apartment until he refused to live there, saying that his doctor told him the lack of daylight was driving him into a depressed state of mind. Grace's older brother, Liam, paid the rent, but rarely visited. She was evasive about where Liam lived; different answers were given, Boston, Mexico City, Tucson. Maybe all the answers were true, maybe none of them. Liam sold marijuana in quantities. That much he had been able to ascertain. The idea of breaking the law was terrifying to Thaddeus, but Grace seemed to take it in stride.

THE PALMER HOUSE. GRACE HAD been working there for two years, starting off in housekeeping and more recently behind the desk in her blazer and skirt. She sometimes complained about work, because that's what you did, but she was proud of the hotel, proud of its luxury and its history. It had been bought and sold a few times, torn down, rebuilt, renovated, modernized, and through it all, it remained a home away from home for people used to the best things—presidents who came to Chicago slept in the Palmer House, as did bankers and movie stars, Capone himself, Mark Twain, Sarah Bernhardt.

"Should I come in?" Thaddeus asked her as they approached the gilded entrance, with its carvings, its bright windows, its fairyland glow.

"Definitely," she said.

"I don't want to get you in trouble."

"We're like a family here," she said, as she took Thaddeus's arm and led him in. The traffic hummed behind them. The heat was epic, the noonday sun. Stanley, the oldest of the bellmen, opened the door for them and touched the bill of his braided cap. Grace stood so straight she seemed an inch taller. They were on *her* turf now. "Here I am not *liked*," she said. "Here I am *loved*." She whisked Thaddeus through the lobby, *her* lobby, which looked like a room in a sultan's palace, red and gold, with inlaid ceilings and soaring arches. There were still dozens of American flags, large and small, scattered through the lobby, left over from the July bicentennial celebration.

"Where are we going?" he asked.

"Surrender," she said. She led him to the elevators, where the brass doors were finely etched with Art Deco designs.

Through the corner of his eye he saw the chimera of his sister crossing the lobby. He always looked. He'd looked a million times. It was a reflex.

When he turned back again, the elevator doors opened and he followed Grace in. The car was carpeted and upholstered and lit with cheerful little lamps.

"You got us a room?" Thaddeus whispered, as the elevator rose with the chains clanking.

She linked a finger through his belt loop and yanked him closer. "I'm sort of a favorite here, if you must know, you terrible boy," she said. "I can do what I want."

He was still trying to decide if she was beautiful, though it didn't matter. There was something hard about her. She was thin, but not the way models are. A pioneer thinness, the scrawn of deprivation. He could imagine her in a gingham dress, in a rocking chair, on a porch, with a shotgun on her lap.

The room was on the tenth floor and it was as stately and full of promise as a box from an expensive shop, everything in it just so, the gleaming bath fixtures, the spotless carpet, the tall mahogany dresser with its double rows of brass handles. Room 1030—they would never forget it—with its triple-glazed windows and view of Grant Park and Lake Michigan, where a ceaseless progression of little waves made their way to the shore, each one showing its frill of white foam like cancan dancers shaking their petticoats.

Next door, however, someone was weeping. Or was it above them, or below them? It sounded like a woman, but it could have been a man. Grief can blur the distinction. They heard the sobs through the plaster. Silence, and then more sobs. Grace turned on the little bedside KLH radio. It was as easy as that.

"So? What do you think of the room?"

"Your boss doesn't mind?"

"I've got my boss wrapped around . . ." She raised a pinkie, grinned.

"Try working for my mother," Thaddeus said.

"Mothers," said Grace. "I can hardly wait not to be one."

"You're already not one."

"I'm too young not to be a mother. You're only not a mother when people start to ask you why you don't have children."

"I still haven't met your mother," said Thaddeus. "I haven't even seen where you live."

"Think of me as living here," said Grace. "In a lovely place with a beautiful view. And all my friends are beautiful artists and we all live for art, and nothing is stupid or boring."

It was art that had brought them together, initially. In the beginning of the summer, Thaddeus had accompanied Libby to the Hyde Park Art Fair, where every year hundreds of local painters displayed their paintings and sculptures and weaving and carving and photographs in a vast outdoor democracy of effort and ambition, yearning and love. Libby wasn't there to buy anything. One simply attended the fair; it was part of living in the neighborhood. Some of the locals exhibiting their work were Four Freedoms customers, and Libby and Sam made it a point for one or the other of them to show their face at the fair. Somewhere along the way Libby and Thaddeus came upon a ratty little card table that, in disregard of the rules of the fair, Grace had wedged between two officially sanctioned booths: one displaying paintings done in the style of Maurice Utrillo, and the other, manned by a thin elderly lithographer in a heavy sweater, showing a multiracial group of children playing on an Anywhere USA street. On Grace's renegade little table were propped a number of her drawings, hyperrealistic renderings of eggs, apples, and artichokes, each done in overwhelming detail, each exuding a kind of mania for verisimilitude.

Libby bought an egg drawing for thirty dollars, and later that day Thaddeus returned to the fair, hoping to buy another of Grace's drawings, perhaps the artichoke, and to strike up a conversation with her. But by the time he made it back, she had already been asked to leave—forcibly escorted out by a pair of furious fair organizers, women in short capes and darkly hemmed nylon hose, and shoes that clacked like castanets across the asphalt playground.

Yet the very next day Grace came into Four Freedoms. The egg drawing had been paid for by a check drawn on the store account, so it was possible she had come looking for Thaddeus just as he had gone looking for her, but if that was the case she never admitted it. She continued to say she was there hoping to find a book of Ingres drawings, which Liam had told her about, having seen an exhibition of the work at the Fogg Museum in Cambridge.

Though she was aware the Kaufmans were not fond of her, it was nevertheless bizarre to Grace that Thaddeus could ever complain about his parents or suggest that staying with them over the summer represented some kind of sacrifice on his part, a trial by fire. Grace would have been more than happy to live as the Kaufmans lived. They had Persian carpets, beautiful pale green glass vases from Hungary in which stood indestructible pussy willows. They had floor-to-ceiling bookshelves. They owned a gigantic Magnavox stereo console, and they owned their own business.

And now summer was almost over, and despite the weeks of physical intimacy, Thaddeus and Grace were still a bit strange to each other. What would become of them once Thaddeus was in New York? "You've got to visit me there, promise me you will" was as close as he'd come to asking her to go with him. "I already miss you" was as close as she came to saying she wanted to go with him.

They fell into the big Palmer House bed. The headboard knocked against the wall and they had to pull the bed away from the wall by an inch or two, but it turned out not to be enough. The banging continued and they let it. . . .

When they were quiet for a while, Grace pressed herself against him. The tidal smell of sex and the sweat of exertion came off her. His feelings were too strong to confidently name—desire? tenderness? worshipful love? lust? "I'm in over my head here," he whispered to her. "It's like I never slept with anyone before, ever in my life."

"I think my father was the first man my mother ever slept with," said Grace. "She squandered her virginity. I shouldn't say that, but she's such a pushover. Always settles for less."

"But she loved him. Maybe?" he asked. He could feel melancholy moving through her like weather. It drew him toward her, the knowledge of it. It wasn't pity, it was simply *knowing* her, being able to feel what she felt. It created in him an intensity of feeling that was almost like a mania. He wanted to cheer her up. To lift her spirits, lead her out of her own darkness. He would have sung for her and danced, had he dared.

"He was good looking," Grace said. "Even with that missing finger. I was obsessed with that finger when I was young. Sometimes he caught me staring at it, the little stump. And he'd press it against my forehead. I'd scream. Like how the teenyboppers screamed for the Beatles. That's how I screamed for that jerk."

"Maybe we can go see him one day. Would you like that?"

"I love that you always want to make things nice, but I don't need to be rejected again. He's not interested. His interests lie elsewhere."

"I'll bet he loves you."

"I don't even think he likes me. Or hates me. I'm just like . . . I don't know. Nothing."

"That's impossible."

"People aren't really drawn to me. I might not be all that likeable."

"You have to stop thinking that way. I liked you so much, from the very beginning."

"Well, that's why you get to make love to me in this beautiful room."

A bar of light, reflected from somewhere unknown, glided across the smooth white ceiling. The music on the radio was Beethoven. Neither of them cared for it, but neither was willing to say so. Thaddeus turned the volume down and the suffering next door could be heard again, but very faintly. Thaddeus stretched, made a sound like a creaking door. The bed seemed larger than a normal bed, more comfortable, too. The exquisite sheets, the goose-down pillows. This is what life could be. He felt himself heading toward it, like someone who has been lost at sea and suddenly sees the first hopeful signs of land.

"What we have here, my dear," she said.

"Yes?" he said. She often paused in the middle of a sentence. When they spoke on the phone, these silences irritated him, but in person they sometimes seemed profound.

"What we have here is so incredibly beautiful and unexpected. I feel like we have both sleep-wandered into something beyond imagination. I just don't know how it happened, what connects us. Because as soon as we saw each other—we knew. When I think of all the ways we could have *missed* each other, I feel such blind terror."

She saw the blood rush to his face and she smiled, knowing she had overwhelmed him. It was what she had, it was something she could do. Most of the standard advantages were his—college degree, plans for the future, a thousand books read, and a few he planned to write. But *intensity* was hers, and she could level him with it. Candor, emotional fierceness, a willingness to risk being hurt, these were all with her. She was not exactly pretty but she was beautiful. Her arms were slender and strong, with dark hair that grew in whorls, like fingerprints. At first the dark hair alarmed him but soon it was part of her allure—everything about her seemed real, the truth of life at last revealed. Her imperfections were perfect themselves, her mild perversities in bed were proof of purity, her aloneness in the world was really a manifestation of her oneness with the universe.

"I agree," he finally managed to say. "A preordained accident. So glad." For a moment, his mind was blank. Words were failing him.

Grace rolled out of bed and stood there for a moment, enjoying the way Thaddeus looked at her. Would he ever be free of her, a boy who looked at her with such helpless longing? Was he hers

forever? She'd always known that eventually her fate would be tied
to a man. Was this that man? She was so young. And she was wary
of early alliances. Her mother had forged an early alliance and it
had been disastrous. Grace's father, more absent than present, more
crooked than honest, more false than truthful, self-pitying and useless. His name was Terrence Cornell, Terry to his friends, of which
there were many. He was a fleshy, wheezing, cheerful, and energetic
man. Terry had been in the navy during the Korean War; he was a
seaman first class on the USS *Iowa* and had lost half of the pointer
finger on his right hand, caught in a hatch door halfway through his
hitch. There was a suspicion that he had done it on purpose. "And
what about this cough and my gunked-up lungs?" he often said. "I
suppose I did that on purpose, too!" His theory was that there was
something in all that on-board fireproofing that didn't agree with
his respiratory system, but he could not find anyone to give his theory credence—no doctor, no lawyer, no one but some old anarchist
who worked in a health food store, a scrawny little yapper who wore
a beret and sandals, and whose breath was yeasty from B vitamins.
While his marriage was still going forward, Cornell supported his
family as a portrait photographer in a little studio he rented on State
Street. He specialized in children, and eventually there were rumors.
Grace never knew if they were true or not and she did not want to
know. Rumors about boys, rumors about girls—it seemed Cornell
was more focused on age than gender. But that he would actually
do such a thing was so very hard to believe; if anything, he'd been a
bit distant with his own children. A bit of a touch-me-not. All Grace
and her older brother Liam knew was that stupid people were saying
their father was doing something wrong at his job. One day two policemen came to the house, like Joe Friday and Officer Frank What-
the-Fuck, and asked Terry a bunch of questions, while Grace and
Liam stayed in the kitchen with Maureen. "You know," Maureen
said (holding beneath the table the bottle of Gilbey's with which she
was lacing her lemonade, keeping the gin hidden as if her children

were not in full awareness of it), "there's a saying that where there's smoke there's fire and I guess whoever made it up was a real stick-in-the-mud, but you have to ask yourself where's the smoke coming from if there's no fire."

The cops left twenty minutes later and Terry was all smiles because as far as he was concerned, they'd been able to see him as the war veteran father husband workingman that he was. But the next day there were four cops at the apartment and they tore the place apart, never saying what they were looking for. Closets, drawers, upholstery, the fridge, even the little bedroom Grace and Liam bunked in, with the butterscotch walls and the red-and-blue hooked rug, every corner of the apartment torn up, ransacked. The next day Terry was gone. His flight from Eau Claire could have been said to speak volumes, but you never knew. At an early age Grace believed that we are privy only to the appearance of other people, rarely their reality. Now her father plied his trade in Akron, Ohio. No talk of extradition, no more talk about what he did or did not do with the children who came to be photographed. There was vindication in that, wasn't there? Grace wrote him a letter to tell him it was safe to come home, but he didn't answer. She decided to never write him, or speak to him, again. Liam was more forgiving and made his own money. He didn't need a handout to see his own father, but he came back from Ohio shaken. It took weeks for him to finally report that their father was now very fat, with a whole new array of symptoms and diagnoses—asthma, diabetes, varicose veins, arthritis. There was reason to believe he was involved in more questionable kinds of photography as well. Liam had seen a check for two hundred dollars from *Sir Knight*, a skin magazine.

"Come back to bed," Thaddeus said.

"I'm going to pee," Grace said.

"Can I watch you?" He had never watched anyone relieve themselves before. He was raised to believe urination and defecation were basically awful things that one had to endure, the body's bad news.

(The only truly good news was the mind.) His mother had taught him to urinate on the side of the bowl to avoid the telltale splash.

"Of course. But let me ask you something, buddy boy. How are you going to survive the real separation?" She traipsed across the carpet and opened the heavy door to the bathroom. He did not follow her in. He was more talk than action. She turned on the lights and the immaculate bathroom sprang into view. There was a fresh roll of toilet paper in the holder, the lead sheet folded into a kind of teepee shape.

"Maybe I'll take a shower," Thaddeus said when Grace came back to bed.

"No. Don't you dare." The more she cared about him, the bossier she became. Having been left to her own governance most of her life, she thought telling someone what to do was a form of affection. She thought that saying *Absolutely not* was sweet and the words *Watch out, buddy* meant basically the same thing as *I'll never let you go.*

He closed his eyes for a moment, savoring the implication: she wanted more of him. More! Desire was like a bird flapping its wings inside his head. Love buzzed within him like a neon marquee on a street where every other business had called it a night. This was happiness as he had always imagined it. The pleasure was frightening. He was in a drugged state in which he did not completely recognize himself.

"This room is amazing," Thaddeus said. "I feel rich here. I wish we didn't have to go back to real life."

"We don't. We have it all day and all night. I could probably get Jerry to send up food. Maybe even wine. Or champagne."

"Don't you worry about being fired?"

"No. It's like family here. At least for me it is. I can basically do whatever I want."

"My parents would hate it here. Especially my father. He doesn't like to go into places where ordinary working people aren't welcome. To him, class privilege is like the smell of shit. It actually makes him sick."

"Should I get champagne?" she asked.

"My parents announced we were having champagne when I graduated," Thaddeus said. "So they brought out this bottle of Cold Duck. In an actual bucket. It was a yellow plastic bucket, like for a mop, but with lots of ice in it."

"At least you graduated," Grace said. She straddled him, kissed his eyes, not wanting him to see the look on her face.

They made love again. At first it was languid, lovely and friendly, easy and slow. But finally Thaddeus started to bear down, the look on his face serious, almost fierce, concentrating on her orgasm as if trying to decipher ancient text. He could not have cared less about his own. He was empty. But hers. Hers. That was the thrill of it anyhow. What happened to her face, her eyes, her breath. Finally, out of pity, she stopped him.

"It ain't gonna happen," she said, smiling.

Relieved, he rolled off her. He lay on his back, breathing in the expensive, perfectly cooled air. They were silent for a while until Thaddeus again announced he had best wash.

"Well, if you must," she said. "The showers here are great. All the guests comment on the showers. Great water pressure. And amazing towels."

"Did you ever read—"

But Grace cut him off. She had not read widely and she was already uneasy with how many times he asked her if she had read this or that. She was tired of saying no. Tired of being the person who knew not. Books were his thing, not hers. She did not constantly drop the names of obscure painters (not that she knew many, but still) and she was waiting for him to take the hint and stop asking her what she had read. She was waiting for him to realize you could not impress someone without depressing them, too.

He showered. All that shampoo. Conditioner, too. From France, no less. The perfume of it was amazing. Ooh la fucking la! The soft and thirsty towels. They made the towels at home seem like waxed paper. He forced himself to leave a couple of dry ones for Grace. *This is how I want to live! I never want to run out of these towels.*

RELUCTANTLY, THEY DRESSED. THE ROOM was cool, but when you touched the windows you felt the heat of the blazing afternoon. Thaddeus lingered before they left the room for good, committing it all to memory. Grace. The feeling of entering her, like a firm welcoming handshake. And the room itself, the bed, the immense, luxurious bed. The long drapes glittering with gold thread. The cool whisper of invisible vents. Oh, to live like this. It wasn't just the coarse, mindless desire to be rich, it was wanting life itself to be rich. To be surrounded by beauty, to be beautiful yourself. And to have this girl, this kind of sex, to wander forever in an orchard of pleasure. Once she said, "I can make myself come just by looking at you." What could ever compare to that?

He dug into his pocket, where there were three carefully folded five-dollar bills. He placed one as a tip on the nightstand before he left.

"Last chance," she said, ready to let the door close behind them. She could feel his desire for her. He was in a kind of agony. It made her want to torture him in a friendly sort of way.

"The summer went so fast," Thaddeus said.

"Are you going to miss me, you terrible boy?"

"I don't even like to think about that." He felt himself at last ready to pose the question: *Why not come with me?* But what if she said no? And what if she said yes? It was one thing to look at the astonishing view; it was another to leap off the side of the mountain, on the chance you might sprout wings.

Into the long hotel corridor. Grace turned the Do Not Disturb sign around so whoever was working the floor would know the room could be made up. The sign showed a cartoon of a little maid with popsicle-stick legs and a black-and-white dress, pushing a vacuum cleaner. The bed would be stripped, the sheets and the towels tossed into the big hamper. The air would smell of furniture polish spritzed out of a can. The pillows would be punched and shaken until they swelled up like new. It took twenty-two minutes to bring the room up to Palmer House standards but Rosie could do it in fifteen and then crack a window and light up a Parliament.

Lagging behind, Thaddeus listened for the sounds he had heard, the weeping. Where was it? All was silence, yet it was going on somewhere: he knew it. When he turned around he saw Grace was halfway down the long mauve corridor, heading for the elevators. Did she even know he wasn't right behind her?

"Grace," he called out. "Wait for me." He stood there until she turned around. The dull, even light of the corridor. The pink-and-green carpeting. Her *Mona Lisa* smile. The hollow deadish ding of an elevator arriving on the tenth floor. A moment later another ding, one going up and one going down.

They necked in the ornate cube as it carried them to the lobby. When the filigreed doors opened, they were facing Mr. Hallenback himself, Grace's boss, who, as luck would have it, was on his way up to the tenth floor with the intention of rousting Grace from the room she had been using in full and flagrant violation of company policy.

"Oh there she is, there she is," Hallenback said.

Thaddeus could sense this was Grace's supervisor. But what was he doing here on his day off? Someone must have ratted them out. He was younger than Thaddeus had imagined—in his late twenties, early thirties. He was not dressed for work, but in shorts, his legs massive, his bare feet in beat-up sneakers. He squeezed and cracked his knuckles as he spoke.

Grace smiled brightly, as if nothing was wrong. "Hello there, Mr. Hallenback," she said. "Working on Sundays?"

"Get out of the elevator, both of you," he said. "Right now."

"Hey," she said. "What's the big deal?"

But there was a tremor in her voice, a crack of fear that went right through it, a place where it would break for good if any more pressure was applied.

"Out of the elevator," Hallenback said, clearly affronted that the order had to be repeated. He had picked up one of the eight-by-twelve-inch bicentennial flags and thwacked it into his open hand as if he were a drill sergeant about to dress down a shoddy recruit.

"We are getting out of the elevator," Thaddeus said. "There's no reason to speak in such a harsh tone."

Hallenback pointed the flag stick at Thaddeus as a warning. The lobby was all but empty, with only a couple of bellmen and the desk clerks, all of whom were doing whatever they could to ignore what was taking place.

"You were using room 1030, is that right?"

Grace was silent. Her face was scarlet and she stared at her feet.

"*Right* as in correct?" asked Thaddeus.

"Who is this?" Hallenback asked Grace.

"Yes, we were," Grace said. "I was. Just for a while. It was vacant."

"It was vacant," Hallenback repeated, as if what she had just said reached the heights of absurdity.

"Well, it was," Grace said.

"Do you know what the rate is on room 1030?" Hallenback asked.

"It's Sunday," Grace said softly.

"Don't you know the first thing about the hotel business? Friday, Saturday, that's when we offer discounts. Sunday through Thursday nights—full tariff, twelve months a year. Those are the workdays, goddamnit, the workdays, and people are staying with us because they are doing business. You *do* know what business is, don't you . . . Grace?" He pronounced her name as if there was something unclean about it.

Grace forced herself to meet his gaze. Thaddeus moved closer to her. He realized he would only be making matters worse by speaking up again or putting his arm around her, but he moved his foot closer and closer to hers, until they were touching.

"I am going to do you a favor, and I am going to give you the employee discount on that room, but as it stands now you owe the Palmer House $105, plus tax, which I will have deducted from your paycheck."

"You can't, Mr. Hallenback," Grace said. "You can't do that."

"Come on, man," Thaddeus said. "Let's be fair about this."

"You can shut your trap," Hallenback said.

Thaddeus's eyes opened wider, his head snapped back. "I'm just saying you should be fair."

"We will put a check in the mail," Hallenback said to Grace. "You are not welcome to ever set foot in this hotel again. You no longer are employed here." For a moment it looked as if he was going to jab her with the flag but he stopped short of her collarbone.

Instinctively, Thaddeus grabbed for the flag, but Hallenback was quick. He hit Thaddeus across the hand with it.

"How about I press charges?" Hallenback said to Grace. "Is that what you want?"

"How about I press charges," Thaddeus said, rubbing the back of his hand, which was already turning rather red. "You're not allowed to hit people."

"Do you have any idea how the world works?" Hallenback asked. "You are, or were, an employee here. You know what *employee* means? You sell your labor—that is your relationship to the Palmer House. You don't help yourself to rooms. You don't help yourself to anything. You have a yearning to stay in nice hotels? Earn it. Go to college. Or better yet, get a high school diploma." He smiled, seeing her reaction. "You didn't think I knew that, did you? Well, I did, and I let you work here anyhow. Out. Of courtesy. To. Your. Mother." With each pause he threatened her with the tip of the flag.

"Come on, Carl," Grace said. "I said I was sorry." She reached out to touch his arm and he smacked her hand quite briskly with the rolled-up little flag.

Thaddeus was astonished. His skin felt pinpricked and icy. Was he meant to do something now? Should he lunge at Hallenback? Would that only serve to make everything worse?

Hallenback turned and walked toward the front desk, reaching behind himself and plucking at the fabric of his shorts.

"What a crock," Thaddeus said to Grace. "Are you okay?" He took her hand. A red welt was on the back of her hand, about the size of a centipede. He sensed the words *I thought you said this place was like a family* forming in his mind and he struggled not to say them.

"Just get me out of here," she murmured. "Let's just go."

She shook her head as they headed for the doors. She shed tears, silently. Raymond the bellman was slouched deep in a club chair, reading the *Herald-American*, which he had expertly folded so it was no larger than a paperback book. This time he did not do them the honor of opening the door for them, nor did he touch the bill of his braided cap. His act of courtesy was to pretend not to notice Grace as she walked past him.

"Some family," Thaddeus said as he gestured for Grace to go first through the revolving doors. He took a last breath of refrigerated air as the two of them were about to be engulfed by the fetid evening that lay in wait for them.

Why would you say something like that? she did not ask him, as she entered one of the pie-slice segments of the revolving door. Thaddeus entered the next segment and she felt him pushing at the door, making it go faster than she wanted. When they were out on Michigan Avenue, he put his arm around her and she pressed her forehead against his chin and said to him what she believed at the moment to be the absolute and unalterable truth: "I'm yours."

Dear Liam,

How's the Hotel d'Inghilterra? I trust, dear boy, that they are treating you in the manner to which you have become accustomed. I got sort of fired from the Palmer House but I got Mom to send a telex direct from the Palmer House to alert them that a VIP was on his way so I hope they rolled out the red carpet for you. Do you have your trusty Leica

*with you? I want you to take a hundred pictures of Rome.
And if Genevieve is not too busy shopping she can take some
of you in your room. I would love love love to see you in your
custom-made hand-stitched, lemon yellow summer suit with
the gauzy curtains of the giganto windows billowing behind
you. One day I am going to get over there, too, so don't cause
any trouble because I would like the royal treatment when
it's my turn. Except I won't have the trusty old Palmer House
telex to pave the way, unless Mom cooperates, which I don't
think will be happening since she is royally pissed off at me
right now. And why? you might ask. And why would our
mother be pissed off at the dutiful daughter who has been
more of a mother than a daughter? Well, my wandering
brother, the answer to both these questions is the same. I am
moving to New York City. Tomorrow. Via jet on American
Airlines. Believe me you, I have been studying crash patterns
and as far as I can see, no accidents have been recorded on
Labor Day, ever. I am worried about Legionnaire's Disease,
though, everyone breathing the same air. Our mother is
pretending she is pleased as punch, but the punch, dear
boy, is poisoned. Since I told her my plans, she is drinking
more and enjoying it less. She is making no attempt to
clean up around this place or even pick up after herself, and
somewhere along the way she has gotten the idea that Roses in
the Snow looks good on teeth as well as lips. Don't think I'm
horrid. I've been doing this my whole life and for the last five
years you've been free. Don't get me wrong. I live vicariously
through you and your amazing adventures. Because of
you, I sometimes feel I am in Rome, or San Francisco, or
Colombia, or Acapulco, though I've never even been on a
plane or a boat. I went to Washington, D.C., when I wrote
that embarrassing essay in sixth grade and came in third in
the National Citizenship Contest, but that's been about it
for me in terms of exotic travel destinations. Because of you,*

you wicked boy, I can pretend I have partied hearty with the likes of Dr. John the Night Tripper and Stephen Stills. Don't worry! I can see your eyes darting ahead in this aerogram, making sure I am not saying something you don't want me to put out there. Anyhow, New York. Labor Day. I am going there because I am in love. (Ooops, there go your eyes again, only this time they're rolling to the back of your head.) But the strange part is, I am in love with someone who loves me. Thought I'd give that approach a try, ha ha ha. He loves my art, and he doesn't mind if I snore. So wish me luck. I'm off to New York, if the plane doesn't crash. Give my regards to Genevieve, if you're still keeping her around.

Chapter 2

French Style

SEPTEMBER 3, 1976

What's with the answer machine? A man of your stature should have a secretary. Anyhow, Tony here. I was able to secure the item we've been talking about so we'll see you at our place Friday. Seven o'clock? Or come earlier if you wish. And for God's sake, erase this message.

H AT, I HAVE TO ASK YOU FOR THE BIGGEST MOST DESPER-ate last-minute favor I have ever asked another human being on the face on the earth for and if my back wasn't acting up, I'd be begging down on my knees," said Tony Boyett with his customary mock humility. Boyett was a drug-addicted lawyer in his late forties, and the man he called Hat was twenty years his senior. Boyett and his wife owned a house called Orkney, named after King Arthur's birthplace, built on a promontory overlooking the Hudson River about a hundred miles from New York City, in the town of Leyden, New York.

Tony and his wife, Parker, were having a hard time holding on to the property. The bills—taxes, repairs, gas, oil, electric—arrived like ransom notes. They did their best to take it in stride. They were not the first to lead irregular lives in the old house—Orkney had been the site of shootings, stabbings, and a century's worth of scandalous copulations. Buried around the property were the bones of

Indians and slaves, banknotes dating from the Royal British Bank scandal of 1856, Krugerrands, manuscripts and maps, and even the body parts of at least one inconvenient mistress. The house's more mundane history was buried in two private dumps on the property, where staff disposed of garbage from the main house. Every now and then rising up from their shallow grave came discarded household items such as a candlestick with its socket stuffed with thick black wax, and countless opaque glass bottles, some clearly from the local apothecary, soda, rye, milk of magnesia, as well as one haunted baby doll, her little mouth a silent scream.

It was a house that defied the standard categories of architectural style, fashioned out of wood, brick, and rough-hewn stone. It sprouted chimneys every which way. It had a steep outdoor staircase that was meant to lead to a third-story widow's walk that never was built. The windows were scattered chaotically, and seemed to go up and down like musical notes on the lines of a staff. But now its ungainliness had been eclipsed by its historical noteworthiness, much as a fool can become a source of wonder and admiration if he lives to be one hundred. The architecture and the legend were not the whole story, either. It had an unobstructed view of the river, with no other houses or anything that suggested the twentieth century. It also came with nearly fifty acres of rolling fields and towering woods, where there lived owls and raccoons, herons, pileated woodpeckers, hawks, eagles, wild turkeys, foxes, weasels, deer, coyotes, and now and again a bobcat.

Tony Boyett worked for Scattergood and Clark, an investment firm where his grandfather and father had worked, and where two days a week Tony sat at a small desk in an out-of-the-way little office, handling his family's gradually diminishing holdings; cousins and grandnephews and other Boyetts had either gone broke or transferred their holdings to other, less moribund companies. Occasionally after work, before catching the train back to Leyden, Boyett went to a bare, boxy little apartment in a high-rise on West Fifteenth Street to buy a week's worth of dope from a woman named Candace, enough for himself and Parker. He took good care of Parker, through whose family Orkney had come. Using the drug was never meant to be a nightly event, but an occasional reward for getting through another day on what the Boyetts called the Most Annoying Planet in the Universe. They had what they considered their own unique approach to drug use and their way of making sure that they did not descend into full-blown Man with a Golden Arm, Hatful of Rain addiction was to make most weekends dope free. Saturdays they took the edge off things with martinis and on Sunday it was cognac.

This Saturday, however, opium was on the menu. Opium was rare in New York, but recently a few Iranians who believed their suave despotic ruler's hold on power was starting to slip had moved to New York, and, just as refugees of yore had secreted diamonds on their person, some of the fleeing Iranians had brought with them black opium. Instability in Iran turned out to be a Boyett boon, since opium was something Tony and Parker had always wanted to try. Cocteau wrote that the smell of opium was the least stupid smell in the world. Julia Lee singing "Lotus Blossom" was one of their favorite songs. Not to mention Coleridge! And now, at long last, they had a ball of the stuff, black and gummy, round and yummy, and their reasoning was that you couldn't really become addicted to it because where the hell were you going to find it again? In the past ten days, Tony and Parker had smoked some of it, brewed some as a tea, and, most efficiently and effectively, shoved a bit up their rectums—French style, in Tony's words, since once in Paris he had been prescribed opium suppositories by a doctor who looked quite a bit like Jean-Paul Sartre, replete with smudged glasses and a face full of blackheads. Both Tony and Parker were looking forward to telling their guests to shove something up their asses. In the meantime, the two of them had never been closer, never more in love. Dope in all its many manifestations, its pursuit, its ingestion, its taboo, its mortal dangers, and its financial obligation bound them as once sex, and then Orkney itself had bound them. They were going to lose the house one day—soon perhaps, and this was obvious to both of them—and all they could say about sex was that with the O around, it ceased to be a source of embarrassment since it turned chastity from a failure of the relationship into a side effect, with Parker dry as toast, and Tony soft as an oyster.

"That lumbar of yours, along with the thoracic," Hat was saying, frowning with what gave every appearance of sympathy—but as everyone along the river said, it was not easy to know what or even *if* Hat was thinking. Few people knew his real name. Even his son had to hesitate when asked what his father's given name was—it was Philip. And though Hat Stratton was voluble verging on logorrhea, he never spoke personally, and if one were to presuppose that beneath all the verbiage and the weird erudition there was an inner life, it would also have to be said that this inner life was something Hat kept to himself. Here's what the Boyetts knew: Hat's wife had died at the age of forty. His daughter left home at sixteen. Hat's son had slept with half the working-class girls in the county and a few girls who it might have been assumed were out of his reach, as well. "Myself, I favor the good old Canadian Air Force exercises," Hat said. "First thing in the morning, before my Chase and Sanborn. I do it by muscle groups. The body is very orderly, if you don't mind my saying. . . ."

"Yes, well, the problem I'm faced with is this, Hat, my friend. We're having people for drinks in about an hour," Boyett said. "Old friends, we call them oil and water because her family owns some wells and his is in shipping, though not in a big way." Boyett was a tall, dry man—everything about him was dry: his parchment skin, his nickel gray eyes, his oak brown hair, his colorless cracked lips, his voice. He was dressed in shapeless khaki trousers and a T-shirt. He thought that if people saw his unmarked arms, rumors about his drug use might blow over. "The plan is to serve them martinis and organize a stroll to the river and come back to the house and have dinner on the patio."

At this point, Tony and Parker rarely invited or even allowed guests into the house. The only people who were allowed entrance were the exterminators who the Boyetts hired to help them deal with the catastrophic vermin problem plaguing the old house—squirrels both red and gray, chipmunks, mice, and even a couple of raccoons raced through the attic, the pantry. The creatures had their own secret passageways inside the walls, up and down, side to side, a world of their very own where they moved unmolested. Sometimes the sound of their scratchy scampering made one feel that madness was closing in. But the Boyetts were far from prompt in paying the exterminators and most of them had not been at Orkney since May.

"The boy and I wanted to get back to the west pasture and do a quick cutting," Hat said. "The power takeoff shaft on the International Harvester is part of the original equipment. Now you will recall that we have done extensive repairs on that temperamental tractor of yours, but we were hoping to stay lucky on the PTO. You know it will run almost . . ."

There were occasions when Boyett would let Hat go on forever. There was something relaxing about the old man's garrulousness, but right now time was tight.

"Hat, the favor I need. It's this. Parker has reinjured her hand and won't be able to cook. I don't know a spatula from a chamber pot so I'm going to be useless here. But you! You, you sly dog, you turn out to be a culinary genius."

"Chemistry was and remains one of my primary interests, Tony," Hat said. He was tall, with a weathered, somewhat caved-in face, deeply lined from the sun. He held himself at odd angles. When his wife was alive—and she was a heavy woman, with a large bosom and sturdy legs—Hat had a bit of a belly, but now his body was lean, with a lonely, sinewy quality. He had a long nose, blue eyes, and a full head of thick gray hair. He was sixty-two but looked older. "If you can remove the fashion from cuisine and see it primarily as a form of chemistry, the combination of elements . . ."

"Yes, exactly. How about that beef stew you brought to us last week?"

"Ah, the bourguignon," said Hat. "A perfect disguise for an overlooked cut."

"Well, it was excellent. And we realize you can't come up with something like that with no warning. Truthfully, we'd like you to just grill up some hamburgers. Done right, there is simply nothing like a good hamburger. Don't you agree? And you can bring your son. The two of you can cook and serve and I think you'll be out of there no later than eight o'clock. Tell your boy we'll pay in cash. Knowing him, he'll head into the village with a pocket full of whoopee." Boyett smiled broadly, though Parker had just an hour ago warned him not to—he was missing an incisor.

"I'll see what can be done," said Hat. "He's his own man, now."

Hat's son, Jennings, was back in Leyden after a stint in Saratoga Springs, where he had been living with a woman fifteen years his senior. Her name was Karen Colton and she worked as a secretary at Skidmore College. She'd gotten Jennings a temporary job with buildings and grounds, where he worked insulating a few of the older buildings. His job was mainly getting rid of the old asbestos, though the mission was confused because he was also wrapping some of the heat and hot water pipes in new asbestos. The school had a limited budget for winterizing, and despite the speculation surrounding asbestos, it was still one of the best things out there for insulation. The job paid decently and Karen herself was pulling in three hundred a week, so together they managed to live well. There were a few months in a row when it seemed to Jennings that every single day had something good in it. He liked where Karen lived, a mile from the racetrack in a ranch-style house built in 1950. He liked the bedroom, liked the bed, liked sleeping with her. She was self-conscious about being overweight, but she was sexually charged and adventurous. (He was a little on the heavy side, too—he had his mother's build—and though he preferred thin, girlish women, he didn't mind Karen's weight.) At first, Jennings had felt reluctant to accommodate her unfamiliar erotic suggestions—he had always slept with many women but his sexual adventurousness was confined to seduction. Soon, however, he found he enjoyed these things, too—both giving and receiving rough treatment, cuffing and blindfolding her, slapping her ass. Other than occasional bouts of what Karen called their Divine Madness in bed, their life was calm, cozy, and affectionate, built around lovely dinners and long walks. However, Karen was in a custody dispute with her ex-husband, with whom she'd had a son, and her lawyer told her that living with a twenty-two-year-old would not look good to the court, and whether this would have been a determining factor or not it frightened Karen into ending the relationship. Jennings moved into an apartment a bit out of town and continued to work at the college, but he missed Karen. Saratoga Springs without her seemed dreary and unlucky and he returned to Orkney, to the yellow frame caretaker's house, where he had been raised. In his childhood, it had been a happier place, while his mother was still alive and before his sister and Hat had had a falling-out and she left the house for good. Now it was just Jennings and his father and all Jennings wanted was to save enough money to move on.

There were few places for employment in Leyden. Jennings tried to stay in the insulation and asbestos business, but the only crew doing that kind of work in Leyden was run by Tim O'Mara, whose daughter Jennings had known in high school and there were hard feelings that made it impossible for O'Mara to hire Jennings, though he wanted to since his best worker had recently walked off the job after seeing a show on TV drumming up a bunch of hysteria about asbestos. There was nearby Avon College, but Jennings was reluctant to apply for B and G work there because they would check at Skidmore and see he had left that job without giving notice. There was Leydencraft, a furniture factory that had been in operation since the beginning of the century, turning out tables, chairs, dressers, armoires, blanket chests, and even little rustic-looking wooden plaques, which they could customize with your name and address burnt into the wood. A combination of inexpensive furniture, manufactured abroad in places like India and Guatemala, and new ways of making furniture parts had gutted Leydencraft. They went from employing over seventy workers to having twenty-two on the payroll, and those twenty-two had had their wages frozen for the past several years, and were working without contracts. The paper mill had been closed since 1970, as part of a government initiative to clean up the river, and the men who used to work there either had moved away or were mowing lawns and plowing driveways. The one expanding business in Leyden was Research Tech, which despite its forward-sounding name was a converted dairy barn used to breed rats and mice, which were used in experiments by laboratories all over the U.S. Research Tech's only foreign competition was from Mexico and Canada, both of which were close enough to ship crates full of rodents to U.S. labs without losing too many to the cold or starvation. But the Canadian mice were expensive and the Mexican specimens sometimes had a hard time getting into the country—once, fifty thousand Wistar rats, with their large heads and long ears, were cooked into a bony-white soup while languishing on the tarmac at Dallas–Fort Worth. RT was getting a computer and already had automatic feeders; they weren't cutting back but they weren't hiring, either. And now a few people from the college and a couple of New York City transplants were picketing Saturday afternoons in front of the barn, saying that it was cruelty to animals to use the rats and mice in experiments, even if it meant curing cancer. The rat lovers marched with picket signs pumping up and down like pistons in an engine, bearing grue-some photos of white rats with electrodes on their heads or their torsos split open and their organs exposed or an unmolested rat star-ing beseechingly, its little pink humanish hands held up as if the creature were begging for mercy.

When Hat asked Jennings to help prepare and serve the meal to the Boyetts and their guests, Jennings was glad for the work. Hat's arrangement with Tony and Parker was that he would be available to them forty hours a week in exchange for rent-free housing and whatever he could cultivate and harvest off the land. If he worked beyond the normal 7 A.M.–3 P.M. workday he was paid five dollars an hour. Hat assured Jennings that he, too, would be earning at least twenty-five dollars.

"If you ask me, I don't see where it takes two able-bodied men to serve a simple supper to four people. With the heat and all, Tony wants us to use the Weber and make hamburgers. I told him straight out we would not be using charcoal. We'll do the whole thing with wood and that way they will get the real taste of the meat. Anyhow, it was Tony's idea. He figured you needed some money."

"Don't call him Tony like him and you are friends," Jennings said.

"You and he," Hat said.

"Yeah. Just don't. Because you're not. Not yesterday, not today, or ever. You're a back and a couple a hands and that's it."

"With that kind of attitude, you'll get us both fired," Hat said. "Don't you need twenty-five dollars?"

IT WAS EASY WORK AND to make it even easier Parker had ventured into town to buy the groceries. She drove the old maroon Buick station wagon, creeping along curvy Riverside Road, fully aware that she was impaired and not wanting to make matters worse for herself by slamming into a tree or clipping a bicyclist. Hat had wired up the tailpipe so it would stay in place, but before Parker was halfway into town, the wires had devilishly untied themselves and the tailpipe was scraping against asphalt, and suddenly she was being stalked by huge hydrangeas of yellow and silver sparks. She switched on the radio and sang along with an old Bee Gees number, to block out the scraping sound, and the anxiety. *You don't know what it's like . . . to love somebody.* At the A&P she left the engine of her car running to keep it cool, and as insurance against her going into a kind of supermarket trance, in which she pushed her little cart up and down the aisles, amazed and appalled by all the crap for sale. She was famously frugal and bought the cheapest chopped meat and day-old hamburger buns from the half-price bin. When she brought her bag of groceries back to the car, it was nice and cool inside. "Parker, you are a very wise woman," she said to herself.

"The buns are stale, Dad," Jennings said as he shook them out of their plastic bag and onto a platter.

"We'll warm them up and no one will be any the wiser," Hat said.

They were on the bluestone patio off the kitchen. Gnarled wisteria vines, swollen and gray, hung from the overhead trellis like pythons. Hat and Jennings had the hamburgers on the grill. Licks of flame rose, and the heat corrugated the evening air. The light was fading. Jennings watched as a long furled contrail slowly dissipated and became part of the sky again. The river reflected the sunset, the pulsating orange of it, the dark blue. He wondered what it meant, any of it. Just another spin in the nothingness of space? How could it be so beautiful? On Hat's insistence, Jennings was in black slacks, a white shirt—he drew the line at the *toque blanche*, though Hat wore his and had brought an extra, in case the boy changed his mind. "If you're going to do something, I always say, do it right," Hat declared. To which Jennings replied, "I'm going to do it right, Pop, just not with a dunce cap."

Tony and Parker and their guests were back from their walk. The guests were in their forties, too—the Longacres, Kenneth and Donna. He was loud and forceful and had a reddish helmet of wavy hair. He had a hanging gut and his shirt was misbuttoned; Jennings had a grudging admiration for the type—this guy was secure, his card had been punched, and he was past caring what he looked like. The wife, Donna, was another matter. She was dark and moody, and the shape of her body was hidden by a gold-and-white caftan. Despite the July heat, she hugged herself and seemed to shiver. She had slipped somewhere along the way on their trek to and from the river's edge and there were grass stains on her caftan, as well as dirt on the heels of her hands, and a little brushstroke of it on her cheek.

The four sat in Adirondack chairs, with their legs extended and their heads tilted back. The night sky was darkening. One by one the stars appeared, like early arrivals taking their seats in an otherwise empty auditorium.

"You sure know how to throw a fucking party, Tony," Kenneth said. "I hope you're prepared to put us up."

"This is very nice," Donna said, in a sad whisper.

"Are you okay?" Parker asked her.

"It's stronger than I'm used to," Donna said.

Jennings tried to catch his father's attention with a quick, pointed glance. More than once, Jennings had told Hat that the Boyetts might be junkies, Hat would just shrug, as if the word was incomprehensible, some new kind of lingo, and then the third time Hat seemed to understand that Jennings was calling the Boyetts dope addicts and he said it was all so sad, and such a waste. But Hat's hands had trembled as he said it and Jennings had regretted pressing the point. In the first place, he wasn't 100 percent certain the Boyetts were actual down-for-the-count junkies, and second, it was unbearable for him to see his father with that look of dread and uncertainty on his face. He didn't want to be the one who forced Hat to face unpleasant truths. With a dead wife and a daughter with whom he was not on speaking terms, Hat had enough to deal with. His sense of well-being was fragile and built on the assumption that he was a valuable man, and in order to fully believe in his own value he had to hold in high esteem the people for whom he worked. If he was hop-to-ing it for a couple of degenerates—what did that make him?

Hat placed the hamburgers on a pewter tray that Tony had scratched up a couple of weeks ago while chopping an onion. Tony, Parker, Donna, and Kenneth waited to be served, with their plates and flatware and glasses of beer on the broad cedar arms of their chairs. Jennings bent his knees a bit to make the tray more easily reached by the recumbent diners. "Oh my God in heaven, my God, my God," said Donna as she lifted the top bun on each of the hamburgers. "Are they all the same?" she asked Jennings.

"Pretty much," he said.

"He's a handsome one," Donna said to Parker. She was open about it, as if they were speaking a language only they understood.

"You think so?" said Tony. "You like the peasant body, with those short arms and round belly?"

"I didn't come here to argue," said Donna. "But there's a manliness to him, and I like a guy to be heavier than me."

"If you're not careful, you won't be able to find such a man," her husband said.

"Hat and his family have been here forever," Parker said. "His father was called Whitey and he worked for my uncle Payson. And when the place came to me." She paused, mired for a moment in the delicious confusion of narcotics, which was like being caught in a spiderweb made of honey. "How long have we lived here, Tony?"

Tony was pointing at the sky, moving his thumb as if it were the hammer of a gun, shooting at the stars as they made their appearance.

"Tony?"

"I don't know. Five years? Seven?"

"Oh, I don't think it can be seven years. Seven years ago we . . ."

"Then five," Tony said.

"Why are those the only choices?" Parker asked.

"All right. We have been here six years. Are we all right with that?"

"Hat?" Parker made the effort to call out to him. "How long have Tony and I owned Orkney?"

Hat's face had turned red from the heat of the grill. A bead of perspiration trembled at the end of his long nose. He stepped back and took off his chef's hat, as if to say the person who would be answering Parker's question was not the person who was broiling up hamburgers.

"It was five years last March fifteenth," Hat said. "The ides of March." He frowned, looked away, as it occurred to him that in Shakespeare this was not a fortuitous day.

Perhaps the mention of the ides of March knocked something loose in Donna's memory. She raised her hand and shook it back and forth like an eager child insisting she knew the answer to the teacher's question. She wore an imposing ring, a cushion-cut sapphire, nearly twenty carats, surrounded by pear-shaped diamonds. "The dogs!" she cried out. "The dogs."

"I said you were welcome to bring them," Parker said.

"We did," drawled Kenneth, "but Donna *insisted* on leaving them in the car. She was afraid they would get lost."

"They've been in the car too long," Donna said. "It's hot." She struggled to her feet and twisted her ring nervously. It was slightly too large for her—it had been her great-aunt's—and it rattled onto the bluestone patio.

"There goes two hundred K," Kenneth said.

"Your dogs can scamper around here," Parker said.

"Martin, Bobby, and John," said Tony. "Is that right? Am I remembering correctly?" The ring had rolled toward him. He delivered it to Donna, who slipped it back onto her finger. The panic in her eyes burned through the narcotic haze.

"No, everyone thinks that," said Kenneth, with evident pleasure. "It's Abraham, Martin, and John. Bobby's not in the song. No, wait. Correction. Dion mentions him in the last part."

"Someone help me find the keys," Donna said. "Please. They've been in there too long."

"You don't have them?" Kenneth asked. He seemed to enjoy catching his wife's mistakes. It was not out of the question that he kept a private tally of them.

"When I fell."

"Why would you lock the car?" Parker asked.

"Force of habit," said Tony. "One of the strongest forces in nature. We just walk up and down the same neural paths, over and over and over, until by the mercy of God we are allowed to die."

Donna continued to search her pockets, but it was clearly hopeless. She gazed out at the long sloping lawn that wound its way down through the high grass, the scrub, until it came to the train tracks and the river.

A party boat was making its way south on the river. It was a
hulking, ungainly craft, filled with merrymakers getting drunk,
dancing. The old tub was decked out in red, white, and blue lights.
The Bee Gees singing "Nights on Broadway" was amped up so loud
that it sounded as if it was playing right there on the patio.

"I can't bear those party boats," Tony said.

"Oh please," said Parker.

"It just breaks my heart," Tony said. "Such a craven, greedy mis-
use of the river."

"I know, baby," Parker said in her Comforting Voice. She frowned
sympathetically. "I just hate to see you get yourself worked up."

"We have to find my keys," Donna shouted. "I can't leave those
dogs in the hot car. They'll die."

"Get off my river!" Tony shouted out at the passing boat.

"Excuse me," Hat said. "Is that old army flashlight still in the
kitchen? It throws out a pretty fair beam."

"I meant to get batteries," Tony said.

Kenneth and Donna's car was off to the side of the driveway,
under an old locust tree, which, inasmuch as they had given the
matter sustained thought, was meant to shade the backseat of their
light blue Impala, rented from Hertz in the city. Donna ran around
the house, with Kenneth and the Boyetts following, and with Hat
and Jennings walking quickly behind them.

"This is not going to be good," Jennings said to his father, and
Hat glared at him momentarily. Despite all of his learning and the
galaxies of facts and figures that illuminated his mind, Hat still had
trouble making a distinction between someone saying what they
thought might happen from what they would actually *want* to happen. He thought, for instance, that predicting Carter was going to
win the election basically meant you wanted Carter in the White
House.

Donna pulled on all four of the door handles hoping that one
of them was somehow unlocked. Her dogs, butterscotch-and-white
King Charles spaniels, were curled up in a heap; which one was

which was indistinguishable. It was a tangle of ears and legs and tails. Donna pounded the heels of her hands against the left-back window, shaking it in its frame, but the dogs, usually so quick to react to the slightest sound, or even changes in the light, gave no sign of sensing her presence, and no sign of life.

"Kenny," Donna said. Tears were streaming down her cheeks. "They're not just dogs. You understand that, don't you? They're life! They're everything. Please."

"We need one of those crafty little car thieves who know how to open a car door with a coat hanger," Kenneth said.

"They're going to die," Donna said. The car was hot to the touch.

"They're fine," Kenneth said. "They're in the shade."

About 120 years ago, when Orkney was completed, and this driveway was suitable for horses and carriages, the borders were marked by white and gray stones, each about the size of a medicine ball. Consulting no one, Jennings picked one up and calmly walked with it to the car. The sun blazed in the chrome bumpers. Jennings lifted the rock and cocked his arms so that the rock was behind his head and—after looking from face to face, giving anyone who wanted to stop him a chance to do so—he brought his arms forward quickly, and heaved the rock onto the windshield.

"Hey, man, it's a rental," Kenneth said.

The rock did not break through the windshield, but created a sudden concave at the center, a deep nest of spidery cracks. Jennings scrambled onto the hood of the car and donkey-kicked at the weakened window, with his back to it. At last, his foot went through. His shoe filled with little shards, his ankle was aflame, and he knew, dimly, that he was bleeding.

"Your face!" cried Hat.

Jennings pulled off his shirt and tied it around his head so that his face was somewhat protected. He had gone from looking like someone serving wealthy people their dinner to someone in a street riot who does not want to be identified. He pushed his way through the windshield that had by now been beaten into submission, but the opening was not large enough. The glass pierced him everywhere—his scalp, along the curve of his spine. A couple of large shards stuck out of him like the plates on the back of a stegosaurus as he made his way to the backseat. Despite the dappling shade of that lovely old locust tree, the car was stifling. He knew the dogs had not made it before going in. But you couldn't just leave them there.

There was barely any weight to them. It was like picking up three gloves. He treated them gently, cradling them in one arm as he unlocked the door. He yanked his shirt down, and took a deep breath. The dogs were a mélange of floppy ears and dark protruding eyes. Their lips were white, covered with thick saliva.

He stumbled out of the car, and Donna stared at him. Her face was red, as if the grief she swallowed in one horrible gulp now scalded her from the inside out. "Are they dead?" she asked in a small voice.

Jennings didn't reply. He set the dogs down on the grass, gently, one at a time. He put them on their side, stretched out their forepaws, their back legs.

"Heat stroke," Hat said. "If it's eighty degrees outside, inside a car it can get up to a hundred in no time. Hundred and twenty, thirty."

"Didn't you leave the windows open?" Parker asked. She was frowning in an extreme way, like a character in a Japanese woodcut.

"A little," said Donna.

"Those dogs are so damn small and slippery," Kenneth said. "Anything more than an inch and they get right out." He put his arm around his wife, who was silently weeping. "What a waste," he said. "And that car. I don't know what the fuck we're supposed to do about that. You know, I must have had a premonition. I swear to God. I must have. I never go for all the insurance they try to sell you, but this time I went for the whole package. I knew we were going to be having a little party and I didn't want to take any chances. Lucky thing."

"Luck?" echoed Donna. "You talk to me of *luck*?" Her sobs began as a kind of breathlessness and increased in volume and intensity, until it seemed she might be dismantled by them. Kenneth shushed and patted her and she pressed her face into his chest and held on to his shoulders. He lifted his chin and pursed his lips and gazed at the Boyetts, wanting them to witness what he was able to do for his distraught wife. Whatever they may think and whatever they may have heard, he was Donna's Rock of Gibraltar.

The Boyetts were reluctant to have guests spend the night, but there was really no alternative to inviting them to sleep at Orkney and deal with matters in the morning. In the meantime, there was a bit more dope—actually, quite a bit, if one counted the two dime bags Tony had secreted away—and enough hamburger to carry them through the night.

"Once more unto the patio!" Tony called out in what Parker called his Most Shakespearean Bellow. They walked in single file and disappeared into the darkness that had settled over Orkney.

When they could no longer hear the Boyetts and their guests, father and son went to the equipment shed. Hat finished plucking out the windshield shards from his son's back and when that was done they both grabbed a digging shovel and a spade. "Get one with a D-grip," Hat said. They walked about a hundred yards away from the house, to the small orchard Hat had planted with his own father right after the end of World War II. The ground in the orchard was soft and offered little resistance, and the dark moist smell of good soil rose into the night air, blending with the smell of honeysuckle, pine, and the distant, ever so slightly brackish smell of the river. Father and son prepared a ditch for the dead dogs. They worked quickly. Hat was always fast and Jennings was trying to burn off his fury.

"When I was a boy we used to think you could dig a hole all the way to China," Hat said.

"I heard that, too," Jennings said.

"The things we didn't know," Hat said. "Your crust, your mantle, the whole lithosphere. Even if you could dig your way through it, you'd have your core to contend with."

"These poor fucking dogs," Jennings said.

"Language," Hat said, without much conviction.

"I guess they'll just get new dogs," Jennings said, as they patted down the loose earth with the backs of their shovels.

"I suppose they will," Hat said. He stepped back to inspect their work, though it was barely visible with only a quarter moon to counteract the darkness.

"Looks all right," Jennings said.

"We can check again in the morning." Hat jammed the tip of his spade into the earth and leaned on the handle to take some of the weight off his legs. He'd been debating saying something since they'd started digging and now he decided he'd go ahead and say it. "You're a good worker, Jennings. It's . . . it's good to work with you. I'm glad you got out of Saratoga. That's a city run by the racing syndicate and the Skidmore bunch. And I must say I never thought much of your lady friend up there."

"You never met her."

"That's right. She never made the effort to come down here and see me. Anyhow, it's water under the bridge. The important thing is, you're home."

PARKER HAD BOUGHT AN ICE-CREAM cake at the supermarket, but Hat had forgotten to take it out of the freezer to let it soften. His distress was unnecessary; by the time he and Jennings were in place to serve the desserts, the Boyetts and their guests were deep in their opium dreams, half-dozing in their Adirondack chairs, except for Donna, who was completely unconscious, with a film of saliva on her lips, quite like the dogs.

"Jennings, you're so strong," Parker said in a desiccated voice. "We need to get poor Donna inside. Do you think you could carry her up to the Rose Room on the second floor? I believe the bed in there is decent."

Jennings glanced at Hat, who nodded yes. Donna's head lolled back and her hair streamed behind her as he carried her across the patio and in through the French doors, into what had once been the dining room and now was called the observatory, a large, high-ceilinged room devoid of furniture except for an upholstered piano bench, and, in the center of the room, a long white telescope on a five-foot-high tripod, perched like a praying mantis on the bare parqueted floor.

As Jennings carried Donna up the stairs, her head lolled from one side to the other and he let it. Sweat trickled down his spine. He stumbled momentarily and Donna's eyes opened suddenly and wide—it was unnerving, like someone in a horror movie come back to life. Her eyes, glassy as a doll's, seemed to register nothing and a moment later she closed them.

He moved through the second-floor hall, a portrait gallery, where Orkney's original owners reigned, the Wohls, with their muttonchop sideburns and unruly brows, their stiff white collars, their enigmatic smiles. Parker was barely a Wohl herself, but the portraits were precious to her, as was the knowledge that moldering beneath Orkney's sod were Wohl bottles and spoons and the bones of servants and pets. Hat often spoke of the Wohls as if he had known them, but Jennings could not recall a single thing his father had ever said about them, could not remember how they had made their fortune or what had become of them.

Jennings looked down on the face of the woman in his arms. His bet was that she was the one in the couple with money. If the husband had his own money, he would have chosen someone prettier. Jennings had been with many girls and women, and his ability to attract females was the cornerstone of his pride, but he had never been with anyone rich. What would it be like, he wondered, to be with such a woman, to be her lover, to know the world as she knew it? What would it be like to be able to have whatever you wanted? You see something you want in a store window and the only problem is, do you have enough time to go in and get it, or do you have to come back some other time and pick it up? Those were the kinds of problems you had! What would it be like to never ever be the one who lifted and carried and fried and scraped and cut and stacked and dug the grave and did without? He lifted her up so her face was closer to his and breathed deeply.

"Donna." He whispered her name. He lowered her onto the bed, and stood back for a moment. She rolled onto her stomach, but quickly rolled onto her back again, breathing heavily, as if that moment with her face pressed into the mattress put the fear of God into her.

"You dumbass," Jennings said, softly. He waited to see if she would respond. "You killed your little dogs," he said, somewhat louder. "Very careless, Donna, you dumbass." Donna's lips parted, as if she might reply, but all that came out were her slow exhalations.

She rubbed the side of her face with her right hand, the hand with the sapphire ring, reminding Jennings of its existence, this small piece of polished stone dug out of some hole somewhere in— what? a jungle? a riverbed? Some hidden spot. He'd overheard what the husband said about the ring's value. *Its worth.* Jennings did not like that word. *Worth.* Who decided? It was all so arbitrary. Gold, diamonds—none of them as beautiful as a ripe apple.

Donna stopped rubbing her face and placed her hand on her stomach and seemed to fall deeper still into her doped-out state. He placed his hand on top of hers and kept it there. He lifted her pinkie, higher, higher, almost bending it, keeping it up, letting it go. It fell with a little thump. Her lips parted but other than that she did not stir. He lifted the finger with the ring, the hundred-thousand-dollar finger, if her husband was to be believed, held it, held it, bent it so far back that her entire hand lifted for a moment. He let it go and it landed on her stomach like a hat tossed onto a bed. He covered her entire hand with his, with a kind of tenderness, and when he lifted it again he had her ring.

He walked slowly down the stairs, and through the house. The leafy sour smell of cigarette smoke came from the patio. He stood in the darkness, wondering if it would be better, smarter, to be seen walking across the patio. That way they'd remember Jennings had had nothing to hide, didn't go sneaking off like a thief but said his good nights and left whistling a little tune. He ran his hand over the pocket of his proper pants, the trousers Hat had insisted upon, and felt the shape of the ring. He pulled it out. What was the deal? How could it be worth more than ten cars? More than the men who dug it out of the earth. He had an impulse to throw the ring into the darkness of the house, where someone would come across it in the morning. He did not decide to do otherwise. He let his body do what his body was going to do and his body put the ring in his back pocket and after that his body pulled his shirttails out, hiding his pocket beneath the cotton blend of Hat's Oleg Cassini white shirt.

"She's asleep," Jennings announced, and bid the Boyetts and Kenneth good night. His voice was relaxed, and as far as he could tell his face was, too, but he could not slow down his gait. He was across the patio in six long strides. As soon as he was away from the house, darkness swallowed him up and he felt such a surge of relief that he pounded his fist into his hand. *Dog killer,* he said to himself, repeatedly. *Dog killer.*

He strolled back to the equipment shed for the shovel and he strolled even more slowly toward the orchard. Though he and Hat had patted the earth flat, he knew exactly where to dig. The dirt was loose, it was like digging through a pile of peanut shells. In no time, he had exposed the dead spaniels. He dropped the ring onto the patch of fur, and moving quickly now, he refilled their grave. He heard the distant sound of music. One of the party boats that Tony raged about, trespassing on *his* river, pirates hijacking the silence of his night. Jennings walked back to the shed to the beat of the music and put the shovel away, locked up for the night. He faced the river as the party boat drifted south. The Mamas and the Papas, an oldie but a goodie. A breeze was blowing. More than a breeze, really, a good stiff wind. The ring would stay right where it was. One day, Jennings would take it far away and try to sell it. In the meantime, it was under—what did Hat call it? The crust, the mantle? The ring was back where it had come from, the part of the world nobody sees. Well, not nobody. Those with the tools and the willingness to dig and get dirty, they saw it.

Chapter 3

Lessons Learned

NOVEMBER 3, 1977

Dear Thaddeus,

How do you like this card? I bought it on the fifth floor, first-time use of employee discount. I'm having a birthday party Friday, but no presents. Your presence is my present. Bring your lady.

Your humble servant,
Gene

I N COLLEGE BACK IN ANN ARBOR, KIP'S FRIENDS USED TO SAY he looked like Franz Kafka, with his deep, dark witnessing eyes; curvaceous lips; and sunken cheeks. But now the resemblance was less pronounced. He'd put on a bit of weight, his gaze no longer seemed wounded, but mocking. He was two years ahead of Thaddeus in college, a comparative literature major, and now worked as a stockbroker for E.F. Hutton. His life was bicameral. By day, working the phones at his little desk on Worth Street, by night in all kinds of trouble—cocaine trouble, tattoo trouble, blackjack in Chinatown trouble, party until dawn trouble. Even his ostensibly wholesome enthusiasms could lead to disgrace—he was an avid collector of first editions, and had been caught stealing a pristine copy of Glenway Westcott's *The Grandmothers* from Bilbo and Tannin's, escaping arrest by promising never to set foot in the store again.

It was Kip who'd urged Thaddeus to move to New York after graduation. More than anyone else Thaddeus knew—with the possible exception of Grace—Kip believed in his talent as a writer and exuded a certainty that one day Thaddeus would publish and be able to secure for himself a modest reputation among the discerning. "You'll be poor but admired," Kip said. Poor but admired? Did those two things even go together anymore? Grace's theory was either that Kip had a secret source of money or that his job at E.F. Hutton was paying a lot more than he admitted to. In support of this either/ or theory Grace noted that the chair Thaddeus so admired was a genuine Eames chair, worth thousands, and had as much to do with Sam Kaufman's BarcaLounger as a brioche had to do with a wad of Wonder Bread. She also recognized that the threadbare carpet in the living room was a Sarouk, made in Persia before it became Iran, and was also worth thousands. Thaddeus would have liked to own at least one suit like Kip's, and it fell to Grace to wise him up to the fact that anything from J. Press was out of their range, and shirts and ties from Turnbull & Asser were so far out of their range that he should do himself a favor and stop fondling the fabric.

Kip kept odd hours. He would never firmly state where he would be or when. Work, he said, work work work as if it were a kind of rain, the rain that made the crops grow but soaked you through and through, the rain that could make you or could ruin you, depending on where you pitched your tent. But there seemed something secret, too, something desperate in his dogged, expensive pursuit of altered consciousness, a kind of internal jet-setting. Those amazing wines, that bottomless jar of gnarled marijuana buds, the kind they used as centerfolds in *High Times*. A jaunty little vial seemed to generate its own coke. Grace found a spent popper in the silverware drawer, along with a postcard from a friend in London showing one of those resplendent Beefeater guards, with the message on the back: *He's mine!* "Kip's a queer," Grace said. "I'll bet you a dollar." Thaddeus did not believe it to be true. He managed to resist giving Grace a lecture on tolerance. Kip made the rounds accompanied by one standard-issue beautiful woman after another, from every aspect of ascendant Manhattan life, bankers and real estate brokers, and all manner of artists. In college, Kip had worn a beret, hair down to his shoulders, had a taste for Stockhausen, Breton, Tristan Tzara. He had worked on his own translations of Mayakovsky, he named his Siamese cat The Cloud in Trousers. He edited the campus literary magazine called *My Heart Belongs to Dada.* Now in New York, despite his long hours on Wall Street, Kip seemed to know hundreds of people in the arts, his "punk pals." The *Village Voice* and the *Soho News* covered the *Wall Street Journal* on his coffee table. He hinted at a love affair with Deborah Harry. He introduced Joey Ramone to an investment advisor and when he had the flu Patti Smith brought him soup. The emaciated singer took one look at Thaddeus and Grace and asked, "What are you two doing here?" And for weeks they wondered if she had meant why were they in Kip's apartment or in New York City. (They finally got themselves some peace of mind by deciding she had meant nothing at all.)

Kip often urged Thaddeus and Grace to accompany him to a performance at some ad hoc gallery in the far West Village, an installation, a concert, a night at the Palladium, a chance to meet Richard Brautigan, a birthday party for Viva at the Chelsea. But the disheveled, slapdash, angry art of New York just then did not appeal to either Grace or Thaddeus. Grace stubbornly admired skill and couldn't understand why any artist would not want to make beautiful drawings like Ingres, or paint like Lippi, with every detail as perfectly placed as jewels in a crown. Thaddeus, though barely writing, was reading Hemingway, Fitzgerald, Cain, and Chandler, and his idea of an avant-garde publication was the *Partisan Review.* Both of them felt inadequate and superior, defensive, confused. They only felt safe and successful in each other's company.

Every generation gets its own New York and Thaddeus and Grace's New York was a city that was loud and dangerous, discouraged and falling apart. It was not a place Fred Astaire would set foot in. It was not a place where F. Scott Fitzgerald or John O'Hara or Mary McCarthy or James Thurber, or anyone else with a light touch and a taste for glamor would feel at home. There was a kind of coarseness to the place: whatever became of savoir faire? Yes, there were still people who drank lovely cocktails and had twinkling views of the skyline, but Thaddeus and Grace could no sooner mix socially with them than they could with Jimmy and Rosalynn.

Thaddeus wanted to write, Grace wanted to make art, but they needed to sleep, shower, shop for food, clean the apartment, and earn a living. What time was left they wanted to spend with each other. To be private, to be enraptured, to feel the drug of it, the exhilaration and the security. So there were a great many things they missed, and people they did not meet. Those their age seemed angry, raw, unprotected, nihilistic, lacking in polish, suspicious of polish, militantly and perhaps somewhat conveniently staked out *against* polish. *Here's what I think of your well-made sentence and here's what I make of your lovingly rendered pear,* these new artists seemed to say, grabbing their crotch, sneering. Grace thought these so-called punks were just a pack of talentless temper-tossing suburban refugees. Thaddeus thought that all those difficult often indecipherable downtown writers, so full of errors and perversity, were attempting to cover up their own emptiness with a flurry of experimentation and *theory*. In truth they were both more than a little afraid of the artists their own age, and exhausted and bewildered by New York. But what were they supposed to do? Go back to Chicago with their tails between their legs?

Where was the middle path? How could you live a moral and creative life and still have extremely nice things, plenty of room, those beautiful towels from the Palmer House?

Thaddeus started working on a story about a young girl who dies and comes back to life the next day, but in Shanghai instead of Chicago, and she surprises everyone with her first word: Elvis. Grace asked him if it was sort of about his sister and they had their first fight.

"It's like me taking your drawing of an orange and trying to squeeze orange juice out of it," Thaddeus had said.

"Well, I'd be flattered," Grace answered. They had to whisper; Kip was in the next room, doing his Jane Fonda exercises in front of the Trinitron.

"Well, you're not supposed to read like that," he said.

"Sorry," Grace said, no longer whispering, *"I didn't go to college and no one gave me the rule book about how to fucking read."*

They found an apartment in an old four-story building, on Twenty-Third Street just west of Madison Avenue. The ground floor of the squat, white brick building was occupied by the Health Nuts, where six days a week cashews, pistachios, pecans, and Virginia Old Style peanuts languished beneath heat lamps, and were sold by the eighth of a pound in waxy little white bags. Business was slow at the Health Nuts and the infrequent customers were an odd lot. They seemed emissaries from a different world, pale, thoughtful men in topcoats and fedoras, women who wore snazzy little capes and pill-box hats with veils.

"I think there's some sort of weird door between dimensions," Grace said while looking out of their apartment's only window that didn't open onto an air shaft. "And I think it opens up right in front of the Health Nuts, and weirdos from the 1940s go in and buy nuts."

"Why don't they just buy nuts in the 1940s?" Thaddeus once asked. "Why do they have to come all the way over to 1977 to buy nuts?"

"How the fuck should I know?" Grace answered. And the laughter that ensued, the frenzy of amusement and arousal left them breathless. They couldn't say what was so funny about her remark, but it *was*, it was hilarious, another in-joke, another gateway to the mad gasping joy between them.

They were each other's refuge in a city that overwhelmed them. Thaddeus called it "New Yorkitis." If they stood at their window, at a certain angle, on certain nights, they could see the swirl of mist around the Metropolitan Life Headquarters, and if they moved a little to the left they could see the lighted tower of the Empire State Building and the moon at the same time, and the thing that was most amazing was that, when it came to glamour, the moon came in second—and seemed to know it. It was Grace who noticed that the moon seemed more confident when it was over Chicago.

They often felt as if they'd been cast into a great production but had not been given an opportunity to learn their lines. The anxiety was epic, especially for Grace. She was used to feeling at odds with her environment, ignored, undiscovered, powerless. It was how she had felt in Eau Claire, and Chicago. But in New York it was worse. She was full of symptoms. The accelerated heart rate, the sweaty palms, the sudden staggering fear of death—not from gunshot or stabbing or botulism or poison or heart attack or cancer or through the criminal carelessness of a drunken driver, or a madman's rage, but death for death's sake. It fell to Thaddeus to protect her from her own thoughts. You're going to be fine, he promised her. Her heart was strong, her body was doing its job, front and center, every corpuscle accounted for. Never mind the tingling scalp, the racing heart. It was merely anxiety. Paranoia. Agoraphobia. He was back to dancing, his arms waving, singing his little tunes.

Kip had helped both of them get jobs. Kip could navigate the waters of Manhattan like a native scout. He pointed Thaddeus in the direction of B. Altman, where he was hired as a junior member of the in-house advertising staff. Able to write about anything the department store sold—suits and ties, books and records, pots and pans, perfume, framed autographs, jewelry—he was praised for his versatility. His own longing for the many things he could not afford gave his copy an extra animation.

For Thaddeus, Manhattan was a crash course in failure, his Ph.D. in pauperhood. He was used to being without money, but he was not accustomed to being around people who seemed to have so much. That afternoon at the Palmer House had affected him like the first drink can seal the fate of a born alcoholic. Those towels! Those sheets! There were people who could enjoy these things and took them for granted. It made what he had seem so sad, depleted, and utilitarian. What was the point of life without access to all the pleasures on earth? Read your Epicurus. Look around you. People were sleeping in better beds, eating tastier food, traveling the world as if the world was theirs, while you and your beloved were holed up like losers in an apartment with virtually no light, drying yourself with towels that just moved the moisture around rather than absorbing it. He experienced his penury as a kind of apartheid, a daily injustice. It might have been easier had they stayed in Chicago, but here in New York all the things he craved were on full display. All you had to do was look through the storefront windows at the cheese wrapped in actual cheesecloth, jackets that made ordinary men look mysterious, and stacks of pastel shirts to make Daisy Buchanan swoon.

If only he could afford just one of those shirts! If only. New York was the world headquarters of *If Only*. If only you had a couple of thousand dollars. If only you had a closet in your apartment. If only your bedroom got even fifteen minutes of sunlight. Everybody knew you came to New York to go up the ladder, not down. To be celebrated, not ignored. And certainly not to be stuck in a subway car stalled between stations, eyeing your fellow passengers in the flickering light, wondering which one was getting ready to vomit on your shoes. Which happened to him.

Kip's helpfulness extended to Grace, whom he helped get a job at Periodic Books, which specialized in scientific books. She was trained to work in the production department, where she earned $10,500 a year. It was more than the Palmer House, though the opportunities to engage in a bit of judicious pilfering were more numerous at the hotel. All she could swipe at Periodic were envelopes, pens, paper clips, bottles of Wite-Out, a couple of metal rulers, and, of course, books. But what the job at Periodic gave to her was a kind of proxy association with educated, upwardly mobile people. She now had a marginal membership in the New York media intelligentsia and when asked what she did, Grace could say, "Oh, I'm a book designer over on Forty-First Street." She thought it was sort of chic to signify her employer through its address, like the Harvard grads who said they'd gone to college in *Boston*—such noblesse oblige obfuscation!

At work, Grace feared detection and expulsion—not for theft but for lying. She knew it was crazy to worry so much about it, but she had gotten her job under false pretenses, and every day she expected to be called into her boss's cubicle and informed that they'd checked on her so-called degree from the School of the Art Institute of Chicago and the only record the school had of her was two summer classes, one of which had taken an incomplete. And this was New York. This wasn't the Palmer House, where they just told you to get the heck out. Here she might be forcibly escorted from the office, here she might be frog-walked through the lobby and tossed out onto the street as if into an open grave.

Thaddeus and Grace met after work and walked back to their apartment if the weather was half decent. They liked to stop at a bar called Dugan's on their way home, and after a few months the bartender and the regulars—a shaky bunch, to be sure—recognized them and even seemed pleased to see them, though from a business point of view it would be hard to think of worse customers. They ordered a Dewar's on ice with a twist of lemon, and a glass of Guinness and traded their drinks back and forth over the course of half an hour, at which point they left a seventy-five-cent tip and were on their way.

It did not seem exactly like a New York thing to do, but they held hands as they strolled home. "Every time I touch you, I know we are meant to be," Thaddeus said, and Grace squeezed his fingers and smiled. The more they were together the more she let him do the talking. His declarations were hyperbolic, and though they were touching and sweet they had a way of silencing her. She simply could not think of anything to say that would match his ardor. *And what about my art? What do you think of that? Do you worry that I hardly have any time left to draw? I worry all the time about your writing. Do you worry about me in that way? Do you? Do you?* Of course she could not say these things. They seemed so small and churlish and needy and lame. But the more she suppressed saying it, the more it was felt.

New York had fallen on such hard times. A cop car was going against traffic, the driver's-side door badly dented, its windshield cracked. The new centurions bombing around in jalopies!

"Your hand in mine," Thaddeus said. "It's everything to me."

"Thank you," said Grace.

"Are you okay?" he asked after a while.

"Mary Ellen? Who I guess is my boss? She asked me if I kept up with my school friends."

"As if it were her business," said Thaddeus.

"And she just stared at me. I think she knows I didn't graduate."

You didn't even attend, thought Thaddeus. *You took a couple of summer courses.* He hated himself when he had such thoughts.

"She's just waiting for me to make a mistake," Grace said. "It makes me so nervous I can hardly even think straight."

They passed a wine shop called Park Spirits, where they once went to a pre-auction tasting of some legendary Bordeaux. They had sipped little dark purple splashes of Haut-Brion and Cheval Blanc, parsimoniously poured from bottles that cost as much as either of them earned in a week, and now whenever they passed Park Spirits, Grace said, "They're in there."

Near Park Spirits was a jewelry shop called Gina's Gems. In all the times they had walked past, they'd only entered once. In the chaos of the display window, with its encrusted bracelets and hammered brass pendants and little beige pouches brimming with Mexican and Indian rings, one thing had caught Grace's eye, and she wanted to try it on—a simple emerald ring. There was not the remotest possibility of their buying such a piece, now or anytime in the foreseeable future, but she wanted to see it on her hand, if only for a minute.

Gina herself had been behind the counter, dressed in a gold-and-black caftan, a large, middle-aged woman, with girlish freckles

and curly hair a curious shade of red. She lumbered to the display
window, unlocked it with her small, stout hands, slid the store-side
panel, and reached in, toppling a display of brightly beaded Afri-
can earrings in the process. The ring itself was not new and Gina
watched with her arms folded over her bosom as Grace held it up to
the light and then slipped it onto her finger.

"It's so green," Grace said, in an awestruck whisper.

Gina explained that she was handling this emerald ring on
consignment from her sister-in-law, who was planning to return to
Brooklyn College, where she hoped to get certified to teach in the
public schools. "I told her, 'Doris, schools are closing, belts are tightening, no one's hiring,' but Doris wants what Doris wants. And for
this she wants four thousand. I don't know if you know very much
about jewelry . . ."

"A bit," said Grace.

"Well then, you see I mainly deal with jewelry of an artistic
sort, from native peoples all over the world. A ring like this would
normally go for twice what she is asking. Emeralds! This one comes
from Zambia. Four and three-quarter carats, nice cut, and you see
the color. Deep, but clear." She pointed to Grace. "Like your eyes,
sweetheart."

"Thank you," Grace said, taking the ring off and handing it
back to Gina. "It's out of our range."

"She can always pick out the one thing," Thaddeus said. "And
it's always the best."

"Well, she chose you, right?" Gina said.

"The exception that proves the rule," said Thaddeus.

"I have some beautiful jade," Gina said. "Which frankly I prefer.
I could put it in the exact same setting."

When they were out on the street again, Grace noticed Thaddeus had a grim expression, and she asked him what was bothering
him, though she half-knew.

"You didn't have to tell her I was too poor to get you the ring
you want," he said.

"*You're* too poor? What happened to *we're* too poor? Anyhow: we're young!"

Over the next few weeks, she continued to glance at the window when they walked past, until one day the emerald ring was gone. She wasn't sure Thaddeus had noticed, but he put his arm around her as they passed the shop, knocked his hip into hers, so she supposed he had.

Lately, knowing that if she and Thaddeus were not careful they would begin to devour each other—Liam had said as much to her in a letter—Grace was pushing herself to meet other artists. But those she managed to meet had little interest in or respect for what she was trying to accomplish, and what had begun as a cheerful, hopeful openness was beginning to turn guarded and even a little sour. Going to galleries she did her best to keep hidden her sense of alarm about the work on display, but the grainy videos of people moping around some filthy apartment seemed incompetent to her. And the physically demanding (and, she thought, demeaning) performance pieces that they would sometimes hear about and be able to attend embarrassed and basically horrified her—she was particularly bothered by a piece called *Failure* in which the naked artist attempted to climb a wall using a rope and her own negligible strength, and the artist, if that's what she was, kept falling to the ground, injuring and reinjuring herself, and grabbing on to the rope and trying it again and again, her legs bruised, her shaggy crotch taking on the appearance of the suffering face of an agonized Christ on the cross. Was that the point? Was it about suffering? It was surely about failure—but whose failure? The artist's? Or the onlookers' failure to discern that they were nothing more than voyeurs? Or was it Society's failure? Maybe Art had failed? Most likely the failure had been Shaggy's parents, who had either underfed or overfed her ego. The entire production made Grace sick with disapproval. She supposed she was a conservative, at least in this.

Thaddeus and Grace were at the opening of *Failure* not through Kip, but through a work friend of Thaddeus's, a fellow named Gene

Woodard, who worked in men's furnishings, selling tie clips, cuff links, and shaving sets. Gene was poorly paid and worked long hours on his feet, but he often said, "This suits me to a *T*." Thaddeus thought men's furnishings was perhaps the most depressing part of the store—all those ties, belts, rows and rows, it was like a morgue. And if you wanted to push it a bit, you could even say it was like Bergen-Belsen.

Gene was fanatically devoted to the job. He never missed a day. He *twice* reported fellow workers for theft. He referred to anyone in a supervisory capacity as Mr. or Miss. He was painfully deferential whenever he came to meet Thaddeus in the room off the mezzanine where the advertising copywriters worked, knocking on the door with one timid knuckle, coming in with an obsequious shuffle and looking around with a sense of wonder at the grim little shared cubicle where Thaddeus worked—two desks, an armchair, and yet another useless window.

Gene was not particularly forthcoming about himself, but even so Thaddeus was able to deduce a history of strife and unhappiness—struggles with alcohol, psychiatric issues serious enough to warrant two brief stays at a hospital called Austen Riggs up in Stockbridge, Massachusetts.

Thaddeus and Grace were invited to Gene's twenty-eighth birthday party. Gene's apartment was on West Twenty-First Street, and that evening the weather was warm, so they could walk from their apartment. The darkness seemed to contain an extra layer. They talked about what would be the best way to describe that shade of blue. Could something so dark even *be* blue? A wind blew west to east; the last of the fallen leaves, the ghosts of summer, swirled from curb to curb. West of Fifth Avenue the neighborhood looked poorer, mainly tenement-style apartment houses, the windows negated by burglar gates, the bricks crisscrossed with fire escapes.

Grace clasped Thaddeus's hand and lifted it to her lips and kissed each knuckle.

"Are you happy?" she asked him.

"Right now?" He made a thinking-about-it face. "I guess."

"I am so insanely happy," she said. "People settle for so much less than we have. You know that, don't you?"

"I do." Less was very vivid to him. "And I wish you were wearing that ring."

After a silence, Grace said, "Yeah, me too, I guess."

"You know what else I wish? That we had a kid." He didn't look at her when he said it.

"How would I ever be an artist?"

"I don't know. You just would."

"Oh my God, Thaddeus. How can you even think about it? We are so lost. Do you really want to pass that on?"

"I'm tired of being a son," Thaddeus said. "Time to be a father."

"It would destroy me," Grace said. "I'd be my mother in no time."

As they neared Gene's place, Twenty-First Street turned suddenly lovely, with half of it given over to a Gothic seminary. The bare trees surrounding the red brick building were spaced as neatly as a pattern on a shawl. Gene occupied the garden and first floors of a town house near Tenth Avenue, with a steep fourteen-step porch. Beneath the porch, a homeless man was preparing to go to sleep in a cardboard shelter filled with rags. He wore fingerless gloves and a World War II pilot's cap. Thaddeus and Grace glanced at him through the spaces between the steps.

"Beneath," Thaddeus whispered.

"What?"

"I don't know. There's always something." Something elusive but powerful, and impossible to hold on to swept through him like a sudden rain, and then it was gone, leaving nothing in its wake but a kind of confusion.

So it turned out that Gene was rich. The job at Altman's for a measly hourly wage was a form of penance, the time he spent there a kind of masquerade. Working in tandem, his father and his uncle had sold Gene on the notion that the (supposed) stability of a sales-clerk's existence and a steady diet of quotidian reality, including an alarm clock, a boss, a budget, and a reason to get up in the morning would offer some respite from his alcoholic episodes. "Better than singing the blues to some headshrinker," his father had said. "And instead of spending ours, you'll be making yours."

The door to Gene's place was painted dark red, with a Hand of Fatima brass knocker. Grace lifted it and let it fall, and a few moments later Gene opened the door. Reeking of irony and mothballs, he wore a tuxedo, a starched shirt, a black bow tie. His trousers were dusty at the knees. He was handsome, with even features, sandy hair, blue eyes; his smile radiated mischievous joy and he was thoroughly drunk.

"What the hell are you doing here?" he said, attempting to glare at Thaddeus while reaching for Grace, grabbing her arm to pull her into the house. "You can stay right there," he said to Thaddeus. "We're stealing all the women and there's no bastards allowed!"

"You didn't tell me it was formal," Thaddeus said, indicating with a gesture his own casual garb.

"I didn't? It doesn't matter, you're not the only ones. Some of us were just thinking that with a president in blue jeans and ratty old cardigans it might be time to bring back a bit of tradition."

"You should have told us," Grace said.

"Oh nonsense," Gene said. "You look lovely. You'll be the loveliest woman here. And this one." He draped his arm over Thaddeus's shoulder. "In evening wear this little genius might come off as a headwaiter."

Thaddeus and Grace followed him into a dark foyer, where several bicycles were haphazardly stored, and into his parlor, with its high ceiling and simple brick hearth, its bare wide-board floors and a Queen Anne sofa upholstered in red. A young man in a kilt playing something mournful on the bagpipes wandered through the parlor on his way somewhere.

"A leftover from the Silver Jubilee," Gene said, in a confiding, slightly derisive tone. "I believe Elizabeth dispatched him to Singapore and now he's here."

"I have no idea what you're talking about," Thaddeus said.

"You don't?" Gene clapped Thaddeus's shoulder. "Well, good for you! We need more of that around here."

Thaddeus and Grace traded looks as they followed Gene down a metal spiral staircase leading to the garden level.

"I'm twenty-eight years old and completely alone in the world," Gene called out to them, over his shoulder. He said it as if he had just discovered a hidden hilarity in his situation.

Watching his friend descend the staircase, Thaddeus had the sense of watching someone going down the drain. The lower half of the duplex was filled with guests and books. Shelves went from floor to ceiling and were so overloaded that the boards sagged in the middle. At no point in their many conversations at work did Gene indicate he possessed such an extensive personal library. He spoke of current events, and various intrigues in the men's furnishings department and throughout the entire store, and now, looking at those hundreds of volumes, Thaddeus was beset by stinging memories of how confidently he himself had held forth about novels and short stories to Gene, giving this personable yet slightly less fortunate man the benefit of his U of M education.

"Nice," Thaddeus said, waving weakly at the shelves.

"Mainly my uncle's," Gene said. "I've squeezed a couple of my own in there, but those are his books. This is his place and everything in it. Luckily for me, he's in Thailand, and if you ask me, he's never coming back. He's been eaten alive by Buddhism." He smiled and held up the wine bottle he'd been carrying, two fingers around its dark neck. "I've been a bad boy."

"Who do I see about being a bad girl?" Grace asked.

Gene grinned delightedly and his eyes glittered. "Where did you find this marvelous girl?" he exclaimed.

"Nobody finds me, birthday boy. I find *them*." Somehow Gene's antic nature, his mixture of superiority and sheer goofiness appealed to Grace and made her more forthcoming than Thaddeus had expected.

"I *am* the birthday boy, aren't I?" Gene said, grinning, rubbing his hands together. "And there's something rather marvelous in that, don't you think?"

There wasn't much furniture and most of the guests stood, drinking from wineglasses, tumblers, and beer bottles, talking with great animation and volume. Sliding glass doors led to a yard enclosed by an eight-foot wooden fence. The yard was paved in flagstones; terracotta planters held frost-blackened ferns. Japanese paper lanterns swung haphazardly in the breeze.

"What a place," Thaddeus said.

"You should buy it," Gene said, with absurd enthusiasm. "Real estate is an excellent investment and I know Uncle Cary would be glad to unload it. The problem is the upstairs tenants, of which there are three. The redoubtable Craig Levitz, a poet, Jeanette Doubleday, no relation to anyone you'd care to be related to, and the inevitable Russian lady with her little dog."

"Like in Chekhov," Thaddeus said, instantly embarrassing himself.

"Anyhow," Gene continued, "New York City housing law makes it difficult to evict tenants. You have to resort to extracurricular methods, such as freezing them out and dressing up as a ghost and jumping out at them when they come home at night. You don't strike me as the type. Or is he?" This directed at Grace.

"Thaddeus is a gentleman," Grace said.

"Sure he is," Gene said. "A gentle man."

"I don't think we'll be buying a brownstone anytime soon," Thaddeus said.

"Well, up to you. But the city's going belly-up and that's always a good time to buy. Say, you know what you two need?" Gene said, pointing at them, first one, then the other. "A trip up the river to Eastwood."

"Eastwood?" said Thaddeus. "As in *Dirty Harry*?"

"Not that Eastwood. It's my family's place in Leyden, which I call Brigadoon. My sisters have banned me from the place. They accuse me of stealing some soup spoons and putting them up for auction at Doyle."

"Are your spoons that valuable?" Thaddeus asked.

"God. They're old and tarnished and taste like a mouth full of dimes. But anything ancestral makes my family extremely tense."

"Where's Leyden?" Grace asked. "We're from Chicago."

"Ninety-nine point nine miles north of here. Straight up the river."

"That's in Windsor County, right?" Thaddeus said. "Where a lot of writers used to be."

"Oh, it's the snoozy-boozy land of used-to-be," Gene said. "I'm sure I'll be reinstated to everyone's good graces by Christmas. Ice boating, Pimm's cup, bridge, and unspeakable food. You have to visit. You must. Come watch the death throes of a way of life. And bring this marvelous girl."

"I don't get brung," Grace said.

Gene made a barking laugh. Loud laughter was everywhere, from the men in tuxedos, and the bare-shouldered women in form-fitting dresses. Laughter! Gaiety! Joy! It had never occurred to Thaddeus that rich people could be so goddamned funny. Gene—who until fifteen minutes ago had seemed like such a lost soul, a hardship case—had somehow inherited all these people along with the key to these luxurious rooms. And a house up the Hudson, like something out of Evelyn Waugh. It would be amazing and illuminating to go—a country weekend with enough witty repartee to choke a horse. With Grace, of course, the two of them getting loaded on those legendary wines, dining on beef Wellington and devils-on-horseback, allowing themselves to be bullied into skating on a pond or shooting skeet, and then repairing to one of a multitude of guest rooms, where they would dissect their hosts' manners and morals, décor, speech, opinions, and dress, and have to place pillows over their own mouths to muffle their laughter.

Thaddeus worried that at any moment Gene was going to abandon them, but instead he stayed at their elbow, steering them through the crush, making introductions, impossible to keep track of, but okay, because just as they would not remember the names that went with all the new faces, the faces would not remember them. Bryan Noy, Patricia Hubbard, Constantine Covey, Mian Jan, Rip Gallin, Xavier Mendoza, Sanjay Ghosh, one after the next, with the preferred mode of greeting a slight shift of the weight backward, a firm handshake, head tilted, a bemused smile, a furrowed brow—as if each person was *almost* remembering you. It was as if they had all learned a dance at the same studio.

And lo and behold in the mix of all the unfamiliarity, Kip Woods emerged, also not in formal wear, but looking lithe and stylish in Burberry suit and tie, his five o'clock shadow darker than usual.

"What are *you* doing here?" Kip said to Thaddeus.

"That's not very friendly," Grace said, laughing—but Thaddeus knew she meant it.

"Old friends?" Gene inquired.

"Best friends," said Kip. He put his arm around Thaddeus. His breath was cold and smelled metallic. Some drug.

He kissed Grace's hand. "*Mmm*," he said. "You always smell so good."

More often than not, Kip's evenings were spent with a procession of stunning, long-legged women, most of them with something machine-tooled in their glamour, some promise of heartless, hydraulic sex—but tonight he was accompanied by a small woman in a dark blue pants suit, a frilly white blouse, olive skin, no makeup.

"This is my friend Anahita," Kip said. "Anahita is from Tehran. Tell them what you were telling me, Ana. I know they'll be interested. Thaddeus, as you know, comes from a long line of political people."

If Anahita objected to being prompted, she gave no indication. She wasn't more than five feet tall and might have relished the extra height afforded by a soapbox. Grace looked at her with open curiosity, as she always did when meeting one of Kip's women.

"Right now in my home," Anahita said, "many students and others are on the street making their protest against the criminal Pahlavi."

"The shah of Iran," said Kip.

"We are not children playing in the nursery with kings and queens and little fairy princesses," said Anahita. "Pahlavi and the horrible Farah Diba were given to us by the United States. We were democratic before our country was forcibly taken away. Your country wants us to live like children, but we are an advanced country. The most advanced and historical country in the Middle East. And such beauty. Our markets bursting, the burlap bags filled with bright green vegetables. We have scientists, poets, surgeons, and great thinkers. We do not want to be ruled by the crazy mullahs who are waiting in the shadows, or the so-called shah and his whore."

"Whoa," said Thaddeus, out of surprise. She seemed so proper, an emissary from a distant, straitlaced time, and to hear her call her queen a whore startled him.

Anahita smiled. Her teeth were white, but with a pinkish sheen, like freshwater pearls, and her gums were dark, almost purple. She wore a serpent ring on her thumb. "The shah will either abdicate or hang. That much we know. His secret police have exhausted themselves hunting down the Communists. And the students in Azadi Square are only the beginning. We also know this. It will grow. The kingdom of lies will crumble. And the United States will have placed a very costly wager on the wrong person. What will happen in my country will haunt you for years to come. You do not stage a coup d'état, and murder innocent people, and install a tyrant, and plunder a nation and simply walk away as if nothing has happened. Your own Dr. King tried to teach you this lesson. The arc of time bends toward justice. My country will find its way, and we could have been friends—"

"We *are* friends!" exclaimed Kip.

"I mean our nations," Anahita said. She shook her head. "This is such a humorous country. It's what the world loves and despises in you. Your incessant laughter. Why are you laughing? That's what the brave young people in the square are asking you."

"We're brave young people, too," said Kip.

"Come on, man, stop," Thaddeus said. His heart was pounding. He wanted to memorize every word Anahita said. She was telling a story he knew was for him, and he didn't want Kip to annoy her. But she wasn't annoyed, as it turned out. She shoved Kip playfully.

"What am I going to do with you?" she said, shaking her head like an easygoing aunt. Kip brought that out in people. You had to indulge him. There was no other way to be in his company.

"You're going to drink with me, my Persian delight," Kip said, spiriting her away.

Thaddeus and Grace wandered through scraps of other conversations. There was an interest in hotels, most of them abroad. La Mamounia in Marrakech. Browns in London. After that, Thaddeus lost the thread. The whole point of travel it seemed was to either visit a well-off relation or stay at a proper hotel or get into some insane scrape—break a leg climbing a ruin, come down with malaria in Samoa. The bagpiper was slumped in the corner, his chanter drooping, his plaid bag wrinkled and deflated. Oliver Onions on the stereo singing "Dune Buggy," the sound track to someone's fond Italian memory.

"Oh my God," Grace whispered to him, "these people. And that music."

"It's what they listen to in Europe," Thaddeus said, irritated with her for a moment, as if she were being obstinate, stubborn in the face of new pleasures.

Thaddeus felt amazed and squashed, almost obliterated by the people in this room, but the destruction struck him as somehow necessary—and encouraging. He was being shunned by the right people, by the people who embodied the New York he had long dreamed of, full of ease and privilege and high spirits. He would keep his head high, and learn from these citizens of the city within the city.

Thaddeus and Grace continued to wander the party, made shy by their own neediness. They helped themselves to drinks at a table

in the garden, a cruddy old knocked-around wooden table, the kind
of table only a rich person would feel okay about displaying in front
of his guests, three and a half legs, the veneer stripped off the top.
Vagabond ice cubes slid around bottles of Popov vodka and Sutter
Home gin, and other cheap brands sharing the perch with pricey
bottles of wine in a kind of democracy of booze.

While helping themselves to glasses of Château Beychevelle, one
of the guests, deciding that Grace was on her own, descended upon
her. His name was James Nichols. He offset his tux with red tennis
shoes. Pudgy, moist, with thinning hair and peeling lips, he nonetheless managed to exude self-confidence.

"I'm the kind of person who," he announced, "when he sees
someone lovely he must go and introduce himself."

"Know thyself," Grace said, good-naturedly.

"That's checkmate, right there," James said. His voice was
hoarse. He sounded like someone who had exhausted himself selling
something, or trying to convince skeptics of one thing or another.
His laugh was something like a cough. "Tell me your name and
everything about yourself."

"Do I *have* to?"

"Okay, fair enough. My name is James, no one calls me Jim,
though my mother called me Jimmy, before I murdered her. Editor at Dodd, Mead. A sleepy old place from which I am planning
to decamp. I mainly acquire history but every now and then they
allow me to buy a novel. I have a decent salary, and have absolutely
no family money, unlike most of the little shits in this room. And if
you're one of them, I'm sorry."

Thaddeus was counting off the seconds this guy would stand
there without acknowledging his presence. He had already reached
140.

"All right. I'm Grace Cornell and I work in publishing, too. At
Periodic. And this is my boyfriend, Thaddeus Kaufman."

"Ah. Thaddeus Kaufman," Nichols said, as if a missing piece had
been supplied. "Gene has talked to me about you."

"He has?" Thaddeus asked. He was going to answer *Has he now*, as a kind of push back, but an actual editor having a discussion about *him* was the main thing on his mind.

"So tell me . . ." *Did he just wink in Grace's direction?* "Briefly as possible: what's your novel about? It is a novel, isn't it?"

"I guess."

"You guess?"

"It's a novel," Grace said. "And it's really good."

"Your accent," Nichols said, pointing to Grace. His fingernail was chewed, his cuticle livid. "I'm the kind of person who can usually tell straightaway where someone was raised, but . . . I don't know. Where are you from?"

"I'm trying to keep away from the typical first-novel stuff," Thaddeus said. "I don't want to do a bildungsroman." His heartbeat was beginning to accelerate. He had a vision of himself simply turning away and fleeing that was so vivid it seemed as if it had already happened, that it was not dread but an actual memory.

"Free advice," said Nichols. "It's not good business to talk about what you're *not* writing."

"My brother says that free advice is worth what it costs," Grace said.

"It's about an old couple in a dying city," Thaddeus said.

"Like Updike's first novel?" Nichols said. "*To the Poorhouse?*"

Thaddeus did not bother to correct Nichols's botch of the title. It was close enough. And, in fact, Updike had been on Thaddeus's mind when he began his own book, so Nichols got some credit there. Nichols was probably brilliant, or close to it, like most of the gatekeepers between Thaddeus and the world. Sometimes in his despair he wondered how he would ever get past them, how he would ever be included. What did he have to offer? His main hope was that he would just simply be able to do it, just as he had hoped as a teenager that when it finally was time to have sex he would know what to do. The preparation for actual sex was two years of masturbation, and the preparation for starting a novel was two semesters of creative writing.

"The saddest thing I see?" Nichols proposed. "And this is something I warn all young writers about."

"How old are *you?*" Grace interjected.

"Older than I look. I take excellent care of myself. And . . ." He raised a finger, insisting on full attention. "The advice is, do not fall between two stools."

"Or two stool samples," said Thaddeus, in spite of himself. *Snap!* went the mousetrap of social regret. *Poof!* went the disappearing promise to stop joking around.

Nichols graciously pretended not to have heard. "There are the avowedly and consciously commercial fictions, the romances and the swashbucklers and mysteries and such, and most publishers can usually make them profitable. But I think it was Mr. Knopf who said the thing about publishing is that it's gone today and here tomorrow." He made a signifying smile. "Returns. They are our ruination. With reliably commercial fiction we tend not to over print and everyone comes out fine. But then there is literature. And what you must ask yourself is: am I writing straight commercial fiction or am I creating literature? Mailer, Styron, your friend Mr. Updike, and I'll throw Kurt Vonnegut in there, too—they are clearly creating literature and they are even getting onto the bestseller lists. Listen, all those guys want to work with me. At Dodd, Mead? Or what I call Dead Meat? No way, Jose. I'll probably end up at Random House and they will be with me there. Mailer, John Gardner, Joe Heller, the lot of them.

"But anyhow: the all-important list. Do you study what's on the list? You should. Right now, we've got old Irwin Shaw, that madman Tolkien, John Fowles—and others who I can stand before you and promise none of us will remember ten years from now, but they're making a good living right now, not only for themselves but for their publishers. Which brings us back to you. Do you see yourself as becoming part of the inner circle? The next Mailer, the next Styron? Because I'll tell you, that's not the feeling I get standing with you. I can smell it." He touched the side of his nose, and Thaddeus felt a swell of horror and shame.

"You seem just like a regular middle-of-the-road person to me," Nichols said, "and there's nothing wrong with that. But there's no place for that kind of writing in this world, not anymore."

"This is ridiculous," said Grace, drawing closer to Thaddeus. "You're being a horrible bully."

"Well, I notice *you're* listening," Nichols said.

"There's a difference between listening and staring," said Grace.

George Eliot, thought Thaddeus. It did not take any great feat of memory for him to recognize the phrase from *Middlemarch*. He and Grace were reading it aloud to each other on the many nights they couldn't afford to go out.

"I am saving your lives is what I am doing. You are going to look back on this and say, *Oh my God, that handsome devil from Dodd, Mead saved our lives.* Here's something I know. A friend of mine, his name is George Atkinson, a bit older than us, great guy. Smart. Talk about smelling something on someone? He's got the smell of a winner."

"And what's that smell like?" Grace asked.

"Difficult to say, but one recognizes it. Anyhow, you know what George is doing next month, out there in Los Angeles? He's opening a video rental store. Like a pay library, but for movies. Betamax, VHS, whatever you want. Right on Wilshire Boulevard. You walk in, pick a movie you want to see, and bring it home. Do you have any idea what that's going to do to publishing? Bookstores? All of us? It's a law of nature, all creatures great and small take the path of least resistance. Even electrons follow this universal law. Faced with the choice of reading a book or lazily watching *The Way We Were*, I think most people are going to opt for the latter. The only books that are going to get bought are the totally pandering, commercial, easy on the eyes, easy on the brainpan kind, or else some kind of event book. And if you're not going to be the person who writes that book, and there's one of them a year, maybe two, then I say get the hell out and find something else to do."

There was no telling how long this advice would have gone on had one of the guests not entered with a blazing birthday cake—a woman in extremely high heels and a strand of pearls that swayed at waist level as she walked. There were cheers, applause, and soon all the guests were singing "Happy Birthday" to Gene, the singing, even in its collectivity, humorous, as if the familiar lyrics were all in quotation marks. "Who me?" Gene silently mouthed, pointing to himself, turning this way and that so everyone could see how he was reacting to the cake and the song.

"We should go," Thaddeus whispered to Grace.

"It's still early. And there's a lot of good wine still to be drunk. What do you want to do?"

"I don't know. Maybe hang myself?"

Now you know how I feel half the time, thought Grace, but instead of saying it, she kissed him.

When they finally got out of there, a cold mist was falling. Or was it rain? Sleet? Was it snow? It was an undifferentiated stinging wetness. They flipped their collars up, put their heads down, and headed toward home.

"If we see a taxi we'll take it," Thaddeus said.

BUT THE NIGHT WAS NOT through with them yet. Every night is a mansion with countless rooms, and the door flew open to the next room. As they walked through the mist, they heard someone calling Thaddeus's name, shredded by the dark wind and barely recognizable. It was Kip, his head out of the back window of a Checker cab gliding to a stop. One of the taxi's headlights was out and it gave the boxy old cab a kind of winking, insouciant look.

"Get in here, you serfs, and enjoy the warmth of my troika!" Kip shouted.

They were relieved to be rescued from the weather and from the sense of failure that walking in bad weather can cause. Kip had already unfolded the jump seat that had been nestled into the floor of the taxi and now he sat facing the backseat, where Thaddeus slid in on one side of Anahita and Grace sat on the other. Anahita wore a floor-length quilted down coat. She had taken an orange from Gene's party and was unpeeling it, releasing a bright citrusy scent and letting the peels fall to the floor. Kip slapped his hands against Thaddeus's knees as if he were playing a bongo drum.

"We're going to drop Ana off at her hotel and then you guys come with me, and the fun will really begin once we get rid of sourpuss," he announced.

"Kip, I'm tired," Anahita said. "Enough excitement for one night. And tomorrow morning there is a vigil outside the consulate."

"Oh sure," Kip said. "Nothing changes history as reliably as a vigil. What about you two? You want to go back to your love cave or accompany old Uncle Kip on his nocturnal adventures?"

Thaddeus looked at Grace, who shrugged, and Kip beat his palms even harder and faster against Thaddeus's knees. "Oh mama mama mama, we are going to get so fucking high!" he sang in a falsetto.

They dropped Anahita off at her hotel. Kip walked her to the front entrance of the Plaza; a liveried doorman met them halfway, holding a striped umbrella.

"She must have money," Grace said.

"One day that'll be us," Thaddeus said.

"Sure, why not," said Grace.

"As God is my witness, we'll never go hungry again!" clowned Thaddeus. He slammed his open hand over his heart, and coughed. It was an old Jerry Lewis routine, the kind he used to do in front of Sam and Libby.

Kip bounded back into the taxi, his hair bejeweled with raindrops. "She is one foxy lady," he said. "But a very serious Muslim. Did you see how she kissed me good night? Completely without warmth or affection?"

The taxi swung around Columbus Circle, and then onto Central Park West to Ninety-First Street, where it turned west. Kip paid the driver while Thaddeus and Grace stood in front of a shabby narrow brownstone between Amsterdam and Columbus. All but one of the windows were dark. Plastic flowerpots holding dead geraniums were scattered on the steps.

"This will be fast," Kip said, pressing the buzzer to apartment 4.

"Mind telling us what we're doing here?" Grace asked.

"I think you know," Kip said.

A buzzer unlocked the door into a vestibule that was a riot of shopping carts and umbrellas. The odor of cat piss was overpowering. Lit by a flickering circular fluorescent light, the steps rose at an extreme angle, more like a ladder than a staircase.

"Top floor, kids," Kip said, his voice bright, manic.

They were calling on a man named Luke, who was fresh out of the shower, draped in a Snoopy towel. He looked like an aging Roman senator from the age of the Caesars, though he hadn't breached thirty. Narrow face, eyes deep-set and guarded. Water dripped from his thinning dark hair, his tufted narrow shoulders, his scrawny legs.

"You're early," he said to Kip.

"Actually, I'm late. Can we come in?"

"Just you," Luke said.

But Kip ushered Thaddeus and Grace ahead of him and Luke offered only mild resistance. His apartment was the source of the cat-piss odor—he had fifteen, perhaps twenty, cats patrolling his apartment, all at different stages of the feline life cycle. He moved a few of them back with a sweep of his leg as he opened the door to Kip and Thaddeus and Grace. The apartment was just two rooms, only one of which had a window. *Who do you have to fuck in this town to get a window?* Thaddeus thought.

There was a bewildering assortment of chairs, all of them in poor repair, as if every time Luke passed a discarded chair left at the curb for the trash collection he couldn't resist bringing it home. His small sofa was covered by an Indian bedspread. The glass-topped coffee table was covered by a triple-beam scale, an empty Chablis bottle, and an open copy of *Screw* magazine, the weekly tabloid in which prostitutes were advertised. A TV set was showing the local access program *Midnight Blue*, with the sound extremely low.

"Hey, look, it's Al Goldstein," Kip said. He took an envelope from the inside pocket of his overcoat and handed it to Luke. "That horny old bastard happens to be sort of a wizard when it comes to picking stocks. One of my buddies over at Cowen is on the phone with him six times a day."

Luke opened the envelope. "Three grams?"

"Three? Five."

"Maybe in Bolivia, but not here," Luke said.

He tried to return the envelope to Kip, but Kip backed away from it, as if he were avoiding being served a summons. Luke kept the money and gave Kip three grams of cocaine, each in its own little origami-like packet. Cats of all colors and sizes paced the perimeter of the room, with sparkling eyes and flicking tails. Kip asked if it would be all right to sample "the item" before they left and Luke made a faux-elegant gesture, inviting them all to sit. There was certainly no lack of choices but it was difficult to tell which chairs were safe.

Thaddeus and Grace rarely used cocaine—too expensive. And they preferred the slow soft languorous forgiving embracing qualities of wine. But Grace was up for it, and Thaddeus, too. He liked the Windex-y astringency in his nasal passages, how his blood charged through the sleeping city of his circulatory system like a Mongol horde, and he vaguely hoped for an extra few hours of wakefulness that he could spend in front of his Olivetti, writing. Night after night, he worked with the diligence of a prisoner trying to dig his way out of his cell with a spoon.

As they were leaning over the dessert plate upon which Luke had portioned out Kip's gram, Thaddeus became absorbed with the television, where Al Goldstein was interviewing a fleshy man in his late thirties with a drooping lower lip and hooded eyes. On the bottom of the screen was his name, Lou Levine. He wore a leather coat, cowboy hat, and long scarf. The conversation was about Levine's sex club called Nero's Fiddle, a mile or so away, at the Marlboro Hotel. The volume on the TV was low and Thaddeus had a hard time making out what they were saying, but it seemed mainly about the club's strict no alcohol or drugs policy, and the wide array of foods available at the buffet—lasagna, meatballs, potato salad, chicken, ribs, macaroni, and cold cuts. "You could come there just for the nosh," Goldstein said, with an air of mild contempt.

Luke noticed Thaddeus's interest in the show. "I've been there once. Plenty of stars. I saw Melvin Van Peebles, Richard Dreyfuss. All kinds of people. Some bridge-and-tunnel types, but there's some hot girls in Jersey."

"We should go," Kip said. "It's close by, right? It's in that place that used to be a bathhouse for the gay boys, listening to Connie Francis and sitting around in their towels. Not unlike you, old buddy," he added, patting Luke's soup-bone knee. "But we could go, right? Like Roman emperors, enjoying pleasures of the flesh once unimaginable to the common man."

"No single men allowed," Luke said. "But if you're really into it, my friend Catherine lives a couple doors down and likes it."

"Would you do something like that?" Grace asked Thaddeus.

"Would you?" Thaddeus said.

"Go into a room with naked strangers and everyone fucking their brains out?" she asked.

"Would you?" Thaddeus asked again.

"You don't have to do anything if you don't want to," Luke said. "You have to take off your shoes, but that's it. You can even leave your socks on." He picked up his phone and started dialing.

"Are you calling your friend?" Kip asked.

"I'll see if she's home," said Luke.

Thaddeus and Grace could never agree on the exact sequence of events, and eventually that night's second half entered into the realm of perpetual silence, beginning with the arrival of Luke's friend and ending with their slipping wordlessly into their own bed at dawn. Thaddeus would have it that they had allowed themselves to be swept into Kip's enthusiasm and taste for debauchery, while Grace would never relinquish her own sense of cause and effect and continued to insist that what had gotten Kip going in the first place was Thaddeus's obvious fascination with Goldstein and Levine chatting away on *Midnight Blue*. What they both agreed on was that cocaine played a part in it, though it was not as if coke was an hallucinogen like LSD or mushrooms, which would allow them to experience (or at least imagine) a different dimension, a counter-reality. Coke was not a disinhibitor like booze. The most that could be blamed on the coke was that it gave them a kind of outlaw sense of rising above the normal world and diminished their sense of consequence, fostering a view of the world like you can have on an airplane, when cities are but twinkling grids, essentially devoid of meaning. *I think I just figured out why people like conceptual art,* Grace said at one point. *It's like coke, it's all mind over matter.*

Luke was feeling generous and the next lines were gratis. Two young calico cats got into it, yowling and hissing and clawing at the air, and occasionally each other, which was frightening at first and then hilarious. What made it particularly strange was that all the other cats just sat quietly and watched. Luke's friend Catherine arrived wearing a burgundy pants suit and a gaudy silver belt. She imported sheepskin jackets from Afghanistan, going to Kabul several times a year and buying dozens of coats for a few dollars each and selling them to boutiques for a 500 percent profit. She was barely five feet tall, but wore platform shoes that brought her up to five three or so. She had a playful voice, and seemed like a person who had gotten herself into and out of numerous predicaments. "I like men and I love sex, but boyfriends . . ." She held out her hand and wobbled it back and forth. "Them I could do without."

"Are we really going to do this?" Grace asked.

"It's fun," Catherine said. "You'll see. It's sort of like a dream."

"No one's asking you to adopt a new lifestyle," Kip said. There was something harsh in his voice, as if they had all agreed on something and Grace was going to wreck it.

"You don't have to do anything you don't want to," Catherine said. "It's all very respectful and easy."

"Let's get going," Kip said. "This is going to be fun. This is what living in New York is all about. Let's just do it!"

"Here," said Luke, laying out more lines. "May as well."

"It's going to be like Rapestock," Grace said.

"No way, Jose," said Catherine. "It's safer for chicks than the subway. The place is women's lib all the way. Girls approach the guys, they don't hit on us. They're not allowed to. Rule. You have to be extremely respectful. But the thing is, you don't even need the rules. The people there are so friendly, and gentle. No one wants to ruin it."

"You up for this?" Grace asked Thaddeus again.

"One more snort and I'm up for anything," he said. And they both knew that he wasn't being completely honest. It was more curiosity than cocaine. The thought of going into a world where everyone was fucking everyone else . . .

Kip ordered a limo from Haifa Transportation. The driver's name was Shlomo. One of his ears looked chewed in half. Mahler's Second Symphony played on the radio, very softly. It reminded Thaddeus of how the music sounded back at his parents' apartment on Kimbark, shrouded and funereal, always out of pleasure's grasp. He took Grace's hand. It was clammy, or his was. The city was still enshrouded in cold mist. Lights from the tall buildings made the fog look like silvery gauze, the buildings themselves all but invisible.

They stood for a moment at the entrance. Across the street was a McDonald's. A woman in a long black woolen coat and a scarf tied under her chin to cover her hair walked by with a Scottie dog on a leash. Thaddeus's heart danced, and the dog walker was swallowed by the fog. Hannah Hannah Hannah Hannah, and then she was gone.

"You okay?" Grace asked.

"As well as can be expected," said Thaddeus, grinning.

Admission was twenty-five dollars a couple and Kip paid. A squared-off man in a ski jacket took Kip's money and shoved it into his pocket. "You do work here, don't you?" Kip asked. His normal bantering tone had returned. The harshness that had set in for a few moments when it seemed that Grace might be an impediment was gone, and the aural mask was back in place. He linked his arm through Catherine's, a legitimate couple descending the steep flight of steps that led to the club.

The first thing: the smell of chlorine and some other odor, sweet and unnatural. A spray? Incense? The darkness that slowly receded into dimness. The music too loud, the speakers full of distortion. Wild Cherry singing "Hot to Trot." The dance floor, some people fully dressed, men in vests, women in pants suits, people in their underwear, and some wearing nothing, breasts flopping, genitals bobbing up and down like rodents trying to leap out of a cage. Spears of light shot down from the crystal disco ball like thunderbolts. *I might be too much for you honey / Do you know what I mean? / I'm just a dancin' fool / And I'm lookin' for a struttin' queen . . .*

Grace said, "This is just like some terrible disco but with a few crazy people who've taken off their clothes." Catherine said they should check out the swimming pool, and above all, the mattress room. Thaddeus said the people weren't very good looking and Kip laughed and told him he was a snob, and then said they would all follow Catherine, who was heading for the buffet. There were people sitting at small tables, eating meatballs and lasagna off paper plates, drinking ginger ale. Mustaches. Big hair.

"'Abandon hope, all ye who enter here,'" Thaddeus said into Grace's ear. She didn't respond. "Dante," he said. "The *Inferno*."

"Wow," she shouted over the pounding music. "You're so literary."

He failed to heed the warning and pressed on. "This is crazy. Like Paul Newman said, why would I go out for a hamburger when I can have steak at home?"

"That's so beautiful, Thaddeus," she yelled. "Unbelievably touching."

Okay, now he got it. "Hey, none of this is my idea," he said.

She kissed him, biting his lip, grabbing his hips. There was something weirdly erotic about being here, as unpleasant as it was.

The arousal was involuntary. It was like being tickled. Someone can dig their fingertips into your rib cage and you might laugh but that doesn't mean you're happy.

"You people are ridiculous," Catherine mouthed. She grabbed Kip's hand and led him deeper into the club's interior.

"There's got to be better orgies than this," Thaddeus said to Grace. "For people who are really doing well."

"Poor us," said Grace, "invited to the wrong orgy."

The swimming pool was not quite so deafening. The water blue as antifreeze. Thirty, forty people floating around, penises sticking up like periscopes. Bellies like the shells of Galapagos tortoises. Tits of all nations. A balding guy who looked like a high school teacher was sitting on the edge of the pool, dangling his feet in the water while a woman (who wore a bathing cap to protect her hairdo) treaded water and fellated him.

Kip and Catherine emerged from the locker room, naked. Thaddeus tried not to notice Kip's body. He was slim and graceful as a greyhound. Catherine was bosomy, thick. She stretched voluptuously, as if here at Nero's she could finally relax. Kip kept his hands in front of his genitals as he and Catherine approached the pool and the two of them jumped in.

"Still think he's queer?" Thaddeus asked.

"More than ever," said Grace. "Are you going to take off your clothes?"

"Are you?"

"Not at the moment." She looked around. "It's sort of boring to just stand around."

"Then you *are* going to get naked?"

"Did I say that?"

Someone was having an ostentatious orgasm, an almost Alpine yodel, genderless, followed by cheers from bystanders, or byfuckers. Who knew, who cared? Thaddeus heard someone say that Sammy Davis Jr. was here. A man with a high, plaintive voice was looking for someone named Andrea, he called her name over and over as he

wandered from the pool to the pool table to the Ping-Pong table to
the buffet, where he helped himself to pastrami, but continued to
call for her as he chewed.

In college, Thaddeus had been a formidable Ping-Pong player.
He was mediocre at every other sport, from basketball to Frisbee,
but he was a terror with a paddle, to his own surprise. He hadn't
played since Ann Arbor, but he drifted toward the club's Ping-Pong
table, where a woman in her late thirties wearing skimpy lace underwear was playing an older woman with one breast, who was naked. They were both good players, standing far from the table. The
woman with the mastectomy was more of a power player, while the
younger woman played a more modest game, based on placement
and English. She was, on second glance, more appealing to Thaddeus than she had been at first. His mind was racing, if only to keep
up with his heart, which had been in a state of great alertness since
the first line of coke and in a state of utter alarm from the moment
they had all agreed to come here.

"Can I play the winner?" he asked.

"We're not keeping score," the woman in panties said.

"Let's," said the older woman. She caught the ball out of the
air. She suggested that she serve first and the game would be to
twenty-one. The younger woman looked tense and took a couple
of deep, steadying breaths. It seemed weird to Thaddeus to be nervous about losing a Ping-Pong match while you were all but naked
in a sex club. That might make for a good short story. First line:
*She'd already been laid seven times but all that faded from memory
once the Ping-Pong match began.* God. Was that the best he had in
him? He was starting to think that maybe it was. The world was
more interested in the guy who had amassed a gigantic ball of
aluminum foil than it was in him and his writing! It galled him
to have his nose pressed up against the glass of the culture. Even
here in this supposed erotic paradise he was on the outside looking
in. Fully clothed, hoping the younger of the two women won the
game, though he would have been hard-pressed to explain why

which one he played made much of a difference, or any difference at all.

As it happened, the younger woman did not win. She was trounced, twenty-one to eight. But the woman with the mastectomy was joined by her boyfriend (who, for a panicky moment, Thaddeus thought was Frank Zappa) and the two of them headed off to the mattress room, where presumably countless couples were squirming like a bucket full of worms, though at this point Thaddeus had not brought himself to even glance in that direction. The vanquished woman agreed to play with him. She seemed not to mind that he was fully clothed. She told him her name was Becky.

"Are you outrageous?" she asked.

"Not really," he said.

Becky slapped herself in the rear with her paddle and offered to let him serve first. Back in Ann Arbor he had a tricky serve, but he couldn't manage it tonight. He kept netting it and was forced to serve up lollipops, which put a look of pure delight on Becky's face before she sent the ball flying back at Thaddeus at what seemed like 100 miles per hour. Finally, one of her smashes resulted in a lost ball and after a futile search they tried to figure out who to ask for a new one. The guy Thaddeus approached wore a pale blue Speedo and had a silver police whistle nestled into his abundant chest hair. "There's a hobby shop on Eighty-Sixth Street," he said. "But they're closed now." Thaddeus tried to explain that he didn't want to buy Ping-Pong balls, but the man interrupted and said, "You'd be a lot happier if you got out of your street clothes, man." Thaddeus said he thought the club policy was no pressure, and the man said, "I'm not pressuring. I'm inviting you to paradise." At which point, he wiggled out of his little bathing suit—his genitals were priapic and to see them spilling out was like watching the emptying of a clown car.

"Whoa," said Becky, backing away. She linked her arm through Thaddeus's. The gesture was more than intimate, it was *tender*. "You're a handsome one," she said. Thaddeus glanced away, wondering where Grace was, and if she was watching him. She was nowhere in sight and when he turned back toward Becky she kissed him full on the mouth, and his mouth cooperated, softened, opened. He was kissing her back and she took his hand and placed it on her breast and said, "Pinch." He moved away from the kiss so he could see her face when he pinched her, which he did gently, as if snuffing out a candle. "Are you going to keep your clothes on?" she asked.

It seemed stupid to him, and contrary to the spirit of curiosity, the spirit of adventure, the spirit of self-confidence, the spirit of irony, the spirit of daring, and the spirit of pleasure, to be one of the few clothed people at a swing club. Fuck it! If Emily Dickinson had found herself in Nero's Fiddle (presupposing that the Belle of Amherst had snorted up several lines of cocaine) she might have decided to go with the flow and stuff her dress and high-collared blouse into one of the club's little lockers, which was where he was heading.

Past the pool, with its multicolored periscopes. A few conscientious swingers were swimming laps. The Jacuzzi accommodated the several customers who were unconcerned about dipping their bodies into a warm bath with twenty strangers who had just either ejaculated or had been ejaculated into. And now the Mattress Room, which was the size of a cozy restaurant, with dim lighting and wall-to-wall mattresses, where some languidly embraced in postcoital peace, while others frantically fucked. Adios and farewell, you thousands of years of religion and law.

Catherine was on one of the mattresses with a young guy who looked like a cop or a soldier on top of her. She had one arm raised and snapped her fingers in time with his thrusts. Kip was watching, propped on one elbow, pleasing himself with his free hand. And that was when he saw Grace, standing in the corner, naked, as if she had awakened from a dream and found herself there. As Thaddeus watched, a middle-aged couple, the man fussy looking with a bristly mustache and small eyes, the woman like a wrestler, were having sex, and the man reached out to Grace and took her hand. Either he yanked her onto the mattress or she put up very little resistance. But when the bristling mustache tried to mount her, she quickly scrambled to her feet, and saw Thaddeus. She stepped over the writhing bodies, the potbellies and pendulous breasts, the hairy backsides and pink soles, over pageboys and crew cuts, braids and curls, over mouths and cunts and socks and armpits and jugular veins, over the moaners, the laughers, the squealers, and the grunters, until she and Thaddeus were face-to-face.

"What the fuck were you doing?" he asked her.

"Am *I* doing? What about you?"

"I wasn't doing anything."

She gestured toward his state of undress.

"Were you about to have sex with that guy?"

"Thaddeus. Come on. You're in no position."

"Can we go?"

"I didn't want to come here in the first place."

"Well, you've sure made the most of it."

She made a small gasp after which they were silent on the cab ride home. The streets were still dark, the sky was black and silver, like the back of a mirror.

"The sun's never going to rise," Grace said, staring out.

Once in the apartment, Grace hurried into the shower. A few minutes later, Thaddeus joined her, but she rinsed quickly and left him alone. By the time he dried himself off, she was in bed, with their extra pillow over her head.

He wasn't even close to being able to sleep. He went to the front room, rolled a piece of paper into the carriage of his typewriter. He wrote: *This is not the city I thought it was. I had it all wrong.* The Olivetti was quiet but it wasn't silent. He found a pen and a legal pad and began to write a story about Americans in a Gulf state country, embassy people, soldiers, journalists. He called the country Tigris; he called the screenplay *Hostages.* What would make it interesting? What would make it real, and not just a polemic based on the ten minutes he'd spent with Anahita? The answer came quickly: they'd all be trapped in the embassy, hostages to a young generation of Tigrians who hated the U.S. for supporting their mad despotic sultan.

He quickly composed nine pages until exhaustion overcame him. He turned off the lamp. Dawn broke gray and dim, like something oozing out of a container. He hated it here. Crime and filth and crazy people. He took off his clothes but getting into bed naked seemed a bad idea. Had nakedness been ruined? Why did Grace flee as soon as he got into the shower? He put on a pair of pajamas, the same pair he'd brought to Ann Arbor when he entered as a freshman. He slipped into bed as quietly as possible, but his presence awakened her. She pulled the pillow off her head and sat up. Their bed was on a metal frame, without a headboard. "We should go to church," she said. "The one next door."

"I'm Jewish," he whispered.

"I don't care and God doesn't care, either."

"Okay. I can do that," he said.

She rolled closer to him, draped her leg over his. "That feels nice," he said, and he thought, *How did this happen to me? How did I become one of the lucky ones?*

Dear Liam,

> *Yes, you're right, it would be totally out of sight if I could have a place to make art. I really appreciate your offer, but right now I think it would be a waste of money. But to have a little work space somewhere that I could call my own? A dream come true.*
>
> *How great would it be if I found a dealer, a gallery, and sold a bunch of stuff and got us out of here? That's my dream, anyhow. There are so many creepy people here. And I don't want to turn into one of them. I want out! Out!*
>
> *But we're stuck here and in the meanwhile I'm thinking of taking a drawing class at the Art Students League on Fifty-Seventh Street, which costs very little, so when I screw up and miss a class I won't feel guilty. All these cool modernists went there but so did one of my secret art crushes,*

Charles Dana Gibson. (First time I saw his drawing of a Gibson Girl I thought, That's me!!!) And Isabel Bishop went there, too. Her studio used to be less than ten blocks from where I sit now. That's the only good thing about NY, just about everyone was here one time or another. But man is it dirty, and is it loud, and is it scary. I don't tell Thaddeus but every Saturday I buy a lottery ticket. Irish sweepstakes, right? And when I win we're going to buy an island somewhere just like old Charlie Gibson did. His was off the coast of Maine. I've never even been to Maine. We went to a party at this rich guy's apartment (you should see it, it was amazing) and he invited us up to his family's mansion just about 100 miles from here. I'd take that just as much as our own island. We could all live there and do our thing and you could maybe stop taking so many chances. I worry about you every day.

Love forever,

Grace

Chapter 4

Potluck on Turquoise Court

JUNE 30, 1978

CARPENTER ONE: Anything happening tonight?

CARPENTER TWO: There's something on Turquoise Court. Couple of guys from New York.

CARPENTER ONE: You going?

CARPENTER TWO: Definitely!

J ENNINGS'S MOST CONSTANT FRIEND FROM CHILDHOOD was Larry Sassone, whose nickname was Itchy, not because he scratched himself any more than the next fellow, or because he suffered from any skin ailments, but because he liked to read and quote Friedrich Nietzsche, which had been misheard as "itchy." And that was all it took in Larry and Jennings's set—Windsor County boys living in tract houses, tenant homes, or trailers, who had been written off by their teachers, and everyone else. They were boys whose prospects did not register on the great Richter scale of American prosperity, hardhanded, proud, physically brave, and intellectually reticent boys at war with school, as they were with many other aspects of organized society, which was a stacked deck from which the assholes got dealt the aces.

Larry Sassone had not been an outstanding student at Leyden High School but he did like school and he *had* graduated, unlike many of his friends. From there he had gone on to Windsor Community College, where the tuition was low and he could take one or two classes at night and still put in forty hours painting houses for his uncle. Larry's plan was to take a few classes at Windsor and if all went well to transfer to a four-year college. But that path was not so much abandoned as lost, like a trail through the woods obscured by new growth and falling leaves and toppled trees. Part of the difficulty was that he was his own advisor, and he signed up for courses that had little to do with each other—small-engine repair, music appreciation, geology, German history. After four years he had no more direction than he had had in high school, and, more important, he hadn't created any momentum behind the idea of leaving Leyden, quitting his job, and getting a four-year degree. The other difficulty was that his uncle and his partner were dyed-in-the-wool Deadheads and smoked pot all day long, from which Larry could not politely abstain. He took one toke for their every five, but still, by the end of the workday he was exhausted from the work and getting high and coming down and getting high again and coming down again and all he could do was watch TV and eat.

When Larry was still making his way through WCC's course catalog, he took a class called the New American Novel, in which he and eleven other students read Norman Mailer, Richard Fariña, Rudolf Wurlitzer, and William Burroughs. The instructor was named Joel Ward, a compact man in his forties with a well-tended beard, and an explosive manner. He felt demeaned by teaching at Windsor Community College, with its part-time student body and its little quadrangle of buildings with all the grandeur of cereal boxes. "Oh, woe is *moi*," Ward said with a sigh before every class.

Glorified high school or not, in Ward's class Larry felt he was getting a taste of what it would be like at a real college. Ward paced, jabbed his finger at whatever page was being explicated, and threw chalk at students he sensed were not paying attention. He talked about the assigned reading as if the students were being given information that would set them apart from ordinary people, membership in a society that was better than they were.

Ward owned a small house outside Santa Fe, New Mexico, and at the end of the semester he asked Larry if he might be interested in coming out to New Mexico and slapping paint on some walls, and fixing things up in general. This meant Larry was Ward's favorite student, as far as Larry was concerned. He was unaware that Ward often used his class as a hiring pool, a kind of de facto shape-up when he needed manual work done.

"I would have gotten an A, but my final paper was late because we were repainting Windsor Diagnostics," Larry explained to Jennings. They were driving his bright yellow Datsun, beginning their journey to New Mexico. Beneath them, the Hudson throbbed with reflected light. Professor Ward had told Larry he could bring a helper and Jennings was more than willing. He was working no more than two days a week—little scraps of employment the Boyetts threw in his direction, and Sunday night at the Mobil station on the dark edge of town, selling cigarettes, beer. Business was unusually brisk when he was behind the counter, since he didn't card. His personal life—that is, his life with girls and women, the only kind of personal life that interested him, or of which he was capable—had traveled its inevitable path, as predictable as the earth's orbit around the sun, to chaos and lies, until leaving Leyden seemed not only an appealing idea, but somewhat necessary.

Jennings was restless. He wanted something to do, but the more he cast about for something that might occupy his body and mind, the less appealing everything around him appeared. He was starting to feel about life the way he sometimes felt about food if he waited too long to eat—there was a state of ravenous hunger that seemed to *destroy* appetite. You had waited too long and now nothing was right, nothing was good enough.

"I want to own something," Jennings said as they headed toward New Jersey. "I want to feel like something in this fucking world is mine."

"Yeah, me too," said Larry, clearly not paying attention. He gripped the steering wheel as if it had a life of its own and might at any moment begin asserting its will. His eyes were fixed on the road, and he was salivating so nervously that he had to keep swallowing. He suddenly felt lost, exiled, though they had traveled less than a hundred miles.

"What comes after New Jersey?" Jennings asked. "Pennsylvania?"

"I guess," said Larry. The farthest west he had ever traveled was Cleveland to visit his uncle Dean, who had three jobs, barber, bartender, security guard: a job for each ex-wife.

"You've got a friend in Pennsylvania," Jennings said.

"I do?"

"That's what the license plates say." He rolled the window down to feel the unfamiliar air, the surge of somewhere else.

IT WAS A TWO-THOUSAND-MILE DRIVE from Leyden to Santa Fe. Larry thought they could drive it straight through—he would sleep while Jennings drove, and vice versa—but Jennings wanted to sleep outdoors and they had brought tents and sleeping bags with them. Jennings had fond, erotic memories of his sleeping bag; he'd lost his virginity in Livingston Park, to the sound of trees swaying and creaking in the wind, and coyotes urging him on somewhere in the distance.

The Datsun behaved, they kept off the toll roads, and found fairly priced food and gas. America was full of places to sleep under the stars—they pitched their tents in Pennsylvania, Indiana, Missouri, and Oklahoma. They got high, met some nice people, and in Missouri a dog adopted Jennings for the night—a silky black mutt about fifty pounds who slinked into his tent, only to be gone by first light.

They both had fantasies about what it would be like to be in New Mexico—courtyards, adobe walls, a burrow tied to a hitching post, mesquite fragrantly smoking in a hearth lined with blue-and-white tiles. But Ward lived in a little split-level bungalow that could have been anywhere, no more distinctive or local than a stop sign, in a neighborhood of similar-looking houses, a kind of lower-middle-class development of which there were several back in Windsor County. And the house itself was in far worse condition than Larry had been led to believe. Here in New Mexico, Ward looked unkempt and unslept, boozed up and pissed off. He was in the midst of marital upheaval. His Austrian wife had left him and taken their seven-year-old son to Klagenfurt. He was on the sofa when they arrived. "You said you would be here yesterday," he said, rising before either of them could sit down. It was stiflingly hot in the house; there were three air conditioners, but all of them had been unplugged. "Treat this house as your own," he told them. "But go easy on the electric. It's a total scam out here." He went over the work he expected to be done and said he trusted them enough to advance them three weeks' salary.

"So I imagine this is the famous Jennings you were telling us all about," Ward said, as he opened a farewell–to–New Mexico beer. He caught Jennings's questioning look. "I was leading them through this great story by Norman Mailer." Ward laughed, and glanced at his beer, as if he had opened it by accident. "It's called 'The Time of Her Time.' It's about trying to get this frigid chick to O. The main character calls his cock The Avenger, and your buddy here said he had a friend back home just like that."

"Not just like that," Larry said, his face redder than a desert sunset.

"That ain't me," Jennings said, rattled.

"Well, you and your avenger will find plenty to do in Santa Fe," Ward said. "Myself, I was married. And stupidly faithful."

He left for the airport an hour later, off to Vienna and to an Austrian court, where he hoped to gain shared custody of his child.

The electric eye governing the entrance to his small garage was malfunctioning; the door rattled up and down unceasingly, hitting the cracked concrete floor of the garage on the downstroke. Jennings and Larry stood at the window, waving good-bye more or less sarcastically as Ward backed his car out of the driveway and onto the curving little roadway that connected the hundred or so bungalows in Turquoise Court.

Even with Ward's air conditioners plugged back in and running full blast, it was blazing hot in the house and the paint fumes made breathing like taking the worst drug they'd ever known. They worked in their skivvies, with handkerchiefs tied around their heads to keep the sweat out of their eyes. The hair on their arms and legs looked frosted from the primer that became airborne as they rolled it onto the walls. By evening they were so tired and dehydrated that they got drunk quickly and cheaply, as they sampled Santa Fe's many bars. *Mark my words,* Larry said, leaning onto the bar at Quixote and Sons. He raised a finger like some wise man about to explain the world, but he was unable to come up with whatever was next, and turned the finger around and pressed it to the side of his head, and made an exploding sound. They both started to laugh, boisterously, with a kind of male insistence on their right to be in this dopey little bar, with its gaudy embroidered sombreros on the wall next to the picture of a naked girl backing into a hornpipe cactus. Their laughter was just short of unhinged, and it drew the attention of three women who were sharing a pitcher of margaritas in the back. They ventured over to find out what was so funny, and when Larry tried to explain, the effort unhinged him further, until you couldn't understand a word he was saying and his laughter was high, breathless and girlish.

All three of the women were short, with overdeveloped calves, porous skin beneath their tans, neon-colored lips. Andrea sold Avon products, Ruthie was looking for a job, and Charlene was a secretary at St. Michael's High School out on Siringo Road. They invited Jennings and Larry to join them at their table. Andrea had short red hair and a wide space between her front teeth, and seemed to be the leader. She called over her shoulder to the bartender, "Another round of 'ritas, Kevin." Jennings and Larry exchanged looks of impending triumph as they followed behind the women.

Larry presented certain obstacles. He was self-conscious about his lack of size and jug ears so he compensated by talking as if he were Professor Lawrence Sassone and everyone else was there to learn from him. No wonder he and Hat got along so well. Jennings mainly drank quietly, but when one of the women asked where the two of them were from, Jennings was quick to answer *New York*, and he frowned at Larry to keep him from saying something along the lines of *Well, not exactly New York City, but a little town up the river*.

Andrea wanted to make it clear to both of them that neither of them fulfilled her basic requirements when it came to men. "To me a man is someone going somewhere, not some dope pounding nails for beer money," she said. "I like a professional-type guy, someone with ambition." She was looking directly at Jennings, and he met her gaze straight on, hoping she could read his mind because he was thinking *Yeah yeah, I know all about it*. An hour later he was riding shotgun in her tan Oldsmobile Cutlass Supreme, on his way to her mobile home park, which was surrounded by high chaparral. Making love with Andrea was not the triumph he had envisioned. She called him Mr. New York in a tone that did not seem particularly warm and when he was on top she poked at his potbelly, as if trying to lift it off her. Afterward, she demonstrated her lack of satisfaction by thrashing around in her bed, folding and unfolding her foam-filled pillow, and finally almost flinging herself out of bed and repairing to the bathroom, only to return a minute later with an electric toothbrush, a bright blue Oral-B, which she turned on and lay across her pelvic bone, hoping the vibration might bring her to orgasm. Jennings found it sort of comical.

"I can help you, if you want," he said.

"If you coulda ya woulda," she said. She seemed to be quoting a song.

"Can do," said Jennings.

"You got all this sexual confidence, man," she said. "And I'm just here trying to figure out where the hell it comes from."

"You're the one hundredth girl I slept with," he said.

"Well, happy anniversary," she said, handing him the tooth-brush.

Larry, in the meantime, had driven Ruthie all the way to Taos, where her old boyfriend was living above a boot maker's shop. They parked across the road and she spied mournfully on him, trying to somehow glean something by staring at his apartment's darkened windows. When Jennings and Larry talked it over the next day they both agreed that, of the two of them, Larry had had the better night.

But the three women, Ruthie, Andrea, and Charlene, formed the nucleus of Jennings and Larry's Santa Fe social life, and it was they who encouraged the guys to throw a party on the last day of June. The potluck was called for six o'clock but by five there were already fifteen cars and pickup trucks jammed into the driveway and up on the lawn, and by six o'clock it seemed as if anyone in or around Santa Fe between the ages of twenty and thirty who was not a tourist and who was not rich was in Ward's house. Some hulking guy with stringy hair, a sleeveless denim jacket, and fingerless gloves brought in a devastating stereo set with speakers the size of coffins, and he set it up behind the house, where the throb of the Bee Gees, Rita Coolidge, KC and the Sunshine Band, and Peter McCann sing-ing "Do You Wanna Make Love?" seemed to chase the daylight out of the sky and hasten the gas-jet blue of the evening. Nobody called the cops, in fact a few people from Turquoise Court joined in, even brought bags of chips. Dave Houlihan from next door arrived with a spiral-cut ham and a bottle of Cuervo.

By ten o'clock there were about two hundred people at the party, and despite the beer, grass, tequila, and sexual energy, people did a good job of respecting the new paint on the walls, though the floors got pretty scuffed up. The guys were going to have to rent a sander and buy a bucket of polyurethane to cover all the marks left behind by many many pairs of dancing stomping spinning Frye boots.

They felt like guests at their own party. Most of the people there had no idea who the hosts were. The locals had known each other for years, some for their entire lifetimes, and for them it was just another venue for the party that had stretched from weekend to weekend forever. Roofers, cobblers, carpenters, trail guides, drywallers, plasterers, electricians, well drillers, highway department employees, apprentice jewelers, chambermaids, security guards, housecleaners, cabdrivers, restaurant workers, auto mechanics, clerks working in shops ranging from little boutiques selling turquoise-and-silver bolos to the new gigantic supermarket a mile out of town, child care workers, and a few visiting relatives who'd come to Santa Fe looking for work, or to escape trouble, or to take time away from their husband, or their wife, or their kids, or to score drugs. Most were white, distantly Irish or German. A few were Mexican, a few were Navajo, there were some blacks and one set of Cambodian twins, who worked at La Fonda on the Plaza, one as a receptionist and the other as a bookkeeper.

Larry was frantic, thinking it was his responsibility to talk to everyone who was there. *Hi, great to see you. You need anything? Take it easy, remember this isn't our house.* Both the Cambodian girls spoke in astonishingly loud voices and the one who was slightly less loud took a liking to Larry and after a while she became a kind of de facto cohost. Jennings was wishing they'd had the party on another day. He was tired. Friday nights were tough, coming as they did after a full week of work.

Turquoise Court was at the border of some undeveloped land. A few years back it had been a horse ranch called the Kit Carson Ranch, where tourists paid by the hour to clip-clop around on old swaybacked nags. But a lawsuit had put the ranch out of business and now its nineteen acres were vacant, except for the slowly disappearing remnants of a barn and some of the two-rail fencing. What had once been pasture was now high chaparral. The land was up for sale and every now and then someone came over with a brush hog and leveled things.

It was here that Jennings walked to get away from the throb of the party and it was here that he found a girl sitting on a boulder with her arms wrapped around her drawn-up knees and her head tilted back. She wore overalls, sandals, and a white T-shirt. Her arms were thin; the sleeves of her T-shirt surrounded them like the edges of a bowl surround a spoon. She gave no indication of hearing footsteps as Jennings approached her, and even when he was practically standing right next to her she continued to gaze up at the star-mad sky, as if waiting for something to happen up there.

Jennings spoke first. "Are you from the party?"

She nodded. She had a narrow face, and long brown hair. He wondered how someone could look spooky *and* so deeply kind. She had a ring on every finger.

"It's my party," Jennings said. "So welcome, even though you're out here."

"You have a lot of friends."

"No. I don't know really anyone. I'm not from around here."

"Me neither," said the girl. "California. I came here with my cousin and her boyfriend."

"What about your boyfriend?" asked Jennings. It was a familiar move and he regretted it.

"Bakersfield," she said. "Sometimes I say California and people think L.A. or San Fran."

"Me too. I say New York and they think I live on top of the Empire State Building."

She unclasped her knees and scooted around so she was facing him. She suddenly moved her legs and a moment or two later was sitting in a lotus position, her spine straight, her hands resting in her lap with the palms upturned. "So's that your house?"

"No. Me and my friend are painting it. Making a few repairs. Just kind of tightening things up."

"Then what?"

"I don't know. We go home. Maybe do a road trip. I have to swap out the carburetor on my buddy's Datsun. Maybe come out to Bakersfield and visit you."

She laughed. "Better be careful if you do. My father's a cop there."

"Whoa."

She straightened her stick-figure arm, extended her narrow bejeweled hand. "My name's Muriel Sanchez."

"Jennings Stratton." He held on to her hand for an extra moment or two. He couldn't help flirting. It was like being in a lake and treading water. "You can sit like that?"

"Like this? Sure. It relaxes me."

"I could never."

"Someone would have to teach you."

Jennings smiled. It was not a smile that lacked sincerity, though he did know exactly what it looked like. "That's friendly of you," he said.

"Everyone I could ever be friends with back home never liked me because of my father."

"Because he's the law?"

"Yeah, and he's so angry. Day and night. He hates the hippies, anyone young, anyone with long hair. And anyone Mexican."

"I heard Sanchez was a Mexican name."

"Sick, right?" Muriel said. "His father was from Mexico City so he has to prove it to the world that he's super white. And I'm his daughter and everyone thinks I might be a narc. Meanwhile my stupid father thinks I'm some kind of drug-crazed hippie earth mother slut or something."

They sat in silence for a moment, Jennings thinking, *Don't go back there. Fuck Bakersfield. Let's go somewhere together.* But there was no way he could say that. If he met the most beautiful girl in the world and right off the bat she said something like that, he'd run like hell.

A breeze was picking up, cooling the evening, carrying the scent of pine and eucalyptus. "So," he said. "It's just you and your cousin?"

"And her boyfriend," said Muriel.

"And they're back at the house?"

"They love parties. They love *people*." This she said as if it were a weird quirk, like a love for marching bands or paper bags.

"So where's your boyfriend?"

"You already asked me that."

"I know. I guess I can't help it."

She regarded him for a moment, and then he could see her deciding. He had always felt there was something stirring about a woman deciding, it was like seeing nature at work, a glacier calving, a red-tailed hawk riding the thermals.

"I don't really get attached to people. But since you're so curious—my *boyfriend*'s in the Marines."

"He joined?"

"Yep. And now he's going to Lebanon." Her voice trailed off and she suddenly unfolded her legs and stood up. "You have to get back to your party? Or do you want to take a walk?"

"I can do that," he said. "You want to walk around the neighborhood? Or we can take our chances on this old horse farm. Probably full of snakes, though."

"I want to walk someplace beautiful," she said. "I want to do something I won't forget."

They walked back to the house to pick up the Datsun. They could smell the weed from the driveway. Music poured out of the open windows: Pablo Cruise singing "Whatcha Gonna Do?" When the chorus played, the guests sang along: *Whatcha gonna do when she says goodbye / whatcha gonna do when she is gone.* Despite the fatalistic nature of the lyric, the voices were exuberant, maybe just a little bit crazy, as if they all knew that soon it would all be over, the fun, the hope. Life had them over its knee, and it was just a matter of time before they were snapped in two. The dancing was so energetic that Ward's bungalow seemed to rock like a houseboat in choppy waters.

Jennings drove through the middle of town, along Washington, past the insane pink Masonic temple and out onto Artist Road, and kept on it until it turned into 475. He was in no hurry. Once they were beyond the city limits, Friday night disappeared and it could have been any time.

Muriel scratched at the back of her right leg with her left foot. A livestock truck was behind them, bearing down. Jennings rolled down his window and waved for the driver to pass him. The cows pressed their pink-and-black muzzles against the slats of the truck. Their eyes were enormous and limpid; it was hard to believe that on some level they didn't know they were screwed. Muriel made the sign of the cross over her heart, and Jennings felt his blood rush to his face, embarrassed, thrilled, feeling at once out of his element and finally home.

"Those poor cows," Muriel said. "I bet they know where they're going."

She was thinking the same thing he was. "I guess we all do," Jennings managed to say.

AT THE SANTA FE NATIONAL Forest he pulled the car off onto the side of the road. The night had a chill in it now. He looked up at the stars, seeing the same things she saw when she looked up. She seemed so familiar to him yet he felt he had never met anyone like her.

"Ready?" she said.

"We're going to fall on our faces."

"Not if we carry the light."

"I don't have a light," he said, to which she just smiled, and before he knew it he was walking through the scrub, somehow avoiding furrows and holes and tangles of vine or anything else that could trip him up.

"Close your eyes," Muriel said.

The idea seemed half crazy but he shut his eyes and saw himself digging a hole in the orchard back home.

"May ALL be happy," Muriel said. "May ALL be free from diseases. May ALL see things auspicious. May NONE be subjected to misery." They walked faster and faster as if they were actually going somewhere. Jennings had a vision of himself falling forward, but soon that vision was gone and in its place was a kind of soft nothingness, warm and pliable and pleasantly scented like the fuzz scraped out of the filter in a clothes dryer. Minutes passed.

"Are your eyes closed, too?" he asked.

"Yes," she said. "But I can see."

"What can you see?"

"Everything," she said. She squeezed his hand. "May WE protect each other," she said, almost singing it. "May WE nourish each other. May WE work together with great energy. May OUR study be enlightening and fruitful. May WE never hate each other."

"We're never going to hate each other," Jennings said. He opened his eyes for a moment. The landscape was unfamiliar, a little scary in its oddness. The smell of piñon trees. The jagged mountains etched darkly against the night sky.

"Om, shanti shanti," Muriel said, over and over.

Jennings felt immense, infallible. How could this be happening? Here was a stranger he had known all his life.

"O dear Lord," Muriel said, "we humbly beseech you. Let us be of service. Give us peace. Give us wisdom. Give us courage. Let us know above all other things that we are part of the universe as each wave is part of the ocean."

It was too much for him. He stopped, opened his eyes, took her by the shoulders, and turned her so they were facing. Yet something prevented him from kissing her. Her breaths were deep and regular.

"Where are we?" he was finally able to say.

"Here," she said, solemnly, but she was beaming, her face full of color, as if it were not the moon shining down on her but the sun.

Chapter 5

Wedding in White

JANUARY 14, 1979

> **GRACE CORNELL** AND
> **THADDEUS KAUFMAN**
>
> request the honor of your presence
>
> *January 14, 1979*
> *1 P.M.*
> *3__ Park Avenue South, #2*
>
> in the home of Christopher "Kip" Wood
> as they are joined together in marriage.
>
> That's right! Marriage!

THADDEUS AND GRACE WERE GETTING MARRIED, AND IN its own quasi-catastrophic way it was a perfect afternoon for a wedding, if only the bride's mother had not gone missing. As far as anyone could surmise, Maureen Cornell was wandering out there alone in the snow-shocked world, making her way on foot or by taxi or—who knew—mush-mushing along by dogsled from the Hotel Edison on West Forty-Sixth Street to Kip Woods's newly purchased loft on Nineteenth Street and Park Avenue South. The question came down to this: was Maureen delayed or was she truly lost? What was the exact nature of the foul-up? Had she lost track of time? Had she slipped on some slick snow or some congealed slush or black ice and landed, as she would have put it, in a phrase learned from the most Irish of her grandmothers, ass over teacup, or teakettle, or whatever-the-hell little saying had been fashioned out of centuries of humiliation? Was the city so paralyzed by the snow that travel of any kind was next to impossible? Or was Maureen in a gin-soaked stupor flat on her back in bed, and one not necessarily her own.

The storm had crippled the city, brought it to its glass and iron knees. The beauty of it, however, was undeniable, and for those without anything pressing, it was a welcome respite from murders and bankruptcies and arson and abandoned buildings, whores, junkies, newsstands festooned with pornographic magazines, and every parked car with a sign on the dashboard claiming No Radio, and a lock on the steering wheel, steel-bar locks that were so suddenly ubiquitous that it seemed a factory somewhere was working day and night manufacturing them. The snow sorted things out, at least for a while, unlike furious editorials in the newspapers or on TV did, unlike prayer, unlike the police. No one was going to steal a car or even a car radio on a day like this. Fire hydrants had disappeared in the drifts. Phone booths were transformed into snowy little warming stations on an Alpine trail. Manic, antic dogs cavorted in zoomy circles. Cross-country skiers went uptown and downtown, and wherever there was a rise in the road red-faced shrieking children launched their sleds, kicking their brightly booted feet, red red red black black black yellow yellow yellow.

It seemed holy. So pure, so full of justice, and forgiveness, a reminder that humans are merely— and gloriously!—a part of nature. A man on a corner in a leather jacket and a Soviet army hat stood with his arms raised high, shouting, *Thank you thank you thank you.*

Sam Kaufman was unimpressed. "What a bunch of sissies," he exclaimed, watching the New Yorkers on the street below. "What kind of person puts up an umbrella in the snow? What the hell are they worried about? Their hair?"

"It's drafty in here," Libby said. She wore a dark brown suit, with black stockings and a chunky onyx necklace. "What is this place?"

"It's Kip's," Thaddeus said, watching his sister along with a few other fun-loving souls on their cross-country skis, heading north on Park. He wanted to bang his knuckles against the glass, somehow gain her attention, but she swirled into white. He turned away from the window, faced his mother with a nervous smile.

"I know who lives here," Libby said. "But what is it?"

"It's a loft."

"A loft?"

"It used to be a factory."

"So it's a bargain?"

"I don't think so. You've got to fix them up. You get a lot of space, but it's not cheap."

"At least that's what Kip says," Libby said, if for no other reason than to have the last word.

Kip was paying for everything. He'd seen to the invitations, bought the food and the champagne, and hired two waiters to keep everything moving efficiently, men who worked at the Hutton executive dining room and who were glad to make extra cash on a Saturday. The waiters were also quite useful when one of the floorboards in the front of the loft popped off like a bottle cap succumbing to pent-up carbonation. Was it contraction or expansion, the cold of the day, or the heat of the apartment? Whatever the cause, one long strip of brand-new white ash flooring was suddenly dislodged, exposing a dark, worn patch of industrial flooring beneath. The old oak floor was installed in 1890 by Irish carpenters when the loft was owned by Sylvester Shirt Makers, and there were black steel bolts everywhere, each one the size of an apple, which once had secured the long lines of sewing machines at which generations of textile workers had labored. The building's new owners had chosen to have new floors put on top of the old floors, but now the loft's previous life asserted itself in a way that was not only dangerous but also curiously depressing. How were you supposed to look at those bolts and not think of the rows of women in long dresses, their hair pinned up, their exhausted eyes fixed on the sewing machine and the needle's deadly dance.

The two E.F. Hutton waiters, ascertaining that Kip owned neither hammer nor nails, pounded the floorboard back into place with the Cuban heels of their brightly shined shoes. The noise was terrific but the two men seemed to enjoy it. Thaddeus stood at the windows, watching the snow. He tried to direct his thoughts to something *positive*. Well, here was something: this storm would be even more alarming if he and Grace had planned a honeymoon! First of all, honeymoons were lame, even the word was saccharine, and suggestive of virginity finally surrendered, the magic moment on a heart-shaped bed, and second, they couldn't afford one anyhow.

Their wedding was largely about things they omitted. They weren't having a priest or a rabbi but split the difference with an Ethical Culture minister for hire. Grace wasn't wearing a white gown or anything else elaborate because they could not afford to spend hundreds of dollars on a dress. Hundreds of dollars was what they spent in a year on clothing, for both of them. Thaddeus could have rented formal wear, but standing next to Grace in a tuxedo while she was wearing something she could have worn to a cocktail party would have looked weird. They didn't have bridesmaids because it never crossed their minds, and they did not have a best man because it just seemed silly—and Thaddeus would have wanted it to be Kip and Grace would have lobbied for Liam. They did not have ushers because there was no place to usher anyone, no aisle to walk down, no bride's side, no groom's. There were no children to be adorable, holding rings or dropping petals.

But what if their guests were unable to make it because of the storm? According to the local news radio station—*You give us fifteen minutes, we'll give you an anxiety attack*—the subways were barely running, the busses were not running at all, and the Brooklyn and

Manhattan bridges were open only to emergency vehicles. They were already missing Grace's mother—what if others succumbed to the storm, as well? Already Gene Woodard would not be here, since he was up (as in locked up) in Stockbridge, Massachusetts, having been checked in to Austen Riggs after a drunken weekend in which he phoned his father and called him a worthless lying penny-pinching palsied old cocksucker. But what about the members of the Celluloid Collective, the playful name given to itself by the screenwriting group Thaddeus had been a part of over the past year? He'd been privately wondering if any of them would bother to show up.

The Collective met for three hours every Thursday evening in a large apartment on West End Avenue, the home of the Collective's oldest member, Jerry Dropkin, who was fifty-five and divorced. Dropkin was barrel-chested, with skinny arms and legs, and he was losing his hair in a kind of random patchwork way that made it seem as if he might actually be pulling it out. He was the only member of the group to have had a screenplay filmed, and shown in theaters. It was called *Indian Killer*, a French-Italian coproduction, filmed in Spain, with Navarre representing South Dakota. Jerry had been fired and replaced, but the basically bitter experience gave him the right to the last word when someone's script was being workshopped in his living room, where bridge chairs had replaced the upholstered sofas and love seats of his married days, and framed family photos had been replaced by flowcharts of the five scripts he had going.

The people in the Collective seemed to think they were Thaddeus's intellectual superiors, and Thaddeus tended to agree. Most of them spoke two or three languages. They had gone to Ivy League schools and, before that, had been prepared at New England boarding schools whose names he had pretended to recognize. (He first thought Rosemary Hall was a singer, but was able to self-correct before discovery.) He shared the Collective's ambitions but not their tastes. He loved *Jaws, The French Connection, Bonnie and Clyde, Rosemary's Baby,* and a French movie none of them had ever heard of, *The Mad Adventures of Rabbi Jacob.* His taste was not only suspect but just the kind of mindless bullshit the others were writing to overthrow.

The evening his script was up, Thaddeus waited in the lobby of Jerry's massive old building, ringing the buzzer every few minutes for half an hour before giving up and heading home. Several days later, he happened to run into Ace Disend, who was furtively shopping for women's undergarments at B. Altman, and learned that Jerry had had a heart attack and gone through open-heart surgery. When Thaddeus said he would visit Dropkin as soon as possible, perhaps after work that very day, Disend shook his head and said the doctors were recommending that visits be kept to a minimum. Only family and the very closest of friends were visiting Jerry, who was dopey from Dilaudid. Nevertheless, Thaddeus paid Jerry a visit a couple of days later and brought Grace along, too, on the theory that every man's recuperation is aided by the sight of a nice-looking woman.

"They split me open like a lobster," Jerry said. He was in a shared room at Roosevelt Hospital. A curtain divided the two beds. Thaddeus saw the silhouettes of the other guy's visitors, moving like puppets in a shadow play.

"You have to guard against depression," Grace said, sitting in the one chair available, with her hands folded in her lap. She wore a loose-fitting dress against the hot summer night. Her arms were bare and the swirling-fingerprint dark hairs on it looked especially prominent in the dingy hospital light.

"Yeah?" Jerry sounded as if he'd already had enough of her. "You think so."

"Yes. Between the hypothermia and the anesthetic. Also, little pieces of plaque kind of bombard your brain. People have as much trouble with the depression as any other part of the recovery after the kind of surgery you had."

"So you're what? A doctor?"

"Better than that," Thaddeus interjected. "She's a children's book designer." He knew it was a mistake as soon as he'd said it.

He'd thrown Grace to the wolves for a little joke. He saw her flash red and he knew it was something she was going to remember.

On the way out of the hospital, Grace said, "He kept staring at my arms." They were at the front entrance. A security guard was posted nearby, half asleep, his long legs stretched out before him. He opened his eyes for a moment to look at them, decided they weren't worth the bother.

"Was he?" Thaddeus answered. It was a subject he avoided. He wasn't certain why it was so, but dark hair on a woman's arms seemed somehow wrong to him.

Grace lifted her left arm, turned it just so. "I love my little monkey arms. I think they're amazing,"

"I do, too," Thaddeus said, uncertainly.

"Good. Because I've been getting shit about this my whole life. I've broken up with people over these little monkey arms."

"Good!" Thaddeus had said, light-headed. It was as if he had luckily stepped back onto the curb as a bus whizzed by.

"I just can't let anyone tell me I'm not good enough."

"Me either. Or neither? Either, neither?" They were outside now. An ambulance was slowly turning toward the ER entrance, as if the patient inside was already lost.

Somehow, the issue of her arms remained unsettled, and they were not mentioned again until on the day of the wedding Thaddeus noticed they had been denuded, and were as smooth as the ring of fat around a steak, though reddened after two burning, buzzing hours of electrolysis, recommended to her by someone at work, a woman named Sophia Krafchek, a good-natured Polish woman with a gold tooth and two grown sons. "I was shaggy like coconut," Sophia said, presenting Grace with a pre-wedding present of a gift certificate to Sonya of Seventy-Ninth Street, where women went to be bleached, plucked, waxed, and zapped.

Sophia turned out to be one of the first arrivals. She had come up on the elevator with Bruce Abernathy. The Ethical Culture minister was a young and hale man; he'd traveled on cross-country skis from his church on Central Park West to Kip's loft, and he entered with his jolly-looking cheeks glowing red. And as it turned out, the guests for the most part braved the elements, and soon they were arriving in waves of icy good cheer, giddy from their adventures, collars and eyelashes wet and sparkling. Some had taken certified taxis, some had settled for so-called gypsy cabs, some had walked, kicking their way through snowbanks. Here were a lawyer, a social worker, a window dresser, a fireman, the guys with whom Thaddeus played basketball at the YMCA, where the hierarchy was based on conditioning and skills—a trust fund couldn't buy you a layup, and if you picked up the ball while dribbling and then dribbled again, even if you were Robert Motherwell it was still a double dribble and you surrendered the ball.

And then came three women with whom Grace shared a painting studio above a pork and lamb wholesaler on Little West Twelfth Street. The studio, redolent of slaughtered flesh and the fumes of the West Side Highway, cost thirty-five dollars a month for each of them; Liam had paid a year's rent as a birthday present for Grace. She admired the other women artists, their energy, their wiry hair, their eyeglasses (either small as silver dollars, or large as grapefruit), the complicated alluring things they could achieve with a scarf, their booming, ribald back-and-forth on the rare occasions when they were all in the studio at the same time. But it was just her luck to find herself with artists who saw no value in her work. These were people who believed verisimilitude was a kind of failure of the imagination. They themselves were proudly incapable of it. They asked her strained, vaguely insulting questions, such as "Is this from a photograph?" and "Are you hoping to sell these?"

STILL NO SIGN OF MAUREEN Cornell. And with the bride's mother missing and the ceremony put on hold, Kip insisted that Thaddeus and Grace absent themselves from the general throng and wait it out in his bedroom.

"You're the stars so you have to act like stars," Kip said, escorting them into his room. Since the night at Nero's, his tone with Thaddeus and Grace had become more and more artificial, careening between the solicitous and the sarcastic, the tender and the teasing. Today, he was wearing an Armani suit in a shade of gray that looked somehow European, a white shirt, and a black bow tie that he had already undone, like a lounge singer at the end of a long set. "We'll give Mom another twenty minutes and then I think you two little bunnies ought to do the deed."

"We can't do it without Grace's mother here," said Thaddeus.

"One of the fat girls from Periodic Books has already damaged the cake," Kip said. "She ran her finger over the icing." He pointed at Grace. "One of *your* friends."

"I hope everyone here is my friend," said Grace.

"Sorry for the delay, man," Thaddeus said.

"It's not like my mother wants to be wandering around in the snow. I'm actually pretty worried about her," Grace said.

"Oh, we'll survive. My date's not here anyhow," Kip said.

"Who's your date?" Thaddeus asked. His face lit up, like a child about to open a present.

"Linda Ronstadt."

"You're dating Linda Ronstadt?"

"Well, that might be pushing things. She said she'll try and make it." There was a burst of laughter from the front of the loft. "I'd better see to our guests. I'm going to close you two in here. Sit tight and no snooping around my stuff."

There was a desk pushed against the wall opposite the bed, covered by a light blue bedsheet. The desk chair was piled high with neatly folded T-shirts. The room itself had been carved out of the loft's once-open space, and the walls did not reach all the way to the high ceiling. An old oak wardrobe was his closet. His bookshelves were filled with first editions—Djuna Barnes, Wyndham Lewis, H.D.

"What do you think is under the sheet?" asked Grace.

Thaddeus lifted a corner of the sheet. A pile of continuous computer printout paper, each sheet with holes running down the left and right side.

"Maybe we can find out a tip on some hot stock," Grace said.

Thaddeus sat next to her on the end of the bed. "You look beautiful," he said. He took her hand, patted it.

"I feel about as sexy as saddle shoes," she said.

"Don't worry," he said. "She'll be here."

"Your parents got here on time."

"I've never questioned their punctuality."

Grace's brother walked in without knocking, holding a plate of Swedish meatballs, each impaled by a frilly toothpick. "You guys hungry?" Liam asked, using his foot to close the door behind him. He had a good-natured, boyish appearance, a conservative haircut, and wore a drab blue suit made even drabber by very wide lapels and fabric-covered buttons. To Thaddeus, Liam always looked more like someone who taught PE at a Catholic school than someone moving kilos of Mexican pot.

"You know," Liam said, "whenever I enter into any kind of transaction I always take the time to go through the variables. I know everything that could possibly go wrong in any situation. I don't care if it's personal or business, ordering a meal or buying ten ki's of product. I don't like surprises. Surprises don't happen to me. But I let this one get away from me. I should have never put her in that shitty hotel." Liam paid his mother's rent and her utilities, and made certain there was cash on hand for extras—beauty parlor appointments, nice clothes, the depression-fighting little luxuries. He had had tickets to New York waiting for her at the American Airlines desk at O'Hare, and a car and driver waiting for her at LaGuardia, whisking her to the Hotel Edison near Times Square. It was not a hotel Liam would have chosen. He was staying at the St. Regis, but Maureen had a sentimental attachment to the Edison. She had stayed there for a week when she was seventeen, when she daringly ran off to New York with a Midwestern boy who played saxophone and was on a mission to meet Louis Jordan.

"Maybe we should look for her," Thaddeus said.

"Where?" Grace asked. "I knew she would do this. We shouldn't have even invited her."

"Grace, come on," Liam said. "She's fine."

"She's not fine, Liam. She's never been fine. She's like a snail crawling around leaving her ooze on everything she touches."

There was a brief knock on the door and Libby walked in. "I think we should proceed with the ceremony," she said, in a nervous whisper. "I don't know what you think is going on out there. But those two waiters? They're very, very angry. They're sitting around watching sports on the TV and making rude remarks about the guests."

"Great. We still have to wait for her mother," Thaddeus said.

"It's almost an hour already. People are getting restless." She looked at her watch, and then her gaze locked onto Thaddeus. Sometimes when his mother looked at him, it felt like the captain from an enemy vessel had just boarded his ship to dictate the terms of surrender.

Liam contrived to leave the bedroom as quickly as possible, as if he was visiting Grace and Thaddeus in a hospital and did not want to overwhelm them. "I'll keep an eye out for Maureen," he said, over his shoulder.

"It's a wedding," Libby said. "It can't wait forever."

"It doesn't matter," Thaddeus said. "There's food out there, drink, and let's not forget the joy of good friends being together for an afternoon of unparalleled conviviality." He put his hand over his heart and smiled with no small measure of desperation.

"You joke around too much," Libby said. "You really do."

"Do I? Nietzsche said a joke is the death of an emotion."

"Since when did Nietzsche know his ass from a hole in the ground?" asked Libby.

"He had insights," Thaddeus said. "Anyhow, maybe he didn't say joke. Maybe he said wit. At any rate, I have plenty of emotions. I can afford to kill a few. It's like thinning out a row of lettuce."

"Who told you about lettuce? What are you now? A kulak?"

"Maybe it wasn't the death of an emotion," Thaddeus said. "Maybe Nietzsche said epitaph. In which case, I am like one big obituary page."

"I'm going to look for her," Grace said.

"Have you called the police?" Libby asked.

"What are the cops going to do?" Grace asked, hoping her tone wasn't conveying the annoyance she felt.

"Find her, it's their job," answered Libby.

"Let's go, let's just fucking find her," said Thaddeus. He rose from the end of the bed, put his hand out to Grace, but she rose without accepting his assistance, or moral support, or ironic chivalry, or whatever it was he had offered her.

Grace and Thaddeus announced their intentions to the guests, and it touched them that everyone wanted to help. They watched with gratitude as people shrugged back into wet coats, pulled on boots. Even under cover of snow, Manhattan was essentially a grid, and searchers were sent in pairs north and south on the avenues, while other pairs went east and west on the narrower, less traveled streets. The north-south searchers were to cover the territory from Forty-Seventh Street to Houston Street, while the east-west crew was to cover from Eighth Avenue to Second Avenue, except for Abernathy, who would zip around on skis, guided by instinct. Kip was to stay home, in case Maureen arrived on her own or Linda Ronstadt showed up. The two E.F. Hutton waiters were in the section of the loft where Kip had set up his largest Sony Trinitron, watching a soccer match, Costa Rica versus Argentina. Kip had a jar filled with change and he gave each person several dimes, with the instruction to call in every fifteen minutes or so to see if Maureen had been found or had strolled in on her own. No one dared worry aloud. A kind of antic spirit prevailed, as if this was all a part of the wedding day, a game they might all play, a scavenger hunt—the first one to find Maureen Cornell wins!

In the lobby, Grace and Thaddeus stood for an extra few moments at the door leading to the street, like uncertain swimmers at the lip of a diving board. The street before them had been plowed, but the sidewalks were matters of conjecture.

The wind swirled the snow from the ground up.

"Well, there goes my new dress," Grace said.

"We can still put it in one of those plastic garment bags and save it for our daughter to be married in," said Thaddeus.

Grace was so far from being amused, she didn't bother punching his arm. She made a little squeak of distress each time she took another step in the snow. Their quadrant was Park Avenue South from Nineteenth Street to Thirtieth, east to Lexington, and Lexington back to Nineteenth Street. What had once been a kind of soft, magical snowfall was sterner now, sparser but swifter, with a stinging, depressing quality to it. It was just past two in the afternoon but the sky was the gray of discarded machinery. Some of the shopkeepers were out, trying to clear portions of the sidewalk. A well-built, Indian man in his fifties, wearing a ski jacket and earmuffs, shoveled a narrow path to his shoe store, perspiring mightily. He seemed on his way to heart failure, and when Thaddeus and Grace availed themselves of the cleared pavement only to walk past his store he glared at them, as if they had taken advantage of him.

"I'm not surprised that my mother is wrecking this," Grace said. "You see now why I could never be a mother? The word, honestly, the very word makes me crazy."

They stood on the corner of Twentieth and Park Avenue South. A massive mound of snow had accumulated and a middle-aged woman in a long coat and a brightly colored Peruvian wool cap watched with pleasure as her long-haired dachshund cavorted at the top of the drift, as if it had just scaled Everest.

"I can carry you across the street, if you want," Thaddeus said.

"Why do we live here?" Grace wailed. She could feel slush packing itself into her instep. "This whole thing is fucked."

"This isn't the only place it snows," Thaddeus said. Since Nero's, hardly a day went by without Grace expressing her unhappiness about their life in the city. His own feelings about New York weren't all that different from hers, yet he often felt compelled to counter her arguments. True, they lived near the theaters and concert halls they couldn't afford to attend, and near the publishers and art galleries who were all completely uninterested in them, and near the avant-garde bohemians whose sexual liberties and iffy grooming were far from the Astaire-like sophistication that Thaddeus thought was going to be the city's dominant style, but for now they were stuck here and he wished she would make the best of it.

"This fucking place," she said. "I wish I was anywhere else."

"Come on, Grace, it's our wedding day."

"Our wedding day," she said, as if the three words described the height of absurdity. She took his arm. "I'm sorry. I'm in a horrible mood. She could be stoned somewhere. She could be with some fat, bald man she met at a bar."

"Why does everyone speak poorly about heavyset men who have experienced hair loss?"

"Fuck you, Thaddeus, I'm serious."

"I know you are. But she's not drunk, and she's not having sex with Chef Boyardee."

"Rilly," she said, forcing herself not to smile.

A few determined taxi drivers made their way up and down the avenue, rear ends fishtailing, hands clenched at two o'clock and ten on the steering wheel. You could see the whites of their eyes, their willingness to risk it all for another hour or two on the meter. Directly ahead of them, a man in a leather jacket and bright yellow boots stood holding a leash while his German shepherd diligently dug at a mound of snow that had been built up around a parking meter. The mound looked like one of those gigantic columns full of termites you see in pictures of Africa. The dog clawed the snow with his forepaws and shot it out under his shaggy gray-and-black torso and through his back legs. He seemed like a dog in a cartoon.

"Busy boy, huh," the man said, soliciting their goodwill. He had a dark narrow face, etched in suffering. Wiry dark hairs stood up from his eyebrows like antennae.

"I can't wait to see what he finds," said Thaddeus.

"He gets like this sometimes," the man said. "Once he dug up a crucifix in Madison Square Park. It blew my mind. I almost converted."

"We're looking for my mother," Grace said. "And we're very worried. It all seems so hopeless."

Thaddeus turned to look at her straight on. This called for more than just a sideways glance because he had never heard her voice so plain and uninflected, except in moments of the most exquisite intimacy, the times the words rose up from a place deep within her and managed to elude all the little baffles and spurs and roundabouts of personality, motive, and agenda.

The man seemed not to have heard her—his attentions were occupied by the dog's vocalizing, the highs and lows of it, from whines that were almost whistles to barks that were almost sonic booms, all accompanied by an ever more frantic digging.

"Atlantis, take it easy, take it easy," the man said. He approached the dog with the leash, ready to snap it onto its collar, but when he touched the dog it turned quickly, snarling, and the man snatched his hand away, almost losing his footing.

"He must really be on the scent of something," the man said, like the mother of a child having a tantrum in a food shop.

"We should go," Thaddeus said to Grace.

"Let's see what he finds."

The man continued to try and get the leash hooked onto Atlantis's collar, but after a couple of feints in the dog's direction he decided to wait, and now the three of them stood in the snow waiting and waiting and waiting still more for the dog to finish its dig, and the longer they waited, with the temperature dropping and the gray in the sky steadily darkening, the more their own speculations about what scent might be driving Atlantis to such great effort steadily darkened as well, until they were all hoping that what the dog was after was merely garbage, and not some urban archaeology of a sterner sort—a severed head, a hand, an ear. At last, with a couple of violent shakes of his head, Atlantis yanked his prey out of the thick icy core of the mound.

A leather glove. It was partially turned in on itself, but surmising from the color—maroon—and its smallness, it was a woman's. Thaddeus laughed with relief and touched Grace's elbow. "We should boogie on, reggae woman," he said.

She nodded, her face grave, her eyes fixed on the glove in the dog's mouth. Atlantis shook it back and forth as if it were a small animal whose neck he was snapping.

"I hate this city," she said, more to herself than to him.

They walked slowly, looking in front of them and on the other side of the street, hoping to spot Maureen.

"I didn't even have a chance to give you your wedding present," Grace said, in a voice that suggested all was lost.

Thaddeus was silent. No one had told him they were supposed to give each other something, as well.

"You want to know what it is?"

"Okay."

"A picture."

"A drawing?"

"Yes. Remember that ring? The emerald? I found a photo of one just like it and I made a drawing."

"Meaning we'll never be able to afford the real thing?"

"Meaning that art is the real thing, or better. And that I am very very very very very very happy with what we have and who we are."

"I am, too, baby."

"But you wish we had the ring, too, right?"

"All I want is to be happy, and for us to be happy. It's the whole purpose of life."

"Happy."

"Yeah. A simple word. But it's not so easily done. You have to seize it from the jaws of the Shit Monster. And once you have it you have to protect it."

"You want to give me happy?"

"Of course."

"You want to give me the best present I could ever get? Give me your word. This is what I want, and it's what I've always wanted. I want us to be each other's main thing, and to know that whatever you say to me in the privacy of our marriage is fine. You're always on my side, and I am always on yours. You will always keep my secrets and I will keep yours. I get it why married people can't be called on to testify against each other in court. What we know about each other no one else knows. And we stand with each other against all others."

"Are the 'others' coming after us?"

"I'm serious, Thaddeus."

"I'm sorry. I'm with you."

"So do you agree? Is that how you see it?"

"I do." He placed his hand over his heart. "I really do."

"I do, too," Grace said.

"So . . . are we married? May I kiss the bride?"

Someone was calling out to Grace, a wind-raked call that turned her middle vowel into triplets. They both looked up and saw Lisa Kaplan, one of the women from the shared studio. Lisa wore a fuchsia wool coat, and her dark curly hair bubbled from her wool cap, like espresso boiling out of the pot. Of all of them in the studio, Lisa was the most forceful in her opinions on everything from art to diet.

"Can I join your search party?" she said when she caught up to Grace and Thaddeus. "Either Jenny and Octavia ditched me or they went home." She placed herself between them and linked her arms through theirs, though the sidewalk, where it had been shoveled at all, was still a narrow path and they could certainly not walk three abreast, or even two abreast. She unhooked herself from them and noticed the distraught expression on Grace's face.

"You okay, little Gracey?"

Thaddeus knitted his brows. He did not much care for that "little Gracey," the diminishment of it, turning his wife into something adorable and unserious, a tchotchke.

"I'm okay," Grace said. "Worried."

"Weddings," said Lisa, rolling her abnormally large eyes, as if snowstorms and disappearing mothers were part of the tedious typicality of people getting married.

More taxis were starting to brave their way north and south, and another snowplow was in sight, its front blade churning up waves of snow and salt. A slow-moving police car appeared, siren silent, flashers on.

On Twenty-Third Street, they found a pay phone on the corner, bolted to the wall of a drugstore. The pharmacist was out, pouring rock salt from a bag, though the pavement had not yet been cleared and the pellets merely disappeared into the snow.

"Is the phone working?" Thaddeus asked.

The pharmacist said, "How in the living breathing motherfucking hell should I know?" before stomping back into his empty store.

"What a pig," said Lisa. "Pig!" she shouted at the closed door.

Grace closed her eyes. *This* was the world her mother was wandering around in, lost and alone.

Thaddeus dropped two dimes into the slot, ignoring the residue of some mysterious goo. He waited breathlessly for a moment—and there it was: a dial tone. He wished he had something other than his finger to put into the holes of the rotary dial, and as he was having the thought, Grace was already rummaging around in her purse and finding an eyebrow pencil, which she handed to him. "Oh my God," he said, "how am I ever going to live without you?"

Moments later, Kip answered the phone. "Wood here."

"Kip, it's me."

"Hello, Me. Nice to hear your voice."

"Any word?"

"She's here."

"She is? Is she okay?"

Grace covered her mouth with her icy hand.

"She's fine," Kip said. "She's getting relaxed. You better get back and close the deal."

"She's fine," Thaddeus said to Grace.

"She's with someone," Kip said. "Wait. I'm seeing if this cord stretches into the bathroom."

"You can—"

"Just wait, all right?" The sound of a door closing. "There. She's with someone. This woman who found her on Thirtieth and Fifth and walked her over here."

"Thank God."

"What do you want me to do? Should we invite her to stay?"

"Of course. She probably saved her life."

"She's fine. There's nothing wrong with her. She's actually pretty. Grace will age well."

Grace made an impatient gesture.

"What's going on?" Lisa asked.

"The thing is," Kip said, his voice lowering. "This woman. I think she might be homeless."

"All the more reason to let her stay."

"Yeah. Marry the girl, *and* do a good deed. Gives you the daily double, you lucky dog."

When Thaddeus hung up the phone, he put his arm around Grace.

"She's fine," he said. "Kip says she looks beautiful."

On the way back to Kip's apartment, Lisa said, "I never even asked you if you were going to keep your name."

"No, she's changing her name to Linda," Thaddeus said. "Why do you ask?"

"Funny man," said Lisa. "But are you?" She leaned closer to Grace, and her expression was serious, expectant.

"Of course I am," Grace said.

"Well, I'm proud of you," Lisa said.

"I keep forgetting," Thaddeus said to Lisa, "that you actually invented women's liberation."

Now that Maureen had arrived, the fear Grace had been holding in check began to flood. Her breath was shallow, and smelled like pennies steeped in malt vinegar. Thaddeus pulled her close.

A snarl of taxis moved slowly behind the snowplow that was clearing Park Avenue. The plow's yellow lights were spinning. The cascades of snow arcing away from the blade looked like waves coming to shore in the moonlight.

"Are you going to keep your share in the studio after this?" Lisa asked, when they reached Kip's block.

"Why wouldn't she?" Thaddeus said, surprising even himself with the vehemence of his question.

"I don't know," Lisa said, unperturbed by Thaddeus's anger. "She might not need it, or want it. How would I know?"

"Her work is amazing. It's radical traditionalism. It makes you love the world. You might not get it, it's out of step with all the mountains of bullshit out there. A bunch of little crappy things pasted onto cardboard. Sorry, Lisa, but you don't even know how to paste right. Didn't you learn that in third grade?"

"I went to Yale, asshole."

"Get a refund."

Grace gave his hand a small secret squeeze. Thaddeus had been moaning for weeks about not being able to get her that old emerald ring from Gina's Gems. For a while, she'd wondered if this was a cover story of some kind, and he had found a way to get it for her after all. But that was clearly impossible. She was prepared to give him something without receiving anything in return. But now she understood that right out here in the snow with their shoes soaked and their eyelashes frozen and their guests waiting for them and getting drunk, he'd come up with a wedding present for her after all.

TO LIAM CORNELL/POSTE RESTANTE/CUERNAVACA, MEXICO

March 19, 1979

Dear Liam,

If this letter reaches you it will give me new faith in the world. Me in Turkey, you in Mexico, all the eyes and hands and cars and planes that will have to pitch in and get this to you. I realize I am a provincial girl after all. This supersonic world doesn't make sense to me. Thaddeus tells me I came up a bit short on the thank-yous when you gave us this trip, but you know I was scared shitless flying from Chicago to New York. And then you're telling me I'm supposed to fly from New York all the way to Istanbul? With all that ocean, with sharks licking their chops waiting for me to fall in? But as soon as we sat in first class all my bad thoughts trotted off to the phobia graveyard. I felt so safe up there with all the vodka and the French wines. I had one terrifying moment during takeoff—the wheels made a noise when they folded up into the belly of the jet—but after that it was perfect. I firmly believe that if anything happens on one of those planes the first-class passengers are spared. I think that part of the cabin breaks off and has its own parachute. T kept singing this song from 1950, Istanbul, no longer Constantinople, *but other than that it was all so perfect.*

I slept for twenty-one hours once we got here. Thaddeus was off sightseeing, kebabbing, and Grand Bazaaring his ass off, but the flight and the time change and the culture

shock was too much for me. I totally conked out. The Pera
Palace is totally out of sight. So dignified and judicious
on the outside, like the Federal Reserve building in New
York. As soon as the taxi dropped us here, I felt safe. Inside
is amazing. Sort of a dusty old museum of past glories, sort
of churchy, sort of mosquey, sort of gentleman's club out of
Sherlock Holmes. Our suite is huge and decorated like a
really hip grandmother used to live here. But the best part
is this: the day manager is this great guy named Galip. He's
over forty, frizzy black hair, except where he's bald. Just for
the hell of it I did a sketch of him, and when I showed it
to him, it blew his mind, if I do say so myself. Next thing
I know he's insisting I show him more of my work, and it
just so happens I have that Fabriano sketchbook you gave
me, already half filled with drawings. Galip spends about
five minutes on each drawing, I swear to God, sitting there
in his linen suit, frowning like he's trying to memorize the
drawings. T walks in in the middle of all this, but I give
him the shush sign and he gets it. When Galip finally looks
up, the first thing he says is, "I see you use the best paper.
That shows me you are a very serious artist." I don't tell him
that most of my drawings were done on notebook paper.
He thinks we're rich, since we're occupying a suite at his
hotel and our baggage claim tickets say first class and we
kept them on the handles of our suitcases—we are never
taking those little beauties off! And the next thing he says
is he wants to show them to his boss, who is the nephew of
one of the owners, because they are looking for artwork to
go in their lounge area and the lobby, too. He didn't even
care that none of the drawings were of Istanbul or anything
about Turkey. He really just flipped out over the work. My
work! T and I spend so much time talking about his work
that it's easy for me to sort of forget my own art. But this
thing inside, this little tender invisible but always present

thing that is the self that is me, I can feel it coming forward when I make my art and I can feel it disappearing when all the other shit takes over, stuff like the job, and relationships, even washing my hands or brushing my hair. And when someone—even a stranger with a voice that sounds like a bunch of flies buzzing in an empty jar, and whose English starts to wobble when he gets excited and he says things like one drawing makes him hear "vague music," and another is "most happily laconic"—when that someone actually SEES what I am doing, and gives me positive vibes about it. Liam my dearer than dear wandering pirate brother—there is nothing like it in all the universe. My art is my soul, for what it's worth. It's my blood and my breath. The fact is, I have been given a lot of shit about my work—by those phony bastards at the Art Institute who couldn't even draw so naturally they HAD to insist that drawing was passé, and Caroline Kovac, that girl who was such a careerist and made me feel like a dope, but whose voice haunts me even though she's in California and I'm in New York, where the artists I meet think art is pasting a pubic hair onto an old copy of TV Guide. "This one is very erotic," Galip said about my newest egg drawing—the one with the little crack on the side. T cleared his throat when he heard that. I felt the rivalry. Galip courting my innermost being and T trying to keep his grip on my shell. I know I sound terrible and like the bitch of all bitches, but the thought that my work might be hanging in this amazing hotel all the way in Istanbul is making me completely trip out with excitement. For the first time since meeting Thaddeus my life feels as if it's about Me. And we all know how long that lasts! Maybe six hours. That night after dinner, T says to me, "Let's have a kid!"

Chapter 6

Lights in the Trees

JULY 19, 1980

HELP US TURN OUR NEW HOUSE IN TO A HOME

Where:

200 Riverview Road
"Orkney"
Leyden, New York

6 P.M.–*Midnight*

JENNINGS WAS PLANNING TO QUIT HIS JOB AT WINDSOR Wheels. The cap he was required to wear was reason enough, but mainly the job was a waste of time—he was making more money cutting firewood, doing lawns, and helping his father around Orkney. And working for tips was against his nature, in his view just a step up from charity, a kind of begging, or being one of those street-corner kids down in the city who danced like crazy, doing leaps and splits and handstands and headstands and grinning like jack-o'-lanterns so some chump will drop a few coins in their cigar box. Before the Boyetts sold Orkney and limped off to Mexico, they emptied the place of their furniture and had a party to which they invited virtually everyone they knew. Jennings, Larry, and a couple of their friends had parked cars, and an old woman, one of the last to leave, pressed a quarter into Jennings's hand when he delivered her car to her. "Here's a little something for you, dear," she said, rubbing her fingers against his hands, plucking at the lines of his palm as if they were zither strings, and Jennings let the quarter drop onto the stones of the driveway, and just walked away.

This evening's run was going to be his last. He drove to Windsor County Airport and idled the stretch limo at the curb. He was a little early and the plane from Chicago was a few minutes late. The old Lincoln was not in the best condition and he had to turn off the engine, or risk overheating. The car was stifling without the AC and Jennings waited outside, half-sitting on the hood, and chewing a stick of Big Red.

His fare was Orkney's new owner. Jennings had driven him down to the airport early this morning and the guy had tipped generously. Fifty percent, in fact. Jennings was glad for the money but it was weird—the guy was roughly Jennings's age, a Jewish guy up from the city, without the slightest idea of what to do with his new acquired property. Could not mow a lawn decently, could barely change a lightbulb. He and his wife excited over the sight of a jackrabbit and transported to a virtual state of wonder over the deer—hint number one that Orkney's long tradition of allowing certain select locals to hunt on the land was going to be a thing of the past. Maybe Hat knew, but Jennings had no idea where the new owners' money came from. As best he could tell, it had come all at once, and there seemed to be a lot of it. Enough for a furniture-buying spree, enough for a BMW, and for a 50 percent tip. The wife was pregnant, and looked as far along as Muriel. Muriel had yet to say a word to the wife, to either of them. When she walked down to the river, she kept as far away as possible from the big house, wading through tall fields of purple loosestrife, her hands raised as if she were under arrest, the stalks chattering on either side of her like shuffled cards.

You don't have to be afraid of them, Jennings said to her. *They're no better than anyone else.*

Suddenly, Jennings noticed his fare coming out of the small airport lounge, and despite himself he quickly slid off the hood and stood soldier straight. He was required to wear an eight-point chauffeur's cap, with a linty crown and scratched patent leather bill, but aside from that he was on his own—faded plaid shorts and salmon-colored flip-flops. The fare was carrying a small leather valise, and he looked tired, in some kind of disarray. He seemed to be looking for someone, though Jennings was standing right in front of him.

"You need some help with that?" Jennings asked, reaching for the suitcase.

"Oh, It's okay. I got it."

"Windsor Wheels at your service." Merrily, Jennings rotated his hand away from his forehead. *Motherfucker,* he thought, but without rancor. He would never let another man carry his burden.

Thaddeus opened and closed his hand, wiggled his fingers, as if to justify what he was about to do by implying he had been carrying the suitcase for miles.

Okay, it had been only a few steps, and he was young and surely did not require any help carrying his own suitcase. But it had been a hellish day—up at 5:30 A.M., early flight to Chicago, taxi to the hospital, four hours in the land of the sick, the land of the moaning, the land of the overgrateful, the land of stink and the even worse smell to cover the stink. His father had had a heart attack, but it turned out to be basically okay (as heart attacks go) and as soon as the doctors said Sam was out of danger, Thaddeus got a taxi back to O'Hare. Had he eaten all day? Had he smiled? Had he moved his bowels? Memory failed.

Thaddeus struggled to remember the driver's name. Ah! Jennings. Jennings Stratton, Hat's son. Son of Hat. Their inherited caretaker. In the giddy chaos of closing on the property, it hadn't been clear that Orkney came with Hat, and Son of Hat as well, and

Son of Hat's lovely post-hippie girlfriend, who Thaddeus referred to as the Translucent One.

"Hey, Jennings, do you mind if I run back in there and make a phone call?"

Again that Ed McMahon gesture, the one in which he tells Johnny Carson, Your wish is my command. It reeked of carefree spirits, with a dash of contempt.

There were three pay phones built into the wall near the baggage carousel. Thaddeus was starting to mourn phone booths. They'd had them at Michael Reese Hospital, where Sam Kaufman had been rushed after collapsing in the shower. The University of Chicago hospital was much closer but Libby would not hear of it—they had not set foot in the place since Hannah. Once he was installed, she called Thaddeus and less than twelve hours later he was there. There was no thought of the expense—those last-minute airline tickets! It was gratifying to Thaddeus to give this demonstration of his new reality—now that he had sold *Hostages* to Hollywood he was a man with a house, a man with land, a man who could be here or there or anywhere else he chose to be without fretting over money. He was, to himself, almost unrecognizable, and he hoped the same would hold true for his parents.

The hospital had good old traditional Clark-Kent-changes-into-Superman phone booths with accordion doors, but here at the airport the phones were hung on the wall like urinals. Now, if only Grace would answer. She had become less responsive. In many ways. But with his child inside her how could he decently complain? He glanced at his watch. Seven o'clock. Grace was probably outside with their guests in the yard, or the garden, or the promontory, he wasn't sure what to call it. The great outdoors. If the situation were reversed, and she had been suddenly called to Chicago, he would have known what time her plane was landing and he'd pick the phone up on the first ring.

But the voice Thaddeus heard at the other end of the phone line was his own, intoning the outgoing message on their PhoneMate.

It had taken him a while to become bored with clever greetings to callers, there were no more trumpet fanfares, Coltrane riffs, or five seconds of the Soul Stirrers; gone, too, were his funny, side-splitting Russian accent and his Walter Cronkite imitation. Now it was short and sweet: "You're in Beep City."

"Hi. You there?" He gave her an extra moment. "Anyhow, I'm back. Everything's under control at the hospital. I'm glad I went. He actually held my hand. And it was good for Mom, too. Having me there. Okay. It's exactly seven minutes after seven. I will see your face by seven forty-five. Sorry you're alone with all those people."

The other passengers on his flight had already left the airport, but the baggage carousel continued its creaky go rounds. Back outside there was a smell of gasoline in the air, and the insect whine of a small plane racing down the runway, its engines torqued for takeoff. The driver—Jennings, Jennings, Jennings—stood outside the absurdly and unnecessarily voluminous limo, still holding the suitcase.

"Home, James," Thaddeus said, lifting his chin and brushing back his hair. The intention was to satirize some archetypal rich asshole, but he could feel the thud of it.

Who the fuck is James? Jennings wondered.

There were four rows of doors on either side of the limo; Jennings opened the second-to-last one for Thaddeus. Thaddeus sank into the oddly uncomfortable seat. The car smelled like a funeral parlor. An unpleasant buzzing noise came from the miniature fridge tucked between the door and the back of the next row of seats. It contained a bottle of white wine, a bowl of hard-cooked eggs, a pair of sunglasses, and a set of keys—the refrigerator apparently also served as a lost and found.

The awkward limo made its way toward the bridge leading to the eastern, more affluent side of the river, as the first layer of darkness slowly mixed with the day's blue sky. Suddenly, colors: peach and tan, purple and gold. In the river, swans paddled back and forth, back and forth, like tin targets in a shooting gallery. A rusted container ship sluiced toward the city, pulling a chevron of foam in its wake. A freight train moved slowly north, carrying its secret cargo of combustibles.

"Hey, man, how's your father doing?" Thaddeus called out.

"He's good, thanks." Jennings looked for the reflection in the rearview mirror. "How about yours?"

Thaddeus wondered if Jennings knew that Sam was ailing, or was he asking to be polite? Or—money created its own hypotheses—was the question posed to prove that the man at the wheel wearing the stupid little cap and the man in the backseat were on an equal footing? Thaddeus looked at his hand, curled in his lap, and replayed the moment he gave up his suitcase to the driver. He wondered if he would ever get used to it, or if he should. Wouldn't getting used to it be the death of something? The severing of his connection to humanity? What was the cost of getting used to someone carrying your suitcase? Did your arm die a little? Or was it your heart?

Jennings steered the car through a sudden turn, taken way too fast. The tires made their fugitive shriek, and Thaddeus struggled to regain his balance.

Thaddeus had made the money and it was like winning the lottery, but to keep matters feeling somehow equal, he demurred to Grace's wishes on how to spend it. She did not want to live in the city. She saw in Orkney a life of beauty. Subliminally, she felt a house with many rooms and extensive grounds was in her lineage. Liam kept promising her a full report on their ancestry, but it had yet to come. Perhaps he was withholding it, having searched in vain for anything grander than a clerk or a local magistrate dangling from a branch of the family tree. Nevertheless, Grace felt magically at home in the house the moment the real estate agent Sawyer Halliday led them in, sporting a walking stick, a tweed suit. Halliday advised them to move fast, and they surprised him with an all-cash offer. Following that, there were a couple of months dashing between Twenty-Third Street and Leyden, hauling books and papers, drawings, and whatever else was too fragile to entrust to the movers, particularly Grace's drawings and the ultrasound picture of Little Nameless floating like a cashew in the amniotic sea.

Tonight was their housewarming party, thrown on the advice of Gene Woodard. "We love parties around here," he said. "And I truthfully do not believe it's because people here have nothing better to do with their time. There's a belief in celebration here, and hospitality. We may not be hip, but we're hip hip hooray."

In a way, Orkney was theirs because of Gene. They had never really thought of (or heard of) Windsor County until Gene told Thaddeus stories about his family up in Leyden. Gene's birthday party was where Thaddeus met Anahita, whose passionate story turned out to be his ticket to the dance. He'd banged out a script that circulated at the height of the hostage crisis in Tehran. It went out on a Friday, and the following Monday, Grace and Thaddeus spent an afternoon that turned into an evening that turned into a night sitting by the phone while Thaddeus's newly acquired agent, originally thrilled and surprised that even one studio was interested in *Hostages*, took offers from four different studios, before a deal was struck at ten in the evening, New York time. Delirious, frightened, Thaddeus and Grace could not decide who to call. Certainly no one at the Collective, no one with whom Thaddeus played basketball, no one at Altman's or Periodic. They knew what envy felt like, and they were free of their own now—why inflict it on someone else? Kip! Of course, Kip. But all they reached was his answering machine.

They pondered the difference between success and money. Money gave you time enough to explore the limitations of money. And money reminded you that life is full of luck, both good and bad. Thaddeus did not want to become one of those people who believe they deserve everything they have gotten. Luck ruled, the dice were always rolling. Luck may be another word for God or Fate, signifying all we can't otherwise explain. Even being born is a matter of luck, which Grace and Thaddeus had learned the hard way, Grace when she was curled next to him sobbing in a taxi on their way to Roosevelt Hospital, blood in her jeans and on her fingertips. Luck was a little Hannah devoured by fever. Luck was four-year-old Thaddeus keeping himself intact with a jar of peanut butter and sitcoms on the TV. And as luck would again have it, he wrote *Hostages* before Iranian students locked nearly a hundred American diplomats and soldiers into the U.S. embassy in Tehran, imprisoning them in an effort to prove the embassy was also an American spy outpost.

Hostages had been begun in a post-Nero's frenzy, a month after Thaddeus finished a comic thriller he called *The Kindness of Stranglers*, and the month before he wrote an adaptation of *Lady Chatterley's Lover*, without legal authority or interest from anyone in the movie business, not even Josh Zoller, his agent, who was really an assistant who had been given the right to take on a few clients in lieu of a raise. The D. H. Lawrence adaptation updated the action to present-day Malibu, California. At first he'd made the crippling war Vietnam, but after *Hostages* sold he changed it to the conflict in the Persian Gulf, figuring the Middle East was now his sweet spot. Thaddeus had never been to Malibu, though he had been in Iran for several hours, thanks to Liam's wedding gift of a trip to Turkey. It was their one honeymoon quarrel, when he and Grace took a day trip from Dogubayazit, Turkey, which Grace kept calling Dog Biscuit, and were driven in a taxi into Iran, where the women were covered from head to foot, and the men smiled at them with easygoing contempt, as if they were circus chimps, amusing and unclean.

How could something so terrible as America's humiliation by a cadre of fundamentalist Muslims bring them such excitement, such joy, such large amounts of money? As the contracts were signed, as the checks arrived and as they were deposited, and as Thaddeus and Grace quit their jobs, looked at real estate in the city and, at Grace's insistence, looked at real estate along points north, the torment of the Americans continued in Tehran. Negotiations proved useless, a mere occasion for insult and mockery. International pressure put on the Iranians had fallen on ears presumably stuffed with scraps of the Koran, and, most shockingly, an attempt to rescue the hostages had led to a catastrophe of sand-wrecked helicopters and death, an announcement that the era of American supremacy was waning. By the time the U.S. helicopters were smoldering in the desert, Thaddeus was at work on the third draft of *Hostages*, this time under the twinkly tutelage of a jovial Canadian director whom the studio had chosen to supervise the rewrites. The Canadian, Neal Kosoff, sleek, evasive, with a half dozen irons in the fire, assured Thaddeus that he needn't concern himself with the actual hostage crisis. *Hostages* was a political thriller, and, if it were to succeed, it would have no closer connection to the actual unfolding of events inside Iran than *The Manchurian Candidate* had to the actual Korean War. He was not to worry about news events, statements from the relatives of the captives, Republican attempts to gain an electoral advantage from the situation, or whatever Hail Mary passes President Carter might attempt as he watched his own political demise.

"This is about a bunch of bad guys holding Dustin Hoffman captive," the director had instructed Thaddeus. "Just think Dustin Hoffman, Dustin Hoffman, and never mind about what's going on in the real world."

GRACE TOOK A MOMENT TO stand by herself, her face aching from smiling. The guests were spread out over the grounds. So many people. Sawyer Halliday, the real estate agent who'd brokered their purchase of Orkney, was in a seersucker suit and a Panama hat. His mother, once a great beauty and now Sawyer's constant companion, leaned heavily on her cane, and looked as if she had just tasted an iffy oyster. Grace and Thaddeus's insurance agents were here, ginger-haired cousins bereft of eyebrows, smiley, liberally cologned (the only thing liberal about them), and so polite that it often seemed they might be kidding. The president of the local bank, who could not handle strong drink, was already in a daze, and stood with his arms folded over his chest, fingertips drumming on his biceps. Dave and Greg were there, the perpetually stoned housepainters, with their beautiful girlfriends who were their assistants. Who else? The owner of the health food store, her quipster husband; the owner of the bakery and her Down's syndrome daughter; the girl from the cheese shop, who exuded a blissful dairyness; the nervous Polish woman who worked at the hardware store, dressed this evening as if for a polka contest, all were there, as were the owners of Leyden Liquors and Windsor Wines, bitter rivals who glared at each other like feuding brothers, while checking bottles of booze to see from whose store they had come. Oh, and not to forget the antique store owners, eight, nine, maybe ten of them—antique stores were where Thaddeus and Grace had done most of their shopping, once they realized the entirety of their own furniture would fill about 3 percent of their new house. "This will look as if it's been there forever," all of the antique store owners had said, no matter if the *it* was a Queen Anne sofa, a pair of painted andirons, or a Persian runner.

The one person they actually *knew* in Leyden at first pretended that they did not exist. When Gene Woodard learned they had purchased Orkney he turned icy at the encroachment. Did he feel they did not deserve to be brushing their teeth and scratching their behinds in such a historic spot? Did he mourn the fact that now anyone with a sudden windfall could buy one of those river houses? Maybe Gene was simply busy, absorbed by other matters and could not find the time or the energy to invite them to dinner or to tea or even for a walk along the Hudson. It was painful for Thaddeus—he felt the rejection as a judgment that went straight to the core of him. Grace was merely offended. Not only was Woodard a snob but he was a jerk. Yet all was forgiven as soon as Gene arrived one afternoon, and when he suggested the party, both Thaddeus and Grace agreed to it at once. It was irresistible. And, besides that, if they were going to have a convivial life along the river, this was the price of admission.

And since the party was basically *his* idea, Gene helped them with their invitations to the neighbors. What Gene considered the neighborhood was anything along the river, ten miles north, and ten miles south. Each house was formidable and some of great historical significance. Some sat at the top of long gated drives, where the grounds were tended like a park or cemetery, while others were merely large, with grounds seedy and overgrown. Gene, of course, knew everyone who lived along that watery corridor, and knew their family trees like a woodsman knows the forest. Here the wealthy begat biblically, every marriage had its round of births involving transfers of property and influence. And, oh, the stories, the scandals and the heartbreak, the ironies and the acts of sheer foolishness, the cruelty and the charity and the gradual slipping down as the cross-pollination of the powerful families followed a predictable course, from hybrid vigor to all manner of misfortune. And what was not undone by misfortune was undermined by the rise of new money and the prices that new money was prepared to pay. It had become a matter of honor to hold on to old family estates, and those who caved and sold out to people with no history in the area and no sense of stewardship of the land or to the Windsor County way of life were considered weaklings, traitors—including the drug-addled Boyetts, who dumped Orkney on the market and decamped to Mexico as soon as those nobodies from nowhere plunked down the asking price.

There was another category of human at the party—the people who were paid to be there. And here, too, Grace was out of her depth. Except for a housecleaner who started coming to their apartment after *Hostages* sold, she hadn't any experience in hiring people. Even engaging a housecleaner in New York had something larky and self-effacing about it, since the cleaner was an actor who arrived on a unicycle, and who seemed to feel culturally and morally superior to them—she once heard him speaking on the telephone, saying something about the Sell-Out and the Sunday Painter, and was damn sure he was referring to them.

When Thaddeus arrived at the party, Grace was standing by herself at the crest of their lawn, gazing west as the evening's last burnt orange light hovered over the river. The crack in the Liberty Bell showed more mirth than her smile, a stop sign made of teeth. Thaddeus put his arm around her anyway and they stood on the patio, looking out at the crepuscular lawn sloping down to the river. Hat Stratton had mowed the lawns and patterned them with a roller, so the grass looked as if it was striped.

"Sorry to have left you with all this," Thaddeus murmured.

"Couldn't be helped. How's your father?"

"He's okay. It's good I went out there. Just to let them know that I am still clinging and obsequious, and will do anything for their love."

"Funny boy."

"And? You?"

"Weird. Our first party in our first house," Grace said, leaning her head on her husband's shoulder.

"I just hope no one goes inside and sees how unworthy we are to live in it," Thaddeus said.

"What are you talking about?"

"It's chaos. It's a mess."

"I think a part of me sort of wishes none of this had ever happened," Grace said. "I feel very small. I liked it when we were both on the same level."

"But the house was *your* idea," he said, plaintively.

She jutted her hip into his. "Anyhow, who the hell are these people? We hardly know one guest."

"Do you think our old friends hate us now we're rich?" he asked.

"They weren't that crazy about us in the first place," Grace said. They had sent their New York friends invitations to the housewarming, but most went unanswered. Grace took it in stride, feeling that the fewer people who showed up for the party the easier things would be, but Thaddeus could not bear to think that their friends would treat them badly, would ignore them, or resent that he and Grace had stumbled into the winner's circle. He was not really convinced that the lack of RSVPs meant no one planned to make the trip north to celebrate their house. Many of the old bunch had wobbly manners, or abhorred making plans too far in advance, preferring to leave themselves open to serendipity. Their friends did not own cars and a few of them never ventured out of the city. Two had asthma, one was fatally allergic to bee stings, and some were broke.

Broke! To be without money in this world! It was like being naked with only your hands to cover you. A twenty-dollar round-trip ticket on the train was not always something you could buy without considering the consequences—the domino theory might not have held true in geopolitics, but it had validity in personal finance for those with limited means. Twenty dollars spent on a train ticket had to come from somewhere, and it might mean having to sacrifice the Con Ed bill, or choosing margarine instead of butter. And for what? To celebrate the purchase of a mansion and a swath of forest? Who could blame them for thinking twice about *that*? Even the ones who were not broke, who were getting by or even better, even they might not want to view what sudden riches could buy.

The only person from the Celluloid Collective to show up was Ace Disend, a gaunt, weirdly lopsided fellow in the best of times and tonight was not the best of times. He had gone from thin to malnourished, and he was literally dressed in rags—his jeans frayed at the cuffs, torn at the knee, held up by hairy brown twine. He seemed to have made the hundred-mile trip north for the express purpose of snubbing Grace and Thaddeus. He had never had a script produced, bought, or optioned, he had no agent, and he never brought any pages in to be discussed at monthly meetings. He claimed he was a surrealist and his favorite film was *Un Chien Andalou*; he also asserted that his aim was to blend the aesthetic of André Breton with that of Johnny Rotten. He prowled the outskirts of the party, feeding wolfishly on a platter of shrimps and hearts of palm. It occurred to Thaddeus that Breton had once said the truest act of surrealism would be to fire a revolver into a crowd of strangers.

Suddenly, Kip Woods announced his presence by grabbing Thaddeus from behind, startling him into heart palpitations.

"Jesus, Kip. We're not in college anymore."

Kip made a show of taking in the surroundings. "I see that, Comrade Kaufman."

"Crazy, right? It's actually not as expensive as it looks."

"Oh, I'm sure," Kip said. "Well, you once said you'd like to have a place where Fred Astaire could take refuge in a time of political crisis."

"So?" Thaddeus said. He hadn't seen Kip in three or four months. Actually more. The last time together was at Max's Kansas City, where over beers and cheeseburgers he told Kip that Grace was pregnant. It was an odd venue to make such an announcement—a dark place filled with the Warhol crowd and people who wanted to be around the Warhol crowd. Kip had frowned, plucked at the stubble on his chin, offering congratulations that were so tepid it would have been better not to say anything at all.

This evening, Kip was dressed as if to parody the upstate bourgeoisie—blue-and-white seersucker suit, white bucks, a pink shirt with a yellow tie. "Been busy. I've got about three more years in me. Then I'm going to buy an island off Maine. And read."

"Buy something up here," Thaddeus said.

"No way. Too close to Wall Street, and all that M and A."

"What's M and A?"

"Murders and assassinations. Well, actually, mergers and acquisitions, aka, what I do, you dumb fuck." Before Thaddeus could show offense, Kip offered up the present he'd brought, wrapped in plain paper. "Here you go."

"Kip! A book?"

"*Go Tell It on the Mountain*," Kip said. "First edition." He turned and took the house in from a distance. "Quite a crowd you've got here. Look at old Gene Woodard. In his element. You guys see a lot of each other?"

"Not really."

"Everyone's in their little niche," Kip said. "The pink-scalp patricians over here, the local shopkeepers over there, I see your little B. Altman crew huddling near the buffet table."

"Did you bring someone?" Thaddeus asked.

"Like a woman? A date? No. Alas."

"Too bad. We were hoping you'd bring that Iranian woman, my Persian muse."

"Ah. No. I actually don't even know who you're talking about."

"The woman you were with at Gene's birthday thing. She changed my life."

Kip shook his head. "I don't remember her. I see a lot of women." He pointed at the house. "I'm curious, does it remind Gracey of the hotel she used to work at? Does it have a gift shop?"

AT LAST, THADDEUS FOUND HIS way back to Grace. She was standing alone on the edge of the patio, half in the light and half in darkness.

"How you holding up there, Mama?" Thaddeus asked. He placed his hand on her swollen middle, hoping to feel the stirrings inside.

"Don't," she said, removing his hand.

"One day this will be his, too," Thaddeus said. "The house, the land, the light on the river. We're giving him an amazing life."

"Or her."

"Yes, or her. It'll be amazing. She'll be amazing. I hope she looks like you." He noticed the look of alarm on Grace's face. She was pointing at the most beautiful tree they owned, a white oak, two hundred years old with no sign of faltering, in full possession of its power and gravity—giant limbs, leaves the size of dinner plates, elephant-hide bark. From the base of the trunk to the apex of the crown, the tree measured almost eighty feet.

"Do you see what I see?" Grace asked.

At the tree's midpoint, the moonlit milky white of Hat Stratton's undershirt was visible.

"What is he doing up there?" Thaddeus asked.

"Remember you asked him if he could put a couple of lights up there?"

"I didn't mean today."

"Well, actually you did. You said you wanted it for the party."

"Really? Are you sure? Suddenly that doesn't seem like a very good idea." Thaddeus's brow furrowed. He could feel himself becoming more serious about certain things—between the money, this house, and a child on the way, he felt he was becoming the man he would remain. And part of that new gravitas was taking good care of the land he now owned, including protecting the aristocratic old trees. He was aware, acutely so, that to many of the people living along the river, he and Grace, aside from being too young to own property here, were cut from the wrong cloth, burped on the wrong shoulders, schooled at the wrong schools. Now they would be wondering why the first Jew to own one of these houses decided to put lights up in the trees.

They were approached by one of their neighbors, a man in his sixties named Hal Marquette. He had a bouncing sort of walk, a merry expression. His face was flushed from several glasses of wine, but even in his slightly dissolute state, he projected confidence and a sense of superiority that Thaddeus suspected was, at its core, racial. With him was Gene Woodard, carrying a highball glass filled with sparkling water.

"I see you've got Hat up a tree," Marquette said, turning again, peering closely, as if his eyes might have initially deceived him. "Will you look at him? My God, he still climbs like a young man."

"Or a monkey," Gene said. "What the hell is he up to, city friend?"

"I'm sure he's safe up there, right?" Thaddeus said.

"Oh yes, yes," Marquette said. "Hat was born to climb. His second home is in the trees. So what do you have him doing up there?" His accent split the difference between Sutton Place and Belgravia, with something of W. C. Fields thrown in, for levity's sake.

"He's putting up a couple of lights for us," Thaddeus said. "Kind of a safety issue."

"Lights? How extraordinary."

The four of them watched for a moment as Hat struggled with a floodlight while keeping his grip on a high branch with his free hand.

"He really should come down," Gene said.

"Lights," mused Marquette. "In that lovely tree. I wonder if you realize yet how much natural light we get along the river. Particularly from the moon."

"Oh, the moon," Grace said. "The moon's okay, but it can be unreliable."

Hat was seated astride one of the oak's thickest limbs, as if on horseback, wrapping the base of the first of the two lights in copper wire.

"This will be a first," Marquette said, adding just the merest trace of regret to his tone, with the same expert care and restraint with which he would have swabbed a trace of vermouth along the side of his martini shaker.

Gene, perhaps out of consideration, changed the subject, and spoke to them about Parker and Tony Boyett, their house's past owners. They were in Mexico now, apparently no longer dope addicts, and no longer in debt, living modestly but well in San Miguel de Allende. "Tony's developed a formula," Gene said. "He's estimated their life expectancy, and made all these calculations based on interest rates and stock market fluctuations, and he's come up with some number, how much money they can spend each year without running into trouble."

"Of course if the price of tortillas goes up, the whole thing goes up in smoke and Tony and Parker are reduced to penury," Marquette added. He patted the breast pocket of his sports jacket. "You wouldn't have a cig, would you?"

"We're both nonsmokers," Thaddeus said.

"Good for you!" Marquette said. A small smile, a little curve of silver in the pink frosting of his face. Suddenly, his attention was pulled to an outpouring of light from the majestic oak. A moment later, the light failed.

"So much for that," Thaddeus said.

"He could use a bit of help up there," Marquette said. "He should have his boy with him."

"Jennings? I thought he'd flown the coop," Gene said to Marquette.

"Back. With a bride no less. A wan little thing from California."

"The Casanova of Windsor County? Married? What is the world coming to?"

Stratton suddenly lost his purchase on the limb upon which he'd been seated and a moment after was hanging upside down, grasping the branch with both hands as well as his feet, which were crossed at the ankles.

"You just watch," Marquette said. "Hat's an old tree man, there's nothing to worry about."

"I just assumed he would have ropes and stuff," Grace said.

"This is so fucked up," said Thaddeus.

"He knows what he's doing," Marquette assured them. He clapped his hands as if at a sporting event.

And sure enough, Hat, by moving his hips and his shoulders rhythmically back and forth, began to sway, five times, ten, and on the fifteenth, like a trapeze artist, he had increased the velocity of his swings and had risen high enough to make a mad scramble. He clawed and hoisted, pulled and shimmied until, at last, he was sitting straight on the limb, where, as a matter of pride, he set immediately to work again, as if nothing unexpected or unintended had occurred.

"What did I tell you?" Marquette said, beaming. "Things have a way of working out around here. And by the way: welcome to Brigadoon."

THE MOON, WHICH HAD BEEN there all along, was suddenly prominent, round and rocky, pale and gold. Hat and Jennings had gotten one of the lights connected and it cast a long spear of brightness onto the lawn. Along the party's southern perimeter, a long table had been set up and the catering staff were making and pouring drinks. People were illuminated briefly before they disappeared into the darkness, and then they would be visible again, drinks in hand. As people in black trousers and white shirts scurried around with trays of food, Thaddeus felt a sudden surge of anxiety. Either the caterer had neglected to tell him what all of this was going to cost or he had somehow forgotten the number, or perhaps had even deliberately deep-sixed it. *Oh well,* he thought, as a way of calming himself. *People seem to be enjoying themselves. Eating well, getting pleasantly hammered.*

Just then, he noticed a tall, thin man with a guitar strapped over his shoulder, wearing a shiny jacket the color of polished gold, straight-legged jeans, and boots. He was tilted to the left, like a tree that has grown on the side of a windswept hill. The man looked like Buddy Klein. It was not completely out of the question. Thaddeus happened to know that Klein lived somewhere in the vicinity. Klein's was one of the names Sawyer Halliday dropped while he was selling them Orkney. The name had meant next to nothing to Grace, but since moving to Leyden Thaddeus had been hoping that one day he might catch sight of his old rock and roll idol. But to have him here on the little patch of the world that Thaddeus himself happened to own? This thrilled Thaddeus more than the Hollywood people he'd met so far—Hoffman, Redford, Lily Tomlin, Richard Dreyfuss, Lee Grant, Sally Field. It did not surprise Thaddeus that Klein's entrance seemed to have been unnoticed. Klein's heyday was ten years gone, and even at the height of his career, Klein was an acquired taste. However, Thaddeus prided himself on his pop connoisseurship, and Buddy Klein had a place on his list of Great Rockers You've Never Heard Of. Not six months ago, Thaddeus had ridiculously overpaid for a vinyl copy of Klein's second album, called *Buddy Klein and the Kleimaniacs in Dusseldorf,* the album title being a small jest, since it was recorded in upstate New York, not far from Woodstock, and nowhere on it was there a reference to Dusseldorf or any other European city. *Dusseldorf* contained—track six, actually—Klein's closest thing to a genuine commercial hit, "Zero Divided by One."

And here he was striding across these newly acquired acres, astonishing under any circumstances, but almost dreamlike in its strangeness now because Klein's name actually appeared in *Hostages*, when the youngest and most appealing of the American hostages talks about music with one of the surprisingly sympathetic Arab insurgents. Thaddeus also indicated that a particularly obscure Klein song—"I Was Never Gone"—be played under the crawl during the movie's final credits, though as he learned more about the limits of his influence in the filmmaking process, either the studio, the producer, or the director taking his musical cues seriously seemed less and less likely.

Yet the question remained: what in the world was Buddy Klein doing at Orkney? Thaddeus hurried toward him.

"Mr. Klein," Thaddeus said, extending his hand. "I'm a huge fan."

There was a long moment of silence.

"Nice of you to say," Klein finally responded. He was neither western nor southern, but even with a slight New England accent, he managed to drawl. "We're neighbors. I'm just over . . ." He waved vaguely in a northerly direction.

"I'm trying not to gush," Thaddeus said. "But this is total fantasy."

"You may feel different after my set," Klein said.

"You're going to play?"

"Yes, it's come to that." He shook his head, laughed. "Hey. I'm not complaining. We're going to have fun and I'm glad for the work."

"You're going to play here, at this party?"

"This is news to you?"

"I'm not sure," Thaddeus said.

One of the caterers, a birthmarked girl with short blond hair and harlequin glasses, drifted over holding a tray filled with little sandwiches. Klein peered intently at the tray, licking his lips once and swallowing. "Do any of these have mayonnaise?" he asked the girl.

"All of them do, Buddy. Sorry."

"Fuck it," he said, helping himself to four of them. And then to Thaddeus, he said, "I'm your housewarming present."

"It can't be true," Thaddeus said.

"I guess I'm also supposed to be a surprise," Klein said. "Well: *surprise!*" He raised his arms, causing the headstock of his guitar to knock into him.

"Are you all right? Jesus, it's really amazing to meet you. I just got a fresh copy of *Dusseldorf,* I mean not six months ago."

"Thank you kindly. But just so you know, the artist doesn't make a nickel out of those secondhand sales. It all goes to the fat guy in the tank top."

"Wait here for a second, would you? I want to introduce my wife to you. Let's just say she's heard a great deal about you."

"If you could aim me at a telephone, I need to make a call," Klein said.

They were standing at the edge of the patio, not more than fifty feet from the back of the house, and the French doors were ablaze with light.

"I'll walk you in," Thaddeus said.

"One day we'll have these little phones like the size of a stick of Juicy Fruit and everyone will carry one in their pocket," Klein said. "It's already happening in Japan. Nippon's got the place all tuned in. The Japanese are eating us alive. The whole place is plugged in. The children glow in the dark."

Thaddeus led Klein to the house, with a longing last glance over his shoulder—how he wished Grace were at his side right now, experiencing the giddiness he felt walking with this old rock icon.

"We're getting more phones," he said, opening the doors for Klein. "But there's one right over here in the kitchen."

"You're right here on the river, man," Klein said. "I can see the river from my crib, but I'm not on it. Movies, right?"

"Movies?"

"The money."

"Yeah, I guess."

"I've got two scripts going. One sort of autobiographical, the other more of a fantasy thing. Maybe you want to take a look at them."

"Sure," Thaddeus said. "I'd be honored."

"I'm calling my boss and yours," Klein said.

"Who's my boss?" Thaddeus asked.

"I'm a present, right? So a present has to be from someone."

A couple of the caterers—a Celtic-looking middle-aged man, with graying hair combed back and dark circles under his wide blue eyes, and a young girl whose russet braids were pinned up on her head, like a Norwegian milkmaid—were seated at the table, chatting and sipping Spanish white wine, now that all of the food preparation and most of the serving was finished. Nevertheless, both rose from their chairs as soon as they saw Thaddeus. The girl, wiping her hands on her apron, said, "Can we help you with something, Mr. Kaufman?" while the man, who in fact had only half-risen from his seat, sank down again and swirled his wine in his glass, peering into it as if looking for a flaw.

"No, no, no," Thaddeus said. "We're just making a quick phone call—we won't be in your way."

"The way is yours, Mr. Kaufman," the man said, in a brogue so lilting and pronounced that Thaddeus was sure it was exaggerated, a subtle way of keeping Thaddeus in his place, keeping the boss at bay. The boss! He was the boss. It seemed preposterous.

Consulting a piece of paper, Klein dialed. While he waited, he said to Thaddeus, "We ought to hang out sometime. I'll cut you in on how things work around here. Oh, hi there," Buddy said into the phone, in a soft, insinuating voice. "This is Jay, Mr. Klein's personal assistant. He wanted you to know that he has arrived at the party. We're going to set up his amplifier, and we'll do a sound check and Mr. Klein's performance will commence in the next fifteen minutes."

Thaddeus heard some sort of reply.

"He wants to talk to you," Klein said, in Jay's voice, handing the phone to Thaddeus.

"Hello?" Thaddeus said.

"Well, happy housewarming, Thaddeus," the Canadian director Neal Kosoff said. His voice was hard and bright as a croquet ball.

"Neal, man, I can't believe you did this."

"That was him, wasn't it? On the phone?"

"Really, Neal. I'm overwhelmed."

"Yes, well, he was supposed to be there an hour ago. I think he's still living in the sixties. But I'm glad you're happy. I'd be there myself but I'm in Toronto visiting my mother. She's gotten round eyeglasses and chin whiskers. She's actually starting to look like Trotsky." Kosoff laughed at his own remark. Thaddeus had been taught as a youth that laughing at your own jokes was coarse and ought under all circumstances to be avoided, but he found the practice rather winning in Kosoff, a kind of vulnerability.

"That makes two of us," Thaddeus said. "I'm just coming in from Chicago. My father is having some health problems."

"Really? Well, those old Lefty Louies are a tough lot."

He couldn't remember telling Kosoff that his parents were hard-charging leftists. What had he been currying, what silence had he been trying to fill when he told Kosoff about his parents' political life?

"Anyhow, I'll let you get back to your party," Kosoff was saying. "But there's one more thing I wanted to tell you about—and it's a piece of fantastic news. Scooter Morris has come on board to work on *Hostages*."

"Scooter Morris? You've got me at a disadvantage on that one," Thaddeus said with a lilt, still feeling insouciant, still riding the crest as he waited for the good news—the *fantastic news*.

"Not surprised you don't know the name. Scooter Morris is one of the business's best-kept secrets," Kosoff said. "The total professional. Starts work at three in the morning and writes until seven, takes his son to this special school for retarded kids, then it's back to work until two. He's got the whole thing down to a science. "

"What whole thing?" Thaddeus asked.

"Seven of the movies he's worked on have been nominated, and two have won. His box office numbers are fantastic. He literally gets as much as me on a movie."

"Wait a second. You're getting a new writer? I'm fired?" Thaddeus noticed that Klein had left and the two caterers were suddenly looking at him, and he turned his back to them. The telephone cord wrapped around his shoulders, a plastic python.

"No, no, listen to me, if they're bringing in Scooter that means the studio is going to make your movie. This guy doesn't get involved in development deals. If he's in, it's on. This is better than pay or play, or getting Hoffman, Redford, and Newman all wrapped up together with a bow on top."

"But am I fired? That's what I'm asking you." The cord slipped off his shoulders and wrapped around his throat. He was having difficulty drawing a decent breath, and turned counterclockwise to extricate himself.

"Fired," Kosoff said, as if the word were childish, absurd.

"Inasmuch as I won't be working on the script. On *my* script."

"You're going to get your start money, your price is going to go up. Watch what they offer you for your next script. This is how careers are made. And you'll almost certainly receive full credit. Scooter doesn't usually even *want* a credit, and anyhow the Guild always finds in favor of the original writer. I'm sure they will back you in arbitration."

"Arbitration? Now I'm in arbitration?"

A strategic silence indicated that Kosoff had now finished trying to put a good face on all of this. "Here's what I think," he finally said. "Go enjoy your party. Listen to Buddy Klein. And I will ring you Monday or Tuesday and I can guarantee that you'll be feeling differently about this."

"You know, Neal," Thaddeus said, but then stopped. There was a certain deadness in the sound of his own voice. "Neal? Are you still there?" He flicked the switch hook once with his index finger and as soon as it was depressed he heard the dial tone. *Fine. Fuck him. What could you expect from a man who makes fun of his own mother's facial hair?*

Life is the worst parent imaginable, embracing you one moment, throttling you the next. As Thaddeus replaced the phone into the cradle, he saw, or half-saw, a flash of light, and heard a kind of fizzing crack. It stopped him from moving, thinking, or breathing. A moment later, Grace was calling his name. She was standing just inches away from him. A lizard-shaped wet spot was on the front of her blouse. Her eyes flashed; they seemed to see everything and nothing. It was how he had imagined the eyes of the student fanatics in his make-believe country of East Tigris.

"Call the fire department!" she said, with one hand over her pregnancy, the other gesturing chaotically, opening, closing, pointing, shaking. "And an ambulance."

"What's going on?"

"Call!"

He dialed. "And say what?"

Her face moist with perspiration, her eyebrows knitted so tightly that they looked as if they were being wrung out, Grace took the phone out of his hands.

"Hang on, Hat," a voice from the party called out. "Hat? Hat?"

"His feet are . . ." His feet were something or other, or maybe his face. Thaddeus was having a hard time understanding what people were calling out as he moved out onto the patio, past Buddy Klein, who was seated on a folding chair, his guitar on his lap, and past a couple of the caterers who were holding their empty trays limply at their sides, staring out at the mighty oak, where one of the floodlights burned a path through the darkness, a bright yellow cone full of moths and other night flyers swooping and darting, oblivious to the human drama. Hat Stratton was thirty feet above the ground, his legs straddling one of the oak's thick, gnarled limbs.

Hat had suffered a long sizzling jolt of electric shock from one of the lights he was attempting to put in the tree. There was a smell in the air, a post-thunderstorm pungency of ozone—metallic, slightly chlorinated.

The crowd took it upon itself to awaken Hat from his shocked stupor. First a few of them began to call his name, over and over, and soon virtually everyone was part of the chant, as if they were in a stadium urging their team on. To Thaddeus's ears there seemed something larky about the whole thing, some shameful nugget of irony in the chant. And really—was that even the man's name? Could he not in what might be his last moments on earth be granted the dignity of his given name?

THE CARETAKER'S COTTAGE, THE YELLOW house where Hat lived, and where Jennings and Muriel now lived, too, while saving money to rent a place in town, had been built in the summer of 1902. It was a cheerful, welcoming place, snug in the winter and cool in the hot weather. The walls were covered in floral wallpaper, roses in the parlor, a riot of huge pink sensuous peonies in the dining room. Hat was certain the yellow house's wall coverings were of historical significance, and to his great displeasure, the wallpaper in the upstairs hallway and bedrooms had not survived, and there the walls had been painted a somber gray.

Most of the time Jennings and Muriel spent in Hat's house was cloistered in their bedroom, to give Hat his privacy, and to avoid any spontaneous lectures that might come geysering out of the maddeningly erudite old fellow. Now, with Hat busy at the housewarming party at the big house, they luxuriated in the parlor.

"If you wanted to go over and check out the party, you could do that," Jennings said to Muriel. "There's all this food and champagne." He was stretched out on the old green velvet sofa, his feet bare, his trousers rolled to the knee, while Muriel massaged him. She pressed her thin, but surprisingly strong fingers into the bottoms of his feet, where the trigger points for all of the body's internal organs resided. She said it was like a switching station for the whole nervous system, as well as digestion, heart health, even eyesight.

"Can I move this?" Muriel said. The floor lamp was right behind her, its tawny shade scorched from the 150-watt bulb Jennings had put into it years ago. Hat refused to change the shade, left it there as a reminder to Jennings that when his father said 75 watts he meant 75 watts.

"Of course you can. You live here."

"I guess I'm still getting used to it." She lifted his foot, regarded it. "You've got beautiful feet." She ran her hand over the dorsal hump. "And so smooth."

"Fresh shrimp at the party," Jennings said. "Champagne. And all these little sandwiches, you know, the kind they cut the crusts off."

"The crust is the best part. Best tasting and best for you." She lowered his foot with inordinate care, and folded her hands around it, holding it as if it were a bird she was trying to warm back to life.

"You want to check it out?" Jennings asked.

"Up there?" She shook her head. "I don't need to do that. Anyhow, we weren't invited."

"I thought you liked champagne."

"I really wouldn't feel comfortable."

Jennings slapped his hands against his stomach, grabbed at the flesh. "I'm getting fat," he said.

"You're the most beautiful man I have ever known," Muriel said.

He lifted his shirt. "Still think so?"

She knitted her brows, tapped her finger against her lower lip. "Hmm," she said. "Maybe not." She waited for his reaction and then dove upon him, kissing his chin, his neck, and half-kissing and half-biting his belly. "I wish you were a total stone fatty," she said. "I wish no other woman would give you a second look."

"You'd like that, huh."

"Oh, I would totally feature that."

"Wait," Jennings said. "Shhh." He put up a silencing hand. From a distance, he heard a crowd of people chanting his father's name, over and over as if it were a joke.

IN MOMENTS, JENNINGS WAS AT the main house, racing down the slope of the lawn, toward his father in the tree. "Dad," he called out, his voice ragged and frightened. The intensity and terror in his cry was not enough to silence all the guests, but those standing closest to Jennings got the message and they stopped chanting, and each subsequent calling out of Hat's name became weaker and more tentative, until, at last, there was silence, save the transistorized twitter of insects and tree frogs. Hat was sitting in a shocked stupor, high in the tree, and everyone stared upward.

"They're on their way," Grace said. "The ambulance." She touched Thaddeus's elbow.

"If he's dead, it's our fault," Thaddeus said.

"We were paying him extra," Grace said.

He didn't want to ask her, *What is that supposed to mean?* If this was anyone's fault it was his.

A long flat cloud moved away from the moon and suddenly Hat was bathed in light. He looked like a man hanging on to the mast of a sinking ship.

"I just cut the power from your fuse box," a voice next to Thaddeus said. It was their real estate broker, Sawyer Halliday.

"Good idea," Grace said.

Jennings, barefoot, his trousers still rolled, moved a ladder from one side of the tree to the other, resting the top of it against a leafy branch. The ladder was wooden, designed for orchard work, and was broad on the bottom, tapered on top, and Hat was at least fifteen feet beyond its reach. Jennings climbed while they watched in silence.

Suddenly, a collective cry went up. It sounded almost joyous, like the voices trailing out of a roller coaster as it makes its great giddy plunge. All they saw was the moving darkness of Hat's falling body. He sped past his son and landed flat on his back. He did not make a sound, nor a movement, but lay there in stillness, not even twitching. No one cried out. No one except for Jennings moved.

"Dad, Dad, Dad," cried Jennings, as he scrambled down the ladder, jumping off when he was five rungs from the ground. He ran to where his father lay, fell to his knees, held his hands near his father's body, but did not dare to touch him.

There was no ambulance, not yet. No squad car, no fire truck, no doctor in the house. Everyone was paralyzed, waiting, waiting.

There was music rising up from the moonlit water as a boat outlined in twinkling white lights floated past, blasting Cheap Trick's "I Want You to Want Me." The captain of the party boat cranked up the volume, defying the people in the big houses along the river, all of whom detested the party boats, none of whom believed other people knew how to treat the river.

Jennings was in an aboriginal crouch, head down, hands folded between his knees. Suddenly Hat stirred. His feet gave a little fluttering kick, and he lifted himself on his elbows. A moment later he was standing straight up, smiling shyly, waving with one hand and rubbing the small of his back with the other. Jennings stood up, and the ladder came whomping onto the grass, barely missing Hat.

"Nothing to worry about, folks," Hat said in a reedy voice. And then to demonstrate just how all right he was he began to dance a kind of jig, with his elbows out and his elbows in and his elbows out again, his head ducking this way and that, as if he were passing under a series of low branches. He grinned with embarrassment and tried to hold on to his pride.

Buddy Klein began to play "Boil the Breakfast Early," the only authentically Irish song he knew.

As his father danced his reassuring jig, Jennings sat with his back to the tree and wept into his hands. Eventually, he looked up toward the guests who were cheering Hat on. He could not tell the drunk from the tipsy, the vigorous from the faltering, the finger snappers from the back slappers, the easy lays from the ice queens, the fat asses from the squash champs, the rich from the crazy rich, the hustlers from the straight shooters, the ones who thought they might be better than the Stratton family from the ones who just absolutely *knew* they were, and the ones who wanted lights in their trees and thought a fat tip turned you into the next Jesus. Right now, they were all in it together, all of them chanting Hat's name, all in on the humiliation, up to their chins in it, up to their eyeballs, over their fucking heads, all of them, all of them.

IF YOU INCLUDED THE HIS and hers sitting rooms, their bedroom was almost exactly to the square foot twice as large as their apartment back in New York. Grace had found a store that sold good wooden hangers and their clothes were at last in a closet. But the work of actually furnishing the place was still in front of them. Chairs, sofas, carpets, lamps, dinnerware, pots and pans, room after room waited to be filled. It was fun at first but it became tedious, and this persistent need to shop created a division of labor between them. Thaddeus had to work on a new script and he also needed to look for what came next—it turned out that being well off was expensive—and so most of the shopping fell to Grace, who was feeling not only the sluggishness of pregnancy but the slowly mounting realization that without so much as a minute's conversation about it she had been relegated to the role of housewife. So far, she had furnished the bedroom with a couple of easy chairs, a small bookshelf, four lamps. The king-size mattress was on the floor because she hadn't found a frame for it yet. It would take thousands of dollars, perhaps tens of thousands to furnish just this one room, and there were many, many others even emptier.

Thaddeus waited on the mattress, running his hand over the new sheets that were still a wash or two away from the softness he had hoped for. He was eager for the comfort of Grace's body, but when she finally emerged from the bathroom, unself-consciously naked, the swell of her pregnancy glistening from her nightly application of apricot kernel oil, her bangs darkly wet from her face-washing routine, which ended with fifteen dutiful lukewarm rinses, she walked past the bed and through the French doors that led to a small balcony. Naked himself, Thaddeus scrambled out of the bed to follow her.

"I can't see a thing," he said, standing behind her, pressing himself against her backside. "We could be anywhere. We could be dead."

"So you'd be trying to fuck me even in the afterlife?"

"That's true."

Someone was having a birthday celebration on one of the party boats and it was still going on despite the hour. They could hear the laughter as the boat moved north, laughter you could tell was mad and drunken, even from a far distance.

"Their party sounds better than ours," Thaddeus said.

Grace turned toward him, placing her hands on his chest so he wouldn't think she wanted to be kissed. "Do you think Hat's okay?"

"He danced. So, I guess."

"What if he sues us?"

"Let him. We're insured."

"We're insured. Wow. You really did it, didn't you? Now we're the kind of people who have to be insured." She relaxed her hands, allowing them to slide down his body. She clasped him from behind and pressed him closer to her.

"This kid is already getting in our way," Thaddeus said.

"It's only going to get worse." She made the sign of the cross on his ass, and then slapped it. "It was really nice of Kosoff to send that singer to play for you."

"For us."

"Oh please. He doesn't even know my name. For now there is no 'us.' It's Thaddeus Kaufman and his pregnant wife."

"Grace . . ."

"No, no, it's fine. Who knows? Maybe it'll get me to work twice as hard. I'm not too good in getting my stuff out there. I have such a horrible fear of rejection. You have so much self-confidence. And people like you so much. I don't go into things thinking I'm going to be liked. Actually it's the opposite."

"I don't care who likes me, as long as you do."

"Look at how much Kosoff likes you and what it's brought us."

He held her closer; he could feel the child moving inside her, or at least he imagined he could. "I think I got fired," he whispered into her scalp.

She looked up at him. It was too dark to see her face, but judging by the sound of her voice he guessed she was smiling. "Rilly? Rilly and truly?"

"Yes. It happens. It's how it works."

She took him by the hand and led him to the mattress on the floor. "It was hard for you to say that, wasn't it? About Kosoff."

"I don't ever want there to be secrets."

She rolled onto her stomach, licked her fingers and wet herself. Sometimes she could be so unromantic about sex, but her frankness was in itself a kind of blunt glamour. He entered her gently, easing himself in as if hardly wanting to be noticed. She was on her knees, her breasts were fuller than they had ever been. She backed into him, encouraging him to let himself go. She closed her eyes and was surprised by what was there lurking in her own mind: an image of Jennings sitting alone, covering his eyes.

"Are you all right?" Thaddeus asked.

She made a noncommittal sound.

He asked the question of the flailing, the lost, and the doomed. "What are you thinking about?" he whispered.

Chapter 7

Stained Glass

FEBRUARY 9, 1981

HAT: Stratton residence.

GRACE: Hello, Mr. Stratton. It's Grace. *(After a silence)* At the . . . house?

HAT: Oh hello. Is everything all right?

GRACE: Well, Thaddeus and I want to have a little dinner party and we were wondering if you and your family could join us on Monday.

HAT: *(After a silence)* Well, you know we have an infant on our hands. It might be difficult for the mother to go out in the evening. You know how those things are.

GRACE: It's just going to be a family party. Of course the babies will be there. Can you make it at seven o'clock?

PUSHING THE BUTTON TO A DOORBELL THAT WAS NOT working, snow on their collars and snow in their hair and snow clinging to their eyelashes, Hat, Jennings, and Muriel waited on Orkney's front porch, their smiles in place. Hat had done everything he could to impress them with the importance and rarity of an invitation to the big house; he had been successful in communicating the evening's importance to Muriel, and even Jennings, with a lifetime of resistance to his father's ideas behind him, had succumbed to Hat's nervous excitement. Muriel held Jewel, swaddled to the point of mummification, beneath her ankle-length down-filled coat. This would be Muriel's first time inside the mansion, inside any mansion. And it *was* a mansion, despite her husband and her father-in-law never saying the word. They called it either the Big House or Over There.

"Are you sure it's tonight?" she asked.

Hat wobbled the doorbell button around in its casing. "There's your problem," he proclaimed.

Suddenly, the front door opened. Light and warmth and fragrance poured out of the house like music.

"I saw your silhouettes through the glass!" Thaddeus exclaimed. "How long have you been out there? Come in, come in, come in."

"Just arrived," Hat said. Since tumbling from the tree, he seldom went out, rarely, as he put it, *ventured forth*, and up until the last minute this evening he wasn't certain he would join them tonight. But here he was, without a winter coat, just a brown wool sports jacket with large leather buttons, patches on the elbows, and birding pants made out of wool thick enough to withstand traipsing through sticker bushes, wild roses, and blackberry vines. His large ears were bright red from the cold, and the skin on his face was scrubbed so vigorously and shaved so carefully it had the sheen of glass. He held his cane over his shoulder, and a small woven basket filled with Cortland apples, their skin dark in the winter light. "This variety of apple was developed right here in New York," he said, handing the basket to Thaddeus. "Back in 1915. Government program, one of the few that was worth the time and money."

Accepting the basket from Hat, Thaddeus asked, "Isn't the dinger working?"

"I'm afraid not," Hat said, and Jennings, sensing a lengthy explanation as to *why* the doorbell was not in tip-top chiming condition, handed Thaddeus a bottle of Veuve Clicquot, festively sealed in its mango-colored box.

"This is great," Thaddeus said. He held the champagne aloft, as if it were something he'd won. "My favorite."

"It was what you served at the housewarming," Jennings said.

"I know!" Thaddeus exclaimed, grinning, though he felt a stir of uneasiness, wondering what other extravagances Jennings had noted at that party, and what he and Hat and all their friends had said about it afterward.

"Mice is what did it," Hat said.

"Did what?" Thaddeus asked.

"Chewed up the wires," Hat said, his face lighting up. "That's why your bell isn't working. Once, Norman Vincent Peale stood on the portico for half an hour. Same thing. The field mice—the brown ones, mind you, not the gray— those critters chew the wires. Now you might want to ask me, why would a mouse want to eat wire? Well, they don't, they don't see it as food. What they're doing is whittling down their teeth. All rodents do this. Left alone, the front teeth of a mouse will grow five inches in a year."

"Sounds like some of the producers I work for in L.A.," Thaddeus said.

"We'll get in there and have a look," Hat said. "If we're lucky they did their chewing near the button. What kind of transformer do you have in there?" He noticed the look of incomprehension on Thaddeus's face. "It's either twelve volts or sixteen. Both perfectly safe, by the way. No one ever got shocked up fixing a doorbell. Right, son?"

"If you say so, Pop."

"The thing is, I don't really know what a transformer actually is, or does," Thaddeus said, motioning them all to follow him into the library. "But it sounds like something I'd like to get into," he said over his shoulder, with a feverishly merry smile.

As she followed Thaddeus, Muriel took in what she could of the house, struck by the beauty of the place. It reminded her of seeing a play at the Mark Taper Forum in Los Angeles, how when the curtain came up and she saw the set—it looked nothing like this, it was just a motel room and a bed—it made her gasp and her eyes fill with tears because suddenly she was in a different world. Here at Orkney, the music room was to the right with its ancient piano and old lithos of composers who looked like British judges. To the left was the library with its floor-to-ceiling bookshelves, its green and pink carpet, a long inlaid table, a blue vase filled with dried hydrangea, leather chairs. Along the long hall, there were ornate sconces on the walls, drawings of eggs and apples in beautiful frames, the beginnings of a staircase. As magical as it all was, it was not like the old photographs in *History of a House*, the privately printed book about Orkney that Hat had given to her. Where were the royal chandeliers, the pleated draperies, the footmen in breeches? In a way it was just a house, only big. And warm! She hugged the baby closer and followed the men into the library.

Buddy Klein was already there, gazing at the unlit logs in the fireplace, perched on a Queen Anne chair in such a way that reduced pressure on his lower back. His pupils were pinned: Percocet. He'd had a rough few months—financial difficulties, on top of ex-wife, estranged daughter, and sciatic nerve difficulties—and it showed. He'd put on weight, the skin under his eyes was pouchy, and his long lank hair showed streaks of gray.

"I guess I crashed your dinner party," Buddy said, as Thaddeus led Jennings, Muriel, and Hat in. "Hat. What the hell? What's with the cane? Now you can't walk?"

"Evening, Buddy. I see you're without your trusty guitar."

"You are looking at that rarest of phenomena, a man who realizes his own limitations," said Klein, saluting.

"Buddy's morose because Bill Haley died," Thaddeus said, and gestured to the low, inlaid table upon which he and Grace had put out cheese and crackers, as well as a silver bowl of cashews, an open bottle of Pinot Noir, a bottle of Russian vodka with an indecipherable Cyrillic label, and a filled ice bucket topped by a pair of pewter tongs.

"I'm going to leave these right here," Thaddeus said, placing the apples on the table. "They'll go great with the cheese. And this . . ." He smiled fondly at the champagne. "I'm going to put it in the fridge, and we can have it with our dessert."

"You can save it for a special occasion," Jennings said.

"This IS a special occasion," Thaddeus boomed, startling himself with the raucous gaiety of his voice. He lingered in the doorway, stealing glances at the staircase, hoping for Grace.

Hat, Jennings, and Muriel sat in straight-backed chairs, the men with their hands folded and hung between their knees, Muriel with the baby on her lap. She touched Jewel's nose and the baby smiled her amazing smile. "So who's Bill Haley again?" Muriel asked.

"One of your original purveyors of rock and roll," Hat said, trying to keep it short. Jennings had already strongly hinted to him that Muriel was afraid to ask questions around him because his answers took so long. Hat felt an obligation to pass along whatever knowledge he had been able to accrue during his years on earth, but at least for tonight he would try to limit his responses to a sentence or two—it would actually be an interesting challenge. Aside from wanting to keep on Muriel's good side, Hat was in pain, especially in his right hip, which throbbed day and night like a heart circulating pain instead of blood. "'Rock Around the Clock' was his somewhat dubious claim to fame," he added, because it would have just been plain wrong to omit that important detail.

He heard footsteps overhead and looked up at the ceiling. It needed a good scraping and repainting.

"Ooops," Thaddeus said. "I forgot something in the kitchen."

"What kind of cheese is this?" Muriel said, after Thaddeus was gone, leaning forward in her chair, sniffing. The cheese, soft and moist and shot through with dark blue veins, looked like her grandmother's feet. Feet that had terrified her as a child. Her father had always told her she'd had an overactive imagination. He made it sound like a glandular problem, like something that made you sweat, or smell. A diagnosis that held no pity and no respect. A diagnosis as hard as his voice, as undermining as his shitty little smile.

"Could be a Roquefort," Hat said. "But I'd put it at a domestic blue—Maytag, maybe. Top of the line."

"Want one?" Jennings asked Muriel, picking up a cracker, and the little cheese knife with its mock pearl handle.

"From the great state of Iowa," Hat added. "The Hawkeye state." He accepted a cheese and cracker from his son, placed it in his mouth and chewed it thoughtfully. "Oh, I could get used to this," he said.

"Guess I better wait," Muriel said. She wrinkled her nose. She had sharp features, a hillbilly plainness, but Hat saw how his boy could find her beautiful. There was something to loving what others overlooked, like finding an Old Master at a yard sale—one of Hat's favorite fantasies. Muriel had spun a cocoon around herself made of daydreams and marijuana. It was obvious to Hat what she saw in his son—a good-looking man who accepted her for exactly who she was and asked little from her. But why, with all the fish in the sea, Jennings had decided Muriel was the one for him, that was a riddle no less mysterious to Hat now than it was when Jennings came home with his California girl wrapped around him like a second skin.

Thaddeus was on his way back from the kitchen, carrying a platter with slices of melon wrapped in prosciutto, but stopped to watch Grace making her way down the staircase. Her progress was languid. She cradled David in one arm, notched against her hip, and had the baby's wicker bassinet in the other.

"Is Buddy still here?" Grace silently mouthed the words.

Thaddeus nodded, and Grace shook her head.

"We're making a huge mistake," Grace whispered.

"It's already settled," murmured Thaddeus. "It's done. And it's the right thing. We almost killed him!"

"Huge mistake," she repeated.

"Oh, there she is," Buddy said, as they entered the library. "Mother of the year."

Thanks a lot, Muriel thought.

"How's that vodka and Percocet treating you, Buddy?" Grace said.

Thaddeus crouched before the fireplace. He was still waiting for Grace to get past her initial reluctance to have a kid, but Grace was dug in. Maybe it was being here in Leyden, maybe it was his career taking off and hers sputtering, but by now her low opinion of herself as a mother seemed to have become a kind of cornerstone to her sense of self. And the argument over whether or not to have a kid continued even after the kid was born. Thaddeus focused on making a fire. He had stacked the kindling and the wood carefully and had gone so far as to surreptitiously squirt a bit of lighter fluid onto the rolled-up newspapers to ensure a quick and easy start.

Five-month-old David was lolling about in his bassinette, less ill-contented than usual. He was dressed in beautiful cotton pajamas, decorated in a pattern of black-and-yellow clapperboards, a gift from the Canadian director Neal Kosoff. David's reddish bare feet looked like newborn squirrels. He was long and thin; there was plenty of room in the bassinet for Jewel, and Grace encouraged Muriel to put her in.

"Lucky you," Thaddeus said to his baby son. "I was in college before I slept with a girl."

"I was ten," Buddy said. "If you count cousins."

"Don't look at me," Muriel said. "My father named me after a cigar."

"That's great," Thaddeus said, his voice booming. "Hilarious." *Calm the fuck down,* he advised himself. He picked up the wine, offering with his eyes to fill his sister's glass, but Hannah shook her head, rose from her seat, and vanished.

"She's not joking," Jennings said. "Her old man loved tobacco. Like an addict. He named his son Kent, after the cigarette. Dog named Lucky."

The conversation went elsewhere. The nibbles were nibbled upon. Wine and more wine was poured. All around the world, people were having parties, and this one was theirs. The women said their breast-fed babies were going to get a hell of a buzz. All partook except for Hat, who said there were certain histamines used in vinification that caused headaches in certain individuals, and was sad to say he himself happened to be one of those people. He drank vodka, which he vastly enjoyed. "Seventy years of Red tyranny has not succeeded in destroying the Russian soul," he said, holding up his glass as if it were a beacon of hope.

"I've been meaning to ask you," Thaddeus said. "Your name. How'd that come about?"

"Oh, well now we get into some ancient history," Hat said. "Back when my father worked here, I often accompanied him on his daily rounds and Mrs. Livermore never paid me much mind, except one winter's afternoon she noticed me with my father. I was shoveling the snow and my father was salting. Back then they used real salt, not the synthetic stuff they sell now. Anyhow, there was a raccoon creating a ruckus in the kitchen and they wanted to get it out of there, and for some reason Mrs. Livermore thought I was the boy for the job. She didn't know my name so she just pointed and because I was wearing a hat she said, 'You, Hat, can you come in here and be a hero?' Of course I wanted to be a hero. What boy doesn't? And I guess the name kind of stuck."

"What's your real name?"

"Philip. But if you called me Philip I wouldn't even think it was me at this point," Hat said.

The library had large four-part Palladian windows. The centers and the narrower flanking panes were white with frost, but the square tops, stained glass representations of standing beavers, glowed purple and gold in the moonlight. Beyond the windows rolled the lawns, and beyond the lawns was the river, and beyond that it hardly mattered because they were all here, the men, the women, the babies. What finer place on earth could there be? A thrumming sound rose up from the cellar, as the old boiler kicked on, sending hot water through the pipes and into the radiators. At least that's what Thaddeus thought he was hearing. He hadn't walked down the basement steps in a while; there were other people who kept things running now. Inside his own house, he was like a passenger on a plane hoping for the best.

Hat, accustomed to finding work orders in the facial expressions of his employers, said, "Don't worry, we'll get Jennings down there and make sure everything's shipshape with your insulation. You'd be surprised what savings can be had." He turned to Jennings. "Tomorrow?"

"Sure. What kind of insulation's down there right now?" This to Hat: Jennings was sure Thaddeus would have no idea.

"I say we do the job right and put in asbestos," Hat said.

"I heard it was dangerous," Thaddeus said.

"Me too," Grace said. "Rilly."

"Well," said Hat. "You hear a lot of nonsense from people who don't know the first thing about anything, but dime for dime you're not going to do better than asbestos. Handled with care? There's nothing better. They feed that stuff to a bunch of rats, and the rats go cross-eyed and next thing you know all the fiberglass companies are up there in Albany trying to get the politicians to pass a bunch of laws. We are turning into the most regulated society on earth, as bad as the Russians. Asbestos is a good product, but it's like anything else. Poison, dynamite, firearms—you have to know what you're doing."

"I don't think we'd want poison or dynamite down in our cellar, either," offered Grace.

The front door banged open suddenly, and a howling gust of frigid air blew in, as insistent as a pack of dogs. The door slammed shut again.

"Mrs. Kaufman?" a tearful voice cried out. It was Laura Duran, their child-care worker. They referred to her as their child-care helper—worker was just a bit raw to their taste. Laura called them Mr. and Mrs. Kaufman. Grace's not taking Thaddeus's name was something Laura averted her mind's eye to, as if it were something Grace would rather not be noticed, like a scar.

"In here, Laura," Grace called out. Her voice awakened both babies in the bassinet.

Laura lumbered in, a large woman in her mid-twenties, radiating the night, its obdurate winds, its freezing implacability. Her blue jeans were tight and her ski parka looked like the outer shell of a hand grenade. Her light brown hair was curly one week, wet-combed the next, then straight and prim beneath a headband the week after that. Today she was back to curly and the ringlets were icy. She had a pugnacious manner and the face to go with it—a blunt nose, a strong jaw, a defiant gaze that warned men away without meaning to.

But tonight she was distraught and in tears. "I'm sorry I'm late," she said. She rarely cried and hadn't developed the skill of hiding her tears. She wept openly, liquid streaming from her eyes and nose.

"It's fine, it's nothing," Grace said. "What happened, what's wrong?"

"I'll get you something to drink," Thaddeus said. "Come on, sit. Sit."

"Love troubles?" Buddy Klein asked, in a somewhat humorous drawl.

"I frigging wish," Laura said. Then, to Jennings: "Oh, hi. I didn't even see you."

"You okay?" Jennings asked, a familiarity and concern in his voice that did not escape Muriel. All these months that Laura had been living in the big house, it had not been evident that she and Jennings knew each other. Muriel had never seen them together and Jennings, as far as Muriel could recall, had never once said Laura's name. But it was a small town, and they probably at one time or another were at the same skinny-dipping party, or got blasted in the back of somebody's van, perhaps they had made out, or worse.

"Laura, honey, what the hell happened?" Grace said.

"My mother," Laura wailed. Her mother was a nurse at Windsor Psychiatric, a looming brick behemoth a few miles south of Orkney.

"My mom was slammed into the linen cart," Laura said. "Right here." Laura touched her temple with three fingers and moved them gracefully toward her ear. "They know who did it. This guy's been locked up since before she even started working. One of the frigging incurables. She took thirty-eight stitches and there's probably going to be a scar. You know how Mom feels about her looks," she added, looking directly at Jennings.

"You know her mother?" Muriel said.

"My mom gave Jennings his first beer, a reward for teaching me to drive."

Jennings smiled, but looked down at his shoes, and Muriel's face colored deeply: stained glass in the church of putting two and two together.

"Oh, look at these two lovebirds!" Laura said, looking down into the bassinet. The infants seemed to have had a tonic effect on her. "Hello, Davey. And is this yours, Jennings? Is this the little girl I hear so much about?" She blotted her tears with her forearm.

"Just don't tell me they took your mother to St. Bartholomew's," Hat said. "Bunch of quacks there running wild."

"It was where the ambulance took her," Laura said, and picked up David. He touched her face with the palm of his hand, and then leaned away from her, watching for her reaction.

"You want my advice?" Hat said. "Get her out of there. You have a constitutional right."

Laura gazed down at Jewel. "If you want, I can take them upstairs."

"You've had a long day, Laura," Grace said, with a faint note of uncertainty.

"It's okay," Laura said. "It can get my mind off of things."

"You want to let her take the babies off our hands for a while?" Grace asked Muriel.

"That could be nice," Thaddeus said. Primarily, he wanted Laura to leave the room. He understood that she had always needed to raise her voice in order to be heard, but sometimes her hoarse honk tightened his nerves. He realized his aversion to certain voices was less than democratic. People raised in large families had big voices. People who worked around machinery had big voices, too. A guy who worked in a body shop is used to making himself heard over hammers, sanders, the hydraulic tire press, and the blasting radio and he can blow your eardrums out with the volume of his conversation. Guys who worked on road crews had outdoor voices, pitched to cut through wind and carry long distances. Cop and army voices finger-poked you in the chest. Masons' voices were white scratchy and dusty and housepainters sounded stoned because they were.

"It's okay," Muriel said. "I'll keep her with me." She took Jewel out of the bassinet, and the baby started to cry.

"See, they don't want to be apart," insisted Laura.

"She's hungry," Muriel said, and undid the many tiny pearlized buttons that ran along the side of her satin blouse, a shimmering antique purchased that afternoon from the hospital's consignment shop.

Grace looked on with considerable amazement while Muriel folded down the shiny fabric of her blouse and just as quickly undid the snap on her nursing bra, revealing a swollen, girlish breast. Jewel made a series of little noises as she groped for the nipple.

"You make it look so easy," Grace said.

"It doesn't look easy to me," Buddy said.

"You don't have to look," said Jennings.

"Still kind of hurts," Muriel said, wincing.

"You got yourself the whole nine yards there, Jen," Laura said. "Happy for you, honest to God."

"You tell your mother I send my best," Jennings said.

"Maybe. Mom never much liked you."

"Nurse Ratched," murmured Buddy.

"You need a haircut, Buddy," Laura said.

"You want to cut it for me?"

"Yeah, right," she said. She was running her ski jacket's zipper up and down its track. "But seriously. A haircut and a shave."

"Oh, I've given up. Surrendered." He peered at her, furrowing his brow. "You sure you're going to be all right?"

"How should I know?" Laura said. She stopped moving the zipper up and down, settling at the down position. She gave the tab an extra yank. The two halves of her jacket parted farther.

Buddy's interpretation: she is saying *I'm available*. He was suddenly emboldened. "What about being my date for dinner?" he asked, placing his hand on his chest. "Not my party, and certainly not my house, but here on the river there's always room for one more."

"It's okay," Laura said. "I'm pretty tired. I guess I'll crash for a while." She stopped and turned before leaving the library. "I'm here if you need me. If these lovebirds start fussing."

They all sat in silence, listening to Laura's percussive footsteps mounting the stairs and making their way down the hall to her room next to the nursery. Jewel made a noise that sounded like humming while she nursed.

Muriel's breast looked like the topping on a dessert, a festive little swirl of sweetness. Thaddeus could not turn away. How could white be so various, with hints of yellow and pink, intimations of silver? Grace cleared her throat, snapping Thaddeus out of his lonely, lustful trance. At last, Muriel disengaged Jewel from her meal. The baby was glassy eyed with satiation; she moved her head in a slow, lolling circle. Shrugging her way back into her blouse, Muriel brought the child to her shoulder and rubbed her back, making quick little circles until Jewel emitted a resonant burp.

"Thank you, Jewel!" Thaddeus exclaimed, clapping his hands. "Dinner is served!" He looked at Jennings but quickly averted his gaze. He wasn't sure if he was conjuring this out of a troubled conscience, but Jennings seemed to have something very close to murder in his eyes. Had he seen Thaddeus glancing at Muriel's breast, or was Hat's fall a wrong that was still waiting to be righted? Or was it as obvious and obdurate as one man was living in a small yellow house that he did not even own, and the other man was rattling around in a mansion?

Buddy eased himself out of his chair, holding the small of his back. "So what's the consensus? Do I go upstairs?"

Muriel was the first to speak. "I think she'd like that."

"And I think you've already made up your mind," said Grace. "So why drag us into it?"

"I just don't think Laura should be alone," Buddy said. "What with Nurse Ratched suffering a broken head and all."

"Come on, Pop," Jennings said. "You want me to give you a hand?"

"There's no ice on these floors," Hat said. "Don't be rushing me off to some home or another." Nevertheless, he held on to Jennings's arm and with his other hand lifted the vodka bottle by its opaque neck. As he allowed his son to lead him out of the library and down the center hall and into the kitchen at the back of the house, he haltingly recited a Carl Sandburg poem:

"A father sees his son nearing manhood.
What shall he tell that son?
'Life is hard; be steel; be a rock.'"

"Whatever you say, Pop. Can you lift your feet?"

Thaddeus had not recovered from the sight of Muriel's breast. He coughed nervously, grateful for the flimsy fingery mask of a hand over his mouth.

THADDEUS AND GRACE DID NOT often have occasion to entertain, and when there were fewer than eight guests for dinner, they served in the kitchen, which was especially pleasant and cozy in the winter. The table was a large oak monstrosity the color of burned honey. It must have been built right where it stood—it was too heavy to budge without risking a hernia, and neither of the kitchen's two doors was wide enough to permit its exit. Thaddeus and Grace wanted to eat off that table for as long as they lived, as would

David, and his children after him, and so forth into the future, even when people just swallowed a couple of gel caps instead of consuming actual food.

Thaddeus and Grace traded glances as they took their places at their ends of the table. The argument they'd been having for weeks, and which seemed to have been resolved, was slowly rising from its casket of silence. All along, Grace had believed there was something naive and egotistical in Thaddeus's desire to make such a large gift to Hat. He was insisting upon going to a lawyer who would draw up an agreement allowing Hat to stay in the house for the rest of his life for a dollar a year, no matter what. From now on the work Hat did around Orkney would be compensated at an hourly wage they would all agree on. Grace understood that this was Thaddeus's way of apologizing for sending Hat up that tree with a fist full of live wires, but the extravagance of the reparation seemed ludicrous to her. *I can be like Tolstoy without having to write* War and Peace, he'd said, trying to joke his way through, but the two of them had fought bitterly over it for days, until Grace finally gave up.

As dinner was served, Thaddeus worried that what they were serving might strike their guests as somehow *stingy*. A T-bone steak on every plate floating merrily in a pool of its own succulence would say "we've spared no expense" in a way that linguini in a primavera sauce simply would not. Would their guests understand that zucchini this small and tender in the dead of winter was a luxury item, the Parmesan cheese came from Thaddeus's favorite shop on Carmine Street down in New York, and that the two bottles of Barolo cost over a hundred dollars each?

Even the nursing mothers were more interested in the wine than the food. Jennings swirled it around his glass before every sip, frowning at how good it tasted. Ah, the things that money could buy!

Hat pushed his chair a little farther out so he might stretch his legs, leaned back, and closed his eyes. "Don't go to sleep on us now, Hat," Thaddeus said. "I've got something I need to talk over with you. We both do."

They had drunk their first glasses of Barolo without a toast, but after Thaddeus refilled the glasses Jennings lifted his glass. "To friendships," he said, moving his gaze around the table—but seeming to skip Thaddeus.

"To friendships!" they concurred, especially Thaddeus, his voice rising.

"And success, and the good things in life," Jennings continued. He was looking directly at Grace now, his gaze calm and unswerving, as if he were observing her through a two-way mirror.

Grace's hand went to her throat, and stayed there.

"Jennings here is looking to go into some kind of business," Hat said. He seemed basically to be talking to himself, though rather loudly. "But he finds himself hoisted on what we call his own petard. Tricky asking a loan officer at Leyden National for funds when you have either kicked his rear in high school or had unlawful carnal knowledge of his wife."

"Thanks, Dad," Jennings said, though he did not sound particularly upset.

Thaddeus noticed Grace giving Jennings a long, appraising look, and finally nodding her head.

"To our children," Muriel said, raising her glass higher.

"Yes, the children," said Grace. "Wouldn't it be something if they actually turned out to be . . . you know: really close?"

"I think we can clear Buddy's plate," Thaddeus said. "I heard him leave."

"Good," said Grace. It hung there for a moment, and she added, "I mean that Laura didn't have to deal with him."

"I didn't even know you and Laura were such old friends," Muriel said to Jennings. She ran her fingertip along the rim of her glass, as if this might create an impression of nonchalance.

"Beaucoup casual," Jennings said. "We ran with the same pack."

"Did you now?" Muriel said, making it sound vaguely lewd. "Oh forget it," she said, and with an angry wave got up to fetch her baby, but Jewel was sleeping peacefully next to David, and Muriel returned to her seat empty-handed. She drained nearly all the wine in her glass in a long furious gulp, and longed to be back in Bakersfield, back in her slanted room with the plywood floor, her too soft little bed with one leg propped up on a compensatory brick, her poster of Nadia Comaneci, who her father called the Little Red Dwarf. As many times as he tore the thing off Muriel's wall, Muriel smoothed it out and retaped it in exactly the same spot. Something about the little gymnast moved her, even though uneven bars and balance beams were as foreign to Muriel as humidors or hockey sticks.

"What do you hate worse?" Thaddeus asked everyone. "The seventies or the eighties?"

"We haven't had the eighties yet," Grace said. "Isn't it too early to start hating them?"

"It's always good to get an early start," Thaddeus said. He seemed to be focusing mainly on Muriel. He refilled her glass, and his own, and it was only then that he took care of Grace and Jennings. "We were lucky to get out of the seventies," he said.

"For most people the labels we give the different decades don't have anything to do with their lives," Jennings said. "Everyone talks about the sixties like the whole country was wearing beads and going on peace marches, but most people were just working their tails off trying to put bread on the table, just like the year before and the year before that."

"The seventies, though, man, the seventies," Thaddeus said, shaking his head. "They were so fucked up. Horrible. I don't know about up here, but New York was ridiculous. Shootings, stabbings, the city completely broke. Empty stores, boarded-up buildings, piles of garbage fifty feet high. And the homeless wandering around like people after a plane crash. Then they call this the me decade? Who the fuck is 'me'?"

"I didn't hear about that," Jennings said. "To me it's the them decade. I guess all of them."

"We're having one of those dinner parties in which the men do all the talking," Grace said.

"Okay with me," Muriel said, laughing. "This is the best wine in the world."

"Did you ever hear about Nero's Fiddle out there in Bakersfield?" Thaddeus asked her.

"Thaddeus," Grace said.

Muriel looked at him keenly. "The restaurant where everyone has to take off their clothes?"

"It wasn't a restaurant," Thaddeus said. "Though they did have food. Horrible, disgusting food."

"Time to change the subject," Grace said, with a false lilt.

"I'm just saying it's not a restaurant," Thaddeus said. "I think it's important to establish that, at least."

"There was nothing like that in Bakersfield," Muriel said. "A lot of titty bars, though." Her expression was placid, as if topless bars were no more notable than taco stands.

"Men who cannot keep their peckers in their pockets, that's the story of Africa," Hat said. "I guess I'll try that wine after all," he added.

Jennings knew full well that Nero's Fiddle was a swingers' club, where people went at it in twos threes fours fives and sixes squirming like maggots on wall-to-wall mattresses. Buddy Klein had told him all about it. Jennings studied the look on Grace's face and knowledge plunked like a stone in a well—she and Thaddeus had gone to Nero's Fiddle. He felt a mixture of satisfaction and revulsion.

Thaddeus's glass: empty as the day it was born. But a third bottle of Barolo appeared; he lifted it for them to behold, and devoted himself to the hard labor of peeling off the foil capsule encasing the cork and of twisting the corkscrew into the center of the cork, followed by the grunting pull of the cork itself.

"Your face is red," Grace observed.

"We need a wine steward," Thaddeus said. He wiped the top of the bottle with his napkin, and reached across the table to fill Muriel's glass. *Breast-feed your child right now,* he thought, *I put a spell on you.*

"Did you really go to that naked restaurant?" Muriel asked.

Filling Jennings's glass, Thaddeus answered, "It's a sex club. A consenting adults swingers' club. They serve food to get around some legal ordinances. Somehow pastrami makes it all kosher." He finessed filling Grace's glass without having to make eye contact with her. "But, yes, we went. Once. Once. And I suppose it could be argued that it was the worst thing we ever did."

"This might be a close second," Grace said.

"The point is, we survived it," Thaddeus said.

"My buddy Larry says what does not destroy you makes you stronger," Jennings said.

"Exactly!" Thaddeus exclaimed. He hadn't meant to, but he clapped his hands, excited that Jennings had more or less quoted Nietzsche. Maybe they would be friends after all!

"The reality is," Grace said, "that what doesn't destroy you actually makes you *weaker*. You get worn out. Pain and misfortune wear you out. Lies wear you out. Hurt feelings wear you out. They kill you by degrees."

Muriel slipped her hand into her blouse and brought her hand out again and touched it with the tip of her tongue, evidently testing for milk.

"I knew if I didn't get out of Bakersfield I was doomed," she said. She peered over at the bassinet, satisfied herself that Jewel was still asleep. "Everyone I ever wanted to like me figured me for a narc."

"Because of her father," Jennings said.

"Yeah. Super Cop. People hated me because of him, and he hated me because of me."

"How could anyone ever hate you?" Thaddeus asked.

"He thought I was a hippie. He really did not like hippies. Once when I was in second grade I found a little orange, one-eyed kitten and I brought it home and Dad said only hippies kept cats, but if I wanted a dog he'd get me one. Then he put me and the cat—I called him Toastie, because he was the color of toast—he put us in his squad car and made me show him right where I found Toastie and I had to put him on the side of the road, right there. He whooped out his siren the whole way, I guess to show me it was some big official business or something."

"I loved hippies when I was a little girl," Grace said. "I thought they were magical, like fairies or brownies."

"Yeah, hash brownies," Thaddeus said. "To hash brownies!" He raised his glass.

"What kind of wine is this?" Grace asked, squinting at the label. "I'm blotto."

"It hails from Piedmont," Hat said. "Good rocky soil, strong sun. Your predecessors the Boyetts visited Piedmont, you might be interested to know. They had good friends there. They all took a hot air balloon ride, though if I were to do such a thing my first choice would be France. I have never trusted the Italians. They know pleasure but they are imprecise. Now the French. The French were the pioneers of hot air balloons. Monsieur . . ." Hat opened his mouth but no sound came out. He shook his head, and his face briefly colored.

Muriel clutched her breasts. "Uh-oh, my boobies feel like they're going to explode."

"These kids are going to get plastered," Grace said.

"I happen to know something about our refrigerator that nobody else knows," Thaddeus said, feeling so expansive he felt he might actually be increasing in size—the helium of his own high spirits filled his chest.

"Oh good," Grace said. "I was hoping we'd be playing guessing games about our refrigerator."

"A bottle of Veuve Clicquot!" Thaddeus said, undeterred. He was silent for a moment. "Oh Jesus," he said, starting to laugh. "That was actually quite guessable." His words struggled not to drown in the roiling sea of laughter.

A silence descended. And in the silence, they heard Laura's heavy footsteps passing over them.

Thaddeus caught the expression on Muriel's face. "Oh please, don't worry yourself over these things. So maybe Jennings taught her to drive. Or something. You know? Something? But what can we expect out of life? It's always a mess. Look at me and Grace going to Nero's Fiddle."

"You really need to shut it down, Thaddeus," Grace said.

"Agreed. I have to get past the idea that I don't exist if I am not talking or fucking or making money. And I need to go to the refrigerator." He pointed at it. It was ten steps away, though to him, for the moment, perspective tromboned. "And get the lovely bottle of Voovarama."

"I don't think we need any more booze," Grace said, as the refrigerator swung open. "We've got two nursing mothers, and you're acting insane."

But Thaddeus was already twisting the cork out of the bottle. A low pop followed by a curl of vapor rising from the bottle's mouth. He filled their glasses, saying ooops each time because the glasses each held a residue of red wine.

"It's such a pleasure having you guys here," Grace said, lifting her glass. A kind of undifferentiated desire swarmed her senses. Color rose from the hollow of her throat, delicate pale pink, the inside of a dog's ear.

"Good to be here," Jennings said.

"Different from what I thought," admitted Muriel. "In a good way," she added.

"To our friendship," Thaddeus said. He pinged the rim of his glass against Jennings's. "And to you, Hat. Who knows this place inside and out. Like no one else. And you, Miss California," he said to Muriel. "Drink deeply!"

"I can't have any more," Muriel said. "My mother boozed when she was nursing me and I think that's why I could never learn math."

"Fuck math," Thaddeus almost shouted—at the last instant he lowered his voice, like a tall man ducking his head before knocking himself silly on a low beam. "Anyhow, I think we better get to the main event before the babies wake up."

"Let's bring out the dessert first," Grace said.

"We don't have a dessert," Thaddeus said. "We're having tomorrow's hangovers for dessert. So listen. Hat? Guys? We never expected to be living like this, in a house like this, with land, and everything else. Until recently, we were living in a small apartment."

Grace looked down at her hands. It was happening, the dreaded thing. It was no longer something they were going to argue about on and on. It was simply going to be put out there in the world. She wondered for a moment if she had married a fool.

"We don't know if I'm a flash in the pan," Thaddeus was saying. "I'm talking about my career. This whole crazy business I'm in."

The phrase turned Grace's stomach—*this whole crazy business*. His career talk embarrassed her. And it diminished her, too, put her in a place she had never wanted to be. What happened to being artists? Living for art and each other? What had happened to the people who wanted something more than to live in a big house and pour expensive wine? She saw it all in a flash, the life before her, the paunchy, jokey husband, the pitiful little punch line of a wife in her home studio making art no one saw.

"So you write what the actors do and say?" Muriel said. She rarely went to the movies, but like most people she was willing to be dazzled by them, and enjoyed hearing about the crazy rich people living unimaginable lives, with their freaky little dogs and their diets and love affairs.

Did Thaddeus even hear her? "Was *Hostages* better than anything else I'd ever written?" he was saying. "No. I can say that without any hesitation. And it wasn't the worst thing, either. So much of it is luck, dumb luck. I never even wanted to write screenplays. I wanted to write books. But I guess I don't have the . . . concentration. Maybe the talent. So right now, I guess I'm on a roll." He shook his hand briskly, as if shooting craps. "I'm getting work based on *Hostages*, but this is what I know—most people end up wiping out. So the thing is, we're here now. But," he added, with an embarrassed laugh, "we don't know what the future holds. And that's a cliché, by the way. A writer told you that."

"Okay, Thaddeus. Please. Don't talk about your career." Grace regretted the sharpness in her voice. She tried to recoup. "It's not like I'm selling paintings or anything," Grace said, in a confidential tone. "Financially, it's all on Thaddeus. It's all kind of nuts. We basically don't know what the fuck we're doing."

Muriel reached for Jennings's hand, seeking reassurance. But Jennings was sitting back in his seat, his hands folded over his stomach, his gaze on the ceiling.

"Hat, you and yours have been living in the yellow house for a long time," Thaddeus said.

"Before me, there was a series of caretakers," Hat said. "Some of them quite dishonest."

"Well, it's yours, Hat. Long story short. No rent, nothing. And when you work around here, you get paid. We'll work that out, but the important thing is the house. Right? It's yours. In case we end up losing this place," Thaddeus said. "It's not my plan. Believe me. But you never know. *Hostages* is going to be okay, I'm sure. But I was fired from it. *Replaced*, as they would have it. The fuckers, the fucking motherfucking fuckers. I'm getting first credit, but still. Here's the thing. We want you to have the yellow house and some of the land it sits on."

Some of the land? Grace sat up. Did Thaddeus just *give* the yellow house to Hat? What just happened?

Thaddeus could read her thoughts, and thought he could somehow make it all work with a smile. It had been a while since he'd felt so certain of *anything*.

Muriel took a small, dainty sip of her champagne during the silence that followed.

"Maybe you can't break up the property," Jennings said, finally. "The old families around here wrote the laws."

Hat had not responded. Was he dazed by the largesse, or had he fallen asleep?

"Hell we can't," said Thaddeus. "We had a surveyor come out when we bought it. We'll have him come back. We bring it to the

zoning board and it's done. End of story." He took a deep breath
and decided he would say what was on his mind—there were things
demanding to be said, they lined up like teenagers waiting their turn
to go off the diving board. "Jennings, man. You remember when
you picked me up at the airport, the evening of the housewarming
party?"

"Sure."

"I can't fucking believe I let you carry my suitcase."

"It's part of the job," Jennings said, looking at his hands.

"I wasn't raised to let other people carry my suitcase."

"Part of the job," Jennings repeated. "Skip it. I didn't mind."

Suddenly, Hat said, "Well, isn't this something." His eyes glis-
tened. He dabbed the corners of his mouth with the back of his
hand. "This one takes the cake."

"I don't see what's happening," Muriel said. "You're giving your
house away?"

"How is it our house?" Thaddeus said. "We don't live there, we
don't take care of it. It's Hat's house. We're just making it official.
And let's face it—we owe it, it's the least we could do. I'm the one
who wanted the fucking lights in the trees. So stupid."

"But I'm fine," Hat said. "A tree man knows how to fall."

"But you should have, Pop," Jennings said.

Jennings had wanted Hat to sue, but there was no case, no doctor's bills, no paper trail of diagnoses and prescriptions. Grace and
Thaddeus had paid for the ambulance and for the emergency room,
but Hat walked out of the hospital an hour after being carted in.

"Well, you've got yourself a deal!" Hat said, moving his hand as
if striking a gong hanging invisibly over his head. Turning to Jennings, he said, "I knew this day would come. I knew it, I knew it, I
knew it."

"He deserves it, if you want to know the truth," Jennings said.
"It's nice of you to do it, but he's given this place everything for—
how long you been here, Pop? Fifty years?"

"No," Hat said. "Not even close."

"How long?"

"It'll be forty-six in March." He sat back in his chair and drew a deep, slow breath. It was taking him a moment to put it all together. Like most men who have earned their living by physical labor, he was years older than his actual age: physically, he was over eighty.

In his glass, a few champagne bubbles were still rising. He drained the glass in one swallow, as if it might have the same effect as pouring a little fuel into the carburetor of a stalled tractor.

"You could move in there, too," Thaddeus said to Jennings. "We could raise our families together."

"I suppose we could," Jennings said, with a smile that was at best enigmatic.

Yes, there *was* a bit of *fuck you* in that. Thaddeus could hardly blame him. But perhaps this whole thing had been a ridiculous, horrible, telltale, destructive mistake. It was as if Sam and Libby, huddled against the cold, were rapping at the icy windows, their angry little knuckles hard against the frozen glass. *Do not do this thing,* they warned their son. *What's yours is yours.*

But what about your socialist principles? he asked them.

Charity is the socialism of fools, they answered. *You're only making things worse, you're pointing out the vast gap between you and them.*

GRACE EMERGED FROM THE BATH dressed for eight hours of non-stop chastity in a flannel nightgown, her face red from scrubbing, her bangs wet, her eyes blurred by exhaustion and inebriation—and anger.

"You feel okay with what we did tonight?" he asked.

"No. Not really. You can tell them tomorrow that you were drunk, and . . . whatever." She slipped into bed, a large California king that afforded ample opportunities for privacy. She sometimes missed the double bed back on Twenty-Third Street, with its little islands of softness and its ability to enforce at least a minimal intimacy, but not tonight, she did not miss it tonight.

"Well, I know we did the right thing," Thaddeus said. "As the Jews say, our names will be written into the book of life."

"So now you're a Jew?"

"I'm always a Jew. Why do you even say that?"

"Well, tell them tomorrow you were a drunk Jew, and when Jews get juiced they get a little carried away."

"I can't do that. We've done the right thing. We don't need to own the yellow house."

"You're such a good boy," she said.

"Well, that's not very nice."

"And I saw you looking at her tits, Mr. Generous," Grace said.

He shook his head, unable to come up with anything that might refute or deflect her observation.

"And if you ever mention anything about Nero's—"

"I'm sorry about that," he said. "I shouldn't have. Sorry sorry sorry."

"When you say it like that it sounds false," she said. "Sorry sorry sorry. Like I'm supposed to feel bad for making you apologize?"

"Okay, I'm sorry about how I said I'm sorry." Yet there was a sense of relief. Grace was leaving the yellow house behind, talking about Muriel, Nero's.

She closed her eyes for a moment. "I can't really figure out how we got from where we were to where we are." She glanced at him. "Why are you smiling?"

"The way you say *rilly*."

"Aren't you tired of that?"

The corners of his mouth turned down. His face was like a Japanese mask. His expression confused her; she couldn't discern if he was furious or overwhelmed with sadness. Maybe *this* was love. The thing we cannot name.

"Never. It was always you I wanted," he said. "When you walked into Four Freedoms. The way you fucked my brains out in my horrible little childhood bed. The way you held my hand when you gave birth to David, the way you squeezed my fingers I thought they were going to break."

"Everyone does that," Grace managed to say.

"But it was you," he whispered. "And not just that. It's everything you do. It's you at the end of the evening. Just washing your face. And then you rinse with tepid water twenty times, early or late, drunk or sober, it never fails, and then you come to bed and your bangs are dark and wet. How would I ever live without that? It's the most sublime kind of crazy. It's this gorgeous commotion, like a flock of birds taking off right in the middle of me. Every good thing that has ever happened to me and every bad thing, too—none of it would mean anything if I couldn't bring it to you. Nothing is real until you see it, nothing is true until you say it. You are the meaning of everything. And I know, I know I know and I know, that's a lot to put on anyone's shoulders, but that's how it is. Without you I am just a series of gestures, a bunch of attitudes, and appetites. But with you it all has meaning, it's all a part of something I believe in, a story that goes on and on. Maybe I will never write a book, but this story, I'm going to tell this story until I die."

"I'm so mad at you," Grace said. "I feel like smacking you."

"Then do it, smack me."

"Would that make you happy?"

"I'm not in it to be happy, Grace. What the fuck is happiness anyhow? It's so stupid. Even the word *happiness* sounds sort of ridiculous. I don't care about happiness. I just want to be with you." He took a long breath and fell silent.

From the cellar, the boiler, hungry for oil, came on with a deep whoosh, shaking the house ever so slightly.

"Jesus," Grace said.

"Vapor lock." He toed off his shoes and lay next to Grace. He reached across the expanse of dotted Swiss duvet and took her hand. To his relief, she linked her fingers through his.

"Hey, I know it's late, but do you mind if I read you a couple of pages of something I'm working on?" he asked.

"Tonight?" She widened her eyes, mocking horror, but feeling it, too.

"Tomorrow will be okay," said Thaddeus. His disappointment was mild; he wasn't really expecting a yes. "Did I tell you I'm up for a Tom Selleck thing?"

"That's nice," she said.

"It's crap. But I should do it. He wants to play a teacher. The working title is—get this—*Tom Is a Teacher.* All they want is three weeks." He rubbed his hands together in a burlesque of greed. "I must take care of my family."

"And now you're taking care of another family."

"Which is going to just . . . it's beautiful. We'll live here, all of us, together. If we ever have to, we can all grow our own food. And what a place for kids. We'll get a dog."

"Thaddeus. It's late. We're drunk. We just gave away a house. And by the way, Laura told me '*we*' gave her a thousand-dollar bonus for Christmas. That was inappropriate, too. It just is. Are you trying to buy people? I really don't get it. Are you trying to impress Sam and Libby?"

From down the hall came David's cries. Not a sleepy baby, he was given to sudden wakings, puzzling tantrums. But tonight's cries sounded especially anguished.

"Oh Christ," Grace said, sitting up.

"Let me," said Thaddeus.

But before he could move, they heard Laura's hurried footsteps toward the baby's room.

"Is Laura even on tonight?" Grace asked.

David's cries stopped; Laura was always so good with him. They heard her pacing back and forth, her indecipherable murmurs.

The sound of a southbound train came up through the darkness, a long, long guttural hum, and then it was gone, leaving silence in its wake.

Thaddeus put his arms around Grace. He kissed her and she kissed him back in that way she had, the way that cleared a path to what was most private and undefended in her. He thought of it as a place, a kind of Garden of Eden in reverse, where you were not expelled by knowledge but gained entrance through sex. *Don't be gentle,* she whispered.

They made love furiously but silently, aware of Laura and the baby. Finally, they slept but somewhere in that unlucky hour near 3 A.M., Thaddeus woke. He had a recollection of kissing Grace's hand and it came to him that the finger that ought to be wearing the emerald ring was bare. The ring she had yearned for when they were poor, the ring he had gone through an ordeal to give her after *Hostages* sold. He had journeyed out to Syosset where Gina of Gina's Gems' sister-in-law lived. Thaddeus had kept a cab at the door while he haggled with the sister-in-law, who kept a Jane Fonda exercise video running on her TV and a Chihuahua on her lap the whole time.

He couldn't contain himself. Sitting up in bed, he shook her shoulder. "Grace," he said. "Did you lose the emerald ring?" He waited for an answer, but she was either dead to the world or doing a first-class job of pretending.

Chapter 8

The Rabbit and the Jewel

JUNE 2, 1983

COME ONE COME ALL

Muriel's Birthday!

When: June 2, 1 P.M.–??

Where: Hat's Place at Orkney

Rain or Shine

**Bring a dish, a bottle, a six-pack,
and a smile.**

JUST TWO DAYS AGO IT WAS CHILLY AND DRIZZLING, AND there wasn't enough sun to burn off the morning mist. It had curled like smoke across the fields and turned into an impenetrable fog once evening came. But now Muriel was having a bit of birthday luck because it was a beautiful afternoon. The sky was dark blue, Smurf blue. The lilac bushes were mad with purple blooms, pumping out their sweet aroma. The fruit trees flowered pink and white, growing just beyond the swath of property that had been deeded over to Hat. Without Hat the trees would probably be dead. He pruned and sprayed them, wrapped the bottoms of their trunks in burlap against the winter's ravaging rodents, and harvested them from August to September, from peaches to pears.

About forty people were on hand to celebrate Muriel's birthday, and you never knew how many more might be on the way. Nearly everyone brought a dish, or a twelve-pack, or wine, or pot. Bob Brody had chips and salsa he brought home from visiting his sister in Texas, the salsa so hot you had to be brave even to taste it. Jennings, Larry Sassone, and a couple of other friends had dug a pit where the main course was going to be fire-roasted. They had woven together sixty or so steel rods, with long handles made of rebar on all corners—a double-sided, homemade grill. Marinated chicken parts were placed on the grill and coated with barbecue sauce that one of the guys swabbed on with a string mop as they sizzled over the fire.

Jennings and Muriel were still living with Hat. Muriel baked pies and sold them to the diner, and Jennings had drifted into doing Hat's work for him. Both of them were off the books; as far as the IRS was concerned, they didn't exist. Jennings could not help but note that most of his guests were doing better than he was, making more money, putting together respectable lives—though he would not have traded places with one of them. One day he would dig up that ring, take it up to Montreal, or down to the city, and with the money start his own business—probably asbestos removal, although he could install it, too, it was still the best insulation out there.

The guests. Some of them worked in the Leyden school system, as bus drivers, lunchroom help, custodians. A few worked at Research Tech, breeding mice and rats for science experiments. Jill Hoover worked in the shoe department at the JCPenney across the river, which was odd since her left leg had been amputated below the knee when she was nine years old. Rory LeBraca carved headstones. Carol and Lois Weber, redheaded twins, worked at the anemone farm, keeping the greenhouses tidy, preparing the blooms for shipment to florists all over the world. Jody Tomjonavic was a mason and had the cough and pallor of someone who'd been on the job for decades. George Zook had inherited his father's job collecting tolls on the Leyden side of the bridge. Even on his days off Zook smelled of auto exhaust. Jerry Neuhauser, Bob Brody, and Oscar Hillman were long-distance truck drivers, all with potbellies that seemed to have suddenly appeared like puffball mushrooms on the lawn after a rain. John Oberman was home from Germany after six years in the army and had opened a karate studio. Mary Beth Quinn, the oldest of eight sisters, had been valedictorian in her class at Leyden High. Once mousy and recessive, she now had platinum hair, wore bright red lipstick; she worked as office manager for a real estate lawyer, whose baby she was rumored to be carrying. Swinging hammers, pounding nails, cleaning gutters, installing flashing, several of the guests spent the working days high above the ground, and one by one they went into the yellow house where they paid their respects to Hat, who rarely left his room.

It was not clear exactly what was wrong with Hat, except to say that since falling from that tree he was not the same. Was it his back, his shoulder, his hip? It could have been he'd lost his nerve, haunted by the possibility of another mishap. Maybe he sensed his luck had run out on him. It was impossible to get him to talk about it. He pretended he hibernated out of choice, not exactly bedridden, not really housebound, but just *there*, his room filling up with an ever increasing accumulation of cups and saucers, magazines, shoes, boots, piles of clothes that Muriel laundered and folded for him but which he had yet to hang in his closet or place in his dresser, and boxes of rocks he had collected over the years and which he now intended to label and catalog. At least once a day, and sometimes two or three times, he tore a sheet from one of his notebooks and in his fragile handwriting made to-do lists for Jennings. They had not been explicit about this, but both father and son were becoming adjusted to the reality that from now on the work on the property would be done by a combination of Jennings's body and Hat's mind.

"Hey, Pop, you want me to get a couple of windows open for you?" Jennings said, letting himself into Hat's room. It was like a convection oven in there, a dry, pulsating heat, though Hat himself seemed oblivious to it. Fully dressed, washed, shaved, his hair combed, his boots laced up, a handkerchief folded neatly into his breast pocket, Hat was stretched out on his bed, reading *North and South* by John Jakes.

"Well, I'm afraid you've caught me reading a real potboiler," Hat said. "It comes highly recommended but what you essentially have here is an old-fashioned soap opera pretending to be history."

Hat held forth on the library book, which was wrapped in thick plastic like an old lady's couch—and Jennings was left with his fixed smile. There were times when he simply could not bear it. His father's love of all that culture seemed like a sad charade, a pretend passion that was useless and embarrassing, like falling in love with a photograph, or with someone who doesn't even know you're alive. Hat liked to wag and wave his finger when he listened to his beloved Beethoven, as if this music was in his blood, and he leaned forward and nodded judiciously when he watched some show about volcanoes or King Tut on Channel 13. And really what good had all these books and magazines and records and hours in museums done the old man? He had no money, his body had quit on him, and without his body, his hands, his strength, his good old-fashioned know-how, he was useless and without value, even to himself. And he was lonely. He and his daughter were not on speaking terms—one spanking was all it had taken! And his wife had been dead for so long he had in all likelihood half-forgotten her, or had allowed a thousand different impressions gleaned from poetry and painting to leech into the precious little pool of true recollection. "Your mother loved this poem," he often said, no longer daring to read so much as a line of it aloud to Jennings, but holding the Robert Burns book or the Gerard Manley Hopkins or the Tennyson, the Longfellow. And it was so clearly a fantasy, so clearly a steaming pile of horseshit. Dot Stratton did not love those poems. Dot Stratton loved Red Matthews, owner of Leyden Stone and Gravel, a married man with soft white hair all over his body like dandelion spores and eyes like bullet holes, for whom she worked as secretary and bookkeeper.

Jennings thrust a cold bottle of Genesee Cream Ale into Hat's hand. "You feeling okay, Pop?"

Hat accepted the beer without looking at it. It was his way of suggesting profound indifference, though he drained the entire bottle in two long swallows. "Brewed two hundred miles from where we sit right now," he said, gazing now at the bottle. "The water they use is from some of the most significant glacial lakes on the East Coast. This is water drawn from a source twenty-five fathoms deep. It's an inexpensive beer, a workingman's beer, but for my money it has qualities far superior to many of your German imports."

"Aren't you hot in here, Pop? How about I get this window open for you?"

"It's painted shut. You're going to have to go to the toolshed and get a putty knife, a finishing hammer, and a mallet. And a rag, too, don't forget the rag. When you use the mallet around the window frame, the rag will protect the paint."

"Let me just give her a try."

"I'm telling you it's stuck."

"I'm just going to turn around and give her a try," Jennings said. He was careful to explain because a few months ago he noticed one day that his father was not speaking to him at all, and in fact pretended to be asleep whenever Jennings came into the room. He let it ride for a few days and finally asked his father if something was wrong, to which Hat replied, *You turned your back on me while I was talking last week.*

Jennings jammed his fingers into the lift and pulled the window up. It offered practically no resistance.

"You got it!" Hat exclaimed.

"Yeah, you musta loosened her up."

"Must *have*," Hat said.

"All right, Pop. Whatever you like."

"It's not about what I like, Jennings. You know how they say a man who will kick a cat will beat a wife? The same goes for mangling the king's English."

"The king ain't here, Pop. Why don't you come down for a while? Jewel would get such a kick out of it."

"Jewel. I'm starting to get used to that name. It grows on you."

"Come on, Pop. It's Muriel's birthday."

"Sometimes I think our friends the Jehovah's Witnesses have the right idea about not celebrating birthdays."

Voices from a few of the guests flew into the room, as suddenly present as birds. The loudest was Larry Sassone's. "Slop some more sauce on the chicken tits," he called out cheerfully.

Hat fluttered his legs, rose up on his elbows, but did not leave the bed. "What's going on out there?" he asked.

"We made a fire pit for the cookout," Jennings said.

"In the hollow? Noise from the hollow carries straight to the big house. They can't be bellowing like a bunch of hopped-up Turks out there. You go down lickity split, mister, and make things right."

As Jennings made his way to quiet his friends at the fire pit, he cringed at the sound of their voices, so hard and boisterous, without nuance, all of them on the same audio errand: to be heard, to rise above the fray, to say, *My turn. Me! I'm here!*

"Hey, guys, guys, come on, you gotta keep it down," Jennings told them. "The sound goes right into their windows."

"Whose windows?" Ricky Smith asked. He was the oldest person at the party, over sixty. Though holding a string mop dripping with barbecue sauce, he nevertheless looked like a priest, with his scrubbed pink skin and snowy white muttonchops, and small eyes that twinkled like blue Christmas lights.

"We are ever so sorry," Sue Petersen said, ever so droll. Her face was flushed from the heat of the fire.

"At least my voice can get in that house," Larry said. "The rest of me would never get through the door." His belly pressed against the fabric of his jokey apron that said May I Toast Your Buns?

"Unless to fix something," said Sue. She had shiny black hair and a sun-blasted face. She'd become a widow at twenty, when her husband, a volunteer fireman, crashed his pickup racing to a chimney fire. She was with Larry now and worked with him painting houses.

Ricky made something of a show of pushing back his shirt sleeve to consult his wristwatch, which was nestled in a thicket of silvery hair. Ricky, day manager at Research Tech, feared he carried on his person an indelible rodent-y scent and wore copious quantities of cologne against it. "It's three in the afternoon," he said. "Don't we have rights?"

"I thought you and them were friends," Sue said. "And anyhow, it's your dad's property, right? You don't gotta big up to anyone."

They were joined by Todd Reynolds, who everyone called Horse—even his teachers, back in school. He loved horses and was rumored to be priapic. After high school he lived with his mother, a cashier at the Grand Union. He chipped in with money he made doing lawns, plowing driveways, selling firewood. But suddenly his life changed, first by marrying Candy Millas, who was distinctly unlike the girls he used to run with. Candy was quiet, prim, she'd been an A student, and would have gone to college if money was no object. And she was religious, the whole family was. They knew about holy days no one else had heard of. She never wore lipstick or any kind of makeup or jewelry, she wore clothes that hid her body, and a lot of people said she was a virgin. Right after marrying Candy, Horse decided to become a corrections officer, though he had hair down to his shoulder blades, was practically Rastafarian in his consumption of marijuana, and had a tattoo on his shoulder of the jaunty-looking dude from the Zig-Zag rolling papers package. In school, tests had irritated Horse, and brought out his rebellious streak—he had not been above writing Who cares? as an answer, and on standardized tests he would pick a letter, most often D, and just go with it start to finish. Yet he prepared for weeks for the civil service exam, and on the Saturday of the test he was in Albany an hour and a half early,

freshly barbered and shaved, in a jacket and tie, as if he already
had the job and was there reporting for work. For work in a federal
prison, there would have been hurdles he might not have scaled, but
for state work there were no problems with any of the requirements.
He had his high school diploma, he had his no felony convictions,
he had his good health. Shortly after the exam, he was a CO in
training, in Binghamton, with a salary of three hundred dollars a
week, good money. Candy stayed back in Leyden, where she was
starting a house-and-office cleaning service with five women from
her church. At the end of Horse's break-in period, he was assigned to
a maximum-security prison fifteen miles from Leyden, just over the
Robert Fulton Bridge, on the mountainous side of the river. He and
Candy could start living together like real married people, though
even with Horse up in Binghamton they still managed to have a
baby on the way.

"Hey, guess who's here," Horse said to Jennings. He stroked his
mustache, his consolation prize for surrendering his long hair. The
mustache itself was crisp and exuded none of the friendliness of a
civilian mustache. "Your landlady."

"Her husband's in Hollywood," Larry said. "A woman gets
lonely."

"Her husband's a piece of shit," offered Horse. He saw the look
on Jennings's face. "Guaranteed," he added, pointing at Jennings.

"Have you even met him?" Jennings said.

"Horse don't meet that many people," Larry said. "He spends
most of his time in jail." Not wanting to take a chance on Horse's
temper, Larry added, "Take a corner, Horse. We're gonna flip the
chicken tits."

Horse stepped back, and looked up, shielding his eyes. "Well,
looky looky looky," he said, as if uncovering some shameful wrong-
doing. He was following an airplane's flight path. "It's a Cessna 150,"
he said.

"A Cessna 150, huh," said Larry. "Sure it's not a 175?"

"You think it's a joke?" Horse asked. "We're under surveillance. All of us. Get it? You're under surveillance."

"Fuck me," Larry said, his default position.

"Could be DEA," Horse said. "Could be stateys, could be town clowns. Who the hell knows anymore, there's so much going on. Circles within circles, wheels inside of wheels."

"Maybe it's someone learning how to fly an airplane," Jennings said. "There's that Windsor Air Field close to here."

"Yeah, *maybe*," Horse said, in a tone that suggested Jennings was naive and pathetic. They flipped the chickens over and Ricky dipped the string mop into a big white stable bucket filled with barbecue sauce and painted the dozens of pieces of chicken—the excess sauce fell onto the burning wood, sending up plumes of smoke and licks of flame.

The plane emerged from the clouds and was beginning the long loop that would eventually bring it directly overhead. The three men watched silently as the Cessna made its way.

"Still think it's nothing?" Horse asked. He cupped his hands on either side of his mouth and shouted up at the plane. "We see you, motherfucker."

"Hey, come on," Jennings said. "There's kids."

"The thing is," Horse explained, "since Nixon ruled that we wouldn't be exchanging paper money for gold, we've had like a thousand percent increase in the number of unexplained small-craft airplanes right in this area, that's all I'm talking about, right here, right where you and I live, and no one's saying shit about it. Someone is watching us. Big Brother's got it all figured out. It's like a chess player thinking ten moves ahead, and we're all sitting here playing Chinese checkers with our thumbs up our ass."

"He can't swear in his own house. He saves it for when he's with us," said Larry, to no one in particular.

"You're sheep," Horse said. "People make decisions about your life and you don't even know it's happening. Who's pulling the

strings, man, don't you ever think about it? Why did they take us off
the gold standard? Whose idea was that? This is your money, folks.
And your money is your freedom. What gives anyone the right to
mess with you like that?" His new muscles were twitching in his
black T-shirt. "When Kennedy started asking questions about gold,
eighty-two days later there was a bullet in his brain. Eighty-two
days. And the whole Nixon thing, that whole Watergate impeach-
ment thing, well, that never made any sense. I was fucking seventeen
years old and I knew that for whatever reason they were kicking him
out of Washington had nothing to do with some stupid robbery.
What I didn't know was how it all tied in to the Federal Reserve.
Gold. The whole history of the world is about gold."

As if to demonstrate the unending reign of gold, Grace wandered over to the fire pit, with little gold crescents studded into her
earlobes. She wore a long white dress; there was a sprig of lilac in
her hair. David was on her hip, naked beneath his blue Oshkosh
overalls, his cheeks flushed, his expression unnervingly solemn. He
seemed nearly half the size of his mother, like a child in an old painting.

"Wow, look at you guys," Grace said. "This is primal."

"Sorry for the noise," Jennings said.

"And look at you, Jennings," Grace said. "You and little David
are dressed the same." Her voice was deep and soft and undressed.
"Where's Muriel?" she asked.

"She's around," Jennings said, with a vague wave.

"We brought her a present," she said. She handed David over to
Jennings without asking and pulled a small canvas from the beige-
and-blue bag that hung from her shoulder.

"A painting," Jennings said. David, resting his head against Jennings, seemed soothed by Jennings's body heat, and appeared to be
falling asleep.

"So what is it?" Horse asked.

Grace had the eight-by-ten-inch canvas turned toward herself
and she inspected it, frowning. Her fingers gripped the stretcher

bars; an absurd overabundance of staples fixed the canvas to the frame. Reluctantly, she turned the canvas around so Jennings could see. "It's not very good."

"It's amazing," Jennings said. The colors were dark, the overall impression somewhat melancholy, though the image was one of childish fantasy: a dark brown rabbit holding some kind of blue-and-yellow jewel in its paws. The craft was painstaking, perfect, a photograph of a world of make-believe. The background was a fenced garden brimming with sumptuous vegetables, and sitting in a lawn chair near the garden was a man snoozing with a book on his lap. The man looked like an older, plumper version of Thaddeus, but with hooves.

"She can just put it in a drawer or something. These days I only make small paintings for easy storage."

"No way. This goes right up on the wall. This goes . . . I don't know. It's really good. It's . . ." He tried to think of something you could say about a painting that didn't mention *pretty* or *beautiful*, something that showed some appreciation of the work, the art of it, the secret language it spoke.

"Really? That's so nice of you."

"I'm not being nice. It's so real, it kind of scrambles the brain there."

"I wish someone would scramble my brains," she said, handing the painting to him and taking David back. He was drowsy and seemed not to register the transfer. One of his little red sneakers was about to slip off. "It's kind of hard taking my painting seriously," Grace said. "I never seem to have enough time. Which is insane. All I *have* is time."

"But you're really good," Jennings said. "My aunt Lorraine is a really good artist, but you're way beyond what she can do."

The guys around the fire pit stood watching them, their eyes going left to right, like spectators at a tennis match.

"I'm glad you like it. Makes me happy," said Grace.

"Let's find Muriel and show her," said Jennings. They made

their way across the newly mown lawn, which Jennings had cut according to his father's specifications. Grace was tiring from David's weight on her right hip and attempted to switch him over to the left without breaking stride. She glanced over her shoulder and noticed her house, her grand house, with its chimneys and porches, and tall windows, looming in the distance like an ocean liner riding the waves.

Someone turned a radio up, a furiously androgynous voice rose up singing: *She says I am the one / but the kid is not my son.*

"If I were Michael Jackson I might not be so fast to deny paternity," Grace said. But the joke suddenly felt cheap, like imitation gold that turns green when it is touched by human warmth. "How many chances is he going to have?" she added, as the sound of the radio disappeared.

"Funny," Jennings said.

The disappointment of that somehow emboldened her. She was like a gambler who responds to a loss by doubling the next bet.

"Remember the night?" she asked. "When your dad fell?"

"Sure. Of course."

"I saw you sitting by yourself. I mean when he got up and did his dance."

A silence, except for the sound of their feet on the grass. "Maybe if he'd just lain still he wouldn't be so fucked up now."

"You looked . . ." She didn't want to say *humiliated*, and she searched for another word.

"I know," Jennings said. "I was." He knew what word she was going to say and didn't want to say it, either. "We understand each other" is what he wanted to say, and he did.

"Yeah." They continued walking, but suddenly everything had changed. The external world was less important than the internal, what was buried more present than the seen. "Thaddeus doesn't understand what it feels like to just be cringing over how the world treats your mother or your father. Even my own brother doesn't get it. Liam loves her, our mother, but he never felt that . . . frustration. I saw it that night, in you."

He thumped his belly, and smiled at Grace. "I'm going to get rid of this. This really ain't me."

They passed beneath a tree whose branches were heavy with small white flowers, each trembling in the wind, awaiting the bees' arrival. Life goes on, the real story, though we think it's about us. Jennings snapped off a twig and gave it to Grace.

"Thank you." She held out the twig. "What is this? An apple tree?"

"Mountain ash."

"Me," David said. Suddenly alert, he reached for the twig as if for an ice-cream cone.

"I dreamed about you last night," Grace said suddenly, as if the memory of it had just come to her, though, in fact, she had been thinking of it all day.

"You did?"

"Sorry. Stupid thing to say. I can't stand people who talk about their dreams."

"I'm complimented," Jennings said, his voice rather stiff. "Should I be?"

Emboldened, Grace asked, "When we first met? What was the first thing you thought when you met me?"

Without hesitation, Jennings said, "You seemed like someone who didn't have a friend in the world. Except for Thaddeus, I mean. Except for him."

"Yeah. I never really got the hang of it. For me, if you're not with someone a hundred percent, then what's the point? I've got this all or nothing thing and it doesn't really work. Out in the world. But I'm okay with it." She forced herself to stop, though she felt she could have gone on talking about herself for another hour.

They were near the pond that now belonged to Hat. All around the shore, Jennings and Muriel had created a funky little paradise, with plaster lions, striped canvas chairs, old beach umbrellas. The grass in spring was a carpet of wildflowers almost indistinguishable from the swarms of butterflies that hovered above them. A thick honey-colored rope had been tied to a low-hanging willow branch and a guy in cutoff jeans and a tank top swung from it and let go over the center of the pond, shrieking with happiness when he hit the water.

Why wasn't she happier herself? The deep, green scent of spring filled the air. When she had first heard someone say that April was the cruelest month of all she thought they were full of shit. If your father is taking pictures for a girly mag, December can be as tough as April—it's when the centerfold might be wearing a Santa hat. And a tipsy depressed mother knows no season. But she was young at the time and didn't realize that when you lost some of your hope and it seemed that most of your stupid fucking dreams were not going to come true, spring was a mockery. Mating season for all that lives. Regeneration? Fresh start? What a joke. But there was David, actually smelling the little flowers of the mountain ash, with the sunlight touching his golden curly hair. And Jennings. Jennings. She felt a slow, sensuous turning within her, radiating down to her legs, up to the back of her throat. Oh! Enthralled and unnerved, Grace stumbled upon her own longing as if it were the beautiful cottage she used to call home, but now she was afraid to open the door and find it uninhabitable. She loathed her own unhappiness. It made her want to shake herself. It was such a waste—a waste of what was left of her youth, a waste of good fortune. Look at all she had. A beautiful son, healthy, smart, *alive*, an adoring husband. She could rise from their bed and look out the window and there was the river, like a shining blue-and-silver scarf dropped from heaven. And still unhappy? It meant there was something wrong with you, you were mad, you were absurd—and how dare you? And that fucking Rilke poem! How many times had she read it, biting back tears, her head spinning, dizzy from the vertigo of self-reproach? One night, hoping to illuminate her own state of mind, she read the poem to Thaddeus.

It was like confessing, she may as well have been on her knees, she may as well have been weeping. He listened with hands folded, his head bowed, making a small show of his reverence for literature. When the poem ended with that stark, urgent, passionate, admonishing line—"You must change your life"—her voice quavered, but she got through it. Thaddeus lifted his head, raised his eyebrows. "Well, I don't see it as a movie," he joked. "Unless we can get Richard Gere for Apollo." He happened to notice her expression—the shock of a tricked child—and he tried to salvage the moment. "I wonder what it's like in the original German," he'd said. "I never know if I should trust a translation."

You idiot, she did not say. *What's happened to you?*

Muriel, lounging near the pond, waved when she saw Jennings and Grace. Raised in an arid zone, where the sky was ochre and the dust stung your face, she was mad for water now, and yet she did not have a proper bathing suit. She could not shake the idea that a bathing suit was a luxury, like a silk nightgown or a platter with indentations you used for deviled eggs maybe twice a year. So she was in gym shorts and a T-shirt, soaked through. You could see the shadow of her pubic hair, indistinct but present, like voices from another room. One of her friends, Jill, sitting on the ground with a towel tied around her lower half, her knees open so that the material concaved into a kind of bassinet, tended to naked Jewel, feeding her blueberries and making funny little sounds to amuse her: "Bungy bungy bungy." Jewel thrust her baby arms and legs stiffly out, as if she were being electrocuted by pleasure.

They were no more than fifty feet from the pond. Jennings gazed at his wife, Jewel, Jill, and the others as if they were angels. Were his eyes bright with tears, or was that the sun, directly overhead? "These are the good old days," he murmured.

What would it be like, Grace wondered, to be with a man who enjoyed life in such a conscious, direct way, who ran his hand over it like a table freshly planed?

"You guys swim in that pond?" Grace asked. "I'm scared to."

"We always have. What are you scared of?"

"I don't know. What lives in there? Fish and turtles and who knows what. Is it deep?"

"In the middle. You should use it when the weather's better. There's nothing like a pond."

"I'm not a swimmer. I'd sink. Drown. That would be it."

"I've taught a lot of people how to swim."

"I can sort of swim," Grace said.

"I could teach you how to swim so you wouldn't be afraid. Here. You give it to her," Jennings said, handing the painting to Grace and taking David out of her arms. David relaxed in Jennings's arms, looking up at him with a serious expression. He showed Jennings the twig from the mountain ash, which had already lost most of its little white flowers.

"Hi, Grace," Muriel said, with the extra energy and emphasis of a shy person.

"Woman to woman?" Grace said. "I think mothers ought to get presents every damn day. For what we went through giving birth, our bodies ripped to shreds."

Muriel smiled uncertainly. "Oh, little Jewel just slipped right out of me, easy as pie."

"Wow," Grace said. "You're so lucky. I'm just not built that way." The remark might have been too personal. *Oh my God,* Grace thought, *not cool.* "Anyhow, I brought you a present. It's really pretty stupid."

"Oh, you didn't have to do that," Muriel said. She leaned over to take her daughter out of Jill's lap. Her long honey-colored hair swayed, a bit of knobby spine showed, her hamstrings tightened. Grace glanced over to see Jennings staring at his wife, who looked like she could try out for the hippie Olympics. This cop's daughter, so wan, so seemingly shy, still knew the way to swing and sway her body like a hypnotist's pocket watch.

Grace tried to give the painting to Muriel, but she wouldn't take it until she thoroughly dried her hands. There was a striped blue-and-white towel on the bank of the pond, and she bent deeply, balletically. It was as if the bend opened her and her loveliness emerged. Grace had had no idea how beautiful Muriel was—she had been misled by the shyness, the few crooked teeth, the pregnancy, the shapeless gingham dresses. When her hands were dry, she approached Grace again and said, "I never had a real oil painting in a frame."

She put her hands together prayerfully and bowed.

You've got to be kidding me, thought Grace.

"Actually, it's acrylic," she said, handing it to Muriel. "Safer for Jewel, in case she decides to eat it."

"Oh no, no, we'll take real good care of this. Oh Jiminy Cricket, look at this! This is so nice. Trippy. Will you get a load of this crazy rabbit. You are really a great artist, Grace, I mean it."

Jewel made a little yearning noise, seeing David in Jennings's arms. The two children reached for each other, their fingers waggling up and down. David's tongue was out. It made him look insane.

"Okay, you two," Muriel said. She put Jewel down onto the grass and David squirmed until Jennings set him down, too.

Jill struggled to her feet and looked admiringly at the painting. "You did this?" she asked Grace. She seemed aggressive but without malice. Perhaps her amazement was meant to be flattering. Maybe she was one of those people who gives you a shove as a way of saying they're glad to see you.

"Yeah," Grace said. "It's not very good."

A little splash from the pond, and Grace's heart seized for a moment. The babies! She could see them in dread's cavernous imaginary theater, little balls of formed flesh sinking slowly through the muck. But David and Jewel were right there, three feet away, safe and sound on their hands and knees in the soft grass, more or less motionless, their foreheads pressed together. It took Grace a moment to regain her composure.

When she looked up, Jennings was smiling. She guessed that he knew what had just passed through her mind.

"I can make you a studio," he said. "If you want. It would be easy to do, if you ever wanted."

"I just work wherever," Grace said. "But thanks."

"I was talking to Thaddeus about it."

"You were?"

"Yeah. He said it was fine with him, if that's what you wanted."

"He did, huh. Well, that's very nice of him. Can I ask you a question? Why would you talk this over with Thaddeus before me?"

Jennings looked unperturbed. "Just did, I guess," he said.

"Well, it's very nice of you. I mean to even be thinking about me and where I do my work. My work is meaningless, but I do love it. I've been doing it since I was little. It's when I'm happiest." She looked away. The last remark had slipped out. She might come to regret it and she might not; it all depended upon where it led.

"The red building just north of the house?" Jennings said. "They used to keep chickens in it when I was a kid. Wouldn't cost much."

"We've got a lot of rooms, Jennings. Right in the house."

"I guess a studio's something else," he said.

"Well, maybe someday I will be worthy of it."

"You want to know a secret?" he said, his voice low.

She knew what he was going to say. He was going to say he had fallen in love with her. No, that wouldn't be it. He'd never say that. He might never have said anything like that his whole life. He was going to say something by which she could infer his feelings. He was going to say something along the lines of *Sometimes I dream about you, too.* He was going to say he'd never met anyone quite like her. He was going to ask her if she'd ever do a painting of him.

"Promise not to tell anyone?" Jennings asked.

"I promise," she whispered.

"I'm looking for extra work because Muriel's going to have another baby," he said.

It was as if she had stepped off a ledge, felt nothing but air beneath her feet, and had one final second of consciousness before the fatal plunge. Grace gathered herself. Her strength was that she had never really expected to be happy. But still. She felt wounded, excluded. But why would she be wounded, and why excluded? Excluded from what? It made no sense, but there it was: the things you feel before you have a chance to think, and smooth everything over on a grinding wheel made of words.

"Really? We might be having another kid, too," she said, a lie not unlike one she'd told as an eleven-year-old girl in Eau Claire when her boyfriend confessed he had kissed Pamela Zeiring and she tried to preserve her dignity with an inscrutable smile, saying it was all right he'd kissed Pam, in fact it was sort of a relief because she'd been cheating, too.

TO: LIAM CORNELL/NOSARA, COSTA RICA

June 4, 1983

Dearest Liam,

Are you going to be there for a while? I want to see those monkeys, too. I want to get those fantastic massages. I want to swim in warm salty water. I think my problem is rich people. I know they're everywhere, but up here in Brigadoon there's not a lot of people so it just feels like rich bastards are EVERYWHERE. I like the poor ones. I think they might be the natural audience for the kind of art I make. Too bad they don't go to galleries or even give a shit about the stupid art world.

Liam, I am really unhappy. I hate money. I hate what it buys and what it can't buy but thinks it can. I can feel myself turning into a hideous creature, the cold abandoned wife, the bored mother, the failed artist. Thaddeus is gone more than he's here, which makes me insane and I end up wishing he was gone even more. Now he wants to buy an apartment in New York. He might not want to be here any more than I want him. I can sense his loneliness and restlessness. It's like a smell, a bad smell. He's going to leave me, or maybe I'll leave him. But if I do, it'll mainly be to get there first. I'm not going to be the one who gets dumped. Me as a single parent. Very scary indeed. T as a single parent, even on weekends? Terrifying. He's more like his mother than he will ever know. Meanwhile, he's wondering, Hey, I make all this money, I work all the time, how come no one appreciates me? He needs constant encouragement and applause. Last time he was home he wanted to do something I found a little distasteful and when I said, Hey, let's not and say we did, he stormed out of our room, and I found him twenty minutes later in the west parlor sitting in the dark and crying his eyes out like someone just backed out of the driveway and ran over his cat.

Liam! We're trapped. If he stops working we'll lose the house and be thrown into a little life with just each other for support, and we've already wrecked things so much we might not be able to survive that kind of change, but the longer we stay in this house and live this kind of life the more wrecked everything gets. Right now, if we had to give it up we'd have maybe a 50–50 chance of survival. So we hang on, because 50–50 is pretty scary if you're talking about survival, but next year our odds of surviving a big downward swoop will be ever worse. Maybe this is all my fault. Maybe if I was as insanely busy as he was, and maybe if I made some money we'd be able to look each other in the eye. But I am making my art and he's way across the house but I hear him anyhow, haw-hawing on the phone with his agent or pacing back and forth waiting for Robert Redford to call. Then he gets tired and I can feel his attention turning to me, like a mongoose that sees there's still one chicken left, and he says in his weary woe-is-me voice, Let's go to bed.

When can David and I come down there? I'll do all the cooking and it's time for your nephew to get to know his cool uncle.

Grace

Chapter 9

Raising Money for a Lost Cause

AUGUST 13, 1984

NEW YORK CITY
THE DEMOCRATIC PARTY AND THE
NEW YORK ARTISTS' COALITION

A Cocktail Party for Walter Mondale and Geraldine Ferraro
The next President and Vice President of the United States

Donation 250 Dollars
Cocktails, Nibbles
And a Surprise Guest

RSVP to the New York Artists' Coalition 212–4____

Hurry!

THADDEUS WONDERED IF THE GIRLS WERE OF DRINKING age. One thing seemed certain: they were Republicans. At least he thought they were. He'd overheard one of them saying something affectionate about Ronald Reagan. What had once been a punch line—that cipher becoming president—was about to become another four years. Whatever they were, the girls stirred his hunger for a human touch. They had peach lips and freckles, they wore black slacks and white button-down shirts. They had a way about them that made you think they were doing you a favor whenever they poured a drink. Maybe it was because they had to bartend a party in a sea of well-heeled liberals. Out there in the world, on the blazing-hot sex-drunk streets of New York, the girls might not be noticeable, but here in his seldom-used New York apartment, filled with media business types willing to spend two hundred bucks on gin and cheese, they were riveting in their pure insolent beauty.

Thaddeus sidled next to his agent, Josh Zoller, who was being served an ironic gin and tonic. Zoller had just arrived from his summer house in Bridgehampton dressed in tennis shorts and a Polo shirt, with a pale blue sweater tied around his shoulders, though it was scorching hot outside. His thinning hair revealed a sunburned scalp, and his nose was peeling.

"Rumor has it that you're shopping around for a new agent," Zoller said, wasting no time. Known for his directness, he took off like a helicopter, straight up and away.

"Where'd you hear that?" Thaddeus asked.

"You haven't been talking to other agents?"

"Hey, I don't know who the fuck I'm talking to half the time."

"That's weak, Thaddeus. It's a small world. I hear things, you know."

"You hear rumors," Thaddeus said.

"Here's the thing about rumors—most of the time they're true. Don't let your friendliness get you into trouble. You can't like everybody and everyone can't like you. Don't be naive. These people are sniffing around because you're currently making money. Sorry to be the voice of common sense here, but that's how it is. Anyhow, where's Grace?" Zoller frowned, contemplating the possibility that Thaddeus was not only a man who would deep-six his loyal agent, but who'd also ditch his own wife.

"In dear old Leyden." Thaddeus was going to elaborate about why—David was being difficult, or maybe David had a cold, or Grace was tired, or the nanny went back to El Salvador. But Grace simply didn't feel like coming down to the city and didn't give a damn about the election. She refused to see the importance of what was happening in the country, of how the Reagans had given greed a deviously benign face, of how unions were being crushed, and trees caused pollution. Even the Democrats nominating a woman for vice president failed to galvanize Grace. She could not get past her initial insight that Thaddeus offering their pied-à-terre for a Democratic fund-raiser was a career move on his part, or perhaps a way of proving to his parents and himself and to whoever else might be keeping score that all those absurd Hollywood paychecks hadn't changed his values. He gave houses away and he hosted fund-raisers! What more could those scurrilous old Trots want of him?

"I tried to interest her in a Mondale fund-raiser, but no such luck," Thaddeus said. *Oh Grace, Grace.* Right now, even hearing someone say her name agitated Thaddeus. With every emotional inch she moved away from him, he longed for her more.

"I think of this as a party for Geraldine Ferraro," said a voice behind him, a woman's voice. "I'm here for Gerry."

Thaddeus turned toward the voice, reminding himself to *Stop smiling, goddamnit, for once in your life.* The speaker was Ann Rosenzweig, who ran United Artists' small New York office. Thaddeus was fond of her and didn't know anyone who wasn't, but she was, in terms of the movie business, strictly a dead letter, with authority to reject pitches and scripts, and none to accept them. She was dressed in a shimmering gray skirt and a white silk blouse. She had large, rather comical ears, which she emphasized with clunky, humorous earrings.

"Honestly, Ann?" Thaddeus said. "I'm stoked about Ferraro. A woman vice president? It would be amazing." He patted his chest, as if his heart was swelling. "If the money we make here tonight can help put a woman in the White House, then I will truly believe I have helped do something worthwhile in my lifetime."

He was surprised by how moved he was by his own expression of sentiment, since the Mondale candidacy was hopeless, and nominating a woman for vice president was a kind of Hail Mary pass. Mondale was a hack, but at least he was humane—a union guy who'd rather do the right thing than screw you over. The Reagan Republicans were different from the Republicans of Thaddeus's childhood, the grocers and the small-town pharmacists, the biddies and the bigots and the Babbitts and the Buckleys. Though Reagan was elderly, the Republicans seemed suddenly young, a new breed who seemed to be working out, slimming down, catching up with the culture, having sex, getting high, while the Dems looked pudgy and exhausted, trudging around the convention center pumping their placards up and down like pistons in an engine running on fumes. One thing remained constant, though: the Republicans were the party of the rich. Yet wasn't Thaddeus himself rather on the rich side of things? At least statistically? Didn't he have a lot to show for himself, and a lot to lose? Did he really want inflation and higher taxes? Did he really want the government's hand in his pocket? Did he want to start schlepping his own suitcase? Not out of liberal gallantry, but because there would be no one there to take it out of his hands.

He ran his fingers through his hair. He was losing touch with what he believed about any given issue. Everything was confusing, verging on the freakish: on the one hand this, on the other hand that, and on the *other* other hand this and that. His life was a crash course in indeterminacy. Pages were written, pages were revised, pages were thrown away. You were hired, fired, promises made, promises broken. You were not supposed to complain, you were not even really supposed to notice.

Ann was with a good-looking man with a Weimar haircut. He spoke languidly, his posture careless. "But Ferarro's husband," he said. "Isn't everyone saying he's mobbed up? John Zaccaro, aka Johnny Z?"

"He's a businessman," Ann said. "And before that he was a Marine."

"Sounds like Michael Corleone," Thaddeus said.

Ann laughed and said, "You," by which she could have meant You jerk or That was such a *you* thing to say.

He was sorry he'd made the joke. "Don't get me wrong." It was a phrase he was using with increasing frequency. "I like her. She's from Newburgh, not so far from where I live."

"Where you live?" Ann exclaimed. "Then what's this?"

"This is extra," Thaddeus said.

"Lucky you." She gestured, encompassing the apartment—the second floor of a Federal town house on Horatio Street. With its whitewashed plaster, polished oak floors, practical furniture, and shallow hearth filled in the summer with eucalyptus branches.

"Well, we'll see how long it lasts."

A man in his forties, tall, balding, with seething eyebrows, a military posture, held a drink in one hand and a napkin filled with canapés in the other. He shoved the canapés into his jacket and extended his hand to Thaddeus.

"This is your joint, right?" he said. "You're Thaddeus Kaufman."

"Welcome. Thanks for coming."

"And you wrote *Hostages*, right?"

"I guess."

"You guess?"

"I wrote it, yes."

"I'm a lawyer, and I'm representing a whole bunch of folks who worked on the set of your movie. Car parkers. Are you aware of any of this?"

"Not really. It's amazing how many jobs a movie can create, though. That's sort of great."

"If the jobs are decent. If the jobs don't strip a man of his most basic human dignity. My clients were hired to hold parking spots for production trailers. Their job was to sit in a car for five, ten, sometimes fifteen hours, so when the production needs the space it's there for them. They just have to sit there. Pretty easy work, huh? Except they cannot leave the car. That's the thing. Leave your car and you're fired. So what happens when you're holding a spot for a director or a movie star or some big shot? I'll tell you. I have a client who lost three toes. Frostbite. I have clients who were relieving themselves in bottles and bags. And I've got two from El Salvador without papers and they are *still* waiting to be paid."

"That's horrible."

"So? Can you help us out?"

"What do you mean?"

"Were you on set? What did you see?"

"I didn't see anything."

"And you didn't know anything about it?"

"How could I know?"

"Yeah, how could you know? That's what they all say." The lawyer reached into his jacket and pulled out his card, handed it to Thaddeus. Thaddeus put it into his shirt pocket without looking at it.

The five-room apartment normally looked neglected, but this evening it had an air of elegance, filled as it was with affluent Democrats. Curious to see if this party was going to be worth the effort, Thaddeus had called someone at the New York Artists' Coalition, an organization for people in the local media business who wanted to pitch in on liberal causes, and under whose auspices this evening's fund-raiser was being held, and asked how many people were expected. He'd been told that 105 people had RSVP'd yes, and at $250 a person that was a respectable haul, enough to pay for tens of thousands of leaflets, possibly enough to put one under every windshield wiper in the city. Who knew? Maybe Mondale could pull off a miracle . . .

Suddenly a crash of cymbals, loud enough to be heard over the noise of the party. Startled, Thaddeus turned toward the noise. Kitchen. Kitchen? It took a few extra moments to realize what he had heard was the sound of many, many glasses shattering, to the accompanying rattle of a dropped tray.

THE CRASH HAD MOMENTARILY CAST a haze of relative quiet over the party, but by the time Thaddeus reached the kitchen the cross talk and the laughter had resumed. Small, with only one window, the kitchen was separated from the rest of the apartment by a swinging door, and when Thaddeus pushed through, it hit the heel of Susan Fialkin from the New York Artists' Coalition.

"Sorry," Thaddeus said.

"Oh there you are," Fialkin said. She was the Coalition's sole staff member. Inefficient, harried, confrontational, and unkind, her employment was a mystery to Thaddeus.

One of the bartenders was slouched against the sink. Her face was pale, and her eyes were bright red. Countless broken glasses were spread over the blue-and-white tiles—the wineglasses, bowl, stem, and foot, the cocktail glasses in great shards. Some of the broken glass had landed on the table, and possibly found its way onto the trays of hors d'oeuvres—they'd have to be disposed of. A stocky, impatient-looking looking man in his thirties, with a broad, Eastern European face and salt-and-pepper hair, was quietly berating the bartender, whose nerves were as shattered as the glasses she had dropped.

"You can't put too many on. How many times do I say this? Nine? Twenty?"

"I didn't," the girl managed to say.

"No?" her boss said, pointing to the floor.

"You're not hurt, are you?" Thaddeus asked. But she seemed not to have heard him. Her attention was completely in the grip of her boss, like an animal in a trap.

"Okay," Susan Fialkin said. "Let's just get this cleaned up. We've got a lot of party to get through." Turning toward Thaddeus, she asked, "Broom?"

"Broom?" he asked.

"And a dustpan. Something."

He thought for a moment. He was quite sure he had a broom and a dustpan, but he couldn't say where they were. He noticed a narrow closet to the left of the refrigerator.

"Did you look in there?" he asked.

Evidently, the door had not been opened in some time; he had to give it a vigorous tug, and when it finally opened there was no broom inside, or anything else that would be of use. It was full of brown paper bags from D'Agostino, a nearby supermarket. Thaddeus remembered shopping at D'Agostino only a couple of times since purchasing the apartment. There was no way he could have accumulated so many shopping bags. They must have been left there by the previous owner, a U.N. translator named Lawrence Winnick, who was leaving New York after the death of his boyfriend from the "gay cancer." Thaddeus had liked genial, soft-spoken Winnick, but now felt a twist of fury at him—what kind of person leaves a bunch of Dag bags stuffed in the closet?

"No broom here," Thaddeus said, closing the door, and then kneeing it shut even tighter.

"We're going to need something," Fialkin said. She moved a chunk of glass with the toe of her tan shoe. She moved it an inch, and another inch, and then kicked it hard, sending it skittering across the floor.

"What are you doing?" asked Thaddeus.

"I'm standing in a kitchen with a man who doesn't know where to find a broom in his own apartment."

"I'm not even sure I have a broom, Susan. What is the big deal?"

"Sweeping. How do things get swept?"

"The housekeeper," he said. He moved a little closer to her, wanting her to know that he was getting angrier. "Obviously." He had donated the use of his apartment out of the goodness of his heart, and suddenly this *mieskeit* is treating him like a sociopath because he can't locate a broom?

"I'm sure you have a broom somewhere in this very beautiful apartment," Fialkin said, holding her ground. "Or a mop? A mop would do."

"Susan, I'm sorry. I'm helpless, okay? I'm pathetic. I'll look around. It's not that big a place."

The other young bartender clattered through the door, carrying a broom; it seemed to Thaddeus that the dark green shaft and bright yellow head were much larger than what you'd find on an ordinary broom. In her other hand she carried a gleaming copper dustpan, also oversize.

"Wow, those are some high-end cleaning implements," Thaddeus said.

The supervisor, who had, while Thaddeus and Susan discussed the broom, gone from berating the girl who'd dropped the glasses to discussing upcoming jobs with her, stepped forward and immediately began berating the second girl, even though she had somehow come up with the mysterious broom.

"Well, I guess this is under control," Thaddeus said to no one in particular, backing out of the kitchen, and resisting the temptation to ask a stranger where his broom closet was.

But wasn't that the whole purpose of success? he counseled himself. *To not know these things?*

THE CATERING STAFF CONTINUED TO circulate hors d'oeuvres, but the bar was now self-serve. Thaddeus looked around his apartment. For the most part these were agents and assistants, producers, publicists. There *were* a few familiar faces. Jerzy Kosiński was there, thin and impeccable. Every few minutes, like a soldier blindly firing his rifle over the top of his foxhole, he raised a small camera over his head and snapped a picture.

A woman from Governor Cuomo's office addressed the guests, making a couple of jokes about the governor's famous reluctance to spend a night away from Albany, and reminding them that "this up-

coming election is perhaps the most important election of our lifetime." She was an imposing dark woman in a sleeveless green dress.
When she was finished she introduced Ed Asner. Stocky, balding,
he had recently fallen; he had a black eye and a large bandage on his
chin, and he leaned on a dark red cane.

"I saw Michael Jackson doing that moonwalking thing of his
and wanted to try it myself," Asner explained, and glowed with pleasure when the line got a laugh, as if an old dear friend had wandered
into the room. In his brief remarks, he seemed less interested in talking about Mondale than in going after Lee Iacocca, the auto exec
whose book had been a bestseller all that year. "When auto execs get
treated like rock and roll stars, you know a country is in trouble."
He went on to defend actors and other people in the creative community who got involved in politics, thumping the black rubber tip
of his cane against the floor as he demolished a series of straw men
who would want to deny entertainers their constitutional right to
affect national policy. It was an odd argument, Thaddeus thought,
since Mondale was in fact running against an actor.

"Question?" a voice from the crowd called out, managing to
pack that one word with an overflow of irony.

It was Kip. Oh shit.

"Who can turn the world on with her smile?" Kip asked.

There were a few laughs, but mainly the room was uncomfort-
ably quiet.

"Who in God's fuck are you?" Asner rumbled. His small dark
eyes scanned the room, squinting as though he were looking past
stage lights.

"And I'm also curious about this whole taking a nothing day and
making it all seem worthwhile," Kip added. "Curious how that is
achieved. What with all that's going on."

Asner's face reddened, making his fringe of cottony hair look
all the whiter. There was something joyful and Christmassy about
his coloring, though his expression was murderous. "We're here because we care about our country," Asner said. "We're not here to

fuck around like a bunch of children. This is a very important election and we're here because we are tired—and ashamed of!—having thieves and murderers run our government. You want to play little piss-pot games? Go to the playground. You understand me?"

Thaddeus wound his way through the tightly packed room and took Kip by the elbow. He hadn't seen him in months—Kip had suddenly left E.F. Hutton and moved to Bangkok without saying good-bye, returning just that week to begin work at Paine Webber.

"Kip, what are you doing? Are you drunk?"

"I don't think so. Why? Are you?" Kip asked, genially. He placed his hand gently on Thaddeus's cheek.

"No."

"Well, maybe I am." He held a glass with a look that seemed to say, *What are we going to do about this incorrigible troublemaker of an empty glass?*

"You need to be quiet," Thaddeus said, momentarily destabilized by Kip's touch, the warmth of it, the suddenness.

"You're so out of it, my friend," Kip said. "Both of you in that stupid house in that ridiculous little town. You live in your own world and you have no fucking idea what's going on."

Several of the guests standing closest to Thaddeus and Kip needed to register their disapproval of Kip's remarks. One young man was practically shaking with rage. "Do you want four more years of Reagan?" he asked in a furious whisper. "Is that what you want?"

"I think my question to Mr. Asner was legitimate," Kip said, drawing himself up to his full height.

"We're trying to do some good here, Kip," Thaddeus said, his teeth clenched. Asner had gone back to his speech, but the people close by seemed more interested in what Kip and Thaddeus were saying.

"Oh please. It's hopeless. It's all hopeless. You're such a . . ." Kip searched for a word to convey his contempt. "Do-gooder. And like all do-gooders, you're selfish. But here's a bulletin for you, old pal.

The meek do not and will not inherit the earth. The meek are going to do what the meek have always done, which is eat shit and die."

"Kip. Please. What's happening here?"

Kip shook his head. "Sorry. I don't mean to spoil the party." He fixed Thaddeus with a furious stare. "A friend of mine is dying."

"Oh God. Who?"

"No one you know." For a moment, it looked as if he might touch Thaddeus's face again, but instead he patted his shoulder dismissively. "Ergo, not your problem."

Meanwhile, Ed Asner concluded his remarks with a request that everyone join together for a verse of "Solidarity Forever." The old union anthem borrowed the melody from "The Battle Hymn of the Republic," but few people present knew the words, so basically it was Asner singing by himself. He didn't seem to mind, and when it was over he thrust his fist into the air. "*Viva La Raza!*"

"*Viva La Raza!*" the crowd replied, and when Thaddeus looked around, Kip was gone.

EVENTUALLY, EVERYONE LEFT, EXCEPT FOR the caterers. The two bartenders walked through carrying crates of steaming clean glasses down to the van. The girls looked tired and unself-conscious, shirts out, covering their sweet Republican derrieres. Thaddeus felt his heart beating despicably in his throat.

The second girl out, the one who had dropped the tray of glasses, might have felt his gaze upon her, sensed his dubious intentions, and turned to glance at him, mainly as a way of confirming her instincts—she was still learning to protect herself from men. She hurried to catch up with her coworker and Thaddeus heard her say, *I feel horrible. I forgot to take my medicine.* A feeling of desolation washed over him.

He went to the kitchen. The leftover booze was apparently for him. He poured a large dose of Stolichnaya. He raised his glass to

commemorate the years he had been consigned to drink vodka with
names like Prince Igor or Dudley's. He had read an annoying piece
in a magazine, claiming that in blind tastings a panel of experts
rated some of the cheap vodkas higher than the pricey ones, but
Thaddeus did not believe it. Such findings contradicted his experience and his faith.

How was he ever going to get through the rest of this night on
his own?

The phone rang, and he hurried to answer it. He had a premonition, which was really no more than a wish, that it was Grace. Grace
to the rescue, calling to assume her rightful place at the center of his
universe. She would be calling to convince him to drive home and
promising to wait up for him. Hint, hint. Or perhaps she was about
to tell him that Doris had agreed to spend the night with David and
that Grace herself was just packing a bag and would be walking up
the steps to the Horatio Street apartment in under two hours. Or
perhaps she was just going to speak loads of lovely filth to him while
he got himself off and she pretended to do the same.

But the call was from Neal Kosoff. Thaddeus supposed the director was a friend, but was always aware that it's called the movie
business not the movie *friendship*, so you couldn't be beguiled by the
flattery, humor, and abundant charms of these people. Helping in
this unsentimental education was his being replaced on *Hostages* by
other writers (finally six of them, in rapid succession), while Kosoff,
who he had originally thought of as an ally, and a kind of partner,
sat idly by. Thaddeus assumed he would never hear from Kosoff after
that, but these guys had no shame and Kosoff's friendliness never
abated. Not only was there that elaborate housewarming present in
the person of Buddy Klein, but there were numerous requests for
Thaddeus's opinions and suggestions while Kosoff went through
the dozen or so drafts that inexorably buried the work Thaddeus
himself had done. When production on *Hostages* commenced, Kosoff occasionally called Thaddeus from the set, and when produc-

tion was completed, Thaddeus was invited to Austin, Texas, for the wrap party. Then the film's premiere at the Ziegfeld on Fifty-Fourth Street, where Thaddeus and Grace were seated in the row reserved for the writers and their plus ones, which Thaddeus feared was going to be a nightmarishly uncomfortable situation, assuming, as he did, that most of the other writers harbored the same resentments that burned within him. But the mood in the Writers' Row was one of dark hilarity and cynical solidarity, in which their shared insignificance was a catalyst for camaraderie. When the character of the ambivalent Islamacist said, "I love many things about your country," one of the writers called out from the darkness, "Hey, that's my line," which began a continual volley of tomfoolery from the writers, as if they were all rowdies in a high school auditorium. One writer called out her ownership of the line, "There's not much time," and another claimed "Step on it," and even Thaddeus got into the act, calling out *Mine!* after Elliott Gould said, "Thanks a lot," though Thaddeus worried that they were all committing career suicide, racing like lemmings off the edge of a riff.

Kosoff was calling from his car, which added some drama. His calls from the car had a way of ending abruptly, and waves of static rolled through the connection as Kosoff free-associated about a script he and Thaddeus were working on about the bombing of the Marine headquarters in Beirut. He offered various names of actors who could play the young Marines, speculating, spit-balling, bullshitting. That was the key to success in the business—you had to continually tell yourself that your dreams were about to come true and that what you thought and said actually mattered. "What do you think of Steve Guttenberg?" Kosoff wanted to know.

"As a Marine?" Thaddeus asked.

"I like Kevin Bacon in this, too. Ellen Barkin as the girlfriend."

"What girlfriend?"

"Terrible idea," Kosoff said, laughing. "Just a thought. I mean if we have a stateside component. It could be good. What's your availability look like right now?"

"I'm working and I need work. I haven't paid last year's taxes yet. I've managed to become rich and broke." He knew you weren't supposed to say you needed work, but he had a theory that by admitting to weakness he might be suggesting hidden strength.

"Yeah, yeah, I know the feeling."

"Hey, Neal, this lawyer was here tonight and he's running a case dealing with stuff that happened on the set of *Hostages*."

"Really? I'm not aware of anything. . . ." He might have been going into a canyon. Thaddeus waited for the crackling to stop.

"A bunch of drivers? Apparently some of them got treated really badly."

"Wow. Good luck to them."

"Do you know anything about it?"

"How would I?"

And with that he was gone, Kosoff vaporized without a word of warning. Thaddeus was sure that the affable director almost certainly made his important calls from a real telephone in his office, and filled the time of the commute between Pico Boulevard and Benedict Canyon with his second-tier calls.

Why did Grace not call? And why was he sure that if he were to call her, all he would hear was his own voice on the answering machine? He understood that his success, for all the pleasures it had brought them, had separated them. He was suddenly celebrated, not by the people he had hoped to impress when coming to New York, not this imaginary tribunal of clever, basically progressive literary types, but by the movie folks, who were so good at flattery, who sent rock legends to your house to entertain at your party, who signed such big juicy checks and had them delivered to you by Federal Express. And in the meantime, there was Grace, making her exacting drawings with the unflagging devotion of a monk illuminating manuscripts, day after day, month after month, year after year.

Had he become so absorbed in the titillating terrors of his unexpected life that he had forgotten to encourage her? What was he supposed to say? How do you discuss drawings and paintings? It did not come naturally; you had to study it. The conversation about visual art was generally conducted in a language he did not know, and to the extent that he was aware of it, it was a language he found pretentious and ridiculous, some weird mix of political jargon and obdurate philosophy. He did not know how to articulate what persuasive theory of art or reality Grace's work illustrated, or if she was a formalist or an experimentalist. Well, no, he knew she was not an experimentalist, that much he knew—but could he say it? Was it a positive thing to say, or was it a knock? Or did it have no particular value, just like those all-white canvases he had seen on one or another of their gallery crawls, big white canvases he stared at to be polite and to appear engaged, and which in time began to strobe with colors, as his own mind, starved for something to do, projected prismatic flashes into the void. It wasn't only Grace's work that he lacked the vocabulary to discuss, and now he wished he had made the effort to learn the lingo. Yet he had resisted it, just as he resisted his parents' arcane patois, refused to learn the difference between Communism, State Capitalism, and Bureaucratic Collectivism, or to admit that there even *was* a difference, or, frankly, to care. Even without the vocabulary, he ought to have been more vigilant about expressing how beautiful he found her work, how the verisimilitude of it, its photographic qualities, impressed the hell out of him, and how indifferent he was to the fact that the style she worked in tended to exclude her from the conversation among contemporary artists and gatekeepers. The last time he and Grace had been to a gallery—a freezing little box of a place on Prince Street, with a skunky smell in the air and a crack the went from one end of the concrete floor to the other—the work had seemed deliberately incompetent, stick figures with childish faces, and cutouts of the Jetsons and the Flintstones. *What shit,* Thaddeus whispered to Grace, resorting to layman's terms because that's how a man gets laid. When his lips touched her ear it was flaming hot, and when he stepped back to have a better look at her she seemed to be fighting back tears. It recalled to him how she had looked when he went after one of her studio mates on their wedding day—the look of adoration and trust in Grace, how it seemed as if the gate behind her eyes had swung open, and for a short while he was in her world. He had come to wonder if, as far as Grace was concerned, that was it, the finest moment of their entire relationship, and everything else, money, house, children, the thousand nights in each other's arms, had all been basically placeholders while she waited for the return of the feeling she had in the snow on Park Avenue South, the feeling of being believed in.

HE RETURNED TO THE KITCHEN to pour himself another Mondale-benefit vodka. The kitchen was cleaner than it was before the party. It was as if something was being covered up, a crime scene wiped down. He opened the refrigerator, and saw the caterers had left him two trays of leftovers, tightly sealed. He unwrapped one and ate a couple of dabs of curried chicken salad on water biscuits while waiting for Kosoff to call back.

The malarial fevers of desire were proving resistant to distraction. He tried to think of someone to call. The night was young! Surely, there had to be someone out there who would want to meet him somewhere for a drink. Yet everyone seemed wrong—either too much time had passed since the last meeting, or there was too much disparity between their incomes. He hadn't made that many friends in New York (or anywhere else, come to think of it). The friendships formed at B. Altman had not survived his leaving the job. His friendships with the Collective had not survived *Hostages*.

He watched the end of a ball game on TV, feeling like a heel cheering for the Yankees after having spent his childhood despising them. But he was in New York now and part of survival was loving what was near you. Wasn't it? And who was near him now? The guests gone, Grace a hundred miles north. He allowed his thoughts to drift toward the woman living directly above him on the third

floor. Occasionally, while alone, he could hear her light little footsteps clicking out their Morse code: *I'm here, I'm busy, I'm happy, I'm
nervous, I'm sad, I'm here, I'm here.*

Her name was Jeelu Ramachandran. She was born in India,
in Delhi. Her family moved to Troy, Michigan, when Jeelu was
three years old; her father had a corporate job at X-Ray Industries.
Like Thaddeus, Jeelu went to the University of Michigan and now
she worked at Chemical Bank in New York, and that was about
50 percent of what he knew about her. The other half was com-
prised of little scraps of information he had gathered during their
brief interactions—she liked baseball, she was allergic to cats, she
was mad for John Travolta. She was not beautiful, or maybe she
was, he kept changing his mind about that. Nor was she particularly
friendly, but there were moments when a desire to simply touch her
was so intense that it muddled his mind and made it difficult to believe she didn't feel something like that, too.

He sank onto the sofa and sipped his drink, numbing one moment, invigorating the next. He listened for her footsteps and there
they were, as if conjured up by his horrible, pointless desire. He
blamed Grace; had she been more welcoming, he would not have so
much untapped desire.

Jeelu's efficient small steps were followed everywhere by the
frantic scamper of her Yorkshire terrier, a butterscotch sneeze of a
dog with long ebony claws. Her dog's name was Jeelu, also. He was
amazed at the goofiness of it, naming a dog after yourself, but the
oddness of it added an element of incongruity that served to draw
Thaddeus all the deeper into the maze. Knowing that he would not
in a hundred years so much as kiss her did not make matters better.
In fact, it made everything worse. His desire's only relationship was
with itself, there was nothing to keep it in check, it was as unsocial-
ized as a child raised in isolation.

The Jeelus were going down the stairs. He allowed himself to
wonder for a moment if she might knock on his door and ask if
he'd like to take a walk. Why would she do such a thing? Who

knew? Maybe she was as lonely as him. Maybe she was as crazy as him. What a lovely thought that was. It was a bit late to be taking her dog out and perhaps she was leery of the dark streets, and had finally figured out that Jeelu 2 could not protect her from anything, not even an assault from a kitten. In the flurry of maybes he almost missed hearing the Jeelus and their six feet passing from the third floor to the second and continuing their way down. He felt spurned. The madness of these fantasy affairs, it was enough to make you loathe make-believe, enough to convince you fantasy was by its very nature toxic. Yet even now he was not quite finished with the matter. He went to the window, parted the narrow slats of the wooden shade and peered down at the street, just in time to see the two Jeelus walking briskly toward Hudson Street.

Thaddeus was up and out of his apartment without any real awareness of his movement. He was a book that slips from your hand when you close your eyes, an apple that rolls off the edge of the table. He was nothing, just atoms moving around. As soon as he closed the door and locked it, the heat of the evening was on him as if it had been poured from a kettle.

For half an hour, he walked the streets of his neighborhood, forcing himself to maintain a brisk pace, for fear of appearing aimless and strange. He was at once looking for Jeelu and dreading crossing her path.

The moon appeared and disappeared, a face looking briefly in on the dark city. Solitary strollers emerged from the muzzy darkness one by one. Approaching was an Asian woman in flip-flops. New York! Was there any place in the world with more beautiful women? She was delicate and private, wearing neon yellow terry-cloth shorts, a white shirt knotted at the navel; she chewed gum furiously and rubbed her hands together, squeezing them, as if trying to wash with only a tiny sliver of soap. Perhaps she had left her apartment to get away from an argument. His eyes widened; he could hear his own breathing. *I'm one of those men,* he thought. *Yet look at her!* Her? There was no her, he did not know the first thing about her. Mo-

ments later she disappeared into the haze of steam rising out of a
manhole, and a woman in her forties appeared, big boned and swag-
gering, wild blond hair, beer can protruding from the paper bag, her
belly swaying beneath her T-shirt. Oh what a ride she would be, no
question about it. She carried the scent of many bridges burned behind her. She detected Thaddeus's interest, and furrowed her brow.
But she saw his harmlessness, his helplessness, and it made her smile.
Thaddeus nodded, touched his eyebrow with one finger, half lost in
an instant of imagining what it would be like to lie down with this
woman, to experience her raucous personality, her pent-up energies,
her tipsy abandon, her desire, not unlike his own, to somehow kick
the plug out of the wall of Self and be plunged into darkness.

He walked south on Washington Street, wanting the closeness
of the river and the possibility of cooling breezes, but not daring to
go to West Street or the docks, where by now the skin trade was running at full throttle. Who would be there? Boys down from Harlem,
and ridiculously muscled men in ripped leather vests, storm trooper
boots. Also, the transvestite hookers who seemed to arrive via space-
craft to ply their trade in the backs of meat-delivery trucks. Venues
reeking of torment and ecstasy. He remembered for a moment when
imagination was like wings, something to lift him above his life; now
it was a jackhammer, pounding him into the pavement.

WASHINGTON STREET WAS SLANTED AND secretive, with the long
shadows of street lamps crisscrossing the gleaming black cobblestones. The utility company had opened a portion of the street and
thrown up a barricade around it. Steam the color of tarnished silver
poured out of the opening, intermittently yellowed by the flashing
light on one of the sawhorses. There was rubbish in the gutters, and
the moronic sound of air conditioners hummed from the windows
of the row houses, walk-ups, and converted factories. On the other
side of the street there was a curly-haired man with an unusually
large head walking a pair of Airedales, but otherwise Thaddeus was

alone. He wondered if he would catch a glimpse of Hannah, but his wondering prevented her from appearing. She could only take him by surprise.

He passed a pay phone padlocked to a cyclone fence, next to a newspaper box selling the *Village Voice*. The moment Thaddeus was parallel with the phone, it began to trill like a mad bird of night. Startled, Thaddeus stopped, looked up and down the street. There was no one around to answer it and no one to see if he succumbed to curiosity's temptations and answered it himself. He picked it up and said hello.

"I see you," a man's voice said, in a harsh tone. "I'm looking right now at you."

Across the street was a modest six-story brick building. A light in the window on the fourth floor flicked off and on.

"That's me," the voice said. Again, his window blinked.

"What do you want?" Thaddeus asked.

"Are you hairy or smooth?" the man asked.

"Is this a joke?"

"Answer me!" The voice was curdled with a fury that sounded just a bit theatrical. Thaddeus looked up at the window, but nothing interrupted that square of bright yellow light, not even a silhouette. Two men in jeans and T-shirts were approaching, walking downtown. They were blasted out on something or other, and sang a Bach fugue, body-bah-bum-bum instead of words, their voices deep and pure—they may have been Juilliard students, or professional singers. Their eyes were bright and wide, like an owl's.

"Are you there?" the voice said.

"I'm here," Thaddeus said. "These two guys just walked by singing so beautifully."

"I'll suck your cock."

"Hey, man. I'm not into it."

"Fuck you're not."

Thaddeus hung up the phone. He hated to leave a fellow human being in the lurch. And his dick registered its own opinion: *Are you sure?* He turned to check the window again. The light was flicking off and on at a furious rate. Thaddeus made a small salute, a jaunty farewell, no hard feelings.

The phone began to ring. This time zero mystery. He did not want to pick up the receiver, yet he could not walk away. On the seventh ring he thought *oh well* and answered.

"I knew you'd answer," the voice said.

"Look, man," Thaddeus said. "You should not be doing this. It's creepy. I'm lonely and fucked, too, but there's a limit. You know? There are things you just have to bear."

"Is Daddy going to teach me a lesson?"

"All right. That's creepy, too." Thaddeus laughed, and to his surprise the man laughed, too.

"You got a name?" the man asked.

"Thaddeus."

"Real name?"

"Yeah, it's my real name. What about you?"

"Leslie, as in Caron, as in Howard."

"All right, Leslie. I have to—"

"Come up. We can talk."

"No way. I'm not that crazy."

"Please." He paused. Thaddeus heard rustling. "For a beer." Another pause. "Or a cup of tea. Iced tea. I've got iced tea." Leslie had abandoned the fiction of his dungeon master's voice and spoke imploringly.

"Sorry. I'm going to hang up now . . ."

"Five minutes. You can't come up for five minutes?"

"All right, Leslie. I'll tell you what I can do. If you want to come down, we can talk for five minutes down here. On the street."

"It's a hassle. I'm on a tank."

"What?"

"Oxygen tank. My lungs are fucked."

"Maybe you shouldn't do that scary voice, probably isn't very good for you."

Leslie laughed until it turned to a cough. "What do you do, Thaddeus?"

"I'm a writer."

"Nice. What kind of articles do you write?"

"Screenplays." He listened carefully to his voice as he said the word, making sure there was nothing apologetic in it. He was sick and tired of apologizing.

"Really? I bet you hear this all the time, but my life would make a great movie."

"I do, I hear it a lot."

Undeterred, the man on the fourth floor went into his story, every once in a while taking time to let his breathing catch up. His lungs no longer fit him. Breathing was walking around in someone else's shoes, three sizes too small. "My sister's boyfriend gets me a job building a squash court in Westchester, and there are a million stories about the client and his wife, both disgustingly prejudiced, she weighs like fifty pounds and he's a tub of lard, but the point is, I end up with a lung full of fine-particle dust, and now I'm part of a lawsuit and maybe I'm walking away with a million bucks. My lawyer tells me that more masons get on-the-job casualties and fatalities than any other occupation, cops, firemen, anything else."

"Oh, man, that's horrible," Thaddeus said. "What is it? Do you have cancer?"

"I've got chronic obstructive pulmonary disease. The big COPD. Which is a lot better than cancer, in one way, because it actually pays more, since no one's arguing about where it comes from and how you get it. Open and shut that it came from the job."

"It's got to be better than cancer." Thaddeus glanced up at the window and a darkness in the shape of a human being had carved out a place in the light. He waited for a reply. A hand pressed itself against the glass. "So what happens in your movie?" Thaddeus asked. "It needs a third act."

"I get the money. I give some to my other sister, and her schizoid kid who needs a lot of extra stuff. My lawyer leaves his wife and lives with me in Santa Fe. I suck his cock and every now and then I look up and there they are, the Sangre de Cristo Mountains."

"Pure Hollywood. We might have to change it a little, for the studio. Maybe Sally Field can be the lawyer."

"You don't think it's too schmaltzy?"

"It's what I like about movies," Thaddeus said. "They tell us to never give up."

"Hey, I really think you need to come up here. Do you see me?"

"I see you."

"Have you ever been with a man?"

"I'm married. I've got a kid."

"And?"

"Talk about never giving up."

"Please. I'm asking. I'll be your slave."

"I don't want a slave."

"Then I'll be your master."

"I don't want either. This is America," Thaddeus added, with a nervous laugh. "Land of the free."

"And home of the brave, too, don't forget that." Leslie waited for an answer. "You're really not coming up, are you," he said.

"No, I'm not. And you're not coming down."

"I can't."

"Then there it is, Leslie. Life."

"Okay. I want to ask you a question. All right? Can I ask you a question?"

There was only the faint sound of breathing on the line. In the interim, Thaddeus's mind began to race, wondering, somewhat fearfully, what Leslie was going to ask him. Why was a married man prowling the streets alone at night?

"So what's your question?" he finally asked.

"It's . . ."

"Just ask it, Leslie. Then I have to go."

"I want to ask you to come up here so I can suck your cock. I'll pay you sixty dollars."

Thaddeus gently hung up the phone, and waved toward the lighted window, but without looking up at it. He turned to walk away and was suddenly face-to-face with Jeelu Ramachandran with Jeelu 2.

"Hello, Jeelu."

"Hello, neighbor," she said. The dog moved restlessly, as if the sidewalk burned its paws.

"I hope there wasn't too much noise," Thaddeus said. Seeing the lack of comprehension on her face, he added, "From the party."

"I worked late."

"It was a fund-raiser for the Mondale campaign."

"Rots of ruck with that," Jeelu said.

"So you're for Reagan?"

"I hate politics." She quickly looked down at her dog. "Yes, yes, I know. Time to go home."

"Would you mind if I walked with you?"

"I'm just going back."

"I am, too."

They didn't bother to make conversation. The silence was agreeable to Thaddeus. It was like something plain and well made, like Shaker furniture. At one point, Jeelu followed her dog into the street where it squatted on the cobblestones, and when she stumbled for a moment, Thaddeus touched her elbow to steady her, but only for a moment.

Still, Jeelu seemed to take it as not completely well-meaning. "Is your wife here, too?" she asked.

"No, she's upstate. I'm Thaddeus, by the way."

"I know your name."

"We're hardly ever here."

"Your son is David and your wife is Grace."

"That's right."

He could see their house on Horatio Street now. The yellow porch light burned with a special intensity, as if the house had seen them and had taken a deep breath.

"Do you know the name of my dog?" Jeelu asked. She jutted out her chin, as if she were hoping he would fail this test.

"As a matter of fact, yes, I do," Thaddeus said, in an insinuating voice. *Don't fucking flirt.*

"Really? Are you sure? What is it?"

"I'm not going to tell you the name of your own dog," Thaddeus said, merrily. *Flirting.* "That's the oldest trick in the book."

"What you are doing is an even older trick. And the person who plays that trick is the person who doesn't know the name of the dog."

"Can I stay with you tonight, Jeelu? I won't even touch you. I would just go to sleep next to you." *There. Not flirting whatsoever.* He had always thought of himself as a tactful person, tactical even. Could Tourette's syndrome come on as suddenly as an embolism?

Jeelu 1 picked up Jeelu 2 and held her protectively against her chest. "I have a very small bed. It's for when my parents come. They're very old-fashioned, and if they saw a double bed or, God forbid, larger, they would say, 'For whom do you need such a large bed? What is going on here?'"

"It sounds cozy," Thaddeus said.

"No, Thaddeus. Tonight, I stay in apartment eight, and you are in apartment four."

She's looked at my door. She knows the number . . .

"Are you sure?" he asked, but he felt something shifting. A fever had broken, the beginnings of relief.

"You paid good money for that bed of yours," Jeelu said, "and you're hardly ever in it." She smiled. She knew her smile was dazzling; you don't smile like that and not know all about it. "I was home when it was delivered. The men were carrying it out of the truck and I came downstairs to let them in."

"Well then, I guess I owe you a thank-you," Thaddeus said. "Saved by a banker."

"You're very welcome." Her hand was on the door. "And why do you say bad things about bankers? If it wasn't for bankers we'd all be dead meat."

"You think so?"

"Good night, neighbor."

"Wait," Thaddeus said. This was something he wanted to get out of the way before she went in. "Since you asked. I know you named your dog after yourself, and I wanted to spend the night with you anyway. I think I deserve some credit for that." It felt as if his skin was cooling down. Thank God he was not going to put further strain on his marriage by sleeping with another woman, even chastely. Nevertheless, he felt the pique of being refused.

How could he have so much and still be this alone? If his life was a book, it was as if a sudden wind had unexpectedly rattled the pages forward and, despite his best efforts to look away, he had glimpsed how the story ended.

BACK IN HIS APARTMENT, HE drank and watched a porn tape purchased upon arrival that day, in case he found himself at the ragged end of the night feeling exactly how he was feeling now. The candy store where he picked up the newspaper and Dentyne also sold these videos, which never ceased to astonish him. He made his purchases furtively, never failing to case the place to make certain there were no women or children present. He tried to limit his purchases in frequency and subject matter, avoiding movies that catered to specific tastes—nothing with teen, ass, bitch, or bondage in the title. He was content with middle-of-the-road raunch, something to take his mind off his worries and transport him to a world of generic in-and-out. Right now, he was glad for his foresight as the first notes of the porn soundtrack played. Of course porn music was the worst music ever made, but his body responded to it, just as it had when, as a child, he heard the distant chimes of the Good Humor truck. It was as if he had a body inside his body that needed to be appeased. All he wanted to do was draw the curtain. *I shall be released.* He watched the actors cavorting beneath the pitiless lights, and as he got closer to completion he closed his eyes and instead of watching strangers—

the men pneumatic, the women old beyond their years—he allowed himself to remember fucking Grace in a way that was similar to how Randy was fucking Brandi. Once he entered into the whoosh of memory's current the trick was to go with the flow and block out the sights and sounds of the tape. As he worked himself with one hand, he groped blindly for the remote control, but he could not find it and the humble reality of his lonely climax was subverted by the theatrical screeches on the film.

HE DRIFTED TOWARD THE FRONT windows and for no particular reason looked down at the street below. There was a man below; he seemed elderly, leaned on a cane and shifted his shoulders, as if trying to establish his balance. On closer inspection, however, Thaddeus saw the man was probably in his thirties—but in rough shape, terrible health. His brown hair was thin, his posture stooped. It was—it *must be*—Leslie. Leslie had somehow tracked Thaddeus's movements from the phone booth back to Horatio Street and right to this building. As Thaddeus had this thought the man below looked up, seemingly at the window at which Thaddeus stood, half dressed. Quickly, he moved from view, pressing himself against the wall, like an escaping convict avoiding the searchlight. He admonished himself to calm down. What would the harm be of inviting Leslie up for a drink, and to hear more about his sister and brother-in-law and that squash court? The lives of the obscenely rich were generally interesting in one way or another; you got to see the human animal released from the constraints of economy. Maybe Leslie needed money. Of course he did. Shoved way under the mattress, Thaddeus kept an envelope with fifteen or twenty hundred-dollar bills, per diem leftovers from trips to L.A. Why not give it all to Leslie, who obviously needed the cash a lot more than Thaddeus? The gesture might be misconstrued—money often spoke with a forked tongue!—but Thaddeus could finesse it. He'd go to the window and wave him up. Or maybe go down to the street, in case Leslie needed help mounting the stairs.

Choreographing his movements so that at no point could he be seen, Thaddeus shut off the Betamax, the TV, the lamp. He collected his vodka glass, took it to the kitchen, placed it in the sink, and ran the hot water into it until he was engulfed in steam. The longer he stood there breathing in the hot moist air, the more he doubted that the man down on the street was actually Leslie. He turned off the faucet, picked up the glass, and put it quickly down again. It was scalding to the touch. He drifted toward the front windows, thinking he might go downstairs just to see who it was out there, but he thought better of it.

He turned off the last of his apartment's lights and went to bed, lest he change his mind again. Yet shortly after going to bed he *had* changed his mind, or at least had allowed it to shift. Had he fallen asleep? He was quite sure he hadn't even closed his eyes.

Naked now, he wound through his apartment's darkness, somewhat unfamiliar with its topography. But the city's persistent ambient light was enough for him to navigate safely to the window.

He parted the blinds and looked down. The man had his back to Thaddeus now and was speaking to another nocturnal walker. A slender woman in shorts the color of a radioactive lemon—it was the Asian woman he had passed on the street. When? An hour ago? Two? Three? She reached behind her and from somewhere produced what appeared to be a Korean-language newspaper, its front-page pictographs suggesting disaster. How could such skimpy terry-cloth shorts have a back pocket large enough to carry that paper? The question crossed his mind, but attending to it was another matter altogether—it was like a shooting star seen through the corner of his eye. A moment later the man who might be Leslie and the woman who might be the Asian woman in neon shorts were joined by the man Thaddeus had glimpsed for a moment walking the two Airedales, only now he was without the dogs and carried a grocery bag filled with yucca, thick, silver-brown-white, jutting this way and that. Thaddeus had seen that yucca before, on the playing cards in a village on the border of Turkey and Iran. Five men in a café on the town square engrossed in a game whose rules or purpose were incomprehensible to Thaddeus—the men threw down their cards one at a time and every few rounds one of them would excitedly grab for whatever had been discarded and gather them up.

He wanted to go down to further investigate this extraordinary situation, as mysterious as the memory of a scent, the lingering memory of the perfume that came off Grace that afternoon in the purloined hotel room, that stale thrillingly human aroma, tuberose, gardenia, perspiration. He scrambled into his clothes—pants no underwear, shoes no socks, his shirt fastened by only two buttons. He felt unsteady as he descended the seashell swirl of the staircase, gripping the railing. The phrase *So many fish in the sea* floated across his mind and he followed it into a kind of oblivion, as his soul left his body. He realized he was on his way to meet his sister, to meet Hannah, but he could not forget that such a thing was impossible. It was that time, three o'clock in the morning. Not at all the dark night of the soul. It was the soul's magic hour, when memory and grief and desire shrugged off the shackles of logic and reason. Hannah would be there even if strictly speaking she was not. But at three in the morning no one is strictly speaking. At three everything is everywhere and it's all at once. Time and its wormholes, and its parallel universes. Coming from afar, Thaddeus heard the wail of a siren, the whooping cry of a suffering world, a crucifix made of sound.

Chapter 10

Sightlines

APRIL 15, 1989

DIGGIN' DEEP FOR BRANDON

Calling All Neighbors and Friends
Join Us for a "Fun-Raiser" to Help
the Reynolds Family Pay for Eye Surgery
for Their Amazing Son Brandon

Sunday 1 P.M. Lord's Fellowship Church
12 Vanderbilt Drive

SAVE OUR RIVER

Cocktails and Art for the Hudson
Sequana 3 P.M.
Auction Preview 2 P.M.

HARD, UNYIELDING, AND GRAY, THE SKY WAS LIKE A PLASter wall waiting for its color. Thaddeus and Grace drove away from their house, up the driveway, and as far as the eye could see, the pasture was covered in snow. But it was not a smooth cover; the snow had been perforated clear up to the horizon by the slender hooves of hungry foraging deer, ten thousand holes. The tops of the bare trees swayed back and forth, searching for spring.

It felt very good to be home. The human presence of his family. The children with their sweet scalps and unclouded eyes, and weird little personalities. And Grace, even moody, even withdrawn, was still Grace. He was used to the idea that their courtship might never end and that the moment when she might have become unalterably *his* might never come or had already passed, and that he would always be in essence chasing after her, like a man who has missed his bus and now must trot behind it to the end of the route, which in his case was the end of time.

Thaddeus had arrived from London the previous afternoon, and had tried to talk to Grace about his experience with Stanley Kubrick, but Grace seemed not to want to hear a thing about it. Her own attitude toward *Lady Chatterley's Lover*, which Kubrick had shown enough interest in to justify Thaddeus running off to London to discuss it with him, seemed to have soured, and now she thought his treatment was lurid, the source material overrated, Oliver Mellors a desk-bound asthmatic's idea of a workingman. She wanted Thaddeus to abandon the project, and from time to time she urged him to do so. But *Chatterley* was a dying project anyhow. Whatever enthusiasm Kubrick himself had for the script had faded by the time Thaddeus was in London. The weekend together was consumed by Kubrick's complaints about agents and executives, as if Thaddeus himself was an ambassador from Hollywood, rather than a fellow artist hoping to turn the system to his own advantage. That really had been the most painful part of the wasted trip—Kubrick's treating him as if he were a hack, some kind of scavenger bird, a squawking hopping gull hoping only to get his beak wet in the rotting carcass of a once-noble art.

When Thaddeus finally made it back to Orkney, all he wanted to do was fling himself into Grace's arms and somehow be reassured by her. But it wasn't to be. She was furious with both of the kids and he could deduce from her fleeting kiss that she had been drinking.

He had hurried back, hoping to somehow please Grace with the promptness of his return. Last autumn, Grace said he was away from Orkney *half the time*, which Thaddeus suspected was an exaggeration, but when he went through his calendars for the past couple of years, he saw that he had been away an average of 135 days a year. The majority of the days had been in Los Angeles, pitching ideas, meeting with producers and directors, sometimes living at the Four Seasons, or the Mondrian while working on a script, engorging himself on expense account meals and spending an hour or two on the treadmill trying not to get fat. There was also some time spent on what he called "refreshing relationships," which meant sharing a meal with a useful person with whom he had worked in the past, though these exercises in faux friendliness (faux on both sides) were generally worked into trips to L.A. that were already ongoing. Also added into the number of days away from Orkney was time spent on-set, though when he went through his calendars there were not as many of those days as he would have guessed. The only significant amount of time he had left Grace and the children was for the filming of *Bread and Wine*, based on the Ignazio Silone novel. Despite the novel's theme of resistance to the rise of fascism, the producers hoped Thaddeus could bring some humor to the story and turn it into a real movie, rather than a well-meaning slog, just as he was able to find the absurdity and laughter in *Hostages*. The filming was in Italy, and the three weeks turned out to be five, which supplied much-needed replenishment of the Orkney Household Account, out of which they paid property taxes, school taxes (for schools they did not use), heat, repairs, land management, and general maintenance. But the havoc his long absence created! As (bad) luck would have it, David was suspended from his twee little school for pushing another little kid down the stairs—the boy was basically unhurt, but that was hardly the point. And Emma was going through a cavalcade of digestive issues. At the time, their nanny was a local girl named Judy

Briggs, but Judy was all but useless at night because she was fearful and felt isolated on the property, and of limited use in the daylight because her driver's license had been suspended for a year.

Hoping to make it up to Grace, Thaddeus suggested she come to Italy, but the invitation only made her more upset. She said she had work to do, and when Thaddeus asked her—this was all taking place on a feeble transatlantic phone connection, full of ghostly whispers—what kind of work did she have that was so goddamned pressing, Grace began to shout at him, accusing him of not taking her seriously as an artist, and of turning her into a fucking housewife. Thaddeus, surprised by her reaction, as he thought she would be thrilled at the prospect of a first-class Italian holiday, and sorely disappointed because he had mentally worked out a perfect itinerary for them, and even had a couple of leads for child care so the two of them could be alone in the amazing tavernas and out-of-the-way little churches he had found, also lost his temper and suggested to Grace that her portraying herself as some put-upon oppressed exploited chained-to-the-sink wife was far from the truth, since she had help and hours and hours of free time and hours and hours after that of *more* free time, not to mention the countless other luxuries and, really, she ought to be ashamed of herself for whining about a life that most people would die for. *You're an asshole,* she'd said, and hung up the phone, forcing him to redial, which in his out-of-the-way location in Umbria was an annoying, time-consuming process. But of course Grace knew it was him calling and didn't answer, so he left his wounded, belligerent retort on the machine: "You're a joke," he said, and she left it there so she could play it for him when he got home. There it was, his awful unstable voice, ten thousand miles away, forty-eight hours in the past, but as present in Orkney's teal-and-cream entrance hall as a dead squirrel wedged in the walls, slowly rotting away. It was three in the afternoon, winter, the sun already sinking, the black-and-white world of icy river and snowy mountains suddenly bright orange and dark blue, and that's when he said it, he finally said it: *It was all for you, you know. All for you. The money, this house, the space and the time and all you do is complain. You think I want to do this bullshit work? I gave up my own work so you could be an artist.* That was bad enough, but then she said it, too, the thing that should not have been said, the thing that could not easily be taken back, but could only be forgiven, and that would not be easy, either. *Your own work? Your own work was too hard for you and you couldn't take the rejection. So don't pretend you gave up some great thriving career as a real writer so you could take care of your family. You had no career and you were fucking ecstatic when you lucked into movies.*

"I'm surprised you want to go to these parties," Grace said, as she drove slowly along their driveway. She had struggled over what to wear; the parties they were about to attend were vastly different. She had settled on a turquoise wool coat, black jeans, and a dark wool sweater. She was letting her hair grow; it was gathered in back by an elastic band and swept back off her high forehead.

"Why surprised?" said Thaddeus. "Why would I let a beautiful woman go out unescorted?"

"Thanks. But honestly? Sorry for saying this, but after a while being charming just creates distance. Charm is just so damned bourgeois."

"Well, I guess that makes me bourgeois."

"I guess we both are," Grace said in a soft, regretful tone. "Not exactly the life we had in mind."

Their marriage seemed stale, maybe it was dying. Grace's eyes rarely met his. Sometimes she looked away, sometimes she gazed over his shoulder. When she heard Thaddeus's voice, she sighed. Last night, during sex, she was looking up at him, with a frightened but also amused expression, as if he were carrying on like a madman. Lately, when they made love he was somehow in the position of emoting for the both of them, groaning and calling out, and even once crying at the end.

They were in her car, a Subaru station wagon, more suitable for country living than the BMW, especially in rough weather. Half consciously, he was running his hand back and forth along the side pocket on the passenger door, looking for clues that might reveal what she did in this car, where she went all those days and nights when he was away. There were secrets she kept from him. He could see it in her eyes, feel it in her body when they made love. Oh well. He didn't begrudge Grace her secrets, surely he was not without secrets himself. We need our privacies, the hidden rooms where we can be alone.

"I HATE MY PAINTING," GRACE said, as she made her way up Orkney's drive. "I hate all paintings. I hate art."

The children in the backseat appeared not to be paying attention, but you never knew.

"Your painting's great," Thaddeus said.

"You don't even know which one is up for auction."

"They're all great. And art's great, too. I like art. It's arty-ness I don't like. And don't even start me on artsy-fartsy."

David and Emma tittered in the backseat. So they were listening after all . . .

"This is where I am supposed to laugh, right?" Grace said.

"Worse things have happened," said Thaddeus.

"I can't believe you're going to Horse and Candy's thing," Grace said. "You're not going to know anyone there."

"Of course I am."

"It's not really your thing. More of a redneck crowd. Your basic white trash."

"Grace. First of all, I like poor people as much as you do, if not more. And isn't it sort of racist to call people white trash? Doesn't it sort of mean that there are white people who don't deserve to be grouped with the real supposedly excellent white people? White people who are so screwed up they may as well be black?"

"Oh, now you're going to lecture me? After flying first class and tooling around in limos?"

"First of all, I just flew coach."

"Oh my God, you poor thing. I had no idea!"

Thaddeus swatted the air, signifying his intention to let the matter drop. "I'm glad we can help Horse and Candy," he said. "And I'm sure I'll know people there. Jennings and Muriel? Aren't they going?"

Grace did not confirm or deny. The most excitable, and tormented part of herself wanted to say, *Don't say his name!* She was out of her psychological depth and she knew it. There were people who could adjust rather easily to the double bookkeeping of infidelity, but she was not one of them. Constant fear of detection coursed through her night and day like a horrible drug she had swallowed by accident. What did Jennings think about what they were doing? How did he reckon with it? She had no idea; they never spoke of it. The conspiratorial whispers that bind illicit lovers to each other were absent between them.

She slowed the car where the driveway dipped and ice tended to gather.

"I just assumed they'd be there," Thaddeus persisted. "They're close with the Reynoldses."

"Jennings and Horse are friends. Muriel and Candy don't get along—Candy thinks Muriel is a hippie."

"And I suppose Jennings slept with her somewhere along the way."

A sudden silence came over the backseat. Grace checked the rearview mirror; the children were staring at the backs of their parents' heads.

"No. Candy's really religious." A trickle of sweat went down her side. She thought it would be best to smile.

"We'll never really be a part of it," Thaddeus said. "The money is like barbed wire. And of course the local gentry hate us, too. We're too . . . I don't know. Too something. They can smell the difference."

"So do you wish you were poor?" Grace said. "Who are you kidding?" She heard the tone in her voice. "Sorry," she said. Sometimes she was appalled by her own moods. Her temper was a little snappish dog dozing in her lap. The slightest provocation.

Thaddeus seemed to feel no offense, yet he did that thing, that irritating, nerve-cannibalizing thing that Grace called the Angry Redirect. He turned in his seat to shower the children with affection, Emma in her Britax car seat, brought back from London, and David next to her, holding the Game Boy, one not yet available in America, which Thaddeus brought back from Tokyo a few weeks ago. "Hey, you guys, party time!" Thaddeus said, drumming his fingers on their knees and adopting his Uncle Goofball voice.

Grace granted that it was not fair, and possibly not *sane* to believe her husband had come up with Uncle Goofball just as a way of plunging her into despair. In fact, there was more than one despair-inducing voice: there was joyous Uncle G brimming with delight; and then there was Poor Old Bozo, the sad clown; and occasionally there was Falsetto Frank, who only said Hello! but said it over and over. And over. But it *was* fair and *true* to say that he turned his high spirits and desire to please on to the children at times when he and Grace were at odds, and these displays invariably took place right in front of her, since they were meant to remind her of all the effervescence that could be hers if she only treated him well.

David was nearly nine years old, tall and underweight, with a nervous scribble of brown hair, a stubborn expression, and dark semi-circles under his eyes. It was his misfortune to have parents with the wherewithal to engage pediatric specialists from New York City all the way up to Montreal in their search of a reason for David looking like a chain-smoking insomniac. There had yet to be a useful diagnosis, and the proposed cures—the diets, the exercise regimes, and the medications—had been a torment to a boy whose nature was basically solitary, sedentary, and introspective. He held the Game Boy tightly in both hands, as if he were a courier entrusted to deliver it from the future. Lately, nothing engaged David except that battery-powered plastic rectangle. The infernal toy was predominantly gray, with two red buttons and a black cross that moved the cursor left and right, up and down. Crosses, cursors, it all seemed to Grace like the death of something.

Strapped into her carrier, Emma moved her foot up and down, hoping to catch her brother's eye. She was the robust one, with full cheeks and a watermelon belly, but she, too, was recessive. She made her needs known with pouts and sighs, rarely crying, rarely venturing beyond a stricken look, as if to say, *How could you not give me what little I ask for?*

"Is this the little foot looking for her brother?" Uncle Goofball chortled, grabbing Emma's little beaded moccasin.

Grace nosed the car onto Riverview Road. The blacktop looked soft in the bright sun. "Why are we bringing kids to a party where they will most likely be bored out of their minds and where they will be left in my care?"

"Because they're beautiful and I missed them and they're great and the whole world wants to see them." He turned to the kids, wagged his brows. He gave Emma's chubby leg an affectionate squeeze. "Whoa. She feels a little warm."

"She's fine," said Grace.

"Did you take her temperature?"

"I actually don't take her temperature every morning. I guess I'm negligent."

Thaddeus could see this was going nowhere, at least nowhere he wanted to go.

"We could have brought Annie with us," he said. "She could look after the kids and you'd be free to have all the fun there is."

"It's Sunday. And we're going to be around actual *people*. Wouldn't you be embarrassed to bring our nanny to a party like this?"

David came out of his Game Boy–induced fugue state for a moment. "Annie the Nanny with the big fat fanny," he said.

"David!" Grace said. "That's very unkind."

"And untrue," added Thaddeus. "Annie has a lovely behind."

Grace looked at him with open-mouthed astonishment.

"I'm kidding," he said, as if that made his remark more acceptable, or palatable, or less insulting, less juvenile, less ill-mannered, more forgivable, cuter, funnier, something, anything.

There were already several churches in Leyden—Catholic, Epis-
copal, Methodist, Congregationalist, two Lutheran. The newest was
a nondenominational Christian church called the Lord's Fellowship,
where today's fund-raising party was being held. The Lord's Fellowship was part of a network of churches, with congregations in
Dallas, Tulsa, Charlotte, Youngstown, Hartford, and Leyden, all in
identical A-frames that looked like ski-vacation lodges. The spirit
of the church was as American as its architecture, free of anything
ancient, medieval, pompous, or formal. Bare wooden pews had been
eschewed for cushioned seats like in a movie theater. For those who
chose to kneel, the kneelers were amply padded with extra layers of
foam rubber. Wooden railings were everywhere, up and down every
aisle, circling the circumference of the place, in the entrance hall,
on the big friendly porch, on the steps leading to the porch. The
parking lot was enormous, and the yellow lines painted far apart to
accommodate vans delivering the handicapped and the elderly, as
well as pickup trucks.

Grace found a slot for their Subaru, next to a robin's-egg blue
Ford pickup with oversize tires. The back bumper was held onto
the body of the truck with copper wire; the red, black, and white
bumper sticker said Puttin' on the Ritz and showed some cheerfully
rendered penguins wearing bright red bow ties.

Next to the A-frame church, a smaller A-frame stood like a dutiful daughter next to her mother. This second structure was the
home of the teen recreation center. So far, not many of the local
teenagers were making use of the place, but one day, it was hoped by
congregants, parents, and local officials, that would change, though
many said the first thing that would have to change was the name:
Christian Fun Zone.

Thaddeus counted the number of cars and trucks in the parking
lot, to get a sense of how much money the Reynoldses might realize
from the benefit. Two hundred dollars? Three? Weren't they trying
to raise money to pay for an operation? Their boy was born with
one blind eye, a dull milky blue. Horse had taken the birth defect

as an unwelcome commentary on his own genetic makeup, and was full of bluster about it. "The only problem with having one eye is if you lose it," he said. And sure enough when the boy was almost four years old he fell out of his bunk bed and hit the side of his head against the floor, snapping the optic nerve of his good eye. Now he was in darkness, and that, as Horse said, still full of bluster, but bluster of a different sort, the bluster of a man who has been dealt a bad hand and will make the best of it, that was a beef no one could cool. Doctors were making headway on cancer and AIDS and heart disease, and all sorts of infections you couldn't even pronounce, but blindness was still basically a one-way street. This one was in the hands of God. But there was a show on *60 Minutes* about an eye doctor in San Diego, a surgeon who was reattaching optic nerves and kids and some adults, too, blind for years were suddenly doing crossword puzzles and whistling at pretty girls. The only catch was money, since no insurance company would touch what they considered an experimental treatment. They'd rather buy Brandon a lifetime supply of canes and dark glasses.

Thaddeus wondered how this benefit could make a dent in what it would cost to operate on Brandon. It would take ten benefits like this to pay for a tonsillectomy. Talk about bad marriages! How about when capitalism and medicine got hooked up? Yet even if Brandon was rich—was there really any chance of restoring his sight? Perhaps the money was being raised to meet other needs—special education, or even a lovely family vacation that might relieve the sorrow of raising a young boy who with every passing day further forgot what his parents, his sister, his house, his friends, his dog, the trees, the sky, the moon, or even what he himself looked like, a boy whose visual memories were being erased by time, plunging him deeper and ever deeper and deeper still into the darkness.

Thaddeus listened to the voracious crunch of the gravel as he and his family made their way from the car to the Christian Fun Zone. He recalled the many times he'd passed by this spot during construction. The one-hundred-pound sacks of cement stacked in

a semicircle like sandbags in a battle zone. The backhoe the size
of a rhinoceros. The razz of transistor radios. The whine of saws.
The ringing of hammers. The smell of tar. The shirtless young men.
The portly older guys crouched over their sawhorses, showing deep
ass cleavage, extreme tans. Boards, nails, screws, bolts, glass, copper
wire, copper pipes, polyurethane, putty, plumbing, paint, and pay
by the hour. Wherever his eye landed was evidence that the world
was made by others, and he enjoyed it like a child enjoys a stuffed
toy dropped into his crib. Out there, somewhere, in the brutal beyond were the road crews, and the logging crews, the masons and
truckers, steelworkers, chemical workers, orderlies and electricians,
paper hangers, bakers, the men in blood-splattered smocks eviscerat-
ing cattle, soldiers in tanks breathing their own stink, soldiers leap-
ing from planes, soldiers ditching helicopters in sandstorms, soldiers
bleeding, dying.

Who made this world?

Who made the clothes on his back? The shoes on his feet.

The fillings in his teeth.

The lost pair of reading glasses. The other lost pair of reading
glasses. The pair of reading glasses he was using as a bookmark as he
made his way through *Love in the Time of Cholera*. The book itself,
the cardboard, the binding, the ink. The pillows he propped behind
him as he read—who raised the chickens or the ducks or the geese
or whatever kind of feathers were inside the pillows, who plucked
the fowl, who stuffed the feathers into sacks and sewed them up?
Who made the mattress, the bed frame, where did the lamp come
from, and how about the shade? His daughter's car seat? His son's
Game Boy?

Monkeys, it occurred to him, knew more about their surroundings than he knew about his.

The first thing everybody saw when they walked into the Christian Fun Zone was Horse Reynolds, dispensing handshakes to the
men, hair tousles for the little boys, pulled punches to the bicep
for the older boys, courtly little bows to the girls, and kisses on the

cheek of every woman over the age of eighteen. A line was forming on the other side of the room, near the long table where the covered dishes had been laid out. About twenty guests waited, holding paper plates at their sides, shaking them like silent tambourines. The whole place smelled of meat and onions and biscuits, and scorched lasagna. The aroma was slightly sickening to Thaddeus. (The tray of gray beef and beige potatoes they had served him in aisle 31 on his flight home from London reminded him that he might not even be *able to* consume food that was meant for the masses. It was as if after a few short years of money he was no longer normal.)

Keeping Horse company were two men he worked with at Willis Correctional Facility some twenty miles west, that fearsome squat red brick building surrounded by barbed wire upon which the desiccated carcasses of low-flying wrens were like notes on a piece of sheet music. Befitting men who spent their workday in a locked-down facility, supervising people who they were sure wanted to slit their throats, gouge out their eyes, or stomp their skulls into jagged chunks of bloody bone, the correctional officers vociferously enjoyed their time off, sharing their volcanic earsplitting laughter. They rarely said what could be shouted. When they partied, it was an endless game of king of the mountain. They were quick to take offense. They were suspicious. And they were bossy. And they were more or less stuck with each other because no one else could stand them.

Horse had bulked up on the job. There was no taper to him anymore; at this point, he could literally darken your doorway. He was always on alert. His clear blue eyes moved back and forth like minesweepers. His hands were like rocks and his neck was as thick as his thigh. His black hair shone but his mustache had turned the color of a tarnished silver fork left in the back of the drawer to oxidize.

"I never thought I'd see you here," Horse said, taking Thaddeus's hand. He had milked cows as a kid and now he had an odd handshake, soft at first, and then a sudden hard squeeze. "And hello to you two," he said to David and Emma, tousling his hair, chucking her chin. He placed a steadying hand on Grace's shoulder and touched his lips against her cheek.

"Oh my, Horse. You've gone continental," Grace said.

Horse had a hard smile that he flashed like a badge.

"Nice turnout," Thaddeus said, looking out at the room.

"Well, it can get pretty rowdy," said Horse. "Not so much here, but next door, where the praying gets done. Things can really really get going. Quite a show, for someone like yourself."

Himself? Was this some form of Jew-baiting?

David spied Jewel across the room and hurried toward her, with Emma following desperately behind. Thaddeus was about to stop them, but saw Grace shake her head.

"Horse tells me you're in the movies," one of Horse's colleagues said to Thaddeus. The middle-aged man's voice was porous and light. It did not seem really to be his. It was as if his real voice was in the shop and they'd given him a loaner.

"Guilty as charged." Thaddeus pointed to the heavyset man's sweatshirt. "Hey, someone took me to that Giants-Jets game. Fucking great, right? Beat the Giants right there in the Meadowlands? Redeemed the season."

"This?" Horse's friend touched his shirt. "This ain't even mine. So what movies you been in?"

"With this face? No, I write. The scripts." He moved his hand as if composing by pen.

"Anything I might have seen?"

"*Hostages*?" He saw not even the slightest spark of recognition, and added, "It doesn't matter."

"Any others?"

"Not really. I mean, not yet. I've got three, well, actually four things in development. Big maybes. A thing about the bombing of our embassy in Beirut." He liked to mention that deal; he thought it gave him some heft.

The guard looked long and searchingly at Thaddeus. Was he wondering if Thaddeus was one to celebrate the slaughter of Marines?

"My brother tells me you said he couldn't hunt on your land," the guard finally said. "He was pretty disappointed."

"Who's your brother?"

"Glenn Milburn."

Thaddeus shrugged.

"Me, I don't hunt. I don't like the taste of deer and I hate being in the woods. I don't need a bunch of ticks crawling up me. But Glenn's been hunting your land his whole life."

"I actually don't know your brother. And no one asked me about hunting. Ever. But have him come by. Maybe we can work something out.

Horse leaned into the conversation. "It was your boy Jennings, he's the one who told Glenn. He's the big barking dog at Orkney now."

A wave of new arrivals distracted Horse and his friend. Thaddeus made his way to a little schoolhouse table with a few chairs around it. In the center of the table was a large green bowl filled with red-and-yellow candy corn, smelling like sugar and floor wax. Thaddeus sat, pulled out his checkbook, and wrote a check out to cash, and pondered the amount for a few moments. A thousand dollars was ostentatious, a hundred was mean. Five hundred was the easiest path. All right. Five hundred dollars. But maybe to Horse himself? To Horse and Candy? No, to cash, good old cash, as David Mamet wrote, everybody likes money, that's why it's called money. Thaddeus tore the check out of its booklet and gave it a couple of ink-drying shakes, a gesture he had learned from his parents, who used to sign their checks with a fountain pen, bringing a sense of solemn ceremony to every transaction. Thaddeus did not even keep a check registry, having long ago decided it would be preferable to run the risk of accidentally overdrawing his account than to go through the tedium of keeping track.

He was on his way to deliver the check, rehearsing in his mind something to say. *Here you go, Horse.* Maybe add: *I wish it were more.* No. Absolutely not. If you wish it were more, then fucking make it more.

A sudden commotion. Brandon himself was on his way in, parting the crowd. He wore a three-piece suit, powder blue, and novelty sunglasses, with Teenage Mutant Ninja Turtles perched on the hinges. Frail, his skin the color of the winter sky, his drab brown hair carefully combed, he gripped his mother's arm and she beamed as she led him in. Candy's face was round and ruddy, crowned by springy blond curls. Her blue eyes moved constantly; she was seeing for both of them.

"Mom?" he piped. "Mom?"

"We're here, Brandon," Candy said. "And a whole bunch of our friends are here, too." She swooped down to lift him in her arms. The child held his dark glasses in place and composed his face in the most serious manner he could manage. He held up his little hand with its skinny thumb and translucent fingers.

The newcomers were filing in, streaming past Thaddeus. Grace had been correct; he didn't recognize these folks. He had been living in Leyden for years, and right now he may as well have wandered into a small town in another state, another country. Precious few had held on to their youthful vitality and good looks; years of hard work had already beaten it out of them. Big hands. Strong backs. Evidence of health problems, a cavalcade of symptoms: swollen joints, burns, scars, one older guy with a glass eye out of *The Pennysaver*. Here they were, tall and short, thin and portly, a slowly turning wheel of blue eyes, bad teeth, jack-o'-lantern smiles, with their double chins, and triple chins, too, daguerreotype beards, sepia sideburns, and shaved necks, gauzy hairdos and press-on nails, in their pastel suits and prewashed jeans. Thaddeus remained poised, mindful that at any moment someone might say hello to him and he would be called upon to pretend to recognize the person. It was possible that some people here had been on Orkney's grounds, running a wood chipper, repairing a roof, visiting Jennings and Muriel. Maybe Glenn Milburn was among them.

It was the last thing in the world he had ever expected to feel. He was afraid of these people. *The* people. He was afraid of the people.

Candy carried Brandon to the front of the room, and tried to bring everyone to order, saying, "Friends?"

At last, Horse shouted out through cupped hands, just one word—*Hey*. His voice was a cannon that echoed in the room. People turned toward him, sheepish and expectant.

"CAN I SIT HERE WITH you?" Muriel was asking Thaddeus.

"Please do. Horse just about gave me a heart attack."

"He's got a strong voice." Muriel looked at home in the little chair. She was wearing a spring dress, sleeveless, and her customary sprigs of flowers in her hair. Today's flowers were tiny and white, and of the utmost delicacy—not unlike Muriel herself. "He's talking about running for politics, and you can see why."

"Horse?"

"I don't like politics," Muriel said. "It's all us against them."

"You look so pretty, Muriel," Thaddeus said.

"Oh you," she answered, without much enthusiasm. She carried an antique beaded purse and poked around in it, idly. "I never know what to wear," she said. "I hardly ever get off the property."

Thaddeus looked at her uncertainly. There was an element of complaint in her voice he wasn't used to. He realized he hadn't gotten to know Muriel, not nearly so well as he had hoped when he'd imagined all of them living at Orkney, sharing their lives.

"Well, I just wanted to say, thanks for being here," Candy was saying, doing her best to project her voice. Brandon was covering his ears, and making a face, as if his cochlea were being pierced. "We don't have a count yet, but when we do I'll let you know how much we collected today. But I'll tell you one thing . . ." Suddenly, her smile, which moments ago had seemed durable, quivered and crumpled, and the corners of her mouth pointed straight down. She dabbed at the corners of her eyes with the heel of her free hand. "This means really a lot to us. We are so blessed. One thing we know. God will never close a door without opening a window. And you are our window, all of you. And we love you."

Horse had his arm around Candy, and nuzzled his face against the top of her head. To Horse, she seemed absolutely indistinguishable from the girl he had courted so assiduously in high school, with her blond hair and small, stubborn mouth, broad shoulders and powerful legs, the girl who had endured months of teasing because she had once gotten down on her knees and prayed before a geometry test, the girl who walked the halls of Leyden High nervously touching the oversize cross she always wore, as if she feared she might be set upon by vampires at any moment, the girl whose success at the hundred-yard dash and the standing broad jump brought a bit of glory to their school. Horse had never expected her to go out with him, but he asked her to the senior prom in the same spirit you'd buy a lottery ticket, and to his surprise, she said yes. But the night of the dance, his father was sick and Horse had to fill in for him at the diner. It was a gloomy Saturday night, with Horse behind the counter, and five or six customers, when suddenly Candy walked in, wearing a pretty little dress and her own apron, saying, "I want two dollars an hour." She got right behind the counter with him, and they decided to keep the diner open late because Candy had put the word out and the Leyden Diner became *the* after-prom destination. After midnight the place was packed, and Horse and Candy were scrambling eggs and slapping patties onto the griddle and looking the other way when their friends emptied flasks of booze into the milk shakes. They'd been together ever since; all Horse had to do to seal the deal was accept Jesus Christ as his Personal Savior, which was no problem since he basically believed that to be true anyhow.

JENNINGS STOOD NEAR THE FOOD table with Emma in his arms. Her mouth was wide open and he held before it a doughnut hole covered in powdered sugar. He moved it back and forth singing the scary music from *Jaws*, all the while bringing it closer and closer to her avid little bite. Grace looked on smiling fondly, her customary vigilance about the child's weight suspended for the moment.

"Oh my God," said Muriel, "the way she looks at him."

"Who?" asked Thaddeus.

"Emma. Jennings. The two of them."

"He better not give her that doughnut hole, though, or Grace will kill him."

"You think so?" She smiled at him as if he were a perfect idiot.

"She worries about Emma's weight. She's like a calorie Nazi."

"Well, Emma might have Jennings's metabolism."

"She should have *yours*. You're so thin. Svelte."

"I'm gaining," Muriel said. She paused, giving herself an opportunity not to say what came next. "And how would she ever get my metabolism?"

"I don't know. How would she get his?"

The temperature outside had dropped, he could feel the cold air closing in on the A-frame like a belt being cinched an extra notch.

Muriel closed the clasp on her little beaded purse. Whatever she had been looking for was no longer of interest to her. "You know, Thaddeus." She took a breath, pressed her lips together.

Candy was going on and on, thanking one person after another.

"I don't want to seem ungrateful," Muriel said. "Gratitude is part of my practice. The Buddha said that even being born is a miracle, and our chance of being here is like you drop a tiny hoop into the ocean and then on the other side of the world you put a blind turtle in the water, and that turtle sticks his head through the tiny hoop." Her hands were tightly clasped and she tapped her thumb knuckle against her chin. "I already wasted a lot of time being angry and feeling like life kind of screwed me, and I never want to go back to that state of mind. I am consciously grateful for the river, the trees, Jennings and the kids, my hands, my health, my mind. And I know I should be grateful for what you did for Hat because that's our home now, that's where we live, but, Thaddeus, I'm sorry I just wish, I wish so much, I wish you hadn't done that. I guess you meant

well. I know you did. But God I wish it had never happened. I wish
we had never set foot in that place."

"Jesus, Muriel, what the fuck?"

"Little Henry peels the paint off and eats it and there's lead in it.
Dr. Schiller says Henry's lead levels are elevated."

"Oh no."

"All I want is . . ." She was momentarily overcome. She breathed
deeply, shook her head. "I love Jennings, that's the whole thing.
He's . . . There's no one in the world like him. He's so strong and
he's so kind. He's the one. If you were walking through Naraka, and
you had to escape. He's the one you'd want with you. He'd get you
through. You don't understand. I never knew I could love someone. And for someone to love me? Even a little?" She waved as if to
dismiss an absurdity. "But he's not happy living with Hat. It's not
good. His father is really hard, you know. Really bossy. I just want
Jennings to be able to relax and be happy, that's all I want."

"Is it the taxes?" Thaddeus wanted to know. "The paint? We can
deal with the paint. I know a pediatrician in the city, a really good
one. We'll get Henry in there. We'll get this all squared away."

"Guys," Candy was calling out, "Brandon would like to say
something." The room was silent as Brandon was stood on the seat
of a chair.

"Hello, everyone," Brandon said, barely audible. "Thanks for
coming over, and helping me to see again."

"Yo, Brandon," a husky female voice called out.

"Gammana," Brandon said, and began to oscillate, his arms
spread out, forming the classic pose of a prophet. The chair threatened to tip until Candy grabbed the back of it. "Bo bo bi eye de
de da da shot tock cop pa," he said. His glossolalia was slurred and
swooping, as if all he had to do was open his mouth for the mysterious language to come pouring out.

"What the fuck?" Thaddeus whispered to Muriel.

Brandon continued to chant, it sounded like a mix of pig Latin,
Farsi jump-rope rhyme, and infantile babbling. People were either

bowing their heads, or raising up their hands as though to touch
the Lord, the hem of whose heavenly robe was but inches away. You
could feel it in the room, the fervency, the power. It was like waking
up to an earthquake or watching a glacier calve. It struck Thaddeus
that civilization was, at its core, a lie, a total scam. Creation is violent
and insane, and so are we. As he listened to Brandon, what Muriel
had been trying to tell him about Grace and Jennings circled his
thoughts, jabbing at him like devils.

Off to the side, in her aqua-and-pink party dress, Jewel was on
her knees, and right next to her was David, in a kind of crouch, as if
to compromise between devotion and his innate skepticism. Both of
their little heads were bowed. And there were Grace and Jennings.
Jennings's hands were raised to the level of his chest, the palms facing upward, as if he were carting invisible trays. Thaddeus did not
know the semaphore signals for varying degrees of piety, but it sure
looked as if Jennings was receiving the Spirit. But the final disori-
entation was Grace, who stood staring at Brandon, her arm raised
nearly straight up, as if she knew the answer and wanted to be called
on by God.

Not ten feet away was Becka Norton, one of the housecleaners who worked at Orkney, with her husband whose name Thaddeus could never remember and who he called Forlorn Mustache,
a likeable fellow who worked at a plant nursery on the other side of
the river. While Forlorn gazed neutrally into the middle distance,
Becka let forth a torrent of her own secret language, which, with
its profusion of vowels, sounded a bit like baby talk. *Ba la la la do
da da da*, benign happy sounds, untroubled, bucolic, so unlike her
actual speech, which could be harsh. She swayed back and forth, her
eyes shut. Was that who she really was? wondered Thaddeus. Near
Becka was an elderly woman in a plum pants suit with her right arm
in a sling, her face contorted as if what she was saying in the secret
language was extremely wrathful. And over there was Oscar King
from Leyden Hardware, the one who was so unjustly fired after he
went into a diabetic convulsion at work. His lips were moving at an

impossible speed, as if he were trying to count to one thousand in under a minute.

Here it was, Thaddeus thought, the hope and terror beneath the skin of daily life. Free of the bonds of so-called common sense. Free of language. Free from decorum. A kind of communal orgasm. Who knew that this church was a kind of Pentecostal Nero's Fiddle?

Who were these people? What did they know? Were they finally extraordinary, were they the human bridge between this fallen world and eternity? Compared to this surging cacophony, the encounters that made up his life were meaningless—the fruitless fetid hours with Kubrick, the egotistical drone of countless script conferences, the pass the salt how was your day of married life. Yes, there was madness in this room right now, but Thaddeus envied it, wished himself capable of it, and he felt the shame and sadness of a life not really all that well spent. "God is real!" someone cried, the one phrase of English in a bombardment of unknown languages. *Star di ba da dora stttttat keesh a na peesh ka na la luchay.* Some of those who were not speaking in tongues were screaming like girls at a rock concert. The screams were a mixture of celebration and mourning, lovely, lonely, urgent, and with something of a high howling mountain wind in them, too. People here were jumping up and down, and some were falling and others were catching those who fell. Candy lifted Brandon off of the chair, holding him as high as her arms could reach, and the hall erupted in applause, cheers, whistles, and whoops, transforming in an instant from a tabernacle to a sports arena.

"I don't want you to hate him, that's all," Muriel said. "I don't."

"Who?" And as Thaddeus asked the question, he saw Jennings and Grace winding their way toward their table. Did she mean Jennings?

Grace and Jennings flounced into their chairs as if they had just run a great distance and their legs could no longer support them. Their faces were red, their lips tight—they looked like misbehaving children doing their utmost not to laugh. Was there any more irritating sight? The privacy of their mirth was galling.

Jennings at least had the good manners to put his arm around his wife. All Grace could manage was to look down at her folded hands and shake her head, little bits of hilarity coming out of her mouth in bursts and gasps.

"What's with you two?" Thaddeus asked.

The simple question set them off. Jennings had long ago learned to laugh without drawing attention to himself and still expressed his merriment with some discretion—his shoulders shook, and his form of laughter was to force air through his clenched teeth. Grace's hilarity made her look pained, contorted, like someone in grief, or childbirth. She pounded the table with her fist.

"What the fuck?" said Thaddeus. "I mean, come on. Really."

"They're speaking in tongues," Grace finally managed to say. "For a minute I thought it was Chinese. But it's even crazier than Chinese. It's . . . tongues!"

"You two," Muriel said. She slid her chair to the left to be closer to Jennings, but the scrape of the metal legs against the floor caused them all to turn toward the sound, as if they had heard a human scream.

Emma, holding a doughnut hole in each hand, toddled over and climbed into Jennings's lap. Grace pried the food away from the little girl, who threw herself against Jennings and cried purposefully. There was her protruding belly, and there, not quite so pronounced, was Jennings's. Where did that little girl get her build? No one in Thaddeus's family was heavy, nor in Grace's. David was skinny, to the point of *feeble*. So where did that propensity to gain come from? Was that pink belly the telltale heart beating in the walls of the marriage? Thaddeus stopped himself from speculating further. He had no desire to pull at loose threads. Why unravel everything because the mind is a fidgety creature, perverse in its curiosity? No. Sometimes the mask is preferable to the face.

IT HAD NOT BEEN THEIR intention, but Thaddeus and Grace had bought their way into the society of river people, the select population of property owners along the banks of Leyden's share of the Hudson, all of whom accepted their responsibility to protect the river from those who would cheapen or befoul it. Thaddeus and Grace did their best to live up to the expectations that seemed to have been listed in invisible ink on the deed to Orkney, but their neighbors were as alien to them as the punks and situationalists and conceptual artists they used to find themselves among in New York. When Thaddeus and Grace first moved into Orkney it seemed that everyone for at least thirty miles to the north and south of them was related to someone who had had a hand in the acquisition, design, and furnishing of their property. But one by one the old fortunes were dissipated, lost, stolen, spent down to the last million, squandered, and new sorts of people were snapping up properties that suddenly seemed remarkably reasonable—especially so as New York City real estate values began to rise. Even the houses still occupied by descendants of the original owners had a compromised kind of ownership. Windsor Meadows had been on the brink of being sold to an archdiocese that wanted to turn it into a rest home for retired priests, but at the eleventh hour Nicky Steinhaus married Mai Chen, a woman from Shanghai whose father manufactured the coaxial cables everyone needed to hook up their TV to the cable box. Another of the old river houses was bought by a Yugoslavian fashion designer who had renamed the place Mamuna, after a Slavic demoness. He liked to loan it out to a bewildering assortment of friends and hangers-on—a bluegrass band, a family of French circus performers, models, jewelers, hat makers, investors, cocaine cowboys, and his own Dalmatian brothers, each drunker and rowdier than the next.

Two of the river houses, one built in 1815, the other in 1877, had gone onto the open market when the families that owned them ran out of relatives who could keep them up. Sequana was snapped up by a fellow from California named Pete Marino, who had been the sound engineer on *Buddy Klein and the Kleimaniacs in Dusseldorf,* and who subsequently produced a string of commercially successful records. Marino had run through three marriages and though his wealth had been cut in half, he was still able to make an all-cash offer on Sequana shortly after Buddy had told him it was for sale. By now, Marino was re-re-re-re-married, this time to a Yugoslavian water polo medalist named Maria who had defected during the '84 Olympics in L.A. For the price of a bungalow in Laurel Canyon, they got a William Strickland–designed Greek Revival main house, a Stanford White barn, and a pristine view of the water, and a sudden relationship with the mallards, the swans, the Canadian geese, and the occasional bald eagle that patrolled it.

To make certain Marino and others could continue to enjoy the majestic views, an ad hoc committee called Greenwatch had been formed to protect Leyden's natural beauty, primarily defending the river but also resisting development throughout the county. This afternoon's fund-raiser was specifically about Capstone Cement, which had announced its plans to build a cement plant directly on the Hudson, using the river's water as an integral part of the process of turning limestone, shale, bauxite, clay, and sand into a thick, moist slurry, to be fed into countless cement trucks that would deliver it to building sites throughout the Northeast. Capstone owned cement factories in thirty-two countries around the world, and sixteen in the U.S., primarily along the Ohio River. A privately held company, its ownership was not easily determined, nor were its finances a matter of public record. Its corporate offices were in Dover, Delaware; Guayaquil, Ecuador; and Hong Kong but they had Albany connections and the savvy to acquire 270 publically owned acres of riverfront property. Some politicians raised mild environmental concerns about the proposed plant, but most of the state officials backed Capstone's plans with great enthusiasm—not only would New York profit on the land sale, but the plant would be a source of tax revenue and (according to Capstone) at least four hundred jobs would be created.

The plant was to be named Paragon, after a venerable Hudson River steamboat. The state senate had yet to vote on the land sale and the governor was also waiting for a final report from the state's Department of Environmental Protection, though, much to the horror of Greenwatch, the DEP was going to be basing its final ruling on such matters as watershed protection and drinking water safety, and would not be considering the irretrievable aesthetic damage a cement plant would do to the life of Windsor County. There was no one in Albany who seemed to care about the value of an untroubled vista, of the sense of reality and tranquility, and, quite frankly, *decency*, it gave a person to see the world the way nature had intended it. No one in Albany seemed to care about the *violence* (there was no other word for it) that would be done to Windsor's little winding roads that were designed for buggies and even now could barely support the automobile traffic that got worse every year, roads that would be clogged with rattling trucks loaded with revolving sludge. And what about the advent of Leyden's first rush hours, when four hundred workers, each in his own Chevrolet, drove to and from work each day? What about the parking lot bordered in Cyclone fencing? What about the litter of beer cans gleaming in the moonlight and windblown Mars bars wrappers scuttling like rats across the empty asphalt?

No property had more directly a stake in this fight than Marino's: the cement factory would be exactly across the river from Sequana. If its view was spoiled, the property could lose half its value. The curving driveway to Sequana was lined on either side by white birch that gleamed like swords in the angled afternoon sunlight. The house itself was modeled after Aspey House in London, with scrolled Roman columns, ochre stonework, and a melancholy air of officialdom. Arriving guests were directed by a couple of ruddy-faced teenagers to an adjacent field, where they were ferried back to the house four at a time in a golf cart driven by a local teen hired for the afternoon.

"This is how we get around on studio lots, when I'm in California," Thaddeus said. He said it mainly to amuse David and, possibly, Emma, but neither reacted. David was sensitive to the cold and his hands covered his face against the wind. Emma was on Grace's lap, with her eyes closed.

"Sounds like fun," Grace said. "Zooming around in the nice weather."

"It's the very best part of it," Thaddeus said. *But I'm always alone,* he did not dare to add.

When they were delivered to the front entrance, the driver gave each of them a blue-and-white campaign button that read Save Our River. Emma was asleep so Grace was carrying her, and David had been reabsorbed by the strange bright flat heartless world of the Game Boy. Thaddeus kept his hand on the boy's shoulder as they entered the house, to remind David that he was part of humanity, and to demonstrate to Grace that he was not leaving child care solely to her.

"I think the food will be a lot better here," Thaddeus said as they mounted the stone steps and approached the tall, freshly painted front door. "Poor people have shitty food." He'd meant it ironically, but his delivery was off and he wished he hadn't said it.

"I'm thinking drinks," Grace said.

"Nervous? Why?"

She scowled, as if *once again* he had forgotten something they had been over and over. Marriage had a way of becoming a test you'd forgotten to study for.

"One of my pieces?" she said, finding it unbearable to supply more information than that.

"Oh, it'll be fine. It'll be great."

"Not to be cavalier about it or anything. Right?"

"Grace. Your work is amazing. Truly amazing." He was starting not to quite believe it—or was he losing all belief in himself and everything he said? Who was he seeing through: Grace the Artist, or Thaddeus the Good Man?

In the foyer was a large print of an Annie Leibovitz photograph of Whoopi Goldberg soaking in a bathtub filled with milk. The party was already well under way. The sound of merry, well-lubricated voices, the smell of wood smoke, perfume, and gin. David managed to keep his eye on the electronic game even as he offered his arms one at a time to his father, who took off his outerwear. Emma's face was slack, her lips parted.

"Maybe we should take her home," Grace said.

"We're here. It'll be fine. We don't want to miss the auction."

Hoisting Emma up so as to get a firmer purchase on her, Grace took Thaddeus's arm with her free hand.

"If everyone goes silent when my painting comes up, get the thing started. Okay?"

It was the most vulnerable thing she'd said to him in months. Thaddeus felt a rush of tenderness, a gust of blind urgent humble abject love and in its wake Muriel's hinting about Emma's paternity was revealed as either a piece of insanity or sheer wickedness. That Grace and Jennings were fucking was beyond belief to him—how could people he cared so much about behave in such a hurtful way? And that his daughter was not biologically his was not only unlikely, it was patently absurd.

"I keep meaning to ask you," he said, taking Emma out of Grace's arms. The little girl clicked into his contours like a Lego. "Do you spend time with Jennings and Muriel when I'm not around?"

"Not really. Why?"

"She says she wishes we never gave the house to them."

"We didn't. You did. And anyhow you gave it to Hat. Because of the *accident*."

He wasn't sure why she said *accident* in such a bitter, mocking tone.

"Well, Muriel wishes they weren't there. I'll tell you one thing. She loves her husband. She's really devoted."

"I have dogs for that."

"Well, maybe *devoted* isn't the right word."

"She's such an idiot," said Grace, in a tone that implied this was an issue that had been settled long ago.

"Apparently the walls have lead . . ."

"I know, I know. But isn't that Muriel's responsibility? Excuse me for being just a little fed up with Little Miss Yoga but all she does is complain."

"I never hear her complain," Thaddeus said.

"Yes, well, you're never here, are you?"

He laughed. "Well, I stepped right into that one, didn't I?"

THE APPETIZERS WERE MEDITERRANEAN, AND the drinks were like shortcuts to oblivion—pink ladies, made with particularly potent Dutch gin, and an extra-sweet brand of grenadine. Whoever mixed them must have been given instructions to get everyone attending the Greenwatch benefit loaded, as a way of stimulating reckless, extravagant, price-is-no-object bidding. It was not an idea without flaws. Some of the guests were rendered practically immobile by the drinks and others remained animated but distracted. In the ballroom where the auction was taking place, the guests seemed to be listing to one side, as if on a ferry crossing a stretch of rough water. The imaginative canapés were no match for the pink ladies. The pink ladies were not only strong, they were delicious. The catering-service workers, in their coal black trousers and ice white shirts, tiptoed devilishly around the room, refilling glasses. When Hal Marquette tried to cover his glass to prevent a refill, the waiter ended up sloshing pink lady on his ruddy knuckles and Longines watch.

While Grace was putting Emma down in a guest bedroom on the second floor, Thaddeus wandered over to stand with Buddy Klein, Gene Woodard, and Pete Marino.

"You look good, Buddy," Thaddeus said. The old rocker had had a cardiac scare of some sort. He wouldn't say exactly what had happened, but he was able to drive himself down to Columbia-Presbyterian, where he stayed for three days, attended to by his ex-wife and their daughter.

"I feel good," Buddy said, a little bit the way James Brown sang it.

"Good. You really do. You look good."

"What about me?" said Marino.

"You look good, too," Thaddeus said. "Stunning. Hey there, Gene. I don't want to leave you out of this. You, too, look ravishing." In the end, their friendship had not survived Thaddeus and Grace buying Orkney. As far as he could figure it, Gene felt that their moving to Leyden was a kind of invasion. *He can go fuck himself,* was Grace's final word on the subject of Gene Woodard. *But I really like him,* Thaddeus said, to which she only shook her head, as if he had confessed to being completely devoid of pride.

"Hello there, Kaufman," Gene said. He made a small smile that could have been friendly but could just as well have reflected some private thought or musing. Thaddeus could not help but admire the manners of the rich, their placid, basically easygoing way of dealing with friend and foe. Before moving to Leyden—well, actually, before meeting Gene Woodard—Thaddeus had a totally different sense of how people acted at the top of the food chain, a misconception based on the political and moral disapproval of those who had gotten more than their share. His family's idea of a rich person was a dentist. In college, Thaddeus might have been casually acquainted with one or two people from privileged backgrounds, but on campus everyone seemed pretty much the same. And in all likelihood, really rich kids tended to avoid the University of Michigan, even if they themselves were from Michigan.

"We should hang out sometime," Thaddeus said to Gene. "I miss seeing you around."

"Good idea," Woodard said. "We always think of you as being . . . away somewhere." He gestured, a little wave into the unknown. "Or perhaps donating a house to someone."

"Oh, you're the one who did that?" Marino said.

"A Whistler etching went for $9,200," Buddy said, changing the subject.

"I think it was a lithograph," Marino said. "It was very small," he added, as if to reassure.

"I recently learned that that painting *Whistler's Mother* wasn't painted by Whistler, it was like by some friend of the family," Thaddeus said.

"That's ridiculous," Gene Woodard said. "Who told you that?"

Thaddeus shrugged. "Some fucking idiot in Hollywood, I guess."

"God, Kaufman," Woodard said, shaking his head. "This calls for another drink."

"I used to see him all the time," Thaddeus said, watching Gene wind his way through the crowd. "I don't think he's forgiven us for buying up here. I think he's a gatekeeper."

"Don't tell his gatekeeper that," Buddy replied.

The rows of red-and-black folding chairs were mainly empty. Most of the guests milled about the ballroom, their Sunday shoes clacking on the parquet floor, the tops of their heads lit by the chandelier that loomed so ponderously. Standing at the front of the room, on a platform originally built as a small stage for musicians, Burton Patty was conducting the auction, just as he did the first Saturday of every month from his barn on the edge of town, where he disposed of the worldly goods of people either on their way up or down. Patty's face was as colorless and unlined as a bar of soap. His expression was impatient, rather unpleasant, and his movements were brusque. Not one for conversation, he seemed practically aphasic, except when running the numbers, when the words came out like bullets from a Gatling gun. His sleepy, frowning son, in his forties now, lumpy and unmarried, and serving a life sentence as his father's assistant, was holding a painting of an unsaddled chestnut horse standing in front of a plowed field.

Charles Vengris, standing behind Thaddeus, exclaimed, "Oh, that's mine and it's worth a great deal of money, everyone!" Thaddeus wondered what *mine* meant—had Vengris painted it himself or just donated something he owned? His mother had made a wise second marriage and was able to leave him some good furniture and a few interesting paintings, though not any cash money. Vengris was slight, not emphatically gendered, and did not own a house on or near the river. He taught dressage to the local girls and in the evenings he was available even at the very last minute for any decent dinner invitation.

"I was supposed to be on at that great No-Nukes Concert at the Garden," Buddy was saying. His cocktail glass was nearly empty, and he scanned the room looking for the girl with the pitcher of fresh fuel. "I was backstage, me, the whole band. But Springsteen ran long."

"I remember that," Marino said.

"And the Doobie Brothers wouldn't get their asses off the stage."

"That I don't remember," Marino said. "But I never remember the Doobie Brothers."

"And now we're here," Buddy said. He wagged his empty glass over his head, as if ringing a bell.

"It's a bit different, I guess," Thaddeus said. "Nuclear power plants that could kill a million people. And a cement factory that's basically an eyesore."

"It's a lot more than that," Marino said. "The river is part of the American heritage. Do you really want to live in a world without natural beauty? And who are these assholes pushing for this thing— without a real environmental study? Do they even care about killing the Hudson?"

"Supposedly the plant will mean four hundred new jobs," Buddy said.

"First of all," Marino said, "who the fuck wants to work in a cement plant?"

"I was asked to rewrite a remake of *Lady in Cement*," Thaddeus interjected. *Who the fuck wants to work in a cement plant?* Had it really come to this? Was this the way the people in his life thought about the world?

The bidding was anemic on Vengris's bay horse, and it went for $130 to Lydia Bishop. Once that was disposed of, Burton Patty's son Marshall made his way to the wall where the remaining artworks

were on display. His movements were bearlike, his shoulders sloped
down, his head swung back and forth. Yet as stunned and without
will as he seemed, he did not hesitate to take down Grace's painting,
somehow knowing that it was next to go.

Thaddeus was surprised she'd chosen the small oil she'd made
of their son last year, a Renaissance-style portrait of David, frail and
shirtless, his skin golden and lit from within. He was posed in front
of Orkney like a Florentine princelet in front of a villa, and he held
a shining chrome toy airplane—a sly reference to an old Blind Faith
record jacket. Thaddeus thought this portrait of their son was somehow a family possession. Grace had countless paintings and drawings stored in her studio—why had she chosen to auction off one
with such sentimental value? He wondered if he had somehow failed
to sufficiently appreciate the painting, failed to communicate how
beautiful it was, *how fine the brushwork, how saturated the palette*—
fucking hell, it was awfully difficult for him to discuss painting.

"What if nobody bids," Grace whispered to him.

"Then I will," he said.

"No! Please. Don't. That would be worse."

"But you said . . ."

"I don't care what I said. Just don't."

"Hey, Grace," Buddy said, his grin crooked. "Where'd you come
from?"

"We were at the benefit for Horse and Candy's little boy," Grace
said. "I thought we might see you there."

"That Redneck Festival at the Fellowship Hall?" Buddy said.
"Man, when those monkeys get going, watch out."

"This I believe is an oil," Burton Patty announced, pushing
his rimless spectacles high onto his forehead, frowning elaborately.
"Contemporary. Signed. Canvas, roughly eight inches by five inches.
Ready-made frame—included." He tapped the frame admiringly,
as if at least *that* had some discernible value. "We'll start at two
hundred." Patty's son whispered to him. "Thank you. This is a local
artist. Grace Cornwall."

"Cornell," Thaddeus corrected, in a fairly strong voice, though Patty gave no sign of having heard.

"Don't," Grace whispered.

"Fuck him," Thaddeus mouthed.

"Two hundred, two hundred, bidding here bidding here two hundred two hundred. One fifty get up and go, one fifty."

"Seventy-five," a wavering voice said from near the front of the room.

"This is really unpleasant," Grace said through clenched teeth.

"Two hundred here," said Buddy Klein. "Actually, make it three."

Thaddeus and Grace both knew that Klein had very little money on hand. In the past few months he had had the electricity turned off at his house for an entire week, and he'd sold a precious Martin guitar in order to pay his oil bill.

Marino bid next, perhaps wanting Grace's painting, though more likely in recognition of Buddy's financial straits—it had been Marino who'd taken the Martin off Buddy's hands.

"Four hundred, four, four, four," Patty nasally half-sang. Patty's personal touch to the art of auctioneering was to point at the bidders with his left hand, moving his finger back and forth as if searching for the right person, the person who understood the value of what was being sold, and then moving his finger in a tight, rapid 360 degrees, to draw a circle around the bidder.

Most of the people seemed not to be paying attention to the painting. They were visiting with one another, concentrating on the ancient Sunday business of getting ginned to the gills.

"Four is standing, looking for four fifty, four fifty, four fifty, who's going to get up, who's going to go," Patty chanted. He glanced at his son, who now paced left to right holding Grace's canvas aloft.

"Four once," Patty said.

"Four fifty," Thaddeus called out.

"Thaddeus!" Grace said in a furious whisper.

"I can bid five hundred." The voice came from one of the few people who were seated, Pierpont Davis, whose family was once prominent in Windsor County but who had lost his estate going short on Xerox shares. He lived now in New Jersey, in a split-level with aluminum siding and a riotous front yard overrun with valerian. He remained a frequent visitor to Leyden, prevailing upon old friends and pretending to be in the market for a place in the area, using up hours of Sawyer Halliday's time, as the real estate agent had no recourse but to take Davis at his word. For today's benefit he'd arrived half-crocked and the pink ladies were the coup de grace. He wore heavy charcoal and burgundy wool trousers, and a matching jacket with big leather buttons, and a bright white hairpiece that rested on his head like frosting on a cupcake. It was a toupee that was not expected to be taken very seriously. He was seated a couple of chairs away from David, who was hypnotized by his Game Boy and seemed to have no awareness of the existence of anything else, including himself.

"Five hundred over here," Patty said, pointing at Davis, and twirling his finger as if to circle a name.

"Let him have it," Grace whispered, grasping Thaddeus's arm.

"For five hundred dollars?"

"I'm serious."

"These people are so cheap. And they talk about the Jews. The Jews are drunken sailors next to these tight-asses."

"Just let it go, okay?"

Thaddeus drew in a deep breath. To silence himself he took a long swallow of his drink. "Motherfucker," he muttered, holding the glass before him and gazing at it with the respect you afford a worthy opponent.

"I know," Grace said. "We're going to have to crawl home."

"David's over there practicing his hand-eye coordination. He can drive us home."

"It's awful. It's like that box is eating his soul."

"What do you think it's worth?"

"His soul?"

"Ha. No, your painting."

"Sold," said Patty, and he drew his imaginary circle around Davis's head.

"Now what the hell do I do?" Davis said. The complaint was jokey, meant to amuse, but everyone there knew he could not afford a painting.

"You bought it, Piers," a voice said, in mock admonishment. "Now it's yours."

"Yes," said Davis, "the rules of the game. Well, I'll tell you what I am going to do." He sprang up to the platform and took possession of Grace's painting. He frowned at it, nodding sagely, as if fully qualified to estimate its worth. Pierpont's great-aunt had had her portrait done by Sargent, and since then the Davis family all considered themselves somehow on the inside track when it came to the arts, especially painting. "I am going to re-auction this very interesting piece, done by one of our terrific neighbors, a local artist."

"I can't watch this," Grace said, shaking her head. "They're treating it like a joke."

"He's broke," said Thaddeus. "He can't pay for it."

"Let's just get out of here."

"Let me bid. Please."

"No!" Her face reddened. She looked murderous. He had never felt frightened of her before.

She turned quickly, and cut a winding path through the standing crowd. Instinctually, Thaddeus followed behind. He saw her for a moment with a cold, appraising eye. Her body had lost some of its youthfulness. Not so much as his—he was a thickening wreck of a man! But Grace? Somehow it had once seemed possible that she would avoid the horns of time with a few deft matador moves. But now—it seemed to have happened all at once—those jeans were tighter than she might have wanted them to be. It may have been the weather, it may have been the light, but it seemed as if her once-shining hair had lost some of its luster. And her legs had lost their gamine quality. He had of course always known that one day

it would happen. Well, welcome to that day. He remembered thinking it on their wedding day at Kip's old loft. Her mother had had a
difficult time pulling off her boots, and when she did Thaddeus had
noted with just the merest trace of alarm the size of her calves. They
were massive and muscular, they put you in mind of hard work,
muddy fields, East German athletes turning around and around in
circles before heaving the shot put. Maureen sensed his eyes on her
and she turned toward him, smiled, and even made a kind of pose.

Davis was capering back and forth holding Grace's painting
aloft, while Patty scowled at him. "All right, fellow custodians of all
that is good and gracious, let's get some real money out here. If we're
going to stop them from turning our river into a factory, we're going
to have to dig deep. Let's start the bidding at one thousand."

"Pierpont," a laughing voice called out. "It's your baby, you
rock it."

"Five thousand," Thaddeus called, and without waiting another
moment he turned and walked quickly across the room, and was just
able to catch up to Grace and follow her out.

"Hey," he said. "Hey hey hey." It was as if he were trying to calm
a horse.

"Oh, just get me out of here," Grace said. "This is humiliating."

"We're already out of there, baby," Thaddeus said. They stood in
the house's central hall, with its compass-mosaic floor.

"Are you insane? I *told* you not to bid." They were both swaying,
far drunker than they realized.

"I want that painting. You shouldn't have donated it. Not that one."

"Sold to the bidder at five thousand," Burton Patty declared
from a distance, without gratitude or pleasure, like a lock snapping
shot. There was a smattering of applause.

"Oh please. Let's just get out of here."

"I'm sorry. I was—"

"I don't care, I don't care, I don't care. Go get your son. There's
no way in hell I'm walking back into that room."

"Let's get Emma first," Thaddeus said. "It'll take a while."

"I'll do it. You get David."

"No, let's both. She *is* my child, right?"

"What is that supposed to mean?"

"Nothing. Everything. Fuck it. Sorry sorry sorry. It's the pink ladies talking."

SEQUANA'S PREVIOUS OWNERS HAD USED this second-floor room as an office, where the various accounts were settled, ledger books kept in order and stored. Though Marino's contractor had instructed the painters to scent the paint with vanilla, the room retained the old tobacco smell, the green and the black of it, the leaf and the creosote left behind by the stogies and cheroots and corncob pipes puffed on and chewed as household accounts were settled, and meager wages were dispensed. Those deep low wet rumbling coughs were still in the air, the tap of a twiddled fountain pen striking the old unlovely desk, the horror house creak of the swivel chair tilting back. Now the room was full of Marino's possessions—his vintage posters announcing appearances by Howlin' Wolf and Roosevelt Sykes at long-defunct Chicago clubs; the photographs he had taken of old people on the Nevksy Prospekt; the gaudily painted ostrich eggs notched precariously on their wooden stands; the queen-size bed with a kind of faux-Storyville frame; the bedspread that appeared to be fur, dyed in black-and-white stripes.

Emma slept on her back, her arms and legs flung wide, her lips in a dainty pout. Her thin brown hair stuck to her forehead—she often perspired while sleeping. Grace had dressed her in a little plaid dress, red-and-black tights, patent leather party shoes. Her belly rose and fell with her deep breaths—the belly Grace had expected her to lose once she was walking, the belly that got just a little bit rounder and larger every month, her intractable belly, her pink and downy belly full of the foods Grace allowed.

How a little girl whose diet consisted mainly of vegetables and poached fish could not only fail to lose weight but was actually still *gaining weight* was a mystery.

Grace and Thaddeus were at extreme odds over the campaign to slim down their daughter. Thaddeus found Grace's hectoring unbearable, and more than once he had stormed away from the dining table rather than listen to another word of his wife's admonitions. His credibility in matters pertaining to the children was not particularly high. They both knew he hated to say no to the kids about *anything*. They both knew he basically thought that the very fact of them was so pleasing, so miraculous, such a blessing, such a privilege, such a run of good fortune in a universe that could—and often *did*—take everything away in an instant, that matters of discipline were almost completely ignored, or, really, simply left to Grace. All Daddy focused on was letting the kids know at every turn how profoundly and unconditionally loved they were. Easy to say this with an overnight bag in your hand. Easy to say with a limo waiting on the driveway. Easy to say with your scalp smelling of the fancy shampoo you brought home from the Royal Excelsior Palace Please Let Us Kiss Your Ass Hotel, or wherever the hell you'd spent the past few nights. And anyhow, what was the virtue of unconditional love? It was a slogan that certainly had curb appeal—but when it led to your son retreating into a haze of snottiness and silence, a world in which his most vital relationships were with poorly drawn characters nuking each other in boxes of light, or it led to a life of obesity, a life of loneliness followed by diabetes, might not love be of more value if it came with a few goddamn conditions?

THADDEUS HOVERED AT THE BEDSIDE and looked down at the child. Her chin, her wispy eyebrows, her oval face, the way her hair curled, all the genetic markers that had once reminded him of himself, or of his mother or father or grandparents, seemed to have disappeared. He did not see Jennings in her, but . . . it remained possible. *Conceivable,* his mind punned. Why not turn toward Grace right now and confront her with his suspicions? Why hint?

Grace was bent over the bed. She was awakening the child in the gentlest manner possible. She placed but one finger on her shoulder and tapped—if you were performing CPR on a mouse you would use more force.

"Let her sleep," Thaddeus whispered.

"What do you mean?"

"Nothing." He would not mention his conversation with Muriel. If Grace had secrets he would not unearth them. It was more complicated than his simply not wanting to know. It was a matter of respect, autonomy. It was also not wanting to destroy the fabric into which the secrets were woven. He could not get to the truth without dismantling whatever structure of lies, evasions, and denials she had constructed in order to conceal it. It would all be destroyed. Sometimes you just had to accept not knowing. The archaeologists finding ancient papyrus scrolls in Pompeii could not open them without having them turn to dust. Inside the scrolls might lurk undiscovered plays by Sophocles or further histories of Suetonius, but they remained unread and preserved.

Was she reading his thoughts somehow? Grace suddenly grasped his shoulders and turned him by forty-five degrees until they were facing and she kissed him hard and full on the mouth, or reasonably close to full on the mouth because they were out of practice with each other and they were impaired. Their minds slid and stumbled through the wreckage of gin and grenadine, and of course he had to spoil it, he could feel himself going too far even as he tried to keep himself in check. He reached between her legs, his stiffened fingers insistent, invasive, and yet strangely resigned to defeat, like doomed soldiers storming a barricade. She intercepted his hand and squeezed his fingers until they relaxed. He yielded to her, and she placed his pacified palm at her center, and moved herself ever so much closer to him to increase the contact.

"Slow," she said. "Gentle."

Though he was no longer able to see her, Thaddeus sensed that Emma had awakened. Her eyes were open, she was watching them. Yet he continued to kiss Grace, his mouth open and yearning, insane with desire. *Let the kid watch, what's the harm? This is life at its best. There is nothing better than this.*

"You're everything to me," he said to his wife.

"Mom? I hungry," said Emma from the bed. "Is there snacks?" She patted her belly, rather hard, as if she were thumping a melon to check for ripeness.

THEY WERE FERRIED BACK TO the pasture that had been designated as the parking area. The golf cart's feeble headlights were no match for the darkness. The boy driving them smelled of cigarettes and cold wind. He wore a Buffalo Bills souvenir jacket. Little bits of frost stuck to the ends of his hair. There was something odd in his manner. He seemed angry or nervous. Something. Maybe, Thaddeus thought, he was just cold.

"We the first to leave?" Thaddeus asked.

Silence. Thaddeus waited. Finally, the boy said, "Pretty much." He snapped the lights of the cart off and on again, four times.

"Well, I bet it'll wrap up pretty soon," Thaddeus said, and then it occurred to him that the kid might want the party to go on until dawn. *How have I managed to forget the concept of hourly wages?* he wondered.

"I'll bet it's quite a party in there," the boy said.

"It's all right. The drinks were strong." He heard scuffling in the backseat and Grace's stern voice. All she had to do was say his name and David settled down.

"I heard they were trying to stop the cement plant from being built," the boy said. He was driving very slowly, still fiddling with the lights.

"Yeah. It could screw up the river."

"Gee," the boy said. It was hard to tell if his tone was sarcastic.

As they approached the pasture/parking area, they heard engines revving high—a convoy was leaving in a hurry. Suddenly, high beams were bearing down on them. First one pickup truck and then another and after that a third came barreling past them, barely able to squeeze by on the narrow access road leading from the pasture, yet making no effort to slow down. Thaddeus could smell the fumes of burning fuel, and the rumble of engines buzzed at the marrow of his bones. The oversize tires lifted up fans of pebbled snow, and a spray of it came into the golf cart. Emma screamed in dismay, while David remained stoic, his hand at his throat, a look of disdain on his face.

Thaddeus turned. The rear lights of the last truck burned through the night and beneath them was the bumper sticker he'd seen at the Lord's Fellowship parking area—the line of cartoon penguins wearing red bow ties: Puttin' on the Ritz.

"Who was that?" Thaddeus asked, but the boy only shrugged. There was only a bit of moonlight, not enough to really see the cars. The boy drove the golf cart slowly through the pasture, waiting to be told to stop.

"I think we were farther back," Thaddeus said. "We were one of the last to arrive." A moment later he added, "And first to leave."

Grace wrapped her arms around Emma and raked her fingers through the child's hair, taking out clumps of dirty snow. David saw an opening and took it—he grabbed his Game Boy out of his mother's coat pocket.

The windshield of somebody's old Jaguar was extravagantly cracked, a spiderweb that spanned practically the whole expanse of the windshield. "Oh fuck," Thaddeus said, too softly for the children to hear, he hoped. Next to the Jaguar was a new Mercedes, and in case there were any lingering doubts about what the people in those fleeing pickup trucks were up to, the windshield of this car was similarly cracked, in fact this one was even worse. A chunk of cement lay on the hood.

"Wait, slow down," Thaddeus said.

"Whoa," David said, his voice riding a wave of admiration. "Look, Mom." He stood up in the back of the cart.

One car after the other stood in the darkness, windshields smashed. At last, after twenty or so cars, the destruction had stopped. Most likely the vandals had heard the electric whine of the golf cart approaching, or the rustle of the wheels moving over the frost. Or maybe they just got tired.

Thaddeus and Grace's own car was parked outside the arc of destruction.

"You better get back there and tell Mr. Marino what's happened out here," Thaddeus said. "Okay? I mean Pete. Right? Tell Pete." Maybe the whole problem was that some people got called Mister, and some got called by their first names, and there were some who didn't even get that—the Whiteys, the Shorties, the Sparkys, and the Hats.

Thaddeus took Emma from Grace and the little girl fit herself into him like a puzzle piece. How could she *not* be his daughter?

"We got lucky," Grace said. She dug into the pocket of her turquoise wool coat and brought out the keys.

"My guess is that people from Party One paid a little visit to the people from Party Two." Thaddeus wondered if the people in the fleeing trucks had recognized Grace's car and deliberately left it untouched.

"I'm sorry I got upset back in there," she said, putting Emma in her car seat. "I realize you were trying to be nice. About my painting."

"I wanted the painting," Thaddeus said.

Grace glanced at him, and decided to let it pass.

"Cold!" the little girl cried out. She flutter-kicked her legs but it was mainly symbolic. She had already learned it was hopeless to protest.

Grace was having a hard time fastening the snaps on the car seat. "Suck your stomach in," she said.

David had gotten in on the other side of the car. His face had a primordial glow, illuminated by dull silver light as the Game Boy slowly powered on.

"In, Emma. Stomach in!"

Thaddeus put a hand on Grace's shoulder and she stepped quickly to one side. "You want to do it? Be my guest."

"Okay," he said. He thought about adding, *After all, she is my daughter,* but that would be ridiculous. He stepped closer to the car so he could deal with the child seat. It was his bailiwick anyhow, the car seat. However, there seemed to be something a little balky in the snaps. *Dear Britax, Thank you for making the best and most expensive car seat in the world. Too bad the snaps don't fucking snap.* His hands were shaking. He was tense and he was cold. And now there was something slimy, wet, and cold on his feet.

He looked down. There was a small crack in the ground, a few inches from the car. Something dark and viscous was bubbling out and slowly spreading.

"Oh shit," said Grace. "Our shoes." She made a defeated sound and covered her eyes with her hand. "Such a waste."

"It smells like sulfur." Thaddeus jumped back. "Did you hear that?"

"What?"

"I don't know. I thought I heard the crack getting wider. Like a ticking. A stretching."

"Those shoes were my favorite," Grace said. She slid behind the wheel, turned the ignition.

"We should get out of here," Thaddeus said. He finally snapped the buckle to Emma's car seat, and he slammed the door.

"Yes. Well, do you notice that you're the only one not in the car?"

Before he knew what he was doing, he grabbed the lapel of her coat and would have lifted her off the seat had she not been belted in. "Everything you say hurts my feelings," he said to her through clenched teeth. He held her for another few moments and let go.

He walked through the headlights to the passenger side. There was pounding between his ears, as if his brain had become a second heart.

Grace rearranged herself on the seat, holding on to the steering wheel as she shifted her weight. She didn't look frightened. She didn't even look upset. She seemed satisfied, as if right before her eyes her husband had suddenly become the person she had always suspected he was.

Chapter 11

Mimosa Sunday

JULY 18, 1989

EPSTEIN PICTURES

It's His Birthday

Arlene Epstein & Bruce Hollander
Request the Pleasure of Your Company

To Celebrate Craig Epstein on his
"27th Year to Heaven"

2___ Briarcrest Drive, Beverly Hills

T HE SHADOWS FROM THE LEAVES OF THE OVERHANGING
willow trees and California sycamore descended upon the
windshield, landing silently on the glass and disappearing at the
next curve. The sunlight poured through the driver's-side window,
illuminating Neal Kosoff's tangerine hair, his freckled scalp, the
screw heads on the hinges of his eyeglasses, the bulbous tip of his
nose, the crown of his Cartier watch. Somewhere along the way,
in Kosoff's journey from his childhood in Toronto as a sickly boy
endlessly at play with his toy soldiers, to university in London, to a

lucky entrance into the theater world, to his first film, his first Hollywood film, his first Hollywood hit, and his current position poised
near the top of the B-list of directors, he had settled into a public
persona almost entirely based on wit—or at least jocularity. Since
picking Thaddeus up at the Four Seasons this morning, Kosoff had
not stopped smiling—he smiled so much out here in California that
the creases near his eyes were fish-belly white.

"I guess you've heard this one," Kosoff said to Thaddeus, stopping at a light on the all but deserted street. "A priest and a rabbi
are sitting at a little café on Melrose and a boy walks by. Four years
old, right? So the priest says, Ooh, I'd like to fuck that kid. Really?
the rabbi says. Out of what?" Kosoff's hand—pale and spotted like a
freshwater fish—reached for the dark mahogany gear-shift nob. The
hairs on his fingers bristled in the light, rigid red spears.

"No, haven't heard that one before," said Thaddeus.

"It's not anti-Semitic," Kosoff said.

"Not particularly."

"I mean it sort of is, but the priest gets the worst of it. You can't
be anti-Semitic and anti-Catholic."

"Well, I don't know about that. Quite a few Nazis managed."

For the first time this morning, Kosoff allowed his smile to disappear. It was a relief to see it go, like watching the owner finally
take charge of his little yappy dog. "Aren't you in a shit mood today."

"I'm fine."

"Jet-lagged."

"I don't get jet-lagged going east to west. It's when I go home
that I get sort of fucked up."

"That's home for you," Kosoff said, his smile restored.

Coincidentally, Neal and Thaddeus were dressed similarly, as
if they were a team, which, for today's purposes, they more or less
were. In blue blazers and light-colored trousers, and stiffly tasseled
loafers, they were on their way to a birthday brunch that Arlene
Epstein was having to celebrate her son's twenty-seventh birthday.
Arlene had secured the rights to *The Strike*, a novel by a young writer

called Gary Shaiken about workers occupying the General Motors plant in Flint, Michigan, in 1937, and for the past few weeks she had been holding court, talking to directors and writers, and by all accounts thoroughly enjoying her position as one who controlled a project whose fervency and good old-fashioned heart-on-the-sleeve progressive politics dozens of Hollywood players gravitated toward, as if the story of young workers risking life and limb to form the United Auto Workers had within it something decent and purifying and all those who participated in the telling would have their former idealism restored. Heretofore, Arlene had only coproduced a handful of cheap, rather broad comedies, and Kosoff barely knew her. Thaddeus had yet to meet Arlene and neither of them had met Craig, her son.

"I get it," Kosoff said, navigating the car around the sun-blasted curves of Coldwater Canyon Drive. "The connection between *The Strike* and *Hostages*. And I think she's going to bring me on to direct. Gut feeling."

"Then what the fuck am I doing here?"

"She brings me in, I bring you. But it'll be easier if she meets you, maybe thinks it's her idea."

"Wow, that's some amazing reverse psychology you've got going, Neal."

"You are really in a mood."

"I'm too old to be charming."

"Never! Anyhow, she's going to like you. Her family is like yours."

"Oh?"

"Old Commies."

"My parents weren't Communists. Trotskyists. Big difference."

Kosoff laughed merrily. "It's like Munchkins."

"Really?"

"Well, yeah, I mean they're both so famous."

As they approached Arlene's house, Thaddeus powered his window down, suddenly desperate to breathe some actual air. The smell

of the outdoors was sharp, piney, with something combustible in
the weave of it, some stray element, or rogue compound turning the
air into fuel for the apocalypse. Everything in L.A. felt unstable.
It was a wonder the trees could stay rooted in the parched, sloping
ground; one good shake and the whole expensive mess would go
sliding down into the Los Angeles basin. The news was full of stories
about environmental catastrophe by which the state's ultimate end
could be surmised. Weird objects washed up on the beaches. Just
two nights ago a hundred swollen black tuxedos filled with water
were spotted near Catalina, looking like the bodies of obese men,
bobbing ten feet from the shore—and no one could say where they'd
come from. Sudden tidal surges washed away fifty million dollars of
real estate in less time than it took to say *May I put you on hold?* Yes,
by all means, put *everything* on hold. Put that hole in the ozone on
hold. Put those geologic squeaks and twitters along the shit-eating
grin of the San Andreas fault on hold. Put those wildfires in the hills
of Santa Monica on hold—was it there or Malibu that temperatures
soared so that horses grazing in the pastures exploded from the heat?
And by all means put on hold the sense of impending doom that
seized Thaddeus the moment his plane touched the runway at LAX,
the sense that here was a place that one day was going to blow up
or burn down or be swallowed whole, and when it happened no
one in all the world would be terribly surprised—sad, yes, horrified,
naturally, but there would not be the slightest element of surprise.
The city would become a vast screaming ward of suffering survivors
and the great unanswerable question would follow them to their
mass grave: What did they expect? How could they have built those
multimillion-dollar houses where they could not stand? The city was
like a display of Fabergé eggs set up on an escalator! Was it really
worth all this for three hundred days of sunshine?

   As Neal guided the Benz into the circular driveway on Briar-
crest, the sun beat against the long brown hood like a fiery hammer.
A ring of vehicles lined the driveway—most of the guests for Arlene's
Sunday brunch had already arrived. There was a sporty red MG, a

dune buggy painted Creamsicle orange, a white Rolls, a Vincent Black Shadow, and an old Mustang with a copperish filigree of rust all over the back bumper. Wearing baggy shorts and a sweat-stained maroon tank top, a slightly built Mexican yard worker was cleaning the dead matter out of the yew bushes with a rake in one hand and the nozzle of a leaf blower in the other.

The house itself was modern, simple and white, and looked like a box from an expensive shoe store. Five broad cement steps led to the entrance. A glass double door offered a view straight through the foyer and out the back to the brick veranda and a view of the distant city, which today looked particularly foreboding beneath a motionless ring of pale brown pollution.

Currently, Craig Epstein was living with his mother and her second husband, Bruce Hollander, the owner of a sports memorabilia shop in the Glendale Galleria. Now that Craig had bought (with his mother's money) a controlling interest in a minor league baseball team out of Concord, New Hampshire, Hollander insisted upon relating to him as if they both were in the "sportsatainment business." Upon rising that morning in his room at the Four Seasons, Thaddeus had wondered how attending a birthday brunch for Craig Epstein would be of any real use to him. True, transactions in the movie business were often a matter of relationships, but attending a birthday party for Craig Epstein was a bridge too far. And now, milling around Arlene and Hollander's living room, with its expensive, uncomfortable modernist furniture, its white vases filled with Casablanca lilies, its white carpeting, its white tiles around a white brick hearth in which were stacked three picturesque white birch logs that would never be burned, Thaddeus was certain he should be back in Leyden doing whatever could be done to spackle over the fissures that had destabilized his home. Or reading. Saul Bellow, maybe *Seize the Day*, one of the short ones. Or poetry! To his great surprise, it turned out Thaddeus was mad for poetry. He ought to have listened to his own internally murmured misgivings and refused Kosoff's request to come out here and help woo Arlene. Thaddeus's first thought had been his best thought (as Allen Ginsberg would have it). Allen Ginsberg! Now *that* would be a way to spend a Sunday, reading "Howl" or "Sunflower Sutra," not here sipping on a mimosa that promised a splitting headache by midafternoon, and looking at the panoramic view of the ongoing catastrophe below. Where was Ginsberg anyhow? Probably in his walk-up on the Lower East Side. His tea brewing in the old kitchen, stacks of books everywhere like a poetry Stonehenge. His lover staring out the window, his fingers laced around the metal bars of the burglar gates, a square of sunlight on his cowboy shirt. Yes, yes, where was Ginsberg? But more to the point: where was Grace? Thaddeus checked his watch. One o'clock here in L.A., four back home. (*Home!*)

"I notice you looking at your watch," a voice said.

Thaddeus looked up and the birthday boy was there in all his Weekend-with-Mom glory. Craig's thick wavy brown hair was matted, he was unshaven, and he wore maroon-and-white-striped pajamas. He was wandering around while holding a jar of peanut butter in one hand and a spoon in the other. His pajama top had been misbuttoned and curls of his body hair were visible, like insulation in a house under construction, or demolition. Craig's green eyes were far apart and sleepy, his nose was oily, and he smiled unpleasantly, as if he had heard something compromising about Thaddeus and was deciding whether or not to use it against him.

"Thinking of my wife, figuring out what she might be doing," Thaddeus said, staring at the peanut butter jar.

"Aw," Craig said, as if Thaddeus's statement was an adorable photo of a kitten.

"Well, happy birthday, Craig."

"Oh, fuck this," Craig said. "Really. Fuck this with a chainsaw."

"The big two seven?"

"Everything." He widened his stance a bit, rotated his hip, trying to rearrange his genitals without actually reaching in.

"Well, you don't look a day over twenty-six," Thaddeus said.

The table was being prepared in the dining room and Arlene could be heard scolding one of her maids. The maid fortunate enough not to be in direct contact with Arlene circulated a tray filled with mini-quiches, moving clockwise, while a young Mexican male servant moved counterclockwise, with a pitcher of ice water in one hand and a pitcher of mimosas in the other.

Even with the rights to *The Strike* to bait the trap, it wasn't easy for Arlene to attract core Hollywood types to her son's birthday party. Two of the guests were real estate agents, one was head of marketing for the Lakers and was clearly Hollander's friend. A couple of lawyers, a couple of studio executives, an abnormally tall man in a Hawaiian shirt who had recently launched a self-help foundation called Yes, Indeed!, and Paula Prentiss and Richard Benjamin, who lived nearby, and breezed in to wish Craig happy birthday, drop off a present, and depart.

Standing to one side, dressed in a short black leather skirt, her bare legs emerging from lavender cowboy boots, her skin pale and dense as the meat of an apple, was Christine McNally, a fellow screenwriter. When Thaddeus's gaze passed over her, she pointed at him, a gesture which of late had taken the place of the wave. She looked amused, as if she had caught him at something. She was Stanford educated, and in Hollywood she had assumed the role of resident intellectual, recommending books to actresses, escorting young directors to obscure performance spaces. Christine seemed out of her element in the daylight, and Thaddeus wondered what she was doing at Arlene's. Perhaps she had come with another director or producer who hoped to get in on *The Strike*.

"Why, of all the gin joints," Christine said, sidling up to him. She was free with her hands, flirtatious but remote. Her bangs were cut Lulu style and her lipstick was dark brown. Christine seemed like one of those people born to be alone, self-sufficient, wary, cerebral, distant. Anyone who spent so much as a weekend with her would end up cramping her style.

"Well, look at you," he said.

"What are you doing here anyhow, Mr. Thaddeus," Christine said. She was from St. Louis; it was anyone's guess whether her slight drawl was an affectation.

"Fishing expedition. And thank you."

"For finding your presence here curious?"

"Exactly."

"I don't know how any of us got here," Christine said. "Look at us, a thousand points of blight drinking mimosas on the San Andreas Fault. It's all very mysterious."

"That's funny," Thaddeus said.

"The thousand points of blight? I've been doing that joke since Bush first said it. Most people react the way you just did. They don't laugh, they just say, *That's funny.* Hollywood, right? Ever wonder how we got here?"

"The original Hollywood guys came out here to avoid patent attorneys because they ripped something or other off Thomas Edison."

"Oh, Thomas Edison was such a pill."

"Was he?"

"Sprockets," Christine said.

"Really?"

"That's what the early moguls pilfered from Edison. The little holes that ran along the edges of the negative? That allow a camera or a projector to advance the film along at an even clip? That was Edison's and the movie guys stole it from him. Or so the story goes."

"And now our job," Thaddeus said, "is to supply content for the sprockets to move along."

"Our main job is to not get kicked out of the Sun King's court. To just keep milling around listening to what's said and what's not said and who's up and who's down, always hoping a little something comes our way. *Courtiers*, it's one of my favorite words. It also means flatterer."

"I leave that to my director," Thaddeus said.

"Well then."

"He's good at it."

"I think you could be good at it, too," Christine said. She raised her eyebrows, smiled innocently.

Thaddeus was momentarily stunned, but decided to overlook the insult, if indeed one had been intended. That was the trouble with quips and snappy dialogue. You never really knew what was intended. And it seemed everyone everywhere was just getting funnier and funnier—was it because people were consuming such massive doses of entertainment? One day, you wouldn't be able to tell what anybody meant. Every conversation would be served with a side of canned laughter.

"Who are you here with?" Thaddeus asked Christine.

"I was supposed to meet Duncan Lee. He wanted to pick me up but I don't much care for riding with someone else. And now he's gone and stood me up." She batted her long, heavily mascaraed eyelashes, the damsel in distress.

The man with the mimosas approached them and they both held their glasses out while he filled them.

"Hello, you two genius writers," Arlene said, appearing it seemed from out of nowhere. "No fair keeping your brilliance all to yourselves. Circulate!" She had a young body, well-moistened and exercised. Today was for turquoise leggings and a Brooks Brothers white shirt and silver jewelry—she looked as if she might at any moment hoist herself up onto the lid of a baby grand and sing a Stephen Sondheim number.

"I meant to ask you," she said. "Are you still trying to get that *Lady Chatterley* thing set up?"

"That's on a back back burner," Thaddeus said. "Basically not even in the kitchen."

Had she heard? The sight of her beloved son saying something to Hollander captured her attention. "Craig," she called. "Get over here, okay?"

"I'm going to show you something," Arlene said to Thaddeus and Christine, as they waited for Craig to wind his way across the room. "Craig is a one-man focus group. My baby just knows what's what."

"Where's your peanut butter, Craig?" Thaddeus asked, doing his best to sound good-natured.

"I was talking to your husband," Craig said, ignoring Thaddeus. "We were talking about baseball and then we were on *Bull Durham*."

"Ron Shelton," Arlene said. "I love Ron. Ron makes me wet."

The remark, crude and shocking, hung in the air for a moment or two. Until Christine said, "Ron."

"Ron Shelton?" Craig exclaimed. "Wrong. It's Kevin Costner and Susan Sarandon and Tim Robbins."

"Ronnie directed, baby, he's the filmmaker," Arlene said, with a delighted smile, as if Craig praising a movie without knowing who wrote and directed it was somehow endearing, like an eight-year-old who still cannot pronounce *banana*.

"Yeah, but people *pay* to see Costner. And Sarandon," Craig said.

Arlene laughed and patted Craig's face. "Look at this. Craig has his finger on the pulse." She pointed at Thaddeus. "You should write something for Sarandon. A strong woman's role."

"With a topless scene," added Craig. He saw the look of consternation on Thaddeus's face and said, "I'm kidding."

"Here's my question," Arlene said. She touched the corner of her mouth and Craig, like a base runner who knows the coach's signals, cleaned the corners of his own mouth with the back of his hand. "What do you make of D. H. Lawrence?"

"The real one or the movie?" Craig asked.

"Either or both." Her eyes shone with pure pleasure. She clasped her hands and the multitude of bracelets on her wrists tinkled like wind chimes.

Thaddeus felt his nerves tightening, like a watch being wound too tightly. As a graduation present, his parents had given him a Swiss Army watch. It was a sturdy red-and-black thing, with a pleasantly pugnacious little face. It was a wind-up watch—neither of the Kaufmans approved of battery-run watches, believing they were a way of selling you a bunch of batteries. They also abhorred digital watches, feeling that the abandonment of the circular movement and its connection to the earth's journey around the sun was an implied refutation of Copernicus, a capitulation to the dark churchy forces of reaction. However, the watch was not to be overwound, Sam Kaufman warned. *You can't wind it and wind it and think it's going to last for the whole week. It needs to be wound moderately once every day.* But, sure enough, the next day Thaddeus was caught overwinding the watch and the watch was frozen. *What did I say to you when I gave this to you,* Sam said, his voice not so much peeved as weary. *I think you said congratulations,* Thaddeus answered. Sam shook his head. *I don't know what to make of you,* he said. *That* was more like it, the admission filled Thaddeus with a sour post-adolescent pride— until the age of posturing gave way to the age of pondering, and he realized that not understanding was a parental euphemism for not accepting. And not accepting was itself a euphemism for not particularly liking.

"Well, in all honesty I don't know all that much about the real one," Craig said. "But the movie was overly long."

"Are you thinking of *Lawrence of Arabia?*" Thaddeus asked, suddenly overwhelmed by a furious dislike for the birthday boy. For Mr. Pajama Bottom. For Mr. Peanut Butter Out of the Jar. For Mommy's Built-In Focus Group. How could Arlene give this boy such power and adoration? Arlene may have been a bit of a barbarian, but she was smart, she was savvy—how did motherhood abscond with her brains? How was this lump in pj's given such respect for merely existing?

Another man might have been slack-jawed with shame over confusing T. E. and D. H., but Craig took the cultural correction in stride. He merely nodded. "Did I make a boo-boo?" he asked, with a smile.

"You know D. H. Lawrence," Arlene said to Craig, in her encouraging voice, like someone urging a child to take his first steps. "Narrow face, that little beard."

"I don't remember," Craig said.

"You wrote a terrific paper about D. H. Lawrence for your English Lit class at Dartmouth," Arlene said. "I kept it. I have it right upstairs if you want to see it."

"You kept it?" Craig said. He smiled beautifully when he meant it.

"Yes. It's brilliant. Well organized, right to the point."

"D. H. Lawrence, D. H. Lawrence," Craig said. He closed his eyes and tilted his head, as if to rearrange its contents.

"Well, there you have it," said Arlene, with a tinkling flourish of her arm. "Here's a college-educated moviegoer, one who studied Lawrence at an Ivy League college, and the name means very little to him. Basing a movie on a classic guarantees you bupkis. At this point. All those classic novels—they have their roots in the nineteenth century. Maybe the novel itself does. But look at us. We're almost in the twenty-first century. The nineteenth century is going to be just for a few nostalgia buffs."

"What's 20th Century Fox going to do with its name?" Craig wondered.

Arlene laughed merrily. "Oh, they'll be fine. The studios always survive."

"So based on this, you think doing *Chatterley* is a bad idea?" Thaddeus asked, in a somewhat lawyerly tone.

"It's a dainty little book anyhow," said Arlene. "Doesn't she put flowers on his pubes? I mean, fuck me with a chainsaw. We're just not there anymore."

"I'm starting to remember him," Craig said.

"I'm going to show you what you wrote," said Arlene. "It's good. Really good."

"You and your son are super close," Thaddeus said. "It's really amazing."

Arlene narrowed her eyes.

"I mean that in a good way," he said.

"I'm sure you do," Arlene said.

"Freud said that a man secure in the love of his mother can never be a failure," Thaddeus said, his grin like a piece of shipwreck.

"Well, we're a team here, Thaddeus. Teamwork is what makes the world run. If you don't understand that you got bupkis."

Oh spare me your Hollywood Yiddish. Thaddeus narrowed his eyes, hoping that their being windows to the soul was an empty cliché.

Near the door to the back patio, Kosoff was talking to a middle-aged man who might have been Paul Anka. The man was frowning thoughtfully as Kosoff's voice rose to deliver his joke's punch line: "Out of what?"

"I don't think there's very much champagne in these mimosas," Christine said, when they were alone again. "The original recipe from the Ritz calls for half orange juice and half champagne. What we may have here is the infamous Buck's Fizz, which calls for twice as much juice."

"I used to be so fucking hungry for all this great food and drink and now everything is starting to make me sick."

"Stick to the Buck's Fizz. Vitamin C."

"I don't know how much more of this I can stand."

"No one quits the mob," she said, in an Edward G. Robinson voice.

"I think Neal is going to be very unhappy he brought me here."

"Oh, I wouldn't worry about that," Christine said with a vague gesture.

"I think I really just went one toke over the line with Arlene and the birthday boy."

"Ah, the birthday boy," said Christine.

For a moment, his annoyance turned on Christine. Did she ever say what she meant? Her deftness, her deep sense of expediency, her instinct for the neutral all seemed like symptoms of insanity, an incurably subtle madness.

"You want to know what I know, chum?" Christine said. "Eagles can tell how much food is going to be available in their habitat over the next six months and if they see it's going to be slim pickings they break a couple of their own eggs so there won't be too many mouths to feed. We're connected to our environment, too. We're aware of what's going on with our species, with our whole world, we can feel it like you can feel a river under a road."

The server with the mini-quiche and the server with the mimosas converged on Thaddeus and Christine. Food declined, orange juice and champagne accepted. Thaddeus was seized by a sense of urgency. He needed to place himself between Grace and whatever door from which she was aiming to exit. He needed a phone. Up to this very moment, he believed people who carried around portable phones were delusional douche bags, but right now he wished he had one.

Now the question was: how could he approach Arlene and ask if he might use one of her phones? In private. He began to wander the room, aimlessly. He tried to arrange his features into something that might appear purposeful. He knit his brows, pursed his lips, and glanced occasionally at his watch. (Yes, Father, I have a Rolex and it doesn't need to be wound.)

His second time around the room, Thaddeus was suddenly arm in arm with Kosoff.

"I saw the great lady granted you an extended audience," Neal said.

Thaddeus saw it all so clearly now: they were all of them in some elevated barnyard, nosing each other front and flank for a better shot at the trough. And the slop in the trough took the form of cars and vacations and extra household help, and tailored suits, education for your children, first-rate medical care, and a comfortable retirement.

"Yes," Thaddeus said, "and I can't say it went very well."

"What happened?"

"Oh, what the fuck? Right? How are we going to have the balls to do justice to the sit-down strikers of Flint if we can't stand up to the Arlenes of the world?"

"What did you say to her?"

"It's that birthday boy."

"Craig? Why in the world would you care about that putz?"

"Listen, Neal, do you have a phone by any chance? I've got problems at home. Big problems."

Kosoff frowned sympathetically, as if compassion had been there just beneath the surface all along. Did this mean Neal was a pretty decent guy after all, or was the compassion a pose? What difference did it make? Thaddeus believed in the Jewish path to morality, believed if you do the right thing and say the right thing, eventually you will come to feel the right thing. Thaddeus's problem was that he could not sustain the right thing, it came, it went, it floated sometimes just beyond his emotional reach, it filled him with righteousness, but, in the end, he simply could not sustain it. Driven by desire, ambition, and a debilitating attraction to ease and comfort, he was buffeted about, with one thing leading to the next, and with no discernible path. He lived and took what came, his decency and his failings tripping over each other at every turn.

"I've got that phone in my car," Neal was saying. "But you have to start the engine."

"Would you mind?"

"Of course not. No one's sick, I hope."

"No, nothing like that."

"Anyhow, reception is terrible up here. You should use one of Arlene's land lines; there's one in the hall."

Kosoff led Thaddeus to the phone, with his hand on his shoulder. His kindness was making Thaddeus wonder if he had the look of a doomed man? He felt a shooting pain in his chest. My God, what a terrible place this would be to die. What a terrible place. The phone stood on a tall, narrow green table, with a small cast-iron Buddha on one side of it and a bowl of M&M peanut candies on the other. The phone itself was made of see-through plastic and its circuits and ringer were visible. He picked it up; the dial tone was harsh and unstable, like the buzzing of a large housefly trapped in a lampshade.

Grace answered on the first ring. So: she was waiting for *someone* to call.

"It's just me," Thaddeus said. Neal had returned with a mimosa, which he placed on top of a monogrammed cocktail napkin.

"Hello, Just Me. What time is it out there?" Grace said.

"I don't know."

"But you always know what time it is."

"It's about one or something." He was gripping the phone too tightly to look at his watch.

"That's my boy."

"Wow. I would have thought it was impossible, but you've turned knowing the time into a personal failure."

"Sorry. So? How's it going?"

"Grace, I can't take these personal crises when I'm out here. It's hard enough."

"Did room service overcook your eggs Benedict?"

"All right. Just tell me what's going on. With you."

"With me? With uneducated, unsuccessful little me?"

"Right."

"Well, I didn't kill Muriel. I think that was an accomplishment."

"Muriel? What can you possibly—"

"She's a complainer. And I miss my brother."

He heard the going-down-the-drain glug of wine being liberally poured; it took that for him to realize she was drunk. Drunk drunk drunk drunk drunk.

"Are you alone?" he asked her.

"No, the place is crawling with gallery owners and art dealers and everyone is—"

"Please. Grace. I'm begging you."

"I caught Emma with a loaf of bread."

"What are you talking about?"

"You want an obese daughter? You want type B diabetes?"

"It's type 2, not type B. If you're going to be a food Nazi at least get your facts straight."

"Oh my God, you are such an asshole!" Grace said, and with that she hung up the phone.

Thaddeus took a small, steadying sip of his mimosa. Nonsensically, he held on to the phone for a few moments, as if the broken connection might somehow be restored.

He heard a burst of laughter from the next room, as sudden as an explosion. Oh what rich fun! He recalled reading something Evelyn Waugh wrote to a friend back in London while laboring here in L.A., how the worst thing about being in Hollywood was seeing the Jews enjoying themselves. What a prick Waugh was, a funny, brilliant, vexing, petty, sniping sonofabitch. He would have been right at home with the river folk in Leyden, with their smooth chests and cleft chins, their flyaway hair, forever boyish, until one day they woke up looking like Auden. Thaddeus strolled into the party again. He didn't know what to do with his face so he decided to look . . . curious. His brows were knotted, his head was cocked, as if all these people and their laughter and their lovely Sunday clothes were of considerable *anthropological* interest, that he was here like that U of Chicago professor who was constantly in the Kaufmans' bookstore looking for anything about circumcision rituals, not because he was necessarily fixated on his own foreskin but because foreskins were his bread and butter.

The laughter had subsided. Evelyn Waugh would be relieved.

The guests were filing into the dining room. Neal was with Christine, and Thaddeus had the sense they might end up working together—perhaps on *The Strike*: who knew? Things moved with the swiftness of assassination in this business, assassinations so casual as to be practically whimsical.

"Hey, Mom says your folks fought in Spain." It was Craig, his hand on Thaddeus's arm.

"Over what?" Thaddeus asked.

"In the war? The civil war? That's what Mom said." His breath was heavy with peanut butter, burnt, sweet, oily, intolerable.

"First of all, no. They did not. And, Craig? Why are we talking about our mommies? Look at you. You don't even have fucking pants on."

"It's my house and it's my birthday."

"Grow up, Craig. Act like a human being."

"What are you doing?"

"I'm giving you some unasked-for advice. Don't go parading around in your goddamn pajamas."

"How'd you like an unasked-for punch in your mouth?" Craig asked.

"I'd be fine with it, Craig. But first thing, I think you better freshen up." And with that, Thaddeus Kaufman tossed his mimosa into Craig's face. Who knew it was so easy? This thing, reality, your life, your future, your reputation, how flimsy it all was, how conditional, how circumstantial, a universe of spun sugar. Nothing was carved in stone. Things were barely scratched in wet sand. Everything could change with a flick of your wrist.

"My eyes!" Craig screamed, stumbling backward, rubbing his hands over his face. "My eyes!"

EXPELLED FROM THE BRUNCH, THADDEUS waited in Arlene's driveway for the taxi. He had hoped Kosoff would drive him back to the Four Seasons but Neal, who was good enough to call for a cab, let him know that if he were to leave with Thaddeus it would give the appearance of support, and it would be best if he stayed at the brunch and did whatever he could to clean up the mess. Thaddeus, feeling the full force of the mimosas, would have liked to sit down, but the hoods of the cars were scalding, even Arlene's BMW, parked in the shade beneath a wisteria-laden carport, was too hot to sit on. Waiting for the cab's arrival, Thaddeus had ample time to consider his options. He needed to empty his bladder, but even in his compromised state he realized that luck was not running in his direction today and the last thing he needed was for Arlene, or Craig, or anyone else in the house to see him taking a leak. He considered letting himself back into the house and using the bathroom, but that seemed tempting fate, and fate had already made it clear that today was not Thaddeus's day. As he thought about what was preventing him from relieving himself, the urgency to do so increased and before long he was desperate. What did homeless people do when nature called? Every bar and restaurant posted signs warning noncustomers away from their toilets; under the cover of night, the parks and bushes could suffice, but what about the daylight hours? Without the right to relieve yourself you had less status, less comfort, and less safety in the world than an animal. How the homeless must envy the Central Park carriage horses. The dogs. The pigeons. Thaddeus tensed and relaxed his calf muscles, believing that this would somehow lessen the urge to urinate. Was there anywhere near Arlene's house that he could take a nice long undetected piss? Perhaps he could walk to the end of Arlene's driveway, find some tree or agave plant to shield him. But the houses here were built close together and for all Thaddeus knew he could end up being seen by a neighbor. Maybe he would be pissing in full view of Benjamin and Prentiss, who lived close enough to walk over to Craig's birthday. What might their reaction be? They were obviously not huge Craig and Arlene fans, otherwise they would have stayed at the brunch for more than two minutes. Would they somehow see in Thaddeus a kindred spirit?

His thoughts, circular and increasingly frantic, were brought to a sudden stop by the arrival of the taxi, a light blue Chevy Nova. A cloud of dust followed it up the driveway, twisting and turning like a massive caterpillar. The driver was an ascetic-looking man in his forties, with a narrow face, sunken cheeks, watery brown eyes, a bristly mustache. His name was Noori Hasseini.

"Howdy," Thaddeus said, slamming his door, wanting for some reason the people at the brunch to know he was leaving, that the monster was gone, and they could all go back to their mimosas and quiche and whatever else Arlene had in store. "The Four Seasons?"

The driver nodded, made a three-point turn.

"I don't suppose the air conditioning is working," Thaddeus said.

"Not today," said the driver.

Thaddeus slunk back and released a long sigh. The urge to urinate had subsided; he wondered if that meant toxins had been absorbed into his bloodstream. A slash in the backseat released a ridge of pumpkin-colored foam.

"We are doing this without running the meter," the driver said. "Forty dollars."

"Seems fair. God, I am so glad to be out of that place." Thaddeus closed his eyes for a moment and leaned back. No. That was not relaxing at all. More like being dangled over the side of a high balcony. He straightened up, pressed the heels of his hands against the sides of his head, as if to reshape it. "I hate this life." He hadn't meant to say it out loud.

He saw the driver's eyes in the rearview mirror, the quick worried glance. The stress of serving the public. How was this guy supposed to know what kind of lunatic might plop down in his backseat? Thaddeus thought it might be a good idea to put the driver at his ease.

"I see your name," Thaddeus said. "Are you Iranian by any chance?"

"Yes. I am here with my family for many years."

"Well, the odd thing is, I'm here—I mean in Los Angeles—mainly because I wrote something that was more or less about your country."

"This is my country," the driver said.

"No, Noori, Mr. Hasseini. Am I pronouncing that correctly? I realize this is your country now." His bladder was once again on high alert. "And what I wrote wasn't really about Iran."

"When did you visit?"

"Iran? Well, that's the thing. Basically never. I mean I was there for an hour. On my honeymoon. The whole thing was made up?"

"You are a journalist?"

"Oh Jesus, no. Screenwriter. Maybe you saw it. *Hostages*?"

Mr. Hasseini gave no indication.

"I made up a country," Thaddeus said. "But people took it for Iran. Because of the timing. I didn't know much about it. I met this woman at a party. But maybe I did, you understand? Maybe we all know about what's going on, a lot more than we realize. Anyhow, it doesn't matter. Because: guess what? I fucked up at the party and now everyone is going to think I'm a maniac."

Mr. Hasseini had the Sunday papers next to him, and he cautiously patted them, and pushed them farther back on the bench to guard against their flying off should he suddenly apply the brakes. Peeking out from below the papers was the handle of what looked like a billy club.

They were halfway to Sunset Boulevard now, and approaching a cleared lot where a house was under construction. The site was deserted, except for one large bulldozer, ochre and forlorn beneath the blazing sun.

"Can you stop?" Thaddeus cried out. "Please. I have to take a piss like a Tennessee racehorse." He was sitting forward now and had his hand on the driver's shoulder, which felt perfectly round and steely.

"You can't do that here," Mr. Hasseini said.

"I can do it outside or in the back of your cab."

They were already past the construction site, but Mr. Hasseini pulled off to the side of the road. He kept one hand on the wheel and the other on top of the newspapers, and stared straight ahead. He didn't say okay, but he made no further objection, and Thaddeus scrambled out of the taxi, closed the door, and made a quick stiff walk back toward the empty lot. *Okay okay okay,* he counseled his bladder. Fifty feet to go, twenty-five. And when he was too far from Mr. Hasseini's cab to catch up to it, the driver ditched him, a full-out, let-me-out-of-here, tire-squealing, dust-raising escape.

"Fine!" Thaddeus shouted. "You fucking idiot!"

He stood there for a few moments, amazed that someone was apparently afraid of him—fearful enough to forgo the fare. A car was approaching and Thaddeus thought about flagging it down and asking for a ride to Beverly Hills, though the act of hitchhiking to a luxury hotel seemed odd. There were a couple of women in their twenties in the car, the driver smoked and the passenger was brushing her hair. Neither gave the slightest indication of noticing Thaddeus's presence. *This is where the hero realizes he is dead, and has been for years.* "Thank you for your compassion," Thaddeus said to the bright red Mustang as it disappeared around the curve. Anyhow, he'd rather pee. He trudged through the building site. The ground had been ravaged, like a battlefield. It was all in huge weedy clumps, difficult to walk over. He stood behind the sad old bulldozer and at last began to relieve himself. At first, nothing came out. Maybe he'd held it in too long. Breathe. Breathe. At last: it came with a sudden hot twist, as if barbed. *Okay, okay. Easy does it.* He wanted his body to hear soft consoling words. His body had done nothing wrong. All it wanted was to be loved, and to have good food and wine, and a nice place to live, and—all right, there was this—enough on hand to be able to pay others to do the unpleasant work, someone to take the suitcase out of his hands after a long trip. Was that asking too much? Since when did wanting a bit of luxury constitute a fucking crime? Wasn't that the whole purpose of the goddamned country?

An old patch-eye bulldog was looking at him from across the lot, and as Thaddeus finished up the dog approached him. It seemed possible to Thaddeus that, given the day, he was now going to be bitten by a dog, but the dog stopped several feet away and stood there, its head down, its tail immobile, its ribs showing on the inhale and receding again when the dog breathed out. "You okay there, Spike?" Thaddeus said. The dog lifted its head and looked him over, but got no closer. It was not going to do him any harm, yet Thaddeus was of the distinct impression that the dog was telling him: you don't belong here.

How many miles to the Four Seasons Hotel? Eight? Ten? The walk would do him good. Even in the pounding sun, the walk might clear his head. And it did. Around mile two he realized that in all likelihood he had ended his career. At mile three he decided that *no matter what* he would never tell Grace what he had done. Also around mile three he started to feel excited about what might be next for him—maybe journalism, as Mr. Hasseini had suggested, maybe that novel. Maybe something that wasn't about writing. He wasn't all that good at writing, it seemed to him, not when he compared what he was capable of to what he had studied in school, or the books his parents bought and sold. And he didn't really enjoy writing. Well, maybe he *enjoyed* it, but he didn't *love* it. Or maybe he did love it and it just didn't love him back. Another unrequited love. One thing was certain and that was in the life to come he would be doing a great deal of walking because walking was amazing, walking focused the mind, walking was like meditation, only better, probably. Around mile four he was starting to see more cars on the road and suddenly without entirely meaning to he lifted his arm, whistled, and hailed a taxi to take him the rest of the way.

Chapter 12

What Was Buried

SEPTEMBER 30, 1990

YOU NAME IT!

Hat's House, Sunday, 5:30

Help Us Name the New Business

Peeps AROUND HERE LIKE PARTIES, THAT'S FOR SURE, BUT I'll tell you this." Thaddeus smacked his fist into his palm.

Grace winced a little at the forced folksiness of his tone, and especially his choice of words. *Peeps? That's for sure?* Who was he pretending to be? The Farmer in the Fucking Dell? He'd been idle and underfoot for several weeks; they'd had more uninterrupted time with each other than they'd had in years. Even the spaciousness of Orkney had begun to feel cramped, and she wondered why he wasn't working on anything. He seemed obsessed with the news—this week it was mainly the upcoming unification of Germany. There was also Mayor Dinkins asking for the hire of more cops in New York, and Thaddeus wondering if former East German secret policemen might be working in Penn Station next year. He was often on the phone with his parents, talking about the impending collapse of the Soviet Union, which he kept saying was unthinkable but he couldn't stop thinking about it. It seemed as if he really wanted Communism to be over with, but it also made him weirdly nostalgic. *My whole life has been about the Cold War,* he declared. That was a new one to her; she would have said his whole life had been about feathering his own nest. She didn't mention anything about how he was spending his time; it was not as if he asked about *her* work. She hadn't been in her studio for months, and she doubted Thaddeus had even noticed.

"This is one party I've been really looking forward to," he was saying to Jennings. "I'm just so proud of you, man. Really."

Oh no. What right did Thaddeus have to pride? What role had he played in Jennings's new venture? It was how he spoke to David, crazily praising the most mundane accomplishments, from finishing his breakfast cereal to cleaning his room to building a robot out of Legos. It struck Grace as ill-conceived on so many levels. The boy was already showing signs of social maladaptation and all this so-called *positive feedback* would only take him further and further out of himself, training him like a dog to look for the little treats and tidbits of parental praise. And saying you were *proud* of someone put you in the mix, where you did not belong. What right did Thaddeus or anyone else have to be *proud* of a kid making a robot out of Legos? You were actually taking or at least sharing ownership of the accomplishment by saying you were *proud*, as if you had something to do with it, either by brilliant parenting or passing on good genes. Grace understood that Thaddeus's own childhood, where compliments were as infrequent as rainbows, was at the core of his incessant cheerleading for David. He was determined to situate himself as far as humanly possible from Libby and Sam's wintry outpost, and Grace's gentle suggestion that overpraising a child can be as destabilizing as underpraising struck him as merely contentious, or worse. She could practically smell the unspoken words on his breath, that she, being raised by a mother treating her own depression with gin, and a father photographing soft-core porn, was hardly in a position to offer theories of child rearing.

"Glad you could make it," Jennings said. He was in a good mood, with a kind of cowboy swing to his voice. "Where are the kids?"

"Home," said Thaddeus, narrowing his eyes.

Jennings took the platter from Grace, breathing in the aroma of the chicken, though it was completely sealed off by plastic wrap.

"I didn't cook it," Grace said.

"Nor I," chimed Thaddeus. "But look at it, so black from being charred and so red from their secret sauce. It looks like a Gorky painting."

Oh no, no no no and no, thought Grace. First of all, Arshile Gorky paintings were about as far from appetizing as you could get. Second—actually she ought to have put this first—why was he dropping the name of some painter to Jennings? What was he trying to prove?

And to make everything just a little worse, Thaddeus had been in town earlier to pick up the chicken and was approached by a couple of teenagers collecting names for a Save Our River petition, and they'd given him a blue-and-white campaign button in exchange for his signature. Grace thought for a moment that she might simply reach over and take the thing off his lapel before anyone else saw it. There was not a person here who would not resent that button. She loved the river—perhaps not with the same heritage-mad sense of ownership that animated some of the other folks whose houses lined its banks—but opposing the construction of a factory that promised to bring hundreds (or even dozens) of jobs to Leyden was a tricky business in a town where most folks would gladly and gratefully trade a stirring view of a waterway or a healthy habitat for fish for the ability to pay off their credit card debts, fix their roof, pay for tae kwon do lessons for their kids.

"Hey," Grace said, quietly, knowing Thaddeus would hear her. He always heard her. He was exquisitely attuned to her voice. She pointed.

He touched his lapel, felt the button. "Ooops," he said, and quickly took it off and dropped it into his pocket.

THE YELLOW HOUSE WAS NOT yet in Jennings's name, but Hat was fading and it was just a matter of time. It was already the official address of the new business, and Jennings didn't think to clear it with his father before inviting about twenty-five people to the house to share a meal and help him choose a name for his new venture. Provisionally, Jennings was calling it J&M Solutions, but he was hopeful that collectively they could all come up with something even better, though he was fond of the "Solutions." Everything else about the venture was in place. He had hired two people to help with the work—his old friend Larry Sassone and Horse Reynolds's younger brother Walter, who everyone called Woo-Woo. But he had yet to take in a dollar. In the meantime, money was leaving his account like air from a punctured tire. Not only did he have to write checks for Larry's and Woo-Woo's wages but he had to put up and feed them both over at the Red Roof in Springfield, Massachusetts, for five days and nights while they took the mandatory course in handling asbestos. From eight in the morning to four thirty in the afternoon, Jennings, Larry, and Woo-Woo sat in a classroom in the summer heat while a cyclone of information whirled around them, everything from making a job cost-effective to making sure you didn't end up with cancer.

The state had its hand in his pocket already and he hadn't even started work. Jennings was well on his way to loathing the government, which seemed to him devilishly designed to keep the lid on your aspirations. Everywhere you looked some pencil neck was telling you no. And even if you got through the forest of no's, there was all that insurance, the workmen's compensation you had to pay for—thousands and thousands of dollars. It was as if the only people who could afford to start a business were people who didn't need money. Maybe Horse was right—the government was like an occupying army. All he wanted to do was put some bread on his table, and the government was right there, elbowing everyone else out of the way, licking its chops, waiting to get fed.

In fact, only some of his contracts were going to be for putting *in* asbestos; the majority would be for asbestos *abatement*, now that some panel of government experts had decided the stuff was bad for you. Jennings himself did not believe there was anything particularly hazardous about asbestos, if you took care installing it and didn't allow it to deteriorate. But the beautiful thing was, there was money to be made in removing the stuff, and hauling it to specially designated landfills, and there was serious coin to be made in burying it, though that part of the operation was more or less locked up by the big dogs.

Even without the government doing whatever was in its power to keep him down, getting started cost money. Jennings needed Teflon suits, gigantic rolls of double-wall plastic, cartons and cartons of duct tape, at least one HEPA vac, and machinery to create a negative air chamber, essential to keeping floating microspecks of asbestos out of the lungs of the homeowner, though it was a virtual certainty that traces of the stuff would adhere to the workers. The teacher at the training seminar liked to joke about "the little lady" needing to wear a Hazmat suit when she did her husband's laundry.

JENNINGS MANEUVERED THE OTHER DISHES on the table—the three-bean salad; ham salad; a copper-colored crockpot brimming with chili; an immense cherry pie with a lattice crust; a lasagna, slightly scorched—making room for the chicken. September light, a mix of bright sun and cooling air, entered the kitchen through its many mullioned windows. Here and there, small crystal globes hung from fishing line and each cast trembling swaths of yellow orange red green blue onto the walls. The radiant prismatic glow on the walls made Grace look away, as if they were somehow emanating from Muriel's wounded soul.

"Wait until you taste it," Thaddeus said. "It's from Johnny Cake Ho."

"The new place?" Jennings asked, glancing at Grace.

She knew what the glance meant. La di fucking da. Johnny Cake Ho was owned by a black couple in their late twenties, he from New York, she from Baton Rouge. One of the three new shops that had recently opened in Leyden, it was mainly a take-out business, selling at hefty prices homogenized versions of traditional Southern fare. It had taken the place of Hoffman Hobbies, which had been there for forty years until hobbies themselves became a thing of the past. It was all said in just a flicker of the eye. Jennings and Grace had come to understand each other through a system of small gestures, undetectable except to each other.

Horse Reynolds came into the kitchen, fanning himself with his paper plate. He wore black trousers, sharply creased, and a tight black T-shirt, against which his shoulders and biceps strained. Streaks of gray shot through his close-cropped hair.

"Hey, I saw you were wearing one of those stop-the-cement-plant buttons," he said. "What did you do? Take it off?"

"I didn't even know I had it on," Thaddeus said.

"So you're with the bigs?"

"Who are they?"

"Your friends all up and down the river."

"I took it off. I didn't even know I was wearing it."

"What does that prove?"

"I'm not trying to prove anything. I see both sides. I don't want the river fucked up, but I get it—people need jobs. But how many jobs are there really going to be? Some people say two hundred, other people say it's more like twenty."

"Maybe it won't be two hundred new jobs," Horse said. "But it'll be a lot more than twenty. And the politicians we got up there who are supposed to be looking after our best interests, they're so worried about what the *New York Times* might say—they're useless."

"It's all really complicated."

"There's nothing complicated about needing a job. There's nothing complicated about taking care of your family. By the way—did you see one of your river buddies got his place trashed last night?"

"Really?" He didn't feel like saying so, but Thaddeus had in fact heard about it. Hal Marquette had returned from Boston after a hernia operation and found several windows broken in his house, smashed through by cement blocks. While the building of the plant on the river was still being debated, most of the vandalism in the past couple of years involved its commodity: wet cement poured over lawns in the middle of the night, mailboxes filled with cement rubble, cement blocks dropped onto the hoods of cars, windows smashed. The lawn signs advertising one side or the other of the controversy had by now faded to illegibility, but the tempers of those who wanted the plant were as vivid as ever. Signs saying Cement=Jobs, had been replaced by homemade signs, such as Take Your View & Shove It, Don't Let Them Pull Our Plants Down, and Windsor County Bass-Lovers, with a line going through the B, and a drawing of a Richie Rich type in shorts and sunglasses going fishing. Using as bait a worker holding a lunch pail.

"You didn't hear?" Horse said. It was his nature combined with the habits learned from working in a prison—he simply never quite believed *anyone*. He always detected a bit of bullshit, the smell of a lie.

"No, I haven't," Thaddeus said. "But these things happen."

"Sure. Always have. Up here, a lot of the people aren't full-timers, so it's easy pickings, right? Kids go in, steal some booze, nice warm bed for some screwing. But this is different, don't you think? I mean when you think about it." He jabbed his finger in Thaddeus's direction.

"Me?"

"You must feel kind of lucky no one's tried anything on Orkney."

"You want to talk about luck, Horse? Try some of this chicken."

"I want everyone to stop calling me Horse. I'm not some kid. It's disrespectful."

"Okay, *Todd*. You got it. Hey, I hear you might be trying to get yourself elected sheriff. Is that true?"

"Where'd you hear that?"

"Grace."

"Yeah?" Todd smiled unpleasantly. "Who told her that?"

There was something in the question that momentarily sickened Thaddeus. His stomach dropped, as if he were sitting in a plane that was suddenly losing altitude. "You want to try some chicken? It's good."

"I do loves me some chicken," Todd said, in his deepest voice, and opened his eyes to their widest aperture, his concept of how a black person would respond to chicken.

"Comes from Johnny Cake Ho," Thaddeus said.

Todd had been just about to take a piece for himself, but suddenly his hand veered over to a giant bowl of potato salad. "I need carbs," he announced. "When you're working with free weights, you need a lot of carbs. Protein, too, but carbs give you energy for workouts."

"You really should try the chicken," Thaddeus said.

"I'm good," said Todd. He piled potato salad on his plate, and then a wedge of lasagna.

"But I insist," said Thaddeus. "I want everyone to know how good their stuff is so they can stay in business."

"I don't really much care if they stay in business or not," said Todd.

Thaddeus flushed red for a moment, stepped back as if pushed. "Jesus, Horse, it's chicken." A queer feeling went through him, as if a ripple of cold water rolled through his brain.

"Horse is over, man. I told you. And I like the way my wife makes chicken anyhow. And if you want to know the truth, I don't go for it when people come here and put locals out of business."

"Well, they're local now, too, *Todd*. They live right above their shop."

"I'm going to tell you something," Todd said. "You can't have a place where the majority of the people feel like they don't even belong. Okay? Either we turn things around or this place is going to blow sky high."

"This place?"

"You're a nice guy, Thaddeus. You made a nice donation for Brandon. That doesn't get forgotten. And you took care of Hat, we all know that."

"Who is this 'we'?"

"Just keep your eyes open, *Thad*, that's all I'm saying."

HAT SAT IN AN ARMCHAIR in the front room, with a plaid blanket over his knees. His tarnished hair was wet and combed straight back, and his clothes—a Harris tweed jacket, a white shirt, blue gabardine trousers—hung so loosely on him that they didn't seem as if they were really his. Muriel was holding his beer while Hat carefully fed himself grapes, eating them simian style, chewing out the meat and carefully extracting the skins from his mouth. It was the only food on his plate.

Had Muriel colored slightly upon seeing Grace? Grace wanted to study her face, but did not dare. Yet she was struck by the thought that Muriel knew everything that was there to be known, and had known all along. Maybe it was perfectly all right with her. Marriages were mysterious, each written in a secret code. A marriage was its own anthropology, similar enough to all the others to fool you into believing you understand it. Yes, it did not strain credulity to consider that whatever passed between Jennings and Grace was fine with Muriel. Maybe Grace was really nothing much more than the safety valve through which the steam of simple human discontent could safely rise. Maybe Jennings was constitutionally unable to sustain fidelity and in Muriel's view Grace was a safe outlet for all that pent-up errant energy, a little fenced yard in which he could run. Or maybe Muriel herself had someone else in her life. She did not act it, and did not look the part. But then: who did? Everyone is inscrutable.

Except to deliver pies, Muriel rarely left the property. She moved freely around Orkney, not only on Hat's swath, but the entire estate—at times it seemed to Grace that whenever she looked up from her drafting table to see if she might draw a modicum of inspiration from all the natural beauty out her window (never worked), or checked to see what her dogs were barking about (never could figure it out), she would catch a glimpse of Muriel, winding her way down to the stand of oaks where the wild mushrooms sprouted after any decent rain, or gathering thistle and rose hips for her witchy teas, or working the orchard with a hacksaw and pruning shears. Her hair seemed always wet, curling down her back in a kind of doomy pre-Raphaelite swirl, and an expression of contentment, a half smile as she gazed at the sky. But maybe that contentment was a pose, or just the way her face looked at rest, the way Thaddeus always seemed to be smiling when all he was doing, or so he claimed, was listening. Yes, Muriel seemed serene. But how could she be serene if she suspected anything was seriously amiss in her marriage? How could she glide around Orkney on her long hairless legs if her heart was broken? She must not know a thing, or must not care.

At any rate, the good and perfect hippie wife held her father-in-law's paper plate while Hat busied himself with his beer. Grace, feeling she must say hello to him, prepared herself for Hat's odd exhausting brand of courtliness and condescension. But the old man's vitality had slipped down another notch or two, and he barely registered her presence. His attention was fixed on the dark sweaty bottle of beer in his hands.

"You look so pretty today," Muriel said. She herself was dressed in an old-fashioned cream-and-orange polka-dotted dress she'd gotten at a thrift shop in California years before. It emphasized the pioneer plainness of her features, her long chin, her aquiline nose.

"Thanks," Grace said. "I think I'm coming down with a cold or something." She couldn't help it; she had a perverse need to complain when she spoke to Muriel—she was either exhausted, unwell, or unable to cope with the dailiness of motherhood.

"Oh! Poor you," Muriel said. "I chew two cloves of garlic when I feel something coming on. If I'm really feeling punk, I Scotch-tape cloves on the bottoms of my feet before I go to sleep and just let it soak into the wrinkles. I'm lucky Jennings doesn't mind. I don't even think he's got a sense of smell sometimes." She reached over and took the beer from Hat. "Here you go, Dad. Let's get some of this good food in you. You can't live on grapes."

Muriel's remark about Jennings's sense of smell went directly counter to Grace's experience of him. She had never had a lover more attuned to the scent of her. He noticed the smell of her shampoo, and even knew when she had switched from Crest to some ridiculously overpriced toothpaste Thaddeus bought from Caswell-Massey. Once, meeting Jennings at the Morpheus Arms, a jokily named but otherwise modest motel about an hour away, she had dabbed a bit of perfume (Obsession, as she recalled) and Jennings had licked her pulse points clean of it, saying he wanted to get down to her natural scent. Why would Muriel point out her husband's lack of a sense of smell when the very opposite was true? Did it mean she knew nothing, or that she knew everything?

Grace was standing close enough to Muriel to see the spidery red zigzags in the whites of her eyes. Muriel, poor Muriel, inconvenient Muriel, blameless Muriel, Muriel the Wronged, Muriel the Innocent, Muriel the Sphinx, Muriel the Sprite, Muriel who heard voices, Muriel the homegrown Hindu, with her long flexible legs and rubber spine, Muriel for whom the world was a yoga mat. Grace had never really hurt another person. The worst emotional damage she had done was failing to love her own mother. A mere sin of omission. But hurting Muriel was different, hurting her was a sin of commission. Yet as bad as it made Grace feel and as much as it filled her with pity and remorse and a desire to protect and somehow repay, it also made her want to never hear Muriel's voice or see her face or even her shadow cast on the long sloping lawn as she trod the deer path, wicker basket in hand, on her way to her weekly rendezvous with the river, to collect stones and wildflowers.

Muriel's basket sat on the table next to Hat's chair, filled with the little treasures she had gathered. Dried lichen, milky white stones, moss-covered bark, tiny pinecones, a bear claw, deer velvet, as well as things she must have had to dig for—a Krugerrand, a shard of pale green and white cameo, a half page of an old manuscript, a scrap of an old map.

"Did you bring David and Emma?" Muriel asked.

"No, they're home," Grace said. She stopped short of *with Vicky*. A Salvadoran woman lived with them now and looked after the children. Maybe not for long. Thaddeus was starting to make noises about economizing.

"Well, too bad," Muriel said. "Jewel was looking forward to playing." Jewel, wearing a child's tiara, a little white dress and blue tights, was across the room, gently shaking the stroller in which somebody's baby peacefully slept.

"Oh," said Grace. "Look at her, she's so good."

"She misses him," Muriel said.

"David?"

"They used to be inseparable."

"Well, you know they get weirdly busy when they get older," Grace said. It was the truth. David was busy with music lessons and horseback riding, and the school he attended was three towns over and with travel to and from that meant his day was two hours longer than the kids who went to Leyden's public school. Yet all of this might be better unmentioned. Sometimes the little privileges were as private as bodily functions. "I don't see Henry," she said.

"He's real shy," Muriel said. "He keeps pretty much to himself."

"He's so cute," Grace said. She feared that at any moment Muriel might start in on the lead paint thing, and Henry's many health issues, and so she picked up the basket. "This is beautiful, Muriel. All this stuff!"

"Oh, there's so much around," said Muriel. "I just think there's so much out there we don't see."

"Yeah."

"Well, tell David he's got a real fan in Jewel. She'd love to see him."

This is where I am supposed to make a playdate for them, thought Grace. But she could not do it. She could not summon the will, the audacity. Her stomach was churning and she was becoming more and more concerned that something was going to show in her expression.

"How are you doing, Hat?" Grace said, turning away from Muriel. "I really like what you're doing with your hair. Sweeping it back like that. It looks great."

Hat appeared to be somewhat confused as to who Grace was, and accepted her remark with a curt nod. "I want to go to my quarters," he said to Muriel.

"Oh come on, Dad," Muriel said. "Jennings wants you to be here for this."

"I'm not one for parties. I'm not one of the party people."

"I'll take you up in a little bit," Muriel said. "We're all going to help come up with a name for Jennings's company. Won't that be fun?"

Hat's expression was sour. He extended his lower lip, and slowly shook his head. "I still would like to know where he came up with the money to buy all that equipment. That's what I want to know and that's what no one is talking about. What we have here is an old-fashioned conspiracy of silence."

Thaddeus stood with Jennings near the front window with its sublime view of the maple, ash, and oak in full autumn color, all the blazing crowns gathered by a ribbon of bright blue sky.

"Color change is early this year," Jennings said.

"Yeah," said Thaddeus, who could not help but notice that none of the other guests had helped themselves to the chicken from

Johnny Cake Ho. Was there some sort of boycott? Did these fuckers have some problem with black people? Or was it really the price of the platter that exercised them? Jennings's friends were consuming potato salad, macaroni salad, Doritos, and Larry Sassone's blazingly hot practically inedible salsa, made from a recipe Larry had learned years ago in Santa Fe.

"Did you try the chicken?" Thaddeus asked the guy standing to his right, a stocky man in his thirties with a somewhat feminine hairdo, a kind of page boy that was in stark contrast to the rest of him—the missing front tooth, the unshaved face.

"Hey! There's my princess," Jennings called out, and pointed.

For a moment Thaddeus thought it was Grace he was talking about. But of course that was impossible and absurd—Jennings was referring to Jewel. And yet the momentary misapprehension continued to unfold within Thaddeus, just as the ripples created by a stone thrown into still water will continue to unsettle the surface whether or not the stone was thrown in on purpose.

Grace and Jewel filled their plates and sat down to eat, each with lasagna and a roll. Was Grace, too, avoiding the Johnny Cake Ho chicken? Awfully suspicious . . . But it was always there, this wondering if his wife and Jennings were lovers, or at least had once been. He did not wish to ask Grace because he did not want her to lie. He didn't want to know—what would he do with the confirmation of his worst suspicions? Leave her? Wouldn't that only make everything worse? Wouldn't that only deprive him of the consolations of her presence, leaving him not only betrayed but bereft, with nothing to distract him from ceaseless contemplation of her unfaithfulness? If he made love to her a hundred times without her making love with anyone else, all adultery would be eradicated. He did not believe this absurdity, but also: he did. Not everything made sense, not everything that was true was, strictly speaking, true. But this was: she was his wife. They lived in the same house, slept in the same bed, they were a unit, papers had been signed, no one would ever know him as she did, and he knew her, too, he was sure of it. That was something that needed to be protected, not prodded and pushed. He did not need, nor would he seek confirmation of his suspicions. What he would do—and by now he was actually good at it—was bury those suspicions in sex, meals, laughter, domestic routine, vacations, and plans for the future. The whole fluttering mess encased in money and property, like a bird of prey in a cage.

When Jewel scampered off, Grace collected her plate and threw it into the trash, took a celery stick and went to the window, peering into the dusk, chewing. She was checking on their dogs, better expressed as *the* dogs, since they were not family dogs whatsoever. The reality was, they were *her* dogs, the Weimaraners, a fairly recent acquisition that had quickly turned into a virtual obsession. She went from one window to the next, hoping to catch sight of them, and when she went out to the porch, Thaddeus followed her and saw the dogs were there—Finn with his large paws on her chest, Molly busily cleaning her own nether region.

"Such a drag," she said. She moved away from Finn and when his forepaws hit the porch, the thud almost moved one of Muriel's flowerpots off the railing.

"What is?"

"Jennings. Doing this. I mean, asbestos is poison. It gets in your lungs. Cancer."

"They wear masks," said Thaddeus. He nudged Molly with his foot to stop her incessant licking.

"He's giving up his life, is what he's doing. He's just completely giving up his life."

"We all do, one way or the other," Thaddeus said. "And I guess we all wear masks."

"Thaddeus," she said, shaking her head.

The dogs heard something quite compelling that was broadcasting on the canine frequency and they bounded off the porch, airborne for a moment, and streaked toward the orchard, where the deer often gathered, eating the fallen rotting slightly alcoholic apples. Moments later Molly and Finn were barking *Come on, we're not going to hurt you* to the disappearing deer.

"We should go in," said Grace.

"Your dogs are out there going crazy."

"They're okay." She made a move toward the door. She drew her hands into the sleeves of her dark purple sweater.

"Hey," Thaddeus said, stopping her. "Kiss?"

They faced each other. A wind came in from the east. He felt it go down his shirt like water. The force of it flattened the fabric of Grace's pants, and he noted the shape of her legs, the bony bulge of her knees, her thighs. She shook her head but he continued to look at her and at last she was forced to say it, the word, a word consisting of just two letters, and the letters were next-door neighbors in the alphabet, but the word was devastating.

BY THE TIME THADDEUS AND Grace were back, Jewel had collected all of the suggestions and handed the bowl to Jennings. He stood next to Hat now, with one hand on the back of Hat's chair, moving his hand in circles, touching the chair as if it were an extension of his father, and he handed the bowl to Hat, who plucked his hardware-store readers out of his shirt pocket, licked his lips, and cleared his throat.

"Hey, Jennings," called out Andy Clark, a baseball star in high school, now working for the town, plowing snow and salting the roads in the winter, and in the summer clearing brush and spraying pesticide on county road weeds at night. "What bank you go to for the money? I've got business ideas, too."

"I saved my pennies, Andy," Jennings said. "Anyhow, it wasn't so much."

"All that equipment?" said Andy. There was a time when he and Jennings were rivals, both handsome boys, Andy on the straight and narrow, with his letter jacket and good grades, and Jennings on the margins, with his truancy and his truculence. The only prizes they could compete for were love and popularity, and in those high school days love was narrowly defined, and was really about *permission*, finding girls who would allow access to the body's secret places. Jennings and Andy competed then and they still competed, though now Andy was losing ground: his twelve-year-old son had been caught with marijuana and got sent to a juvenile detention center, where the very first night he hanged himself. He was cut down in time to save his life but there was some kind of brain damage. Andy's older brother John had served in Vietnam and tried to convince Andy that the chemicals in Roundup were the same deadly chemicals used in Agent Orange, and the inconvenience of this information enraged Andy; he and his brother, upon whom he had depended for most of his life, and from whom he was renting his house, were no longer speaking. Added to the unlucky slant of his life, it was almost certain that the town, strapped for cash, was going to cut Andy's hours in half. That Jennings would begin to rise as he felt himself sinking was more painful than failure itself to Andy. He had been fully aware that Jennings had been serially unsuccessful in securing a loan from any bank in the area, and these turndowns had all kinds of reasons—Jennings had no credit history, no credit cards, and not even a lease. And of course there was the personal dimension, too, meaning that Jennings still bore his old reputation as a wild man, and a seducer. Yet now he had somehow gotten his hands on enough money to make a serious capital outlay and Andy was grimly curious about where this money had come from. Did the Orkney Jews give it to him, just as they had given crazy old Hat a house? Had Jennings talked his poor, dying father into using the yellow house as collateral and gotten some bank money after all?

"Come on, bro," Andy said. "You're getting us to come up with all these names for you. How about giving us the secret of your success?"

"More than one way to skin a cat, Andy," Jennings said.

"Uncle Buddy has an idea!" Klein called out. He was in a neck brace and wore loose-fitting clothes. He'd put on twenty pounds during the convalescence after falling off his roof, where he'd been sunning himself and had the bad luck to fall asleep and the good luck to land in the forsythia. "Why don't we all mind our own fucking business?"

After a smatter of polite cheers, Todd pointed at Buddy. "Listen up, Big Star, there's kids here."

"He can kick the shit out of prisoners but he don't like no dirty words," Thaddeus whispered to Grace.

"Everyone can see you," she said without moving her lips.

Jennings explained what he was going to do, sounding large and strong and full of joy, a man whose life was taking shape. He would read off the suggestion and if more than ten people thought it was a halfway decent name for his business, he'd hold on to it, and if less than ten people thought it was good, he'd just drop it on the floor, no hard feelings.

"That's ridiculous," Thaddeus whispered.

Grace pursed her lips, slowly shook her head.

"Peace of Mind," Jennings said, reading the first suggestion. He looked around the room expectantly. "So?" He waited. "Anyone like it?" More silence. "No one?"

"Not even the person who wrote it?" Thaddeus called out.

The scrap of paper floated to the floor. Jennings continued to read off the suggestions. Windsor Insulation. Done-Right. Tight and Tidy. The Money-Savers. Windsor Environmental Solutions. The room was still after each, except Tight and Tidy, which got a couple of snickers.

"You know what?" Todd said. "The only one in the whole lot that's any good is Money-Savers, and I'm not saying it just because it was mine."

"Because it wasn't, it was mine," said Maggie Coolidge, her hair the color of cranberry juice, overdressed for the occasion in a skirt, high heels, madcap earrings. She was a home health-care worker, new to Leyden, imported from Florida to tend to Gene Woodard, who'd run his Austin-Healey into an oak tree. She and Larry Sassone had been spending time with each other for less than a month but Larry was optimistic about their chances. Maggie was not only familiar with Nietzsche but had a parrot named Zarathustra. In his maze of paint fumes, pot, and exhaustion, Larry still remembered believing Nietzsche was important, though now he'd be hard-pressed to say why.

THADDEUS HELD ON TO GRACE for balance and closed his eyes. His heart seemed to suddenly kick into overdrive. Anxiety, the distant coppery taste of doom on the roof of his mouth—it was like being in New York, in the old days, when often he had pictured himself crumpling to the sidewalk and people simply stepping over him.

"Are you okay?" Grace asked.

"I think I'll go home," Thaddeus whispered.

"Arc you okay?"

He nodded his head yes but said no.

"You want me to walk with you? I can leave."

"No. Stay. I'm all right. Nerves. I'll see you when you get home."

Thaddeus walked through the kitchen on his way out. Robert Altman once told him that he had saved his own life by drinking a glass of water and preventing a heart attack. Thaddeus knew he was not about to have a heart attack, but something was happening to him. As he stood at the sink and let the water get colder, he saw that someone had stubbed out a cigarette on the otherwise untouched platter of chicken from Johnny Cake Ho.

Who would do such a thing? And it occurred to him that just about anyone in the front of the house could have done it. He did his best to freshen up the chicken, the cost of which he was suddenly acutely aware, and as he looked around the kitchen for the garbage receptacle so he could get rid of the cigarette butt, an unwelcome memory was suddenly delivered: the look on Susan Fialkin's face when all those wineglasses got broken at the Mondale fund-raiser and Thaddeus didn't know where the broom was kept in his own apartment. The shattered glass, the pregnant pauses, the contempt. *Oh fuck them all,* he thought. *I fucking earned the right not to know where some ridiculous broom is.*

He deserved what he had, if not all of it then at least most of it. And if not most of it then some of it. And if not some of it . . . well, that was as far as he could go. It was not inherited wealth, it was his. He was not a thief, he didn't push people around, he was just trying to live in the world as he found it, the world of haves and have-nots, the lifters and the lifted. *May I take that suitcase off your hands, sir? You most certainly can.* So, yes, he no longer had to entirely fend for himself, but he was not some Craig Epstein pattering around Mommy's house in his pj's. Yet thoughts of Craig in his insolent informality only further destabilized Thaddeus. It could very well be that his days of expensive take-out food were drawing to a close. That tossed drink may have extinguished the little flicker of heat that had up to that point been his career.

And speaking of his film career: Where the hell was the garbage can? Under the sink? In some corner? He just wanted to get out of there. The Trotskyists used to talk about the dustbin of history—well, he couldn't find that, either. He dropped the cigarette butt into his pocket and walked quickly to the back door, and into what minutes ago was evening and now was night, pure dark cold night, nothing but night.

The dogs materialized, as if conjured up by the darkness, panting, wagging, gyrating with excitement. But a few moments of that was all they had in them, after which they trotted off to points unknown.

"ARE THE DOGS BACK?" GRACE asked, as soon as she returned home, her face bright from the night air and the exertion of criss-crossing the property in search of them.

There's my princess.

Thaddeus was in the library, reading a novel, trying to get back into the groove of it, just reading for the sake of reading, nourishment for the soul. He looked up at Grace with his features carefully arranged, as close to neutral as he could manage. He had been hearing people leaving the party at the yellow house for some time and though he was in no particular hurry for Grace to return home he could not help but note she was staying out late, which he could also not help taking somewhat personally. And now here she was, flushed, and the first thing out of her mouth was an inquiry about the fucking dogs?

"No dogs here," he said, placing the book down on the side table. "I tried to round them up on my way home. But you know they don't really listen to me."

"So where are the kids?" Grace asked. She checked her watch. Nine forty-five. "Asleep?" She noticed the down on her arm could no longer reasonably be called down. She wondered if Thaddeus was going to say anything about it.

"I think so. Vicky said they were fighting. Do you worry that maybe they hate each other?"

"You're an only child, but take it from me, Emma will one day adore David and he at the very least will adore being adored."

"I'm not technically an only child."

"What do you mean?"

"Let's find those dogs of yours," he said, rising from his chair, rubbing his hands together.

"Aren't they your dogs, too?"

"Yes. I suppose so."

"You suppose so?"

"Would you feel better if I said let's find those dogs of ours?"

"It's okay. I can do it. You're feeling a little iffy anyhow, right? But I appreciate the offer."

Because they were all but impossible to see in the darkness, the dogs had reflecting tape on their collars, but the orange material needed street lamps or moonlight or something else to spark it to

life. Out on the porch, Grace put her fingers in her mouth and whistled, the way Liam had taught her to five million dollars ago in Eau
Claire.

She walked toward the glow of the yellow house. The dogs
regularly found their way to Jennings and Muriel's porch. Grace
suspected that Muriel fed them. Molly and Finn were friendly and
adorable and gorgeous, but basically they were in it for the protein.

Shivering, Grace followed the curve of the driveway, veering
right five hundred feet from the house, and walking to a rise in the
land from which she could look down into the slight hollow where
cars were still leaving the yellow house, their headlights crisscrossing
in the darkness, silver clouds of exhaust pouring from their tailpipes.
She saw Jennings standing on the porch, illuminated by the porch
light. His hands were clasped and his chin was raised. He looked
pleased with himself in a way that made her furious.

The cars left the property in single file, the beams of their headlights bouncing up and down.

Grace stepped out of the trees and waved. An expression of *something* crossed Jennings's face—was it curiosity, concern, or perhaps
disapproval? Disapproval! As if she were trespassing. He slowly unclasped his hands, and raised one in greeting. Grace started down
the hill, as if beckoned, making her way carefully toward him. The
last thing she needed was to slip and fall.

"Looking for those damn dogs," she said. She had decided to
be casual, good-humored, but her voice was curdled with irritation.

"I asked Mur not to feed them," Jennings said. "You want some
help finding them?"

Mur? When did that begin?

"They often hang out at the orchard," Grace said. "I'll go over."

"Okay."

She didn't move.

"Want some company?" he asked.

"Of course," she said.

The grassy ground had been coarsened by the early frost, its sponginess seeping through the soles of her brown-and-white pumps. She wondered what the effect would be were she to even momentarily take his arm for balance. It was what she had come to know about illicit affections: every gesture was measured, everything had to be titrated just so. The structure of a secret romance was so complex and so flimsy that everything you did either added to or subtracted from its ability to survive. She decided against taking his arm. No casual contact. No appetizers before dinner; it was the main course or nothing. They followed the curve of the land, the slight downward slope. The yellow house disappeared but the light coming through its windows created an arc of brightness in the night. One of the party boats passed, unseen by Grace and Jennings from where they stood, but clearly audible. The owners of the estates along the river had complained about Rock the Hudson, saying that the noise pollution was insupportable, and it seemed that since then the throb of the passing boats had become all the more pronounced. The band Foreigner singing "I Want to Know What Love Is" blasted from the boat's sound system, the urgent, indefatigable voice of the lead singer echoing against the Catskills.

"Hideous," Grace said. "They really have no right."

"It doesn't bother me," Jennings said. "Mur likes that song."

"Since when is it Mur?"

"I've always called her that," Jennings said.

"Really? Have you? I never heard it, not once."

"What can I tell you?"

They were at the edge of the orchard now, and Grace sensed the dogs weren't there. She would have at least heard the jingle of their collars. The music from the party boat grew distant—when the music was close it annoyed her but as it drifted away it all seemed so sad.

"I wonder how many people are on that boat on a night like this," she said.

"Yeah," said Jennings. "But the boats make good money."

"I miss you so much," she said, emboldened by his indifference. "Don't you even think about me?"

"Sure. You're Grace. There's only one of you in the whole world."

"That's not what I mean."

"I care about you, Grace."

"Oh come on. Really? You're saying this to *me*?"

"Don't you want me to care about you?" he asked.

"I was thinking you might love me."

"I do. Of course I do."

"Oh God."

She could not see but heard him shrug, the rustle of his shirt.

"I mean for real," Grace said. "Physically. Desperately. I want you to be thinking about me while you are trying to go to sleep."

"I fall asleep as soon as my head hits the pillow. Like nine thirty. It's already past my bedtime."

"Oh fuck you." The words hung there, violent as the smell of cordite. "I'm sorry," she murmured, at last. She wondered if he was telling her about the early bedtime as a way of indicating he and Muriel were no longer having sex.

"You're unhappy," he said.

"I wouldn't be if you kissed me."

"As simple as that?" he asked.

"Yeah."

He took her in his arms, and kissed her hard, with a little throb of brutality. When she increased the intimacy of the kiss—opened herself, let him feel her tongue—he stepped back.

"There," he said.

There? As if it were a little chore he'd just completed.

"How dare you?" she said, in her old Audrey Hepburn voice, long unused. It felt somehow centering to bring it back. Surprising them both, she slapped Jennings hard across the face. She felt the flesh and stubble of him on her open palm. She hadn't slapped someone's face since high school, when all the girls in her set were doing it. It was kind of a fad to make out with a boy, and smack him one if he touched you beyond the prescribed areas.

"Don't put a mark on me," he said. "That would not be cool."

"I'm sorry. I can't believe I did that."

"We do things. It's okay. We just have to . . ."

"Have to what?" she asked.

"We have to be cool."

"When was the last time we fucked?"

"It's been a while."

Her eyes filled with tears.

"Do you love me, Jennings? Seriously. What's happening here, what are we to each other?"

"I'm going to tell you something. Something only one other person knows."

"Who?"

"It doesn't matter."

"No, but who?" she asked. "Who else knows?"

"Buddy."

"Buddy? You're putting me on the same level as Buddy Klein?"

"It's about the money I got to start the business."

"That's all anyone at the party could talk about."

"I could be in trouble."

"We're all in trouble."

"You don't understand, Grace," he said. He put his hand on her shoulder, not in a particularly loving way, but as you would check a child about to cross a busy street. Nonetheless, the feel of his touch created a kind of churning within her, alive, luminous, sickening and thrilling at once. "I stole a really valuable ring," he said.

"From me?" she asked. She wouldn't have said that if she'd given herself one extra moment to consider it.

"From you?"

"Well, you're telling me."

"Before you came here. There was this woman."

"There always was, always is, and always will be," she said.

He pulled a cigarette out of the pack in his shirt pocket and got it going with his lighter. The little lick of flame illuminated his face for a moment.

"You shouldn't smoke," she said.

"Yeah, I heard." His laugh had something bitter in it, self-pitying.

You're the one who wanted to get involved with asbestos, she thought. But how many things could she quarrel with him about? You had to choose. "So this woman?" she asked.

"She was a friend of the Boyetts."

"By the time we bought Orkney they were in Mexico."

"They should fucking stay in Mexico," Jennings said.

"Isn't *'Mur'* Mexican?"

"What's that got to do with it?"

"Nothing. So what about this woman? Was it Boyett? I don't remember her first name. Gene Woodard always refers to her as the Lady Boyett."

"It wasn't her. One of her friends. She got high and killed her dogs. Little yappers, but still."

"She killed her dogs? You slept with a woman who killed her dogs?"

"Who said I slept with her? She passed out and it was up to me to lug her upstairs."

"And then what?"

"I took a ring off her. I didn't know what it was worth but I figured it was a lot."

"You took it off her?"

"And I buried it right over there, by the Italian plum tree. I figured I got myself a plum, so I wouldn't forget."

"Where you buried it."

"Right. I wasn't going to forget *that* I buried it, just where. I can tell you this—I was nervous."

I can tell you this. Grace noted it: wasn't that a classic standby Hat-ism? Thaddeus did a funny imitation of Hat, the way he wagged his finger as if conducting an orchestra of assorted facts and figures, rubber plantations in Congo, the countless varieties of apple, the best way to lure bluebirds, which were, after all, the official state bird—and interspersed with this deluge of information were the foundational phrases, including *I can tell you this.* Slowly, inexorably, Jennings was coming to resemble his father. His ears were growing larger, his nose a bit longer. Father and son both had a bit of Lyndon Johnson in them. The belly must have come through his mother. If Jennings had once hoped to fuck and snarl his way into eternal youth, if he had in any way imagined that he could fold his arms over his chest and stand to one side as time rushed past him, the nose, those ears, that belly, and the way he was starting to talk would prove him wrong, if not this year then the next.

"It's grand larceny," he said. "You steal something from somebody poor it's petty larceny, but if you steal something that really is worth something then you're looking at five to ten."

"Did she call the cops?"

"Yeah. They questioned me." He smiled, letting her know it was something he could handle. "I know all the local guys but she brought in her own people. And the stupid Boyetts were out there for weeks, crawling around. They made my dad look for it, too. That was the worst part of it, seeing Hat on his hands and knees looking through the grass. But there was nothing I could say. I buried it and I kept it buried, until last year. I figured by then no one was thinking about it anymore. I dug it up, and I got Buddy to help me find a guy to take it off my hands."

"Like you took it off hers," said Grace.

"Ha. You and Thaddeus always have something funny to say."

"Thaddeus is the funny one in the family." *That's right: family.* She could feel herself moving away from Jennings. It felt like the time she'd gotten on one of the moving walkways at the airport. Thaddeus had veered off at a kiosk to buy a Heath bar and she turned and watched as the conveyor belt moved her farther and farther away from him. The weirdness of it, its intimations of some sad future being previewed, must have struck Thaddeus, too. He waved good-bye to her as he—or was it she?—got smaller and smaller.

Go back to Mur. Good luck in your new business. I should have guessed it: you're a thief.

Yet if he were to touch her, it might stabilize her. And hadn't she, too, taken things that were not hers? Those pearl earrings she'd found at the Palmer House and given to her mother as a birthday present? Maureen's thank-you had been icy; she knew the earrings were stolen. She wore them once and put them away, in the blue-and-yellow Salerno butter cookie tin where they became part of the glittering jumble of junk jewelry.

"So here's what happened," Jennings was saying.

"Why even tell me?"

"We're friends, aren't we?"

"If you say so."

"Me and Buddy took the train into the city. Right into Pennsylvania Station. He was more nervous than me, I'll tell you that."

"I hate the smell of that cigarette. I'll tell *you* that."

He looked at the cigarette in his hand, as if surprised to find it there, and then took a long drag. "First thing he wants to do is go to this bar right in the station. Then he waves a taxicab over and we get in. The driver has this turban on. It's snowing and this guy's from a place where it never snows so he's gripping the steering wheel and sweating and I'm thinking, Well, this is what I get because I'm pretty damn sure this guy's going to wipe out."

"But he didn't," Grace said, hoping to communicate via tone that every word Jennings was saying was the wrong word, and what he ought to be saying was, *We need to find a way for us to see each other.*

"He takes us to Forty-Seventh Street and Avenue of the Americas where this guy Buddy knows from the old days is working. Allan Levitas, *Big Al.* He used to be Buddy's bass player, but now he works for his uncle in the Jewish diamond district."

"It's just a diamond district, Jennings. Diamonds can't be Jewish."

"You know what I mean. He's in this huge place, with like fifty different businesses going on, everyone's got their little turf, you know? They even have a secret restaurant, in the back, you go up the stairs and there's like forty guys in black hats eating sandwiches. We show Allan the ring. He's not dressed like the other guys, he just looks normal. But he's carrying one of those jeweler eye things on a chain around his neck and he says it's worth thirty thousand. Me, I'm about to flip out. I never held thirty thousand dollars in my life and I'm never going to hold that much money ever again. It probably doesn't seem like much money to you."

"Of course it does," she said, with some emphasis.

"I didn't even know what to do with it. I wanted Buddy to keep it for me, but I was too embarrassed to ask. You know?"

They were silent. The distant sound of sirens. Someone had fallen, or crashed, or there was a fire.

"So there you have it," Grace at last said.

"You told me you used to steal things. When you worked in the hotel."

"I was a kid."

"You were poor."

"I'm curious about something, though," Grace said. "Your telling me this. Now. Tonight. I'm wondering why."

"I'm not sure. I just wanted to. I trust you."

"You know what I think? I think my dogs are in the shed with the shovels and rakes. They like to go there. You want to check it out with me?"

"No," he said. "They're not there. All kinds of critters were getting in and we closed it up good."

"*Critters* is such an annoying word, Jennings." Her eyes had finally adjusted to the darkness and she saw the look of puzzlement on Jennings's face. Or was that a frown of mild disgust? No, he wouldn't do that, not his style. Then dismay, it must have been a frown of mild *dismay*. "All right, since you're in full-disclosure mode, why not tell me something else? What was the purpose of it, this whole thing between us? You were never going to leave *Mur*."

"And you weren't going to leave Thaddeus."

"You never asked me to."

"And you never asked me."

"All right. I'm asking you."

"Grace." He smoothed her name out as he said it, like the gentle downward sweep of a hand closing the eyes of the deceased.

"That's your answer?" As well as she knew that if you drank a half bottle of Ketel One you were going to feel like shit in the morning, she knew that the more she pressed Jennings to make some massive declaration of love, the worse she was going to feel.

But could she actually feel any worse? Maybe it was already too late for self-protection. Why put up an umbrella when you were already soaked to the bone? She had already demeaned herself in front of him, all but begged him to kiss her—how much worse could she feel? Why not just drop to the ground and throw a full-out tantrum? Why not threaten to tell the police about the source of the financing for his new venture? That he would not love her was, for the moment, more than a disappointment, it exceeded ordinary heartbreak: it was an affront. She could make his life so much better than it was, and that was not even taking into account certain material advantages she might be able to offer. Why would he be so needlessly protective of his relationship with that lunatic from Bakersfield? It was not as if the sex was anything special. *Mur* was on a short leash, sexually speaking, and as she aged the leash lost links, became even less flexible. Her breasts were sensitive and she would cry out if his touch was heavier than a butterfly landing. Doggy style was for dogs. Because once she had gotten an ear infection, which she was certain came from bacteria introduced by his tongue, her ears were out of bounds.

Grace wondered if what was wrecking everything between her and Jennings was that she had somehow failed to communicate to him how *fond* of him she was. He may have been under the impression that her attachment was mainly physical and did not know that loving him and *being* with him kept her sane. Put simply, he was an essential piece of the Rube Goldberg contraption that kept her alive, as essential to her heartbeat as a pacemaker, and if he didn't know that, he was an idiot. And it seemed suddenly quite possible that that was exactly what he was. An idiot and a dunce, someone who slips a ring off a drunk woman, buries it for years, and then swaps it out for a bag full of cash. Grace was not wed to the law—life as Liam's adoring sister was a crash course in moral relativism—but there was something pathetic and abject about the kind of theft Jennings had committed. It was grubby.

"Nothing good can come of it," she said.

"Of what?" Jennings asked. The neglected cigarette had gone cold, but he still held on to it.

"Any of it. The ring, your business. Us."

"I'm sorry, Grace. You're beautiful. You know that, don't you?"

"I am aware of how I register in the commodity market," she said. "Let me ask you something. And be honest. Has this whole thing been like your *revenge*?"

"I don't need revenge."

"Your father. Sending him up in that tree. Everything."

"I protect you, Grace. If you want to know. You may own this place but Orkney is under my protection. Things are happening up and down the river, and it's only going to get worse. There are a lot of really angry people here. And I make damn sure nothing happens to your house, anything of yours."

"Oh please."

"You'll see. Just wait. You'll see."

"We haven't even talked about Emma," Grace said.

TODD AND CANDY SAT AT their kitchen table, sharing a beer. Todd glanced at the clock above the stove. It was almost ten. He had to be at Willis Correctional at five thirty, and the prison was a good forty-minute drive. He could shower before going to bed, or he could get up a half hour early and do it before leaving for work. Either way, it meant maybe five hours of sleep. The last time he'd gone to work that underslept he ended up losing his temper and slamming a prisoner against the wall. Unluckily, the prisoner had an uncle who was a lawyer and the family kicked up a fuss that almost led to Todd being suspended without pay. If he ever got caught being too physical with an inmate again, who knew what action the warden might take?

"Don't Bogart that bottle," he said to Candy. It was sexy, it was almost indecent, the way she drank her beer. Her cheeks filled and then deflated as the cold beer coursed down her throat. Her deep throat! It never failed to arouse him, Little Miss Purity walking the halls of Leyden High, now a woman, his.

"You have to start being nice to people, Todd," she said, passing the bottle to him.

"I was kidding! Take the whole beer, there's more in the fridge."

"I mean to other people. You want them to respect you, but you don't want them to fear you. You know the difference, right? Respect means they come closer, fear means they run and hide. You need friends."

"Got plenty."

"Better friends. Friends who can help you."

"I don't have to big up to anyone."

"Well, actually you do. You can't just have your old buddies running around smashing things. You need money, you need organization. You want to be in the Republicans, then you have to *join* them. That doesn't mean you walk in and all of a sudden you're the boss. You want to be sheriff, don't you?"

"I'm going to be sheriff."

"You *want* to be sheriff. So far no one's even nominated you. You have to go slow."

"What's that mean?" He pushed his chair back; the legs squeaked loudly. He looked up at the ceiling, hoping to God he didn't wake the kid. "I'm getting another beer. A whole one."

"I'll take one, too," Candy said.

"Thatta girl."

Candy rolled her eyes as he handed her the open beer. Their marriage was full of little transactions like this one, and the second beer meant *I want you.*

"It means if someone doesn't go along with one of your little theories you can't bite his head off."

"I don't have any *little theories.*"

"Contrails? You think that's a conspiracy up in the sky, right?"

"It's chemtrails, baby, and it's not just my theory. The majority of people think that. Like eighty percent."

"Conetrails, coattails, whatever. It's all bull-you-know-what. And I have to tell you, Todd, you're the only one I ever hear talking about it. You want to talk about what's up there? Try talking about God."

"I do."

"Not about how the Russians killed Kennedy."

"Jack. Not Bobby."

"Or how the Vatican got us off the gold standard."

"Come on, Candy. That's been proved."

"Or this Bilateral Commission—"

"Trilateral."

She raised her eyebrows and laughed, and he laughed with her. He wasn't sure what they were laughing about, but he never could resist her laughter. When she laughed it meant she loved him.

"You can't sell yourself short, Todd. God has a plan for every one of our lives. And God has a plan for you."

"And I guess you've got a plan for me, too, Candy."

"I sure do," she said. "And I heard what some of the guys were saying tonight. I know what they're up to."

"Not me, I'm right here."

"I know. You're different. I always knew you were special. When you talk, people listen. That's why I want you to go easy on some of the conspiracy stuff."

"The thing is," Todd said, getting up, walking to the sink, and looking out the window. He'd heard that something was going down tonight but he'd walked away because it was better in the long run not to know. He thought he might have heard something, car wheels, footsteps, but the night silently pleaded its own innocence. "Do you think people would really vote for me?" he asked.

"What counts is *we* stand up and be counted," Candy said. "But they will, I know they will."

"Sheriff Todd Reynolds."

"Look who we've got doing that job now. Tomczak is an old man, drunk on his behind half the time."

"We just got to straighten things out around here."

"Not just here."

"Straighten it the hell out, all of it. And these people with their hundred-dollar fucking chickens?"

She winced. "Come on, Todd. Don't. You've got a beautiful voice, so say beautiful things. Be strong and courageous! Do not tremble or be dismayed, for the Lord your God is with you wherever you go. You know what I mean, baby? You understand?"

He nodded briefly. She wasn't certain he had heard her. He was pacing now. He went to the sink, ran the tap, and threw some water onto his face. When he turned to face her again, it looked as if he'd been weeping.

"You know what I can't stand? The way everything has to be so friggin' special. Special schools, special food, they don't even drink the same water as us. You see them? They get their water in these little bottles. If they love the river so much, why don't they drink it? Are you part of America? Okay, then drink American water out of the tap like everyone else. But they don't respect anything. They sure as shit don't respect us. We're here to do their dirty work, end of story. They get drunk and wrap their car around a tree—who answers the call? Their tennis buddies? Their stockbrokers? No, it's us. Us pulling them out, us mopping up the blood, us racing them to the hospital, risking our own damn lives to get them there before they bleed out. Storm comes, trees fall, lights go out. They're squealing like a bunch of stuck pigs but you don't see any of *them* out in the weather, you don't see any of *them* up on the cherry picker, getting the chainsaws going, patching it all back together again. It's us. Who's plowing the roads so they can drive their little German cars?

Who's emptying their bedpans? And when it's wet-ass time? They *hear* something, or *see* something, or if some jigaboo wanders up out of the Bronx . . ."

"You can't say *jigaboo*, Todd. I don't want to hear that kind of thing. I really don't. This isn't about black and white, it's about right and wrong. We can't be what they think we are. We're not rude and dumb. What we're doing—it's bigger than us. You know that, don't you? We have to make sure we don't get in our own way. Remember, baby: we were put here for a reason."

"You think?"

"I know."

"We were," Todd said. "We were put here for a reason."

"I've always known that," said Candy.

"Someone's got to straighten this out," Todd said.

"I'm looking at him," Candy said.

"Amen to that, Candy," said Candy's mother. Her voice startled them for a moment.

"Did we wake you?" Candy asked.

Dressed in baggy gray sweatpants and a T-shirt, Candy's mother had made it down the stairs, holding Brandon in her arms, his downy legs dangling, his hair sticking to the sweat of his brow.

"Brandon's awake," Candy's mother said.

Brandon, who had been cast into darkness so he might see the real world, spoke to them in the tongue of angels. "Shaa po kuh," he said. "Oh mo dee yo. Koo koo yah bah. Sen dow mo dee ya." The blameless big-hearted boy reached longingly toward his father's scent, his fingers moving like little underwater creatures, his dark brown sightless eyes like those of a deer head mounted on a wall, glassy reminders of all that was lost. He heard the familiar thudding sound of his parents' devotion, their knees touching the kitchen floor, and he, too, began to sink, as his grandmother joined them in kneeling. "Koo koo yah bah koo ko yah," he said. "Koo koo yah ban ya brata shot koa ban ya ran ya shot kay baya shot ya baya shot kah baya shot kah."

THE DOGS WERE COLLAPSED IN front of the fireplace in the library, looking at Thaddeus with glittering eyes. "I'm not building you a fire, if that's what all these loving glances are about," he said to them as he stood at the window looking for Grace.

The night had gone from nippy to just plain cold and she was somewhere out there traipsing around in search of those elusive Weimaraners, who were now dozing nose to nose. He considered using the golf cart, an electrified four-seater, a recent acquisition, and a sore point between them. Grace said it was a needless and senseless extravagance, and a shortcut to "fat assitude."

Thaddeus stood for a moment at the bottom of the stairs, his hand resting on the newel post, thinking about Grace and her growing obsession over Emma's weight. He was going to call up to Vicky to tell her that he was leaving for a little while, but he changed his mind and left without saying anything. He thought about how wonderful it would be to be a ghost, and to make occasional visits to the world, to see it for all of its folly and not feel sad or thrilled, to not feel anything at all, just to experience the whole thing like a story you could read for a while, put down, and pick back up whenever you were in the mood.

The golf cart was in front of the house—he had wanted to drive it to the yellow house, but Grace objected. "It's enough we're bringing fancy take-out food," she'd said. "Do we have to arrive by chariot?" That wasn't very nice of her to say, but as part of a story, a piece of make-believe in a world in which everything was an illusion, it wasn't so awful. In fact it was sort of amusing.

The key was in the ignition and he turned it. He placed his foot on the brake and put the gear shift into drive and the cart rolled forward, at first with a couple of jolts and then smoothly, with a pleasant, busy hum. The property looked strange to him in the darkness, the rise and fall of it, the dark sky cut into crazy angles by the even darker trees, the smell of the fields and the soil and the secrets of the earth. He kept to the driveway, whose ruts he had memorized.

He had the feeling of not being alone. Of being watched? No, it was something else. The coyotes were yipping it up. An owl was at its post, hooting and hooting, and no other owl replied. The wind blew through Thaddeus's coat, and seemed even to breach the barrier of his skin, and go right for his heart.

Suddenly, the coyotes went silent, and Thaddeus was plunged into a kind of despair. The hopelessness of life seemed undeniable. Life, liberty, and the pursuit of happiness, what a joke. Happiness was fool's gold. Happiness was a consolation prize for those who could not sustain passion and could not create art. He agreed with some novelist whose essay he'd read in the newspaper, some lucky bastard who had his ticket punched and now was free to pontificate. Thaddeus hated and envied them all, the people who had stayed the course and made him feel like a failure, but he liked what this guy had written: *Happiness is for amateurs.* Thaddeus heartily agreed, yet he had not spent his life pursuing passion and art. He had chased after happiness like a greyhound in pursuit of a mechanical rabbit, around and around the track, his jaws snapping at nothing. And now? And now he was going to lose his wife, and without Grace, without the knowledge of her, the warm eternity of her body, her breath, simply knowing she was there—what was left? The beautiful rooms, the curtains moving in the breeze, the smell of exquisite perfume, the thirsty towels, the wines that formed sensory anagrams on your tongue, the massages and manicures, the stretch limos and the Egyptian linens, and these windswept acres that streamed past him like useless footage on a Moviola, all of it destined for the cutting-room floor, as was he.

HE MADE IT ALL THE way to Riverview Road, swung in a wide arc, and headed back toward Orkney. The main driveway had three forks—one leading to the main house, one to the yellow house, one to the pastures and what remained of the old barns. This time, he headed toward the yellow house. This spur was actually in better shape than the main drive; apparently Jennings and/or Hat had done some repair work. For a moment, the main house emerged from the night, like a sunken ship that through some miracle or some horrible perversity has risen from the deep, its portholes blazing with light, the passengers trapped inside, their faces pressed against the glass. He swerved right and the mansion was gone. In front of him now was the yellow house, and just as it came into view the downstairs lights started going out one by one. The sweep of the golf cart's head-lights caught something moving. Grace! Away from the orchard, across the driveway, up the small hill that gave the mansion and the yellow house privacy from each other, a buffer of trees and grass and soil, and the unseen world coursing below. He shouted her name and she stopped, turned toward him.

She had never looked more beautiful. Her chest was heaving, her hair was moving in the wind. He wound his way toward her. She did not move to meet him, but waited, the golf cart's anemic little headlights illuminating her face. She looked possessed, a mixture of Mary and the archangel Gabriel who had come to deliver the news, that moment in the garden, the story repeated so often that it may as well have been true, the image rendered over and over and over and over in reverent detail, each brushstroke an invitation to prayer. The glowing paintings, the lost art of them, the faces magically lit, the diaphanous round disks of the halos. Golden David in Grace's ethe-real painting, holding the silver airplane, the canvas thrown into the fireplace in a tearful row a day after the auction, rescued, and now black in one corner and somehow more precious having survived its trial by fire.

Why had she been running? Why did she look at him now as if afraid? He heard something rustling off to the side, to the left, or the right, hard to pinpoint out here. Without manufactured spaces to limit the reverb, the noise of life seemed to come from everywhere all at once: the staticky sound of crushed twigs, the yearning of that sleepless owl, the madness of the coyotes, the eternal wind, the roar of a jet pulling its sound behind it like a horse dragging a plow across a stony field.

"Grace!" he called, and she came to him, slowly at first, and a few steps later with purpose, until she was standing next to him and placed her hand on the cart's roll bar.

"The dogs are back," he said. "I've got them in the house."

"They are?"

"Hop on."

"Are they all right?"

"They're fine. Come on. Hop on."

She climbed in beside him and he took the yellow house's driveway to the point where it intersected with the main driveway, which led to the big house.

"You want to take a little ride?" he asked her. "Maybe go down to the river?"

"I'm freezing cold," she said. She rested her head against his shoulder. "Thanks."

"For?"

"For finding the dogs, and coming to get me."

"Of course."

"What would I do without you?"

"Don't make it sound so sad," he said. He was driving as slowly as possible. Their house was in view now but through a trick of the darkness it seemed to be drifting away.

Home.

"Maybe after you make a fuss about the dogs we can make a fuss about each other," Thaddeus said, as they walked onto the porch. He offered his arm, and Grace took it with a sense of gratitude she hadn't felt in a long while. He was here and she needed him.

Just as they touched the door, Vicky pulled it open for them. She was holding Emma, whose chubby little face was wet with tears. How could a child look so tragic?

"Here's Mommy now, just when you thought there is no hope," Vicky said. She had taught herself English from books while she still lived in El Salvador; she had a large vocabulary, but her accent was a problem. "She's hungry," Vicky explained to Grace. "But I know we are trying to be careful."

"Come here, you," Thaddeus said, reaching for the child. "The great food-rationing campaign is over. You want a bowl of cereal?"

The girl slowly nodded her head yes, as if confessing. He carried her into the kitchen, and sat with her while she devoured a bowl of Rice Krispies. He noticed that she took as much as her mouth would hold, and was already reloading her spoon while she chewed. He was convinced that if she could correct these two things the weight would gradually disappear without having to force a Draconian system of self-denial on the poor child, who was clearly being traumatized by her mother's campaign to slim her down. There was a middle path. After Emma finished the cereal, she asked for a cookie. She patted her stomach as she asked, as if to prepare it for the insult that usually accompanied her requests for sweets.

"I'll split one with you!" Thaddeus said, with great enthusiasm.

For a moment, it looked as if Emma might argue for the whole cookie, but she thought better of it. They stood together in the kitchen, and when their halves were consumed Thaddeus said it was time for bed and Emma slipped her hand in his and the tenderness of this, its utter lack of artifice or agenda, its simultaneous submissiveness and sense of ownership was almost devastating in its loveliness. She was his child.

In Emma's room, illuminated only by a night-light in the shape of a rearing palomino, Thaddeus sat on the edge of her bed and slowly patted her back to help her fall asleep. She felt a little spongy to his touch and he was irritated with himself for noticing. It usually took five or ten minutes of gentle patting for Emma to fall asleep. Thaddeus had perfected the routine, beginning with pats that came regularly, one per second, and slowly decreasing the frequency. But tonight as his hand slowed down, Emma suddenly turned over, wide awake.

"David was mean to me," she said.

"Oh no. That's terrible. Are you sure?"

She nodded. "He never lets me in his room."

"Well, you know. Some people."

"You never even had a brother."

"I know. I would have liked one, I think. It might have been nice." He was whispering, still holding on to the idea that she might drop off to sleep at any moment.

"Or a sister," she said.

Without fully considering where this might lead, he said, "Actually, I did."

Even in the near darkness of her room, he could see she was amazed. "Where does she live?"

"In my heart."

"Why?"

"Well, she died. She died when she was very little." As soon as he said the words he realized his error. She was far too young to hear about a little girl dying. She was a little girl herself—what was he doing? Had he become emotionally incontinent?

"What was her name?" Emma whispered.

"Hannah," Thaddeus managed to say.

Emma reached for his hand and he took it and pressed it to his forehead.

"It's okay, baby. It was a long time ago."

"Do you miss her?"

"In a way. But I didn't really know her. I was little, too, when it happened. Hey, you know what? It's really late and Mommy's waiting for me, so I better . . ." He had managed to regain control over himself, but it felt temporary. He stood up, light-headed, and Emma's room momentarily flapped like a sheet in the wind.

"Am I fat?" Emma asked. Thaddeus had already opened the door; the light from the hall trembled around the shape of him.

"You're beautiful and you're smart and you're *good*," Thaddeus said. "And don't let anyone ever tell you anything different."

In the hallway, with his hand on the doorknob, he backed slowly against the door until he heard it click shut. He stayed there for a few more moments, listening for her, gathering his wits. Closer than usual, the coyotes were wailing. At least he thought they were coyotes.

Downstairs, he found Grace in the library. Fresh logs were on the andirons and the dogs slept their deep canine peaceful slumber as sparks ticked against the fire screen. The wind had picked up and the windows shuddered in their frames. Grace was on the pale green sofa with the rolled arms, the damask upholstery, the lion-claw feet, and she was drawing. She had her art face on, intense and concentrated in a way that seemed painful. He wondered what their lives would have been like if neither of them had wanted to be an artist, if they had not wanted to be one of the anointed, and to make something out of nothing. What if they could have been happy with each other, with the pleasures of life, what if they could have just taken things as they'd come?

"She's asleep," he said.

"I know what you did," Grace said, without looking up.

"Yes, the cardinal sin of the late-night cookie."

"Ha ha, big joke."

"Grace, please. She's our daughter. We want her to be healthy but we can't have all this pressure. We don't want her to think there's something wrong with her, do we? Who knows how long any of us will even *be* here?"

She chose not to pursue the conversation. She went back to her drawing, and Thaddeus stood silently, wondering if he should simply leave the room.

"Do you want a drink? I'm going to pour myself something."

"No thanks."

"You sure?"

"I'm going to work."

"What are you working on?"

"Liam's asked me to do something for him. He even offered to pay me."

"Good!" Why not tell her right now that in all likelihood his little gallop through the pastures of plenty had ended at Craig Epstein's birthday brunch? Yet the shame he felt silenced him.

"It's not movie money or anything like that," she said. "But earning money with my art? It was always the thing I wanted. To show the world what I saw and what I felt. It's really so awful when the world shrugs and walks away. You have no idea."

"I'm sorry, Grace. I really am."

"I guess it didn't work out that much better for you."

"That's true."

"Well, we have that in common."

"We do!" He felt his spirits lifting. It was a new and unexpected kind of union between them, a new equality. They were runners expired halfway through the marathon, holding on to each other as they fought for breath on the side of the road. Was there any greater intimacy?

"So what do you think? They're labels for his avocados." She moved a floor lamp so the light shone directly on the two avocados, one whole, the other neatly split. Grace had been rendering avocados with colored pencils for many years, the dark rough shell, the pale green meat with its gradations of color, the dark ripples where the flesh had begun to spoil.

"Amazing," Thaddeus said. "Beautiful."

"I hope Liam likes them."

"I kind of miss your brother being an outlaw," Thaddeus said. "The journey from pot to guacamole is a little disheartening."

"It was always the plan," she said, her gaze fixed on the drawing. "He just needed to make a certain amount of money."

Thaddeus kneeled in front of her and to his surprise she ran her fingers through his hair and then pulled him toward her. From the distance, they heard the party boat with its full complement of revelers, and the sound of the Allman Brothers singing "Whipping Post."

"Oh, those party boats," said Grace. "Don't they know there are people trying to enjoy the peace and quiet of their homes? We don't want to hear their stupid music while they stuff their faces with chips and salsa."

"Well . . ."

"Oh, don't pretend. You can't stand their food."

He patted her hip and she made room for him to sit next to her. "Remember back at that benefit for Brandon?"

"More chips and salsa."

"Well, I never wanted to bring this up. But Muriel . . ."

"Oh Muriel," said Grace, her face twisted into a sneer. "*Mur.* She started off crazy and has only gotten crazier. I can't stand her or her stupid baskets and all the little found objects, as if she and she alone can appreciate the beauty of forgotten things. You know what I think? We should buy them out. Just get them the hell out of here. After Hat dies. Jennings will take the money if we make an offer. I know he will. He comes on like this free spirit of the woodlands, but he's very focused on money."

"I don't think so, Grace."

"Don't I have a say in this? I never wanted to give them that property to begin with. Your stupid Communist parents. Excuse me. *Trotskyist.* Whatever they are, they filled your head with a bunch of shit they don't even live by themselves. You don't see them giving away their stuff. They gave us a check for one hundred dollars for our wedding."

"I'm not in a position." He stood, walked over to the hearth. He used the poker to take a hard whack at a burning log, launching an eruption of embers that rose in a bright orange cloud and then drifted up into the flue.

He turned toward Grace, the heat of the fireplace on his back. "I want to tell you something."

"Maybe put the poker away. I don't like being *told something* by a man with a weapon."

He looked at the poker, shrugged, and put it back with the tongs, the ash rake, and the shovel.

"Better?"

"Perfect."

"Last time I was in L.A., I was at this party . . ."

"Oh Christ."

"What?"

"Nothing. Just say. You were at a party."

"And I lost my temper and threw a drink in someone's face."

"Rilly?"

"You look pleased."

"I thought you were going to say something else. Worse. That's not too bad."

"I was going out there for a job, and I didn't get it."

"So you'll get another one. You always do."

"I don't think so. I really fucked up."

"Should we be worried?"

"My agent seems to think so. I don't have an assignment right now, and he says he's not getting any inquiries."

"But come on. That's crazy. You always get work."

"I've got no real prospects. I don't know what we're going to do for money. And I'm sorry. I had no right to act so rashly. I realize everyone here is counting on me."

"You actually threw a drink in someone's face?"

"Yes."

"I'm trying to imagine it. What kind of drink?"

"A mimosa."

"Why did you do it?"

"I'm not sure. He was wearing pajamas. I didn't think he ought to be wearing pajamas when everyone else was dressed."

"So you did it on a whim?"

"It felt like inspiration."

She closed her eyes, hoping in the darkness there might emerge some pattern in the shattered pieces. "Are we broke?"

"No. Not yet."

"Soon?"

"Depends on what you mean by soon." He was sitting close to her again, patting her knee, as if she had let her emotions run away with her and needed calming.

"Tomorrow?"

"No."

"In six months?"

"Maybe. Yes. That could happen."

"Can you stop patting my knee?"

They looked at each other like two people on a suspension bridge who can hear over the raging water below the fatal ping of one of the cables snapping and then another and another.

"Men are such idiots," Grace said, finally.

"Okay, your turn," he said, taking her hand. "I told you something I didn't want to. Now you. Tell me something I need to know about. Something I don't know but I should. Something important."

"What makes you think I've got anything?" she asked.

"You said men are such idiots. You can start there. What you're thinking about? Who?"

"Thaddeus, if there's something you want to know, you should ask me."

"And you'll answer?"

"Yes," Grace said.

"Answer truthfully?"

"I won't dignify that."

"You have to promise. There's no point to it if you won't promise to tell the truth."

"I will tell you the truth, Thaddeus. Ask away. Anything you want."

"All right."

He waited. He studied her face. He was still holding her hand and he placed it gently on her lap.

"Okay." He breathed deeply. "Here's my question."

"Just ask, Thaddeus."

"Okay. Here it is." He stood up, walked across the room to the windows, turning his back to her, choosing not to see her face when she answered. "My question is this: are you absolutely one hundred percent sure you won't join me in a drink?"

Ah, a joke. Another emotion toppled into its waiting grave. Relief shivered through her as bright and cold as the thawing of a stream. She would live to lie another day.

"Daddy!" Emma's voice called from upstairs.

"Mom?" called out David. The two of them were standing at the top of the stairs. "We smell smoke."

Thaddeus parted the curtains and looked out into the night. He moved his head left and right, trying to see around his own reflection. Silence, privacy, a world of your own: it was what the house had been built for, no one could see you, but that meant you couldn't see them. He never thought he'd have to worry about a *them* before, but now he wasn't certain. All that he could see were the pebbles on the driveway, the back wheels of the golf cart. Everything else was as invisible as luck, fate, time, love, everything that actually mattered.

He, too, smelled smoke, but if there was a fire it was far away. How could it not be? Wasn't the fire nearly always somewhere else?

"Daddy?" Emma called out.

"It's okay, guys," Thaddeus said, turning to their voices. He went to the staircase and saw them peering down, their faces bewildered, frightened, their hair askew, their limbs bare. They were holding hands. "It's fine, kids," he said, as he rose toward them. "Don't worry."

He gathered them in his arms and kissed them as he carried them down the stairs, wishing he was stronger. Once he was off the staircase and on level ground their weight was easier to bear. He carried them to the library, where their mother sat silently on the sofa, twiddling a green Prismacolor, looking down at the drawing on her lap, and where the dogs sat alertly in front of the hearth, their slumber interrupted by the smell of smoke. He knelt in front of the window, balancing David on one hip, Emma on the other, and the three of them peered out at the night through their own reflections. "You see?" he said. "Everything's quiet, everything's nice."

"But I hear sirens," said Emma.

"And I smell smoke," said David.

"But look, look," Thaddeus said. He started to point but Emma almost slipped off and he gripped her again. "What do you see?"

"Us," said Emma.

"Nothing," said David.

"That's right," said Thaddeus. "You're both right. Something's going on out there, but it's not us. There's a fire, I guess. But it's far away. And we're safe, you guys, me, Mommy, Finn, and Molly. Someone's in trouble, but it's not us."

Acknowledgments

Thank you, Jo Ann Beard, for everything from inspiration to stern warnings.

Thank you, Lynn Nesbit, always wise, always strong. Thank you, Dan Halpern, my editor, publisher, and perfect reader. Thank you, Gabriella Doob, for herding cats.

Thank you, poker players and tennis partners who provided distraction, amusement, and emotional sustenance during my long journey through this novel: John Kurowsky, Steve Leiber, Jody Apap, Paul Cohen, Sheila Maloney, John Corcoran, Griffin Dunne, Wally Carbone, Steve Siegel, Ralph Sassone, and Henry Dunow.

Thank you to Ariella Thornhill and Emma Singer for charting the river under the road by researching everything that was happening around the world while this novel's parties were taking place.

About the Author

Scott Spencer is the author of eleven novels including *Endless Love, Waking the Dead, A Ship Made of Paper,* and *Willing*. He has taught at Columbia University, the Iowa Writers' Workshop, Williams College, the University of Virginia, and at Eastern Correctional Facility as part of the Bard Prison Initiative. He lives in upstate New York.